STORMVAULT

STORMVAULT

ANDY CLARK

BLACK LIBRARY

A BLACK LIBRARY PUBLICATION

First published in 2020.
This edition published in Great Britain in 2021 by
Black Library, Games Workshop Ltd., Willow Road,
Nottingham, NG7 2WS, UK.

Represented by: Games Workshop Limited – Irish branch,
Unit 3, Lower Liffey Street, Dublin 1,
D01 K199, Ireland.

10 9 8 7 6 5 4 3 2 1

Produced by Games Workshop in Nottingham.
Cover illustration by Vladimir Krisetskiy.

A CIP record for this book is available from the British Library.

ISBN 13: 978-1-78999-200-7

See Black Library on the internet at

blacklibrary.com

And find out more about Games Workshop
and the worlds of Warhammer at

games-workshop.com

Pr̶   by CPI Group (UK) Ltd, Croydon, C̶   ) 4YY

Fo̶   e and

From the maelstrom of a sundered world, the
Eight Realms were born. The formless and the divine
exploded into life.

Strange new worlds appeared in the firmament, each one
gilded with spirits, gods and men. Noblest of the gods was
Sigmar. For years beyond reckoning he illuminated the realms,
wreathed in light and majesty as he carved out his reign. His
strength was the power of thunder. His wisdom was infinite.
Mortal and immortal alike kneeled before his lofty throne.
Great empires rose and, for a while, treachery was banished.
Sigmar claimed the land and sky as his own and ruled over a
glorious age of myth.

But cruelty is tenacious. As had been foreseen, the great
alliance of gods and men tore itself apart. Myth and legend
crumbled into Chaos. Darkness flooded the realms. Torture,
slavery and fear replaced the glory that came before. Sigmar
turned his back on the mortal kingdoms, disgusted by their
fate. He fixed his gaze instead on the remains of the world he
had lost long ago, brooding over its charred core, searching
endlessly for a sign of hope. And then, in the dark heat of
his rage, he caught a glimpse of something magnificent. He
pictured a weapon born of the heavens. A beacon powerful
enough to pierce the endless night. An army hewn from
everything he had lost.

Sigmar set his artisans to work and for long ages they toiled,
striving to harness the power of the stars. As Sigmar's great
work neared completion, he turned back to the realms and saw
that the dominion of Chaos was almost complete. The hour
for vengeance had come. Finally, with lightning blazing across
his brow, he stepped forth to unleash his creations.

The Age of Sigmar had begun.

PROLOGUE

Bronvynne Karrobeth put one foot in front of the other as she tried very hard not to die. She didn't look at the mountain road winding up towards the storm-lashed peak above. To do so would rob what little strength her elderly body had left. She didn't look down at her feet either, lest the ragged remains of her boots and the crimson stains left in her wake remind her how she had walked them bloody these past days.

Not walked, limped, came a vague thought, tinged with the ghost of her usual impatience.

Bronvynne looked at the battered leather tome she clutched to her chest with spindly, bandaged arms. That was what this was all about, what all this effort and pain was for. She held it close, striving to keep it from the grasp of howling wind and lashing, faintly acidic rain. Dying would most certainly have been the easier choice, but it wasn't the right one. Lief was relying on her, after all. Wherever he was.

Bronvynne started as she realised that, in her delirium, thoughts of her brother had almost led her straight off the side of the mountain road. The drop wheeled beneath her, green-lit chasms yawning like maws far below. One bloodied foot skidded on loose gravel and for a horrible moment the old cryptoscholar's heart slammed to a halt in her chest. She staggered back from the edge and by a supreme effort of will managed to stay on her feet. Beyond the lip of the ledge, the chasm-split plains marched away into a grey haze and lightning reached down from the clouds to blacken them with its touch.

Fall now and you won't get up, you stupid old woman, she scolded herself.

She couldn't allow that to happen.

Too many lives were at stake.

Maybe Lief's.

It was hard, though, so hard to keep pushing on. It wasn't as though she were young and strong, not any more. Her vitality was not what it once had been. Much of Bronvynne's body was numb from shock, blood loss and exposure. Those parts that could feel sang a dirge of agony that she ignored only by dint of focusing instead upon her fear of failure. The wound in her midriff was bleeding again; she could feel blood oozing through the filthy bandages and trickling down her legs. She shook with cold, or maybe fever. It was hard to tell any more and really what did it matter? If she didn't make it to the mountaintop she'd be dead one way or another.

In a moment of weakness, Bronvynne looked up and felt the last wisps of strength ebb from her body. Miles to go yet, miles of switchback roadway flanked by looming bladepines, lashed by screaming winds and scattered with jagged rocks. Stern faces graven into vast boulders and outcroppings stared down at her, judgement welling in the shadows of their eroded sockets. Lightning flashed again and she saw it for a moment, the Stormkeep silhouetted against the divine light of Sigmar's wrath.

The structure was huge, imposing. It promised merciless might to its enemies and blessed sanctuary to its friends.

It was a sanctuary she would never reach. Bronvynne swore weakly as she thought of the miles she had crossed to get this far, the Realmgate she had braved and the dangers endured. To die now, in sight of her goal, seemed desperately unfair.

Yet Sigmar has a plan for all of us, she thought as her knees buckled and she fell painfully to the unforgiving stone. Her temple struck the ground and the world spun. She felt tears prick her eyes. She reasoned there was no sense holding them in any longer. Leif wouldn't see, and if somehow he did, well, he would understand. He was her brother, after all. *Sigmar has a plan for us all, and my part was to come as far as I have come,* she thought as she listened to the howl of the wind and the creak of the trees. *I got the tome this far. Perhaps they will find it. Perhaps they will do the rest. They must...*

Sound became distant, as though she had fallen down a deep well. Lightning flashed, a muted glare that offered cold comfort. For a moment, Bronvynne imagined that she saw angelic figures framed in that glare, winged servants of the God-King come to snatch her up and bear her soul away to the Underworlds in honour. She hoped that it was true.

Perhaps Leif would be there.

Then darkness.

Kalyani Thunderblade strode down the corridor towards the healers' sanctum. Her armoured footfalls echoed from walls adorned with trophies: severed heads and fallen banners and captured blades of myriad foes. She and her warriors had earned those trophies across the span of a half-hundred battles and more. They had paid for them in blood. Yet as a Lord-Celestant of the Celestial Vindicators, Kalyani expected no less of herself or those who followed her. Sigmar had created perfection when he forged his Stormcast Eternals. Perfection was what they would deliver him in return.

To do less was to fail.

She passed a mirrored shield, torn from the grasp of some twisted Champion of the Dark Gods on a long-ago battlefield, sanctified with prayer and holy blood and mounted upon the Stormkeep's wall as a mark of honour. She caught a glimpse of herself as she passed. It was a figure she both recognised and, on some level, still did not after all these years – tall and powerfully built but moving with predatory poise; armoured in the turquoise and white of her Stormhost with a lightweight crimson cloak at her back and Sigmarite prayer-scrolls flowing from belt and roundel; strong-featured face framing dark, intense eyes; caramel-brown skin dotted with pale scar-lines and gold studs; onyx-black hair chopped short and threaded through with gold-beaded honour braids.

She still affected such cosmetic flourishes from her life before her Reforging, and sometimes Kalyani wondered whether it was a mark of respect for those she had lost or simply a way of clinging on to memories she was frightened to lose. Sigmar's gift had made her stronger, faster, a better warrior than ever she could have been before, and Kalyani was grateful. Still, she saw what became of Stormcasts reforged time and again, saw their personalities eroded and the lessons of their mortal lives lost or forgotten until they passed the apogee of their abilities and began a slow descent into being something lesser, something little better than golems wielding blades.

That will never be my fate, she thought fiercely, one fingertip brushing her honour braids. *I will never lose what I am, who I am. I will fight always to prevent it. But I will not let such fears keep me from my duty.*

She let her hand drop to the pommel of Song, her sigmarite

longsword, belted at her hip and all but thrumming with the need to kill in the God-King's name.

'Soon,' Kalyani breathed to her blade.

The Lord-Celestant reached the end of the corridor and turned into another, similarly lined with the trophies of fallen foes. So many she and her warrior chamber had slain in the God-King's name. It was never enough. There were always more fools determined to set themselves against the Heavens, and Kalyani never tired of teaching them the error of their ways.

She halted as she came abreast of a strange figure hunched within a recessed alcove and lit by blood-red candles. It was humanoid, yet its body, its limbs, even its visage, all were fashioned from artfully forged and decorated blades. Kalyani made a brief gesture of deference, leaned in to light one guttered candle from the flame of another, and then was on her way again.

Ahead, lightning crackled in lantern-cages and threw dancing illumination along walls, floor and ceiling. Two Paladins stood beneath the lightning cages, flanking the arched door to the sanctum. They saluted with their stormstrike glaives as she approached.

'Hail the Once-Forged,' they chanted in unison. 'Hail the Thunderblade.'

Kalyani returned their greeting with a one-fisted salute slammed against her armoured chest.

'They are within?' she asked, not slowing.

'They are, my lady,' came the reply.

Kalyani passed through the gem-studded archway and into the healers' sanctum of her Stormkeep. The chamber was long and high-ceilinged, housing rows of sturdy sleeping pallets scaled and reinforced to accommodate wounded Stormcast Eternals. Around each, strange brass armatures and gauge-studded mechanical devices hunched like quiescent insects. Huge crystal-paned windows took up much of one wall and provided a magnificent prospect of the storm-lashed mountains that marched away to the south. The lightning that leapt ferociously without mingled with the glare from the lightning cages within and lit the sanctum with a flickerstrobe brilliance. Kalyani saw fledgling corposcaris flowing sinuously through the skies outside, the iridescent air-serpents frolicking through the raging storm.

In the vivid light-flashes, Kalyani saw several aelven healers clustered around a pallet at the room's far end. Its armatures had been pushed back, suggesting that whomever they were attending did not possess the miraculous physiognomy of the Stormcast Eternals. Two of her crystal-winged Prosecutors stood a little way outside the busy circle of healers, flanking the formidable figure of her Stormkeep's Lord-Castellant, Rojavi Sundershield. Sundershield was a big man, ice pale with white-blond hair pulled back into a severe queue, and his heavily scarred face was set in its usual dispassionate mask.

To the untrained eye the bulky warriors might have looked out of place, maybe bored or awkward in their apparent uselessness. Kalyani knew better. If what her Prosecutors had brought back from the mountainside proved in any way dangerous, they would slay it in an instant. It wasn't as though the agents of the Dark Gods hadn't tried such tricks before, after all.

'What is it?' she asked as she marched up to her warriors and saluted them. They returned the gesture before one of them replied.

'Lord-Celestant, they found her collapsed near the foot of the Warriors' Way,' said Sundershield, his voice deep and sombre. 'Human, elderly, badly wounded but with no trace of taint about her.'

Kalyani glanced towards the pallet, but the gathered healers mostly obscured her view. She caught an impression of a slight figure beneath the bed's heavy furs, a nest of dirty, steel-grey hair, one bony arm flung out from under the covers as though in denial.

She considered for a moment.

'Any indication of from where she hails? Or what her purpose was?'

One of the Prosecutors gestured to a side table behind him. A meagre handful of battered objects lay upon it and Kalyani moved to examine them.

'Her effects are limited, and tell a strange tale,' said the Prosecutor. 'A haversack, Freeguild issue, torn down one side and hastily patched. A map-sphere, command device, something that should have been in the hands of a general, not… whatever she is. Parchment. Ink. Several stone tablets, all broken apart but inscribed with an odd mixture of runes and sigils.'

'And this, which she had clutched to her chest,' said Sundershield, handing Kalyani a sizeable tome bound in brass and black leather.

'Looks old,' commented Kalyani as she inspected it critically. It was locked tight, she saw, an ornate clasp holding the covers shut and requiring a key to open.

'Whatever it is, my lady, it is clearly of great importance to the captive,' said the Lord-Castellant. One of the Prosecutors gave a wry chuckle.

'My lord understates,' he said. 'She didn't release her hold upon the damned tome even in a state of near death. We had to pry it from her unconscious grip before the healers could begin their work.'

Kalyani gave the book another speculative look, wondering whether she could force its clasp and deciding that she probably couldn't without damaging it. A last resort, she decided, and set the book back on the table. As she did so, she noticed the spots of blood that patterned its spine. She looked again at the muffled figure.

Yours? Or someone else's? Kalyani wondered.

'She bore no weapons?' she asked.

'None that we have found, my lady,' replied Sundershield. 'And it seems any provisions and medical supplies she might have set out with were all used up by the time she reached the foot of our mountain.'

More curious still, thought Kalyani. Who was this stranger? What did her arrival portend? If she was a threat, then it was the duty of the Lord-Celestant to deal with her swiftly and mercilessly. Yet the crumpled figure on the pallet and her odd assortment of personal effects didn't speak to Kalyani of danger. Rather, they suggested something more mysterious.

The stranger felt more to her like some harbinger of fate.

'Maethrias, when will she be conscious?' she asked the chief of the healers. 'Questions need asking.'

The tall, spare aelf straightened from where he had been running a glowing green crystal wand up and down the lines of his patient's torso. He turned to regard Kalyani coolly over his pomander mask, pulling the bulky thing down to his neck with one long-fingered hand to allow himself to speak.

'My Lady Thunderblade, this woman is human. If that weren't bad enough, she is elderly, physically weak, utterly exhausted, half-starved… From the condition of her feet she has walked an unthinkable distance to reach us. Her wounds have festered, and she must have wrestled for days on end with a fever that should have killed her in hours. It is nothing short of a miracle sent by Sigmar that she lives at all. For all of our healing arts it will be a wonder if she ever regains consciousness again.'

'Oh… I don't know about that…' came a parchment-dry voice from behind him. The aelf and the Lord-Celestant both looked down in surprise to see the elderly woman regarding them from beneath the piled furs. Her cheeks were hollow, her skin pallid and sweaty, but Kalyani saw a strength in the old woman's stare.

The healers immediately set about waving a fresh set of crystalline wands over their patient, one muttering incantations and sprinkling powdered herbs that ignited and burned away to nothing as they settled on the woman's scalp. Another poured oily liquids of dubious hue from several slender decanters into a crystal glass, then gently but firmly raised the patient into a sitting position before making her drink its entire contents.

Kalyani watched impassively through it all, studying the woman and finding herself studied in return despite the patient's obvious weakness. All the while, the Lord-Celestant clamped down on the impetuous temper that characterised her Stormhost. She wanted answers, but she wouldn't have them at the expense of the woman's health.

It was the patient herself who lost her patience first.

'Oh, enough!' she barked, her voice carrying a snap of authority despite its weak and reedy state. 'If Sigmar's going to take me then he is, but by the hammer and the storm I'll deliver my bloody message before he does!'

'You have been sorely wounded and suffered extreme exposure and exhaustion–' began Maethrias, but to his obvious consternation he was interrupted by the woman's irritated sigh.

'I know all that, you pointy-headed twit. I was there, wasn't I?'

Kalyani had to stifle a rare snort of mirth. Sundershield blinked slowly, about as much emotion as Kalyani ever saw him show about anything other than battle. Maethrias' low opinion of humans was hardly a secret, and the aelf's bewilderment at his scolding had left him blinking and speechless. Before his surprise could turn to haughty anger, Kalyani stepped up to the bedside.

'I am Lord-Celestant Kalyani Thunderblade, leader of the Eviscerators warrior chamber. You are in my Stormkeep, brought here from the road below. Who are you? And how did you come to be bleeding to death at the foot of my mountain?'

'The Eviscerators?' repeated the elderly woman. She nodded, as though she had tasted something and found it to her liking. 'Yes, you sound as though you'll do the job.' Kalyani waited, her silence pointed. The patient hacked out a weak cough, then gestured at the aelf with the pitcher to refill the glass. Looking uncertain, he did so and handed her the vessel, which she drained before leaning back, eyes watering.

'Don't know what that is but it hits the spot,' she sighed. The aelf went to speak but Kalyani raised a finger to forestall him.

'I asked you who you are and how you came to be here,' she said, her tone no longer amused. The old woman looked at her with an expression half defiant and half hopeful.

'My apologies, Lord-Celestant, but I'll answer better now that I don't feel as though I'm about to cough myself to death,' she said. 'My name is Bronvynne Karrobeth and I am an arcanotranslocutor in the service of the holy armies of Azyrheim. I came to you for aid, and for vengeance.'

'An arcano…?' Sundershield let the question hang.

'A cryptoscholar,' Bronvynne elaborated in the tone of one well used to having to do so. 'Specialising in translations of ancient and arcane texts, lost languages of the Age of Myth, and the handling of potentially hazardous literary weapons in the service of Sigmar's armies of reconquest.'

'You spoke of aid and vengeance,' said Kalyani as Sundershield nodded slowly to himself. 'Say on.'

Bronvynne gave a small sigh and a shake of her head. Bony fingers gripped the furs and pulled them up to her neck, and in that moment Kalyani saw the fear and pain, the horror and loss that had all but hollowed the scholar out from the inside. *What must she have gone through*? she wondered. Bronvynne's bravura, such as it was, was the last means this elderly woman had of keeping herself from falling apart.

The glimpse was gone as swiftly as it appeared. The scholar's defiant stare returned in force.

'I was attached to an expeditionary force out of Azyrheim,' she began. She paused, throat working, and Kalyani saw the old woman remonstrate with herself before proceeding. 'Our commander was Freeguild, Koriam Kaslyn, a good man and a good soldier. He had human, aelf and duardin all under his command and he got them to work as one. I travelled with the army. I recorded their great deeds. I applied my scholarly talents to unusual artefacts and lost languages, did what I could to translate that which our officers couldn't read and gathered intelligence to be ferried back to Azyrheim. I did my part. They were good days.'

Kalyani waited while Bronvynne took a few slow breaths, gathered herself and pressed on.

'We were on the Basalt Flats south of Lionshold when we got the order to push for the Scatterlight Realmgate. No one said as much, but I've a sense that certain fragments of arcana and lore I had sent back had been pieced together with Sigmar knows what else by Azyrheimer scholars, so I suppose it might all have been my fault, what followed... The army was bloodied from a messy engagement with a horde of ghasts, but General Kaslyn sent the wounded to Lionshold and got everyone else rallied and moving quick as you please. We...'

There was a pause for coughing before the scholar carried on in a hoarse voice.

'We passed through the Scatterlight and pressed south down a half-erased highway so old it no longer had a name. We wound between jade-hued mountains whose peaks glowed with strange lights. Cold, they seemed. Dangerous. Saw a few natives on our march but never more than beastback scouts who watched us pass from the heights above. Saw more eerie lights at night, too, dancing witchfires deep within the roadside caverns that had the soldiers clutching their hammers and praying to Sigmar. Nothing came of those, though, either. Nothing but a sense of menace. Our destination was ten days' march south of the Realmgate. We knew it only as Mordavia, and we came to it without challenge.'

'You were fortunate to travel so far in such times without a battle,' commented Kalyani. 'Since the Necroquake, the dead maraud at will.'

'Fortunate, were we?' asked Bronvynne. 'I don't think so. Mordavia was a wonder, albeit a faded one. A city from the Age of Myth by my reckoning, half-subsided into canyons and tunnels yet still its crumbling structures filled an entire valley. I still recall my first sight of it as we crested a rocky rise. The dawn light shone on the lake that had drowned the city's western districts, transforming the still waters into a sheet of glowing glass. Time-worn spires and crumbling arch-bridges and the sprawling hollows of old buildings marched away, sunken streets winding between them, rocky outcroppings thick with grass and ferns pushing right up through them to set the place all askew. I remember the dim shadows of forests, just visible to the south. How I came to hate those forests soon enough.'

Bronvynne paused so long that Kalyani thought to prompt her. However, as she drew breath to do so the scholar went on.

'The orruks hit us there, in that very moment. Savage beasts with green skin and jagged tusks, daubed in warpaint and bursting from the ruins and rocky outcroppings that bordered the road. How our scouts missed them I don't know. Cunning, maybe, or sorcery? They set up that terrible cry of theirs, that monstrous roaring, and it hit us like physical blows. Then they descended. Thousands of them, many, many thousands. They poured down the mountain slopes and… well. We never stood a chance.'

'The army was destroyed?' asked Kalyani.

'Massacred, would be a more accurate term. I and a handful

of others managed to escape into the city, and our reward was to be hunted from pillar to post for days. I dragged General Kaslyn with me for the first two days, I and his adjutant Thrent. Poor man never did wake up.'

'That is how you came by this?' asked Kalyani, plucking the map-sphere from the table and twisting its hemispheres in her hands. The duardin-crafted device spiralled open with a whisper of oiled cogs, minute gems glowing within its layered planes as they ticked steadily around one another.

'It is,' Bronvynne replied, eyeing the device protectively. 'By that time, it was just me, Thrent and two Freeguilders. The rest were dead, I was sorely wounded… Someone needed to make it out, you see. Someone needed to bring a warning of what we found there, the danger.'

'If the horde of orruks is as large as you say then they cannot be allowed to continue their rampage,' said Kalyani, frowning at the map-sphere. 'You look to have travelled some days south to reach the Emberspan gate before… Sigmar's heavens, before crossing half the Blasted Lands to reach us. That is no small march, it truly is a miracle that you live.'

Or something more sinister, she thought, appraising the scholar anew. Bronvynne waved a hand in a tired gesture of dismissal.

'I know what you're thinking but I've made no dark deals to get this far. It was the lives and pilfered rations of those I travelled with that did that. Thrent knew a measure of healing and he saw to my wounds as best he could. The others fought on my behalf more times than I'd wish to count.'

'Where are they now?' asked Sundershield, but Kalyani thought she already knew the answer to that question.

'They lie where they fell along our road,' replied Bronvynne, her voice sombre, her eyes flashing in defiant challenge. 'I put cairns over them to stop them walking again and buried them with what holy words I could remember. Sigmar knows I hope their spirits remain quiet.'

'And what of the book?' asked the Lord-Celestant, lifting the tome from its table again. This time the old cryptoscholar recoiled a little. She stared at the book with outright loathing.

'That, Lord-Celestant, is what I've been trying to tell you. The danger isn't the orruks. I mean, it is but not in the way you imagine. There is something *in* that city or lurking below it or...' Bronvynne gestured weakly as though fishing for a word just out of reach. She slumped back, frustrated and clearly exhausted. 'It is why we were sent there, Lord-Celestant, I'm sure of it. I found that tome in the tumbledown remains of something that resembled a temple. It was inside a lead-lined chest that had broken open in a fall. Just chance, you understand. Or perhaps Sigmar's hand at work. I laboured to translate what I could of it as we made our way through those hateful, damned woods, greenskins still pursuing us, night after night...' She stopped, shook her head, looked away with one fist pressed to her lips as tears leaked from her eyes.

'My lady, she needs rest,' said Maethrias, his tone brooking no argument. Still, Kalyani frowned at him and shook her head.

'In a moment,' she said. 'Miss Karrobeth, the book is locked shut. How did you open it? And what is it you know? Speak the warning you travelled all this way to deliver. Let me act upon it.'

'In the map,' the scholar replied. 'You see the disc representing the Heavens' alignment? Yes, that's it, give it a quarter-turn clockwise and then a half-turn back the other way.'

The device clicked as Kalyani manipulated it and then a small slot opened in its side and a stubby metal key slithered out. The Lord-Celestant caught it before it hit the floor and raised it to her eyes. It was made of verdigrised metal and had a sense of great age to it.

'I'll save you the trouble of opening it, as the dratted thing is in a dialect both time-lost and convoluted,' said Bronvynne, her voice now growing faint. 'What little I've managed to decipher speaks of a weapon, something forged for a god to wield in the days before Chaos blighted the realms. It is that weapon that hides somewhere in the city, its power that lends such direction-less menace to its streets, I know it is.'

'And the orruks must not be allowed to lay hands upon it,' said Kalyani, her tone grim.

'If, by the grace of Sigmar, they haven't already,' replied Bronvynne. 'I… I can't say what the weapon is, what it does, but there's no telling what damage those brutes could do if they had such an ancient and powerful thing.'

Kalyani Thunderblade stood and thought for five slow, steady beats of her heart. Her mind whirled, assessing, considering and discarding one possibility or plan after another. Her eyes flickered over Bronvynne's pilfered map-sphere. One armoured finger tapped against the device's brass shell. Then she set down both book and sphere with a decisive thump and straightened to look down upon the scholar.

'I thank you for your warning, Bronvynne Karrobeth, and I honour you for the strength and determination that it must have taken to reach us as you have. The Eviscerators will aid you in recovering this artefact before the God-King's enemies can do so, or if they already have then we will slay them and prise it from their dead hands. But we shall do none of this alone, for though we are a full warrior chamber the horde of greenskins you describe is vast indeed. I have allies upon whom I can call. Messengers shall be despatched.' She gave a nod to Sundershield, who swept from the chamber with his cloak billowing behind him.

'And me?' asked Bronvynne, her weathered brow creasing in a frown that marred the obvious relief on her face.

'Sigmar has appointed you this task, that much is clear,' replied Kalyani. 'Rest. Recover your strength. Do whatever you must to make peace with the ghosts at your heels. In two days, we depart for Mordavia to achieve what your former comrades could not. By the time we reach the city, you will have achieved a sufficient translation of that text that we understand precisely what it is we fight for, or face.'

And in the meanwhile, I shall watch you like an aetherwing on the hunt, thought Kalyani as the old scholar slumped back into her bed and at last allowed herself to pass back into unconsciousness. *And if I suspect the slightest hint of duplicity, then may Sigmar have mercy upon you and whatever fell powers you work for.*

Beyond the inner wall of the healers' sanctum, in an interstitial space gnawed through the very stuff of reality, a trio of black-clad figures hunched. Their forms were wiry and darkly furred. Large ears and whiskered snouts twitched beneath dark cloth. Long tails switched back and forth, one tipped with a jag-bladed knife. Strange, green-black mists drifted about them, glowing with eerie lights.

One of the skaven held a bulky brass device of pipes and tubes with a fluted end. This he held up against the wall of the gnaw-hole while the smaller of his comrades held the device's other end to his ear and listened intently. He in turn recounted Kalyani and Bronvynne's conversation in a snarling whisper while the third ratman scratched ugly runic script onto a roll of mouldering parchment.

The listening skaven stopped speaking. The transcriber paused for a moment then aimed a vicious kick at his small comrade, who replied with bared fangs and a savage snarl.

'No more speak-words, done-done they are,' snapped the smallest of the trio. 'Kick-strike at me again and you lose that footclaw, Switchfang.'

Switchfang sneered at his small comrade.

'Threaten me again, Skritt. Switchfang rip-tears your throat and takes your share of the warp tokens, yes.'

'Shut your muzzles, fools, and listen to Blackclaw,' hissed the first skaven, who was even now folding down the listening device and lashing it to his back by frayed leather straps. 'Switchfang, put-safe the scroll in its tube. We have learned a great secret here, one that will give-grant many-much power to Eshin Clan Skwyrm.'

'Or to… us?' asked Skritt. The others leered down at him, fangs bared.

'Or to us,' repeated Switchfang. 'But who do we pledge-sell our secrets to? Who pays-pays best reward?'

'Splichritt?' asked Skritt after a moment, and Switchfang swished his tail appreciatively.

'Splichritt,' echoed Blackclaw, then set off at a swift scurry through the cloying shadows and unnatural angles of the gnawhole. His comrades followed, just two more shadows soon swallowed by the gloom.

CHAPTER ONE

UPON THE EVE OF WAR

Mordavia, before the Battle of the Dead City

WHUMP – WHUMP, WHU-WHUMP!

The beat of the Big Drum rolled through the still air of the evening like the colossal heartbeat of a godbeast.

WHUMP – WHUMP, WHU-WHUMP!

Brognakk the Skinner felt its basso boom vibrate in his barrel chest. The sound sent a surge of exhilaration through the old megaboss. A spike of aggression tightened his fist instinctively around his massive double-bladed choppa, Krump, until its gnarled leather bindings creaked.

WHUMP – WHUMP, WHU-WHUMP!

The sound bounced off the mountains that towered like Gorkamorka's tusks to the north. It boomed like thunder over the ruined cityscape that sprawled before Brognakk, its sunken streets and canyons black with shadow, the hard planes of its ruined buildings daubed bloody down one flank by the setting light of Hysh.

WHUMP – WHUMP, WHU-WHUMP!

The Big Drum itself had been hauled to the top of the ruined watchtower that overlooked the road north of the city. Crude block and tackle winches and a great deal of gargant muscle had got the drum into position, and now a pair of hulking ogors pounded away at it with double-handed beaters made from obsidian and monster-bones.

Beneath him, Brognakk's maw-krusha steed shifted restlessly. It hunched on a crag overlooking the watchtower and the drum. He had named the enormous beast Smash; this was in part because of what Brognakk had seen it do to Boss Graznak's 'ardboyz the day he killed Graznak and took the monstrous steed for his own, and partly because he didn't have time for all that imaginative mucking about. Let the weaker races mess around with fancy names for their weapons and mounts and what have you. While they were wasting time with such nonsense, the orruks would be kicking down their castle doors and smashing their teeth in.

'Steady, lad,' growled Brognakk as Smash stirred again. The maw-krusha pounded one huge, scaly fist against the lip of the crag, dislodging a spill of scree. Brognakk gave his steed an affectionate whack on the back of the skull with his own clenched fist, asserting dominance as naturally as he breathed air. 'It's da drum, innit? You feel it too,' he said. His maw-krusha gave a deep, rumbling snarl that sounded like wet rocks grinding together deep beneath the earth. Brognakk chose to take that as assent. It was the Big Drum, he thought, the war beat of Gorkamorka pounding out until it filled the valley. How could Smash not respond to that? How could any of them not?

At the thought of Gorkamorka, Brognakk spat superstitiously, first right then left. One for each head of the Great Green God.

'Come on, lad. They'll be gavvered by now,' said the leathery old megaboss, and gave his steed another whack to get it moving.

Smash let out a deafening roar then launched itself from the lip of the crag and spread its wings wide. Maw-krushas couldn't really fly, per se, not like the fancy winged beasts of Sigmar's storm ladz or the twisted-up terrors that the biggest Chaos boyz rode to battle. They were too big, too tough, solid lumps of muscle and bone that even the widest wingspan wouldn't keep aloft indefinitely. Instead they leapt and glided, as Smash did now, launching itself high into the air with a tremendous shove of its heavily muscled forelimbs then catching the air and soaring upon it with the wide flaps of skin that stretched bat-like between its wrists and hind legs.

Brognakk grabbed onto the pommel of his saddle and enjoyed the sensation of acceleration. Smash shot over the watchtower where the Big Drum still pounded, greenskin shamans and warchanters gibbering, dancing and adding their own drumbeats about its base. The maw-krusha sailed down over the lower slopes and as it went its shadow swept over a sea of shanty-encampments. Fire smoke billowed around Brognakk, parting in a whirl as Smash plunged through it. Crude idols to Gorkamorka jutted up everywhere, ramshackle agglomerations of rubble, hewn wood, war trophies and dung daubed with vibrant colours and jangling with cheap bells and trinkets. Smash clipped a few of the tallest and Brognakk leered at the cries of shock from below as rubble crashed down on surprised orruks and ogors. Thousands upon thousands of warriors marched beneath Brognakk's flayed-skin banner, and they teemed underneath him as he rushed like an angry wind towards the valley floor.

The slopes raced past below, thick with grass, undergrowth and giant emerald-green ferns that broke like green waves against the rocky outcroppings jutting amidst them. Ahead, the ruins of the city swelled larger with alarming rapidity as the horde's forward positions approached.

'Dat way,' barked Brognakk, wrenching Smash's head around as they whipped past a hillock crawling with chanting Bonesplitterz and the Morkagork hove into sight. The enormous war fort had been wheeled all the way to the fringe of the city's crumbling northern districts and now loomed, huge and menacing, as its two wood-and-iron visages watched the city sink into twilit shadow. Brognakk's black old heart swelled with pride at the sight of the Morkagork, as it always did when he saw the colossal war engine. He had enslaved an entire nation of Spiderfang grots to build it, working most of them to death as they hacked down the web-festooned trees of their dank valleys and mined their shadowy caverns for the materials to make Brognakk's rolling tribute to the Great Green God. It was a veritable castle on iron wheels, moved by gargants chained into its lowest level, bedecked to resemble Gorkamorka and loaded up with deck upon deck of spear chukkas. For now, its presence was a brazen challenge to any enemy entering the valley. It said, 'Orruks is 'ere, get gone or get ready fer a fight.'

It would rain spears down upon the enemy in support of his horde when the big fight came, as it always did.

And there was a *big* fight coming, thought Brognakk.

Of that he was sure.

His warchiefs had gathered in the shadow of the Morkagork as instructed. He could see his sail-like Waaagh! banner rising from amidst the tumbled ruins of an ancient structure that squatted on the very fringe of the ruined city. Mobs of orruks and ogors lolled about the courtyard before it. The hand-picked ladz of Brognakk's best warchiefs eyed each other belligerently across the cracked and sprouting expanse of stone. It wouldn't take much to spark a fight between them, he knew. Greenskins and ogors alike forgot quickly who was in charge, started getting ideas in their heads about being biggest and best.

And nothing proved supremacy amongst Gorkamorka's teeming offspring like a good bit of violence.

'Time t'remind 'em who's in charge,' snarled Brognakk and leant forward over Smash's scaled neck, his tusked leer widening. The rushing wind squeezed tears from the corners of his right eye, though it had no power to trouble the glowing green gem that had long ago replaced his left. It sang through the metal plates hammered into Brognakk's flesh and rattled the assortment of tribal charms that hung about his thick, green neck.

Smash came down with meteoric force amidst the warchiefs' bodyguards. The maw-krusha hit so hard that stone shards splintered and burst up around its great knuckles, rattling from its thick hide. The beast let out a stupendous bellow of rage, so deafening that luckless orruks fell back with blood squirting from their ears and noses.

WHUMP – WHUMP, WHU-WHUMP came the endless drumbeat from the slopes above as Smash ploughed a path through the warchiefs' retinues. Its huge clawed fists left deep craters in the stone, more than one painted with the remains of Ironjawz orruks too slow to get out of the way. The beast's club-like tail swung behind it, swatting an ogor from his feet and breaking the arm of another armoured orruk. One greenskin, a real monster with spiked shoulder guards and a double-handed choppa, stood his ground and bellowed a challenge as Smash ploughed towards him.

Brave, Brognakk thought, *but really,* really *stupid*. Smash's head shot forward on its saurian neck. Its gaping jaws stretched wide then slammed shut like a mantrap. Fangs thicker than Brognakk's arms punched through iron, flesh and bone. Blood jetted as the orruk's legs flopped to the ground, relieved of the rest of his body in a single monstrous bite. They were mashed to pulp an instant later as Smash ploughed on, head thrown back and gullet working as it crunched the challenger down – armour, blade and all.

There was a gaping rent in the far side of the building that his warchiefs had gathered in, but a megaboss of Brognakk's station didn't go around. He went through.

Smash reared up on its stubby hind legs like a massive simian and pounded its huge green claw-fists into the side of the ruin. Ancient stonework cracked and gave, and the maw-krusha ploughed through amidst a rain of tumbling rock and billowing dust. Cries of shock and alarm met Brognakk as his steed shouldered its way through the hole. Indistinct shapes tumbled away amidst dust and shadow.

Brognakk pulled in a huge breath, rose high in his saddle with Krump brandished high above his head, and bellowed at the top of his lungs.

'WAAAGH!'

Coughing and retching, his warchiefs answered his bellow as best they could. As the dust began to clear they raised war cries of their own, fighting to stand their ground and show neither fear nor weakness to their boss of bosses. Bloody evening light spilled through cracks in the ruin and spread crimson fingers over the assembled warchiefs.

As he loomed above them, Brognakk nodded grimly to himself. There was Thrugg the Wrecker, Big Drekk and Gazblagg, the lesser megabosses who commanded the thousands of Ironjawz that made up the core of his horde. Big Drekk's gore-grunta steed, Trampla, had deposited a sizeable heap of dung at the sudden arrival of the megaboss, but was now pawing and snorting as it squared up to Smash. Drekk's luckless grot slaves were even now digging their way out of the piled ordure with squeals of revulsion.

There was old Shrakka One-Tusk, who carried Brognakk's banner into battle lashed to his muscled back. There was Zag Zagog, the wurrgog prophet of Brognakk's Bonechewer allies, squatting atop a rubble-heap with his masked head cocked sideways. A few steps below him stood Crushes Gitz, the monstrous

Bonechewer big boss who served as Zag Zagog's right hand. Across from them loomed Gormm, the corpulent, gold-bearded tyrant of Brognakk's ogor followers, and his chief butcher Kurrg, a stinking mass of blubber, gore-stains and hate.

To Brognakk's right lurked his own complement of weirdnob shamans, gathered in a shuddering, gibbering clump around the biggest of their number, Gobblagabba. The weirdnob's bulging eyes met Brognakk's for a moment and flashed with the bloody light of the evening.

There were other leaders there, dozens of them, orruk warlords and swaggering big bosses, lesser Bonechewers who stomped and yelled, even a smattering of grots whose tribes had managed to keep up with the horde thus far and hadn't yet been trampled or eaten. Brognakk hadn't bothered to learn any of their names. What was the point? They were no threat to him, and most of them probably wouldn't live long enough for him to remember them anyway.

'What're yooz lot doin' dossin' around here?' roared Brognakk. He was gratified to see surprise and panic flash across many faces. Always best to keep them off balance, he thought. He glowered around, Smash stomping and snarling beneath him. A steady pattering of liquid hitting stone sounded through the taut stillness; the beast drooled in anticipation of devouring any who displeased its master.

'Well?' Brognakk demanded in a furious shout. 'Come on, zoggers! Who's got da guts to answer me?'

Thrugg the Wrecker apparently did. He stomped forward through the haze, massive cleavers in hand, and planted himself four-square before Smash.

'Yooz told us to, boss,' he snarled, managing to make it sound like a challenge. At a thump from Brognakk, Smash craned its head forward until its slablike muzzle was inches from Thrugg's face. Hot wind blew from the monster's nostrils and set the buckles of the orruk's armour to jingling. Drool splattered his iron-shod feet, but Thrugg didn't so much as flinch. That one would bear watching, Brognakk thought.

'And *why'd* I tell ya to, eh?' demanded Brognakk. He saw Thrugg fish for an answer, come up with an empty net then heft his cleavers in case he had to defend himself from his megaboss' wrath.

The weird, singsong voice of Gobblagabba pulled Brognakk up short.

'Coz Gorkamorka told yooz dat was what we 'ad to do, and when da Great Green God tellz ya sumfing, all da orruks and da ogors and da grots gotta do it!'

He'd been looking forward to making an example of a few choice gits, put the fear of him back in the rest of them. Reasoning out the answer he was after would have been beyond all but the most inspired of them – frankly, he was amazed a couple of these monstrous war leaders could even manage breathing and walking at the same time while off the battlefield – but his chief weirdnob had spoiled the moment by getting it right.

Of course, that was hardly fair, thought Brognakk, being as it was Gobblagabba who had had the vision in the first place.

He turned in his saddle and stared sourly at the rag-clad weirdnob. Hulking but oddly scrawny, the shaman leaned heavily on a staff hewn from a snarg tusk and wore a peculiar crown of squig fangs and stone fragments bound around his skull with wire. His eyes bulged, wide and mad amidst a crude skull-mask of face paint, yet though his gaze roved madly here and there, Brognakk always had the sense that Gobblagabba saw right into him.

The lesser shamans that made up Gobblagabba's peculiar retinue shuffled subtly away from their boss as Brognakk's regard fell upon him. Bonkers they might be, gibbering and smeared in their own fluids in several cases, but none was deranged enough to stand their ground in front of the megaboss' anger. None but

Gobblagabba. But then, Brognakk reflected, he had surely been struck by Gorkamorka's own fist. Brognakk would never follow his visions so slavishly otherwise.

'Yeah, dat's right,' growled the megaboss, his tone dangerously low. 'Yoo'z all 'ere coz Gorkamorka hisself said you 'ad to be, and I speak for Gorkamorka!' Brognakk paused to spit right then left, then tapped one splintered claw against his biggest Waaagh! charm for luck.

'So you say, big orruk, but why?' came the deep rumble of Tyrant Gormm's voice. Brognakk turned, bristling, to stare the massive ogor down. You always had to be ready for a fight with that one, thought the megaboss. Ogors took more bossing than most, on account of them being bigger than everyone except the gargants, and smart enough to be trouble.

'Wotcha mean why?' roared Brognakk. 'Ain't da word of yer megaboss and yer god good enough?'

Gormm stroked his golden mustachios with fingers thicker than a grot's arms and shifted his massive bulk with apparent unconcern. The wealth of golden trinkets that pierced his flesh jingled against the slabs of armour bolted in a hotchpotch across his frame. He hadn't even drawn the colossal hooked sword that he wore across his back, Brognakk noted; the tyrant was doing everything in his power to tell the megaboss that he wasn't scared of him at all. Another one to watch.

'Maybe is, maybe isn't,' replied Gormm as though he were giving the matter deep thought. 'Thing is, what's the point? What we doin' here? No fightin', 'cept with each other. No loot, 'cept wot we nick off each other. Nothin' to eat… 'cept each other…' This last was delivered with a meaningful stare and a heavy pat of the ogor's massive belly. Brognakk's lip curled back from his jagged tusks. As though he'd end his days as ogor fodder, he thought scornfully. Gorkamorka had bigger plans for him than that!

Brognakk kicked Smash's scaled flanks and urged his steed to stomp across the ruin until he loomed over Gormm. Crimson light fell across the tyrant through a rent in the walls, turning his gaudy finery to fire and gore. Beside him hulked Kurrg, piggy eyes glinting. The stinking butcher fished a decaying orruk arm from the burlap meat-sack he kept stapled to his backflesh and slowly and deliberately began to crunch upon it.

'Dis is why I'm da boss, and you ain't,' said Brognakk in a tone clearly reserved for the terminally stupid. 'Dis is why it's my zoggin' great banner flyin' over dis city and not yours. You ain't got da smartz to see beyond your next bellyful, do ya?'

Gormm bristled and let one hand stray to the grip of his blade.

'It's 'cause you're the boss that we're sittin' on the edge of a dead pile o' rocks doin' nothin'. And now you got the big boomer going, and what's gonna happen when your mates hear it and show up but there's nothin' here but us, eh?'

Brognakk felt the eyes of all the assembled bosses on him, on this confrontation. He felt the tension crackling in the air, taut and violent enough to make the weirdnobs and the wurrgog groan and gibber. They twitched spasmodically, green sparks crackling around them and strange lights glowing from their eyes. He relished it. It made him feel alive. He drew himself up to his full height and sneered down at Gormm.

'Gorkamorka sez dere's somethin' shiny somewhere in da city. Somethin' so shiny and so powerful dat everyone's gonna want it. He sez when da big ghostyquake 'appened it zogged up wotever was hidin' da shiny wotsit and so now everyone's gonna come lookin' for it. And when dey do dere's goin' to be da best scrap any orruk ever set eyes on! Dat's why we's 'ere, ya dung-skull mound o' gutz, coz when everyone comes lookin' for the shiny fing we's goin' to clobber 'em all! Gettit?'

Brognakk waited while the slower of his war leaders slogged their way along the path to understanding. Some of them had heard bits of this already, he knew; some of them had been there the night Gobblagabba had had his Waaagh! vision. Some still bore the scars from the searing torrent of ectoplasmic vomit that had erupted from the weirdnob's distended maw as the Great Green God bellowed through him. Still, there had been too much grumbling, too much second-guessing; orruks and ogors got bored extremely quickly and sitting around for more than a day or so with no one to fight was bound to make them mutinous.

Hence the need for him to assert a little dominance.

'You says fight's coming, but where is it?' snarled Gormm, metal scraping as he drew his massive blade. 'I reckon you don't know nuffin'. I reckon you're out of ideas, hopin' Gorkamorka gets you out of mess before we work out our megaboss gone soft between ears. I reckon time for a new leader.'

The tension filling the ruin seemed to billow and expand until the walls fairly creaked with it. Orruks, ogors and grots watched with avid eyes. Wurrgog Zag Zagog shook his fetish-laden staff until bones rattled eerily together like the rattling of some huge serpent. From somewhere near the rear of the structure came the sound of a weirdnob being violently ill.

'Can't yooz feel it? Is you too stupid?' growled Brognakk, casting one hand out towards the ruined city even now sinking down into the gloom of night. On the slope above them, countless campfires belched smoke and fume into the darkening sky.

At that, Gormm faltered momentarily. He *could* feel something, thought Brognakk triumphantly. They all could, had done since they got here. Something calling to them from deep within the sprawling, half-subsided ruin of the city. Something that whispered of power, that teased the mind with hallucinatory echoes of glory then faded so suddenly it felt as though it had been imagined all along. It was all the proof Brognakk needed that Gobblagabba's vision was true.

'All I feel is hungry! And I hate feeling hungry! Time for a new boss!' roared Gormm, rallying and swinging his blade in a mighty arc. Brognakk, who had seen the blow coming from half a league away, leaned forward and swung his own blade to meet it. The two weapons crashed together, the echo of their impact ringing around the confined space of the ruin. Smash reared back with a deafening roar, swung its massive fists up and brought them crashing down on Gormm. The tyrant heaved himself aside, Kurrg falling backwards with a growl of surprise and dropping his half-chewed orruk arm. Stone smashed and shrapnel flew, peppering both ogors with bloody but superficial wounds.

Even as the butcher scrambled backwards, spitting blood and curses, Smash swung around to follow Gormm. There came a shriek from behind Brognakk's back as the maw-krusha's club-tail caught a luckless grot chieftain and flung him away to land in a bloody and broken tangle. The megaboss barely noticed, all his attention fixed on Gormm. The tyrant stepped back as though gathering momentum for a leap, then swung his blade high over his head and lunged in again, aiming to hack through Smash's scaly neck. Brognakk flung himself from the saddle, his double-bladed choppa shuddering as it met Gormm's weapon again with thunderous force. Sparks flew. Weirdnobz howled and chanted. Green energies crackled through the air.

Gormm staggered back and Brognakk the Skinner hit the ground boots first. He kept his balance and stormed forward, swinging first one blade of his massive polearm then the other, almost as though he were paddling a crude canoe. The tyrant smashed the first blow aside, swung to block the second one, just managed to block the third. Then his heel caught a chunk of rubble and he staggered. Brognakk struck, Krump's blade slicing into Gormm's thick neck. Blood gushed as it cut through flesh, muscle and fat, but Gormm was far from done. Despite the grievous wound he bulled forward with a roar, body-checking Brognakk with his sheer bulk and sending the megaboss staggering back in his turn.

The hooksword whistled round in a disembowelling cut that Brognakk just managed to parry. The tip of the ogor's blade skated upward from the clash and snagged in the megaboss' bottom lip, ripping away a sizeable chunk of flesh as it sailed past. Pain and anger drove Brognakk forward again, spitting blood as he rained blows on his larger opponent. From behind he heard Smash roar, but he replied with a furious bellow of his own.

Stay out of this, it said, an alpha beast asserting its dominance. *This isn't your kill.*

He heard his steed's pounding fist-falls recede, heard Smash give a truculent snarl, but he had no time to look around. Gore was sheeting down the tyrant's right side now, spilling in pulsing floods from his neck wound and draining his strength with every pumping heartbeat. Still Gormm put up a mighty fight, blocking and parrying with brute force, letting more than one of Brognakk's blows ring from his heavy armour plates, then managing to get a right hook through the orruk's guard hard enough to ring his head like a bell and dislodge one of his huge tusks.

Brognakk hadn't got as far as he had simply by being big, or strong, or tough. To be a megaboss you needed to listen to *both* of Gorkamorka's heads. He went with the blow, stumbling back, feigning worse injury than he had truly taken. Seeing his opening, Gormm roared as he swung his blade up, ready to bring it down for the killing strike. Fast as a thundering avalanche, Brognakk swung Krump up and sliced into his opponent's gut. He split the ogor's belly-plate with a resounding clang and spilled Gormm's capacious innards across the floor in a wet spill before spinning the double-bladed weapon up and around to hack through his forearms.

The tyrant's face twisted into a mask of horrified agony as his brain caught up with the fatal wounds he had suffered and his blade, still clutched in two severed hands, clanged to the ground. Gormm crashed down on his knees, pawing with bloody stumps to regather his emancipated intestines, then crashed face first into his own spilled guts and did not move again.

For a heartbeat, silence reigned through the ruin. Then Brognakk's war leaders raised a bestial cheer for their megaboss' victory. They stamped their iron-shod feet, bellowed their war cries and punched one another exuberantly while the weirdnobs wailed and howled.

Brognakk turned his gaze on Kurrg. The butcher still sat amidst the rubble, staring with wary hunger at the carcass of his former master.

'You got a problem wiv lissenin' to Gorkamorka?' asked Brognakk, then spat first right then left.

Slowly, Kurrg shook his head and wiped slobber from his purple lips with the back of one scarred hand.

'Good. Den yoo'z in charge of my ogors,' said Brognakk. 'Eat wotcha like of 'im, but don't knacker his skin. I wants dat for my banner, gottit?'

Kurrg nodded again, more enthusiastically this time. Then, grabbing a cleaver and a meat hook from his belt, the bloated butcher fell upon Gormm's corpse with eager appetite.

Ignoring the revolting sounds of crunching and slobbering coming from behind him, Brognakk swung back up onto Smash's back and gave the beast an affectionate clout. He looked around at the gathered war leaders, all staring at him in the gloom, ready once again to follow his lead.

For now. No doubt more examples would have to be made. They always did; that was Gorkamorka's way and it was as close to holy as his teeming children got.

WHUMP – WHUMP, WHU-WHUMP went the drumbeat

from high on the hill. Chanting and roaring rose to meet it, both inside the ruin and without.

WHUMP – WHUMP, WHU-WHUMP!

It was the pounding of Gorkamorka's mighty green heart, and Brognakk's own beat in time with it. He knew Gobblagabba had spoken true. He knew a great fight was coming, maybe the best he'd ever had.

WHUMP – WHUMP, WHU-WHUMP!

He felt again that strange tug from inside the city, thought for a moment he saw a shadow of great towers rising around him and glimmering energies spilling from his blades in roiling clouds. Then the feeling was gone, and he found himself hungry as he always was after a good scrap.

'Now wotcha waitin' for, ya gang of zoggers? Let's break out da meat and fungus brew and celebrate da fight dat's comin' our way!'

Another ragged cheer, almost drowned out by the drum's incessant beat as it rolled away across the dark, still ruins of the long-dead city.

WHUMP – WHUMP, WHU-WHUMP!

CHAPTER TWO

MEETINGS

South of Mordavia, the dawn of the campaign's first day

Kalyani Thunderblade dug her toes into the craggy slope and drove herself upward, attacking the climb like it was a foe to be defeated. She gripped jutting spars of bone-white architecture where they stretched out from the crumbling mass of the Echo-lith's flanks, trusting whatever ancient artifice had wrought them to take her armoured weight. Kalyani climbed the mysterious structure alone, for those she went to meet would be offended if she brought bodyguards with her. It would suggest that she did not trust them. They were proud, stiff-necked, and would take that ill.

Never mind that I do not trust them, she thought as she climbed. Still, a debt was a debt and she knew that none took such things more seriously than they. Besides which, she had instructed her Vanguard-Raptors and celestar ballistas to conceal themselves in the overgrown crags that reared to the south and east of the Echolith. If things went awry, the storm's fury would strike swiftly.

Kalyani and her brotherhood had passed through the Ember-span Realmgate some days earlier. Their march north from there had been relentless, and thankfully untroubled. This was a wild and mysterious corner of Ghyran they found themselves in. It was so out of the way that, to Kalyani's knowledge at least, no Storm-cast army had ever travelled it in force. Certainly, she had never seen it upon any map, save the sphere that Karrobeth had liberated from her fallen commander.

'Quiet doesn't always mean peaceful,' she told herself as she climbed. Thus far though they had met no resistance save the swift-growing tangle of the forest through which they travelled. Its vitality was aggressive. It sprawled immensely, a green ocean in full flood that snatched at the lands about it with possessive savagery. The ancient road that had once connected the Ember-span to ruined Mordavia had been buried by undergrowth and eroded by the creeping passage of root and tendril until it was all that Kalyani's scouts could do to find the route forward. She felt a new respect for the formidable little cryptoscholar who had survived this wilderness alone.

No, not alone, she corrected herself. *She left the bodies of her comrades behind her in this place. They gave their lives that she might bear her warning to my gates. Or so she says, at any rate.*

General Kaslyn's map had marked the Echolith as a potential vantage point a day's march south of the ruins of Mordavia. Karro-beth had opined that the map had been fashioned as much from the scrying of seers as the first-hand accounts of scouts, which accounted for the wealth of geographical information it contained but also for its lack of useful specificity about conditions on the ground. Thus, when Kalyani sent her message to her allies and suggested a time and place for their rendezvous, she had known only that the Echolith was likely high, sizeable and a compara-tively secure location to meet.

She hadn't expected its alien beauty. Before beginning her climb, Kalyani had swept the Echolith's perimeter alongside a handful of her Vanguard Rangers and had swiftly come to the realisation that the structure was, at least in part, an artificial construction. The exuberant tree-cover of the forest petered out low down on the Echolith's southern flank, but soil, moss, grass and jutting boulders clad it so thickly on that side that it could have been mistaken for a natural hillside, or perhaps a small mountain rising from the forest floor. Only the profusion of bone-hued spars that protruded like quills from its hunched back gave any clue that a purpose-built structure lurked beneath.

Circle round to the north, though, and the truth was revealed in all its inexplicable glory. Rearing to well over a thousand feet above the forest floor, the Echolith was a massive concave oblong that reminded Kalyani of a peaked cowl pulled up against a storm. Its encircling arms and jutting crest put a wide oval of forest into shadow, and there the trees grew sparse and pale. A great fringe of trailing creepers spilled over the lip of the Echolith like a green waterfall and fell most of the way to the ground; they stirred constantly in the wind and gave off a susurrus that could be heard for miles around. The sound had made Kalyani think of the ocean when she first heard it, but she had swiftly clamped down on those thoughts lest they bring reminders of tragic battles long since fought and lost.

The projection of those rustling sounds was surely some work of the Echolith itself, she thought as she neared the structure's peak. Sigmar alone knew who had built this towering edifice or why, but the name given it by the cartographic seers of Azyrheim seemed as good as any. It snatched up sounds made within its curving arc and threw them outward magnified tenfold. Those were its echoes, she thought. And perhaps the memories they sought to stir within those who heard them, also.

Kalyani saw wild, hate-filled eyes for a moment, heard sibilant hissing, panicked screams, the ring of steel and the spatter of blood. She felt it on her skin as though it had sprayed hot and fresh from the artery onto her body that very moment. Alarm bells tolled distantly in her mind. The Lord-Celestant shook off her hateful memories and applied herself to the climb, shutting out the Echolith's murmurs by will alone and striking hard for the summit. Now was not the time for introspection. She had a task before her.

By the time Kalyani neared the Echolith's crest, the wind was whipping around her with enough force to make her cloak flap and snap. It wasn't enough to drown out the drone of endrins, however. She heard them approaching from the east, the sound of their sky-ships still high off and far away but drawing closer by the moment.

Kalyani took a moment to glance about at the breathtaking view. The forest stretched away in all directions, hungry and belligerent as an infant deity. To the north, faint in the morning haze, Kalyani could see mountain peaks towering higher and higher until they vanished amidst crowns of cloud. Strange lights glimmered amidst those peaks, cold and eerie beacons that came and went before her sharp eyes. To the east, the land sloped slowly downward before shattering apart into a tangle of fanged ravines and jutting mesas whose flanks were studded with irregular masses of green crystal. She could dimly see avian shapes swarming above the maze of chasms, shapes large enough to give her pause.

Whatever they are, they would be a fine test for my blade, she thought, then discarded the notion just as quickly. Duty compelled her. She and her warriors did not have time for distractions. As always, she would simply have to master her impulses and save them for a time when she could vent them against the proper foes. Kalyani knew better than most the importance of discipline, of self-control and temperance in the face of naked aggression. She realised she could hear the ocean again, could see bloodied hair tugged by the outgoing tide, broken blades protruding from wet sand.

'Next time I arrange a rendezvous with potential allies, I shall meet them on a bare expanse of unfeeling stone,' she said to herself, thrusting the memories aside irritably. Despite her private horror at the spiritual entropy of multiple Reforgings, in some ways, Kalyani envied those of her brothers and sisters who had been reforged many times. They had had their histories and memories abraded, their present honed like blades sharpened on a whetstone. Yet she could not pretend to herself that she was not rightly proud of her title, and again the thought of lessons lost and agency stolen made her skin prickle with discomfort. Kalyani had died once, or as good as, and that was enough; no foe would ever be as deadly as Anjalia. No foe would ever best her again.

Kalyani took a look back down the rugged slope she had climbed, down over humps of mossy earth and tumbled boulders and jutting off-white spars to where the main strength of her army waited beneath the forest eaves – several hundred Celestial Vindicators, bloodlust simmering close beneath the surface of each and every soul; more Stormcasts in the rich purple armour of the Celestial Warbringers, warriors of Lord-Celestant Galabrith's Extremis Chamber mounted upon hulking dracoths; Galabrith himself, sat astride his stardrake, Sablewing. It was a great assemblage of heroes, an army of warriors worth many times their number of foes, a force capable of toppling cities and sundering hordes, and it was at her command. Somewhere down there, an isolated mortal amongst reforged demigods, was Bronvynne Karrobeth. Most likely she would be bent over that ancient tome, thought Kalyani, striving to unlock its obscure secrets. Well and good; anything the cryptoscholar dug up from her dusty book might prove useful in the battle to come, and at least while she was intent upon research, she was not bedevilling Kalyani's brothers and sisters with irksome questions.

The drone of endrins was closer now. With it came the creak of leather and rope, the hiss of steam and the gruff shouts of duardin voices, all subtly amplified by the Echolith. Kalyani stood, cloak billowing in the wind, one hand raised to shield her eyes from the golden glare of Hysh's dawning. She scanned the undersides of the scattered clouds where they stretched amber and rose across the skies to the west.

First, she saw small figures emerge from the cloud cover, dropping down into sight suspended below strange brass orbs nearly as large as themselves. They maintained a loose 'V' formation, its point aimed towards the summit of the Echolith as they thrummed closer. Soon Kalyani could make out the detail of metal masks and bodysuits, gold-glinting eye-lenses, vicious harpoon launchers and the weird brass contraptions into which the duardin were securely lashed. These last were clearly holding them aloft through alchemy Kalyani couldn't begin to fathom. She discarded her questions half-formed. The duardin could fly, she'd already known this; how they did it wasn't relevant.

Now came the sky-ships. Their undersides split the ragged clouds as they descended, parting them like waves before a boat's prow. Dawn light glimmered upon brass and iron as the armada of aircraft dropped through the clouds in formation and powered towards the Echolith peak. There were dozens of them, ranging from small gunboats bristling with cannons, repeaters and bombs, through to sizeable warships over whose hulls and rails swarmed duardin crewmen clipped to trailing harness lines. Despite their ornate decoration and wildly varying silhouettes, all the craft shared similarities. All were formidably built, their riveted metal hulls and rune-marked armour plating bespeaking the finest duardin craftsmanship. All were suspended by metal cables and sturdy girders from huge versions of the brass flying endrins that their skirmishers hung from. They looked for all the world like brass balloons that left shimmering trails of gilded cinders and aetheric smoke in their wakes as they thrummed through the skies.

It was a formidable assemblage, thought Kalyani. More craft than she had hoped for. That was either excellent news or, if for some reason her allies planned duplicity, it was a deeply unwelcome development. The duardin of the Kharadron sky-ports were honourable enough, she knew, but wholly in their own way and upon their own painstakingly negotiated terms. Profit was their master, expediency the star they sailed by. If it had proven more lucrative to draw up another contract with one of Sigmar's enemies without her knowledge, to come here and bomb Kalyani's army out of existence then pay off the resultant debts some other way…? If that were the case, Thunderblade vowed that the Kharadron would regret their decision within moments of their first cannon firing. She gripped her weapon and stood her ground. Closer the airships came, and closer, and still the crash of guns did not sound nor the ominous clunk and wail of bombs detaching from their cradles.

The skirmishers had reached the Echolith now, yet they did not seek to land. Instead they peeled away to either side and soared past Kalyani. They hefted their harpoon-launchers and regarded her coldly from behind impassive metal masks as they flowed to either side of her, their aether-endrins puttering, their legs dangling weirdly in their harnesses.

Most of the airships had slowed now. Some drifted lazily back up until they were half-lost amidst the lowest wisps of cloud cover. Others circled away to patrol the surrounding area or hang menacingly over the Stormcast army down below. One craft kept coming, a massive dreadnought whose aether-endrin was taller and wider than the gates of Kalyani's Stormkeep. Rows of cannons, bomb-launchers and other, more incomprehensible weapons jutted over its deck rails and shoved their muzzles through gun ports. Alone amongst the sky-craft its prow bore a towering brass figure-head, a stylised duardin woman with a huge shield on one arm, a repeater pistol levelled over its rim and an expression of merci-less determination on her broad features. Kalyani saw the name *Shieldmaiden* blazoned upon the ship's flank in Kharadron runes. This was Norgssen's ship then, she thought.

The *Shieldmaiden* rumbled in overhead and, as it did so, shouted orders rang out from its decks. Duardin in light leather boiler suits clambered in and out of hatches, worked levers and spun dials as they brought the craft in above the Echolith. Four loud bangs cracked like thunder. Kalyani's hand had already dropped to Song's grip before she realised that the sky-ship had discharged its mooring anchors. Fired from pneumatic launchers built into the vessel's underside, the harpoons whistled down and struck the surface of the Echolith with sharp cracks. They buried deep, penetrating windblown topsoil and puncturing the skin of the structure itself. Each harpoon-anchor trailed a metal cable as thick as Kalyani's wrists. These now quivered with tension as they held the *Shieldmaiden* in place.

The sky-ship hung massively above her, its dark shadow engulf-ing her. Still, the Lord-Celestant took care not to move or react. Let them see her impassive in the face of all their martial might. Negotiations such as these must never be entered into from a position of anything other than strength.

''Ware b'low!' came a loud shout and metal cables sailed out over the sky-ship's deck rails. They uncoiled with a steely ringing sound, slapping against the *Shieldmaiden*'s hull as they unspooled until their ends hung just above the ground to either side of Kaly-ani. Then bulky figures were sliding down them, each gripping a contraption of metal plates and cogs about the size of a Stormcast helm. The devices meshed somehow with the cables and trailed sparks as the Kharadron rappelled swiftly down from their ship. Their boots thumped heavily as they hit the ground and immediately Kalyani found herself under the hungry muzzles of a dozen duardin firearms. Multi-barrelled cannons, stocky brass blunderbusses and an array of pistols covered her. She noted with respect that the duardin had not simply surrounded her, but instead had arrayed themselves in such a fashion that, were they called upon to open fire, their crossfire would angle away from one another instead of running the risk of hitting their fellows.

'Sigmar's greetings, trusted allies,' Kalyani said, her tone dry. She received no response from the metal-masked figures around her. They were shorter than her by a foot or so, but far bulkier even than she in her full armour. Red coals flickered to her right and she glanced to see a metal pipe jutting incongruously from the faceplate of one duardin. Smoke drifted thinly from its bowl as he took a puff, gun unwavering.

Another cable unrolled from above and her old ally Vornn Norgssen descended to the peak of the Echolith. She appraised him as his boots hit the ground. Norgssen was clad in a resplendent suit of burnished armour that looked like it had cost more than the wages of an entire Freeguild regiment for a year. Cogwork joints purred smoothly as he moved. Lights winked and gauges ticked on built-in aeronautical devices beyond her ken. A double-handed hammer was clamped to his back by elaborately worked clasps, while more of the same held a menacingly large pistol locked to his right thigh where it could be drawn swiftly at need. Norgssen's face was hidden behind a magnificently worked faceplate whose eye-lenses were thin-cut sapphire and whose fixed snarl of rage was wrought in precious metals.

Norgssen regarded her, unreadable. Kalyani stared back. The

wind soughed over the peak. The smoking duardin's pipe crackled and puffed as he took another sulphurous lungful.

'Where did we meet?' asked Norgssen, his voice rendered tinny and artificial through the mechanisms of his mask.

'Thostorr Peninsula. Fort Hallowhame,' replied Kalyani.

'How long ago?' he asked.

'Three years, near to the day,' she said.

'Under what circumstances?'

'Hallowhame was besieged by mordants and you and your crew were contracted to fly in supplies,' said Kalyani, remembering the brutal conflict with perfect clarity. She could almost smell the pungent smoke of the warding braziers, hear again the hissing pelt of the rain and crack and crunch of the scavenging cannibals feasting upon the battlefield fallen. 'Your craft went down beneath the assault of a pack of winged horrors, hit the ruins of the outer vigil-tower and broke up in the midst of the foe. You and your first mate Grafi Hengin survived the crash and made your last stand atop your aether-endrin as the mordants closed in. I sallied out with a force of my Celestial Vindicators and cut a path to you. We brought back as many supplies as we could salvage and saved your lives. Hence our alliance.'

'Contractual bond,' corrected Norgssen, holding up a finger to emphasise the correction. 'What did you salvage from our hold that day, Lord-Celestant?'

'Medical tinctures and salves, four weeks' worth of rations for the Freeguilders, four thousand rounds for the handguns.'

'And?' he asked, and Kalyani sensed the moment of stillness amongst Norgssen's crew. This was the real question, the test that all the rest of it had led up to. All that she had answered so far might have been gleaned by others, should they wish some deception, but this last detail had passed between her and Norgssen alone and he had asked that it remain thus.

Until now.

She smiled slightly at the memory.

'An artificial limb, cogwork, Threggsson manufacture. Exquisite piece. Child's size. It was for the garrison captain's daughter. You asked me to keep it a secret because you had agreed to give the man the arm free of charge after learning the tragic circumstances in which she'd been maimed but you didn't want your crew to suspect you of profitless altruism.'

A few of the duardin shifted their stances at this. Leather under-suits creaked and eye-lenses were turned in Norgssen's direction. This would have been the instant to strike, Kalyani knew, and part of her was tempted despite the nihilistic stupidity of such a course of action. Just to draw her blade, to bury it in those who surrounded her with their weapons and their suspicion. That was the essence of her Stormhost talking though, the boon and curse both of the Celestial Vindicators' rage. Learning how to muzzle her natural ferocity had been part of Kalyani's journey to earning her rank, yet every time it was an effort. Kalyani's boon had always been the lesson she had learned at Anjalia's hands, or rather, at the edge of her blade. *Control before ferocity, and never lose sight of yourself amidst the fires of battle,* she thought.

Norgssen grunted then reached up and unhooked the faceplate of his helm. He removed it to one of the many hooks on his belt, revealing a face as weathered and craggy as a coastal cliff. His bushy eyebrows and close-cropped beard were both shot through with more silver than Kalyani remembered, but otherwise the grizzled duardin looked little different.

'Aye, you're she, right enough,' he said.

'Cap'n?' asked the pipe-smoker, his voice rough as thannok-fur.

'Lower 'em and stow 'em, lads. The Lord-Celestant is who she claims to be.'

'But she said–'

'Aye, and she's the only one I'll hear make mention of it, now or ever again, eh? Terms clear?'

'Terms clear, cap'n,' replied the pipe-smoker dubiously, slinging his gun and standing back.

'Captain Norgssen, what is this caution in aid of?' asked Kalyani, relaxing her stance as the duardin around her stood down.

'*Admiral* Norgssen these days, if you please,' he corrected her sourly. 'I've had cause to be cautious since the day I signed my first contractual agreement with the followers of Sigmar. There's plenty abroad in the realms who take ill to such allegiances, even be they mercantile and obligatory in nature. It pays, literally pays, to be cautious.'

'And yet here you are, offering your aid in this endeavour when, so far as I can see, it promises potential risk and precious little profit,' said Kalyani with the ghost of a smile.

'Hengin,' barked Norgssen, snapping his armoured fingers with a dull clang. The duardin to his right removed his helm to reveal a bright red beard and elaborately braided mustachios, above which twinkled ice-blue eyes. Hengin, Norgssen's first mate then and now, fished a blue-and-gold scrollcase from amidst a nest of them stored in a metal rack on his back. The duardin unscrewed one end of the case and then carefully tucked its cap into a pouch on his belt while all about him waited. He slid a scroll from the tube into his waiting palm, unfurled it with crisp motions and then cleared his throat. His voice, when he spoke, was a basso baritone so low that Kalyani felt it as though it reverberated in her chest.

'In the presence of all pertinent witnesses, all but one of whom have signed and countersigned their comprehension of terms and soundness of mind and body prior to the delivery of this document, and in proper accordance with the artycles of the Kharadron Code, let the following be recognised and understood. That Admiral Vornn Norgssen, hereafter referred to as the indebted, does confirm that he does, at this time and in the sight of the ancestors, owe a debt of honour to the value of his own life, that of his associate and a substantial quantity of his cargo to Lord-Celestant Kalyani Thunderblade, hereafter referred to as the creditor. Let it be further witnessed that the indebted owes additional and substantial assistance to the creditor in lieu of her ensuring the continued good reputation and mercantile honour of both the indebted and his associates. Let all here be notified that, in the undertaking of military aid to the creditor in the prosecution of a swift and desirable resolution to her armed campaign the indebted will consider said debt paid in full. To wit, the indebted and his associates will provide whatever military assistance and transportation is requested by the creditor during the prosecution of said campaign, and will extend all reasonable efforts to secure or destroy the – and here I quote the creditor for clarity's sake – the "weapon or item of prodigious power and menace that lurks somewhere beneath the ancient city of Mordavia." So let it be witnessed and agreed in the sight of the gods and the ancestors of the duardin peoples.'

Kalyani blinked as her mind caught up with the spiel of Kharadron legalese that had just spilled from Hengin's mouth.

'Simple, eh?' said Norgssen. 'May I have both your verbal and written agreement that you will consider our business satisfactorily concluded and my contractual obligation to you fulfilled once the terms of this document are met?'

'You support us in whatever fighting there is between our forces and the orruks. You aid us in securing the prize beneath Mordavia, whatever its nature, or in destroying it if it proves too perilous. And then we're square?' asked Kalyani, wanting to check her understanding out loud and to make sure that every other duardin present heard and understood what she required of them.

'We will provide military support and any transportation that you request, and will offer all reasonable efforts at acquisition or destruction of the prize,' Norgssen paraphrased. 'That's correct.'

'Agreed,' said Kalyani, taking the proffered copper quill and signing her name thrice at the bottom of the Kharadron contract. Her signatures joined a forest of scrawls that marked where Norgssen's chosen crew witnesses had already completed their parts of the pre-battle paperwork.

The moment Kalyani had finished her third signature the quill and parchment vanished, stowed efficiently by Hengin, who then stepped back after offering her a polite nod. He then fished a device from a pouch at his belt, a small brass cage wrapped with wires and housing two glimmering crystals perhaps an inch in length. As Kalyani watched with interest, Hengin depressed two brass studs on the device and held it close to his face. The crystals shimmered with sympathetic magical energies and as they resonated the ghost of a voice shuddered from them.

'*Aye, first mate? All concluded satisfactorily?*'

'Well enough, stand the fleet down and await admiral's orders,' Hengin replied before stashing the device again.

'Ingenious,' she commented to Norgssen, who grunted again.

'I flatter myself as something of an inventor,' he replied.

'You fashioned that device yourself?' she asked, genuinely impressed.

'That one and others like it,' he said, though if he took any pleasure in her reaction it didn't show through his dour façade. 'Issue them to my captains. They only work across short distances, and the crystals aren't easy to come by, but they've proved their worth more than once. We're not here to discuss my contributions to the advancement of duardin endrinering, though, are we? What can you tell me of this endeavour?'

'Little, beyond what my messenger conveyed, though I have a scholar labouring as we speak to learn more of the nature of the weapon.'

'A scholar,' echoed Norgssen, his tone dubious. 'Are they of use?'

'She seems skilled enough and determined to discover what manner of thing awaits us beneath the city's streets,' replied Kalyani. 'She's attempting to translate a mythic tongue, though. Since we set out on this march, she has established a little more of the weapon's probable location, but beyond that all she's translated seems nonsensical. Warnings about waning sparks striking the hottest fires and a shadowy figure seeking mastery...'

Norgssen harrumphed.

'Sounds about as useless as most academia to my ears, Lord-Celestant,' he said. 'What of these heading details though?'

Kalyani didn't acknowledge his criticisms; Norgssen owed her and he was a sound enough ally so long as he was contractually obliged to be, but she had found little enough to like about him when first they had met and found her disposition no warmer now. Barring that one spark of aberrant kindness he had shown amidst the blood and mayhem on the Thostorr Peninsula, he appeared sour-tempered and pedantic, a cynic most concerned with keeping up appearances.

For all that, his aid in the coming fight would be invaluable, especially if she wished to carry off her audacious plan of attack.

'There is a large structure with a substantial domed roof and a number of towers that overlooks a wide square near the city's centre,' she said, recalling the details that Bronvynne had painstakingly recovered from her tome. 'My scholar believes that the weapon is located somewhere within or beneath that structure. She also believes that it may well lie beyond the territory currently claimed by the orruks, if indeed they have not rampaged off into the wilds in search of fresh conquest.'

'She *believes* that, does she?' asked Norgssen.

'She was there, admiral. She has seen the city and its invaders for herself and escaped both with her life. I trust her in this.'

I have to, for now, she thought. *If the threat is everything she warns then I must deal with it. And if she is some agent of the enemy sent to lead us all astray, well...* Her hand fell to Song's pommel again.

'Have you a plan of attack, then?' asked Norgssen.

'I do, and it is why I asked you to meet us here. According to my map, Mordavia is another day's march yet for my warriors. We will likely reach the city sometime during the hours of darkness and be forced to wait for the dawn before we can push into the ruins in force. However, I dislike the thought of leaving the weapon unclaimed for any longer than we absolutely must, not when the orruks may stumble across it at any time.'

'Or be drawn to its power, if it is all that your scholar asserts,' said Norgssen with a scowl. 'Such primitive beasts have a way of sniffing out powerful and dangerous things, usually to the ruin of all.'

'Just so,' agreed Kalyani. 'That is why I ask you to furnish me with your fastest ship and to transport myself and a band of my finest warriors ahead of the main advance. We shall strike this very day, before Hysh has passed its apogee, and if fortune is with us and Sigmar smiles then we may resolve this matter with minimal cost to either of us.'

And in truth, you chafe for action, she chided herself wryly. *You wish to confirm the truth of the scholar's tale. You wish to see this city and these deadly orruks for yourself, and to seize the prize with such speed and skill that all will marvel. The Once-Forged has proved herself the dynamic heroine yet again, and you have proved to yourself that you are still the master of your wrath and able to direct and use it rather than letting it become you.*

Kalyani knew there was truth to this, that it was in her to be reckless when battle and glory were at hand. But such bold strategies had worked for her before, many times, and if she could spare the lives of Sigmar's faithful by risking her own then so be it. She knew how bloody matters were likely to get should the Celestial Vindicators meet the orruks in open battle, and she would spare her brothers and sisters from themselves if she could.

'Swift, decisive, unexpected and economical,' Norgssen pronounced, nodding slowly. He sniffed in a 'well then' sort of a way and gestured up at a sleek frigate currently circling away over the treeline to the west. The morning light glinted from the sky-ship's guns. 'The *Exactitude* will bear you hence. She's Captain Skarlig's ship, swift as they come and deadly as a fall from the clouds. How long will it take you to assemble your warriors?'

'They are already gathered at the base of the Echolith,' she replied, flashing him a wolfish grin. 'No sense wasting time, eh?'

'No indeed, an hour wasted is a shipment missed,' said Norgssen, sounding vaguely scandalised at the thought. 'And the rest of us? You would have us follow in your wake?'

'I would,' she said. 'Would you do us the honour of escorting our forces from the air?'

'I am obligated thusly,' he said, and she sensed that closed the matter. *Not quite the vows of heroism and fealty I am used to,* she thought to herself, *but it will suffice.*

'I will gather my followers from below and return to this peak with all haste,' she said. 'With luck, by the time the rest of you catch us up, your attendance will be nought but a formality.'

CHAPTER THREE

GLUMM'S GLORY

Mordavia, the first evening of the campaign

Wings thrummed, their insectile drone rolling like sickly thunder as the swarm of rot flies swept over the lake. The creatures were huge, each larger than a full-grown warhorse and considerably more corpulent. Chitinous armour plates gave the daemonic insects a hunched look, and glinted with weird iridescence in the light of late afternoon. Their gangling limbs trailed down until they skimmed the still waters. Where they touched, ripples spread outward, suddenly seething with foul blooming algae and scads of diseased foam. Rancid juices drizzled from the rotting rents and myriad pustules that proliferated across the rot flies' distended bodies; the swarm left a diseased slick across the lake-waters in their wake.

Sat astride each fly was a rider every bit as corrupt and dis-figured as their steeds. They were pusgoyle blightlords, worship-pers of Nurgle, once mortal men and women now swollen and made monstrous by the Plague God's fecund blessings. Rotted innards spilled through blubbery skin, swarming with maggots and dribbling filth. Their rusted armour plates fused directly with their puffy grey flesh and lent them even more bulk. They wore helms that boasted jutting horns, racks of rotting antlers and jangling tangles of verdigrised bells, and each hefted a grotesquely outsized weapon. Some had axes or maces. Some bore hammers whose heads were forged into the shape of leering plague daemons' faces. Most wielded tall scythes of warped rotwood from which fluttered ragged pennants bearing the tri-lobe sigil of Nurgle. Several riders had lashed chains about their revolting steeds and hung huge bells below them; even now the rust-caked tocsins skimmed the water. Once in a while one would clip some jutting rock or protruding spar of ancient masonry, letting out a warped and mournful *bonggggg*.

At the head of the swarm, slouching easily in his saddle and trusting accumulated rust and crust to hold him in place, Cankus Glumm rode upon his enormous rot fly, Ghrottle. He was larger than his followers, fattened and made putrid by the foul gifts of his patron. His pus-white flesh bulged through rents in his armour as though ready to burst. In several places it had, leaving trails of diseased meat and swollen innards hanging down about him like foul garlands. A tri-lobe of milky green eyes stared and rolled madly in his straining breastplate. One shoulder guard had warped and grown until a twisted gnarlmaw sapling rose from it, branches thick with poisonous thorns and hung with jangling bells. Glumm's helm swathed the top half of his head entire, a curving horn rising from its faceplate where eyeholes should have been. Below it, his rotting jowls were split by a grinning maw that belonged on a shark, not a man. His needle teeth were black with rot.

In one hand, Glumm easily hefted his enormous trident, which he called Benignance. In the other he gripped the neck of his incubatch, his plague allotment, the nursery bed for all his finest afflictions. Yakob, rot-raddled, legless, one-armed and at first glance no more than a corpse, was all those things, yet to Glumm he was much more. Yakob was his oldest friend, his most honest counsellor. His brother. Yakob had been with him since Nurgle first planted a seed of power in Cankus' flesh.

Now, as the lake swept below and the ruins of Mordavia drew closer ahead, Cankus Glumm raised Yakob up so the incubatch could get a good view.

'There it be, old chum,' said Glumm with an expansive grin. 'Mordavia.'

'*Just... where the Great Gardener... said t'would be...*' replied Yakob in his landsman's rural drawl. His voice had always sounded similar to Glumm's own, just more strangled, more rasping.

'Aye, he's led us true, like he always does,' said Glumm. 'Now 'tis time for the real work to be startin'.'

'*The... weapon...*' croaked Yakob, his voice bereft of the relish that coloured Glumm's. Yakob was never very happy about anything. It was one of the few small sorrows of Glumm's otherwise blessed existence. He wished he could find a way to bring his brother joy.

'Ar, the weapon. The desolator, right 'n true enough,' said Glumm. 'Can't be lettin' that fall into the wrong 'ands, now, can us?'

'*Not since... the Gardener... told you not to,*' offered Yakob by way of agreement. He sounded despondent and Glumm frowned at him.

'You'm don't sound too pleased 'bout all this, brother,' he said, wobbling slightly as Ghrottle jinked to avoid an ancient stone column jutting from the waters. The light of Hysh was settling low above the mountain peaks to the north as the day moved on and its beams lanced long and amber over the lake and the ruined city as they drew nearer.

'Just got… a troublesome feelin'… 'bout it all,' replied Yakob, his tone morose.

Glumm stared ahead as he pondered this, seeing without eyes, watching the lakeshore race closer with its half-submerged ruins and ragged accumulations of undergrowth. Mordavia was a place dead and yet not, he thought to himself, a sprawling ruin that Ghyran had long reclaimed and yet it held on to its shape. It clung to its purpose. Just as the Great Gardener had said, this city had a secret yet to keep and it wouldn't surrender itself to dust and undergrowth while its task remained.

He sighed, a low, bubbling sound.

'Lissen, you 'eard what the Gardener told, brother, when he came to us in that filth pit outside Bleker's Peak,' said Glumm, speaking in the tone of one who has had the same debate now several times but has the patience to hold it again. 'A weapon that'll still the life of all. A thing that leeches through the veil, that spreads entropy 'n stillness like a shroud.'

'I 'eard… same as you…' replied Yakob, sounding truculent. Glumm looked about him to his nearest blightlords, shooting them a 'what can you do?' shrug. They returned his gesture, stoic and neutral. His followers always acted that way when it came to Yakob. Glumm supposed they just didn't understand the bond that he and his incubatch shared, didn't know why he indulged Yakob so.

'So, what ails you?' asked Glumm, unable to suppress a too-wide leer at his own terrible joke.

'This weapon's been 'ere… all this time, ain't it? But no bugger's come along 'n… had it away in all them long years? Why's… that then?' asked Yakob. Glumm was surprised to hear anger in the incubatch's clotted rasp.

'You've 'eard, same as I, 'bout these 'ere vaults as what got uncovered when the Necroquake hit,' Glumm replied, his tone one of a patient adult explaining something to an obstreperous child. 'Got to be one o' they, ain't it? All bound up with forgettin' magics and hidden away by oh-so-'igh-and-mighty Sigmar so's no one else would know where the most powerful weapons were planted. Seed to be watered when all he had left for the waterin' was blood, that's what we 'eard, remember? Only now Old Bones 'as given the realms a glottin' good shake and look what comes a-tumblin' out.'

'*All right... so why don't the Gardner... come and get it hisself if'n it's so... bloomin' important?*' Glumm felt annoyance take root in his chest and fought to stop it growing. He hated it when he and Yakob fought, and the incubatch could be so stubborn about things sometimes. Though not, he admitted to himself, without good reason. Glumm was an optimist through and through. Yakob had been his festering voice of caution for many long years.

'He said he was goin' to send help, don't you remember? I reckon your brains is rottin' away at last, brother. We'm the advance guard is all. First chance at the glory.'

'*Could've at least... waited for the rest o'... the warband...*' gasped Yakob, sounding sulky.

'Don't reckon we'll even need that bunch o' slugs, eh?' Glumm replied with forced cheer. 'Us'll be in, grab the weapon from where 'is Gardnership said it were, and be back out quickr'n a dose of the screamin' flux goes through a swampland village.'

'*He said... there'd be others...*' said Yakob. '*He said... they'd fight...*'

'Then we'll rottin' well kill 'em all and sow lovely new plague beds in their corpses!' exclaimed Glumm, his patience fraying. Ghrottle's trunk-like proboscis quested up and slathered at Glumm's leaking juices, the daemon made eager as it scented bitterness in the air. Glumm slapped it away irritably. He couldn't understand his incubatch's reticence towards a perfectly good opportunity for glory, but he could sense his followers shifting uncomfortably in their saddles and shooting glances at one another as the argument escalated. Leadership of a warband like this, even one as harmonious as the followers of Nurgle, was a perilous affair. He couldn't afford for Yakob to keep undermining him before his followers, lest one of them catch a bad case of ambition. That particular ailment spread faster than any amongst the worshippers of the Dark Gods, in Glumm's experience.

He pulled the incubatch close, his nostrils filling with the ripe stench of decay as he did so. Things squirmed from Yakob's putrid flesh and dropped onto Glumm with squeals of delight, but he ignored the little daemon maggots.

'We're almost over the city. Won't be long after then 'n we'll be in the square what the Gardener showed us. Then it's straight to the prize. So if you got somethin' on whatever's left o' your mind, Yakob, sick it up, eh? Or else keep your peace an' stop sowin' malcontent.'

For a few thrumming wingbeats, Glumm thought Yakob had subsided. He did that sometimes, went quiet for hours, even days at a time until Glumm began to fear that his brother truly had become just the cursed remains he appeared to be. Then Yakob spoke up again, quieter, his voice little more than the hiss of corpse-gas escaping a dead man's throat.

'What if we're bein'... spent like coin?' he asked. 'Us are mortals still, still expendable. If this thing's as terrible as'n the... Gardener said, then what if we're being chucked... in first t'fertilise the ground with our blood 'n toil... then he comes... after 'n reaps the... crop?'

Glumm's ill humour evaporated as he realised that Yakob was only thinking of him, of all their warband. The Horns of Plenty had fought long together in Nurgle's name. It was only natural that Yakob would be concerned for their wellbeing. Rot alone knew Glumm certainly was.

'We're favoured, and by all the blights we're tough as they come,' he told Yakob with a vicious grin. 'Ain't no good crop sowed without sweat 'n toil, and the harvester's scythe cuts sharp no matter who it be slicin'. No chance we're doin' this thing without a fight, brother, but we'll do it all the same. That weapon has to go into Nurgle's cauldron, s'the only way it'll be destroyed. And the Gardener'll reward us proper when we do, eh? Mayhap we'll finally get you a new body to stroll aroun' in. That'd be a fine thing, eh?'

Bells bonged and boomed as the swarm of rot flies thundered in over the beach and wobbled heavily up and over the half-drowned ruins that marked the city's edge. Glumm looked up, searching the jumbled landscape for the landmarks he had seen in his vision. There, he saw the cadaverous tower rising near the city's eastern edge, its peak like a clawing hand. There, closer, was the bifurcating ravine that had swallowed an entire district, ruined buildings still clinging to its lip like rotten teeth in a gaping maw. There the three low hills that hunched amidst the city's northern districts, each crowned with the crumbling remnants of what might have been fortifications.

'Now if all o' they be in their rightful places, then...' Glumm's voice trailed off and his grin threatened to split his head in half as he saw it rising amidst the ruins. A proud if shattered building, with the cracked-egg remains of a dome stretching wide over it, four mighty bell towers whose peaks had toppled into the surrounding streets, and the eroded and crumbling shapes of robe-swathed statues looming huge at its cardinal points. The building was as big as a district in its own right, while the square stretching before it was so wide that he could make it out just from the gaps in the skyline that it created.

'There we are, the Old Temple. Thank'ee, Great Gardener,' Glumm said. He turned in his saddle, drawing in a rancid lungful to shout orders to his swarm. Before he could, Pulgh the Sighted raised his scythe and pointed with it.

'Foes, m'lord, soaring through the skies!'

Glumm spun in his saddle and his unnatural sight fixed upon a sizeable airship sweeping in over the city from the south. *There will be others*, he thought, recognising the burnished brass and strange mechanisms of a Kharadron vessel. *There will be others, and we shall make such offerings of them to Grandfather Nurgle.*

'Ain't no harvest without a little rain, is there, my beauties?' he bellowed, brandishing his trident and giving a gurgling laugh. 'We was sent 'ere to reap, an' that's what we'll do, and if'n they wants to stand before the scythe we'll reap them too! On! Fly on to the square and be ready when they comes our way!'

His followers raised a rumbling war cry and leaned forward in their saddles. They thumped iron-shod heels into the flanks of their sour-tempered mounts, eliciting squirts of pus and angry buzzing as the rot flies swept on towards the Old Temple at the city's heart.

'Foes dead ahead,' cried the lookout from his observation dome atop the airship's aether-endrin. Stood upon the foredeck of the *Exactitude*, Kalyani Thunderblade leaned upon the fore rail and stared hard over the patchwork of rubble, shadow and rampant greenery that was the ruined city. She saw the massive bulk of the Old Temple looming at the city's heart, its silhouette matching that sketched roughly by Karrobeth just before the *Exactitude* set out. It took her a moment to pick out the bulky shapes of giant flies wobbling madly through the air towards the building from the east.

'Several dozen at least,' commented Koris the Breaker, who stood to her right shoulder. The Retributor-Prime hefted his massive hammer with eager purpose. 'Seems we are not the only ones making a dash for this weapon, Lord-Celestant.'

'Enough to make the battle interesting,' said Melandra Brightbolt, the Judicator-Prime to Kalyani's left.

'We cannot allow them to take possession of the weapon,' called the Lord-Celestant, turning to address Captain Skarlig, who stood some way behind them at the *Exactitude*'s helm. 'Can your craft beat the Chaos worshippers to the Old Temple?'

'You're asking me if my warship can outpace a wallowing swarm of fat and sickly flies?' the Kharadron captain called back, genuine affront in his voice.

'Don't shout about it then, captain. Do it,' Kalyani replied before turning back to the railing and drawing Song from its scabbard. Lightning crawled along the length of the blade, dimly visible in the late afternoon light.

'What are they doing here? What chance they'd reach this place just as we did?' asked Brightbolt.

'They seek the same prize we do. The same thing that the orruks, too, were drawn here to find,' replied Kalyani, narrowing her eyes and staring past the flies towards the distant temple. 'It's out there, calling to any with the strength to reach out and take it. Can't you feel its pull?'

Kalyani had been feeling it ever since they came within a hundred miles of the city. It was as though some undertow were drawing her on, faster and faster, towards a dark and thundering whirlpool. Part of her wanted to turn away in fear, to strike out with everything she had and get as far away from whatever this was as she could get. She tightened her grip upon her blade. There was duty to do, and enemies between her and it. That was enough to stoke the fires of her battle-rage and burn away all other concerns. She was the Once-Forged, never bested in battle since Sigmar had raised her up to the Heavens. She would not die this day.

'More power to the terculators,' shouted Captain Skarlig, sending his crew swarming through hatches and along clamber-lines between thrumming islands of machinery. 'Double rotation on the foiling caps! Open valves three through eight. An extra share of the victory profits to every duardin aboard if we reach that temple before the rot-botherers. Let's show 'em what *Exactitude* can do!'

The deck shuddered beneath Kalyani's feet. The powerful thrum of the aether-endrins rose to a basso roar as the sky-ship accelerated to flank speed. She heard the rattle and clank of cogwork turning as the bulky fore turret revolved nearby and brought its massive harpoon launcher to bear.

'Breaker, Brightbolt, ready your retinues,' Kalyani ordered as the sky-ship swept in over the ruins of Mordavia. They saluted her and turned to call orders to their followers, who were even now piling from the hatches of the craft's interior. Kalyani did not understand what unnatural artifice allowed there to be so much space within the stocky sky-ships of the Kharadron, and she didn't have time or inclination to question it now. She leaned over the railing and watched the sky-ship's shadow flicker and flux as it played over rubble-strewn streets, corpses of balu trees and giant ferns, ragged chasms, shattered buildings and toppled statues. Kalyani almost fancied she could have reached down and slapped the highest spires of stonework as they passed above them.

Skarlig was bringing his craft lower as he aimed her prow towards the Old Temple. He sought to put its armoured flank between the rot flies and their destination, Kalyani realised, probably planning to hammer them with gunfire as he did so. Sure enough, arkanauts were taking up firing positions on the port side of the sky-ship as it hove closer to the swarm. They checked the actions on multi-barrelled cogwork guns and hefty blunderbusses as the wind sang around them and the endrins roared.

There were a lot of rot flies, Kalyani thought. Enough to tear the *Exactitude* out of the skies if matters went ill. But she could see from his manoeuvring that Skarlig wasn't content to leave so great a swarm on their tail; what use was reaching the destination first if they were overrun just moments after getting there?

No, he aimed to maul the foe with a close-range broadside then pull ahead of them, giving the Stormcasts a far better chance of victory once they reached the Old Temple. It was a bold move, equal parts bravado and bravery. The Lord-Celestant approved.

'Brightbolt, be ready to add your fire to theirs. This volley needs to tear the enemy apart lest they seize the chance to board us,' she called over the scream of the wind. The Judicator-Prime saluted again.

'What of my Retributors?' Koris shouted from across the throng-ing deck.

'Be ready in case the broadside doesn't do its job,' Kalyani replied, shooting him a savage grin. She knew that their duty lay ahead in the temple square but as the enemy grew ever closer and the sky-ship's acceleration squeezed tears from the corners of her eyes, the Lord-Celestant couldn't deny the grip of the battle-rage that was her Stormhost's inheritance. She could make out details now: the rot-ting hides of the revolting flies; the equally disgusting hulks of flesh, muscle and rusting metal that rode upon them. She saw the giant that rode at the head of the swarm, a lamprey grin upon his face and a massive trident brandished in one fist. Kalyani marked him; this one would be hers, she thought, fitting tribute for the God-King.

'Come on… come on…' she willed her enemies as the *Exactitude* pulled ahead of them. Sure enough, she saw their horn-helmed leader realise that the sky-ship was going to outpace him easily, that if he wished to win this uneven race, he had only one option left to him. He gestured, and the rot flies swarmed in towards the *Exactitude*, putting on a burst of manic speed as they sought to close the gap. As they did so, they put themselves in point-blank range.

'Fire!' roared Captain Skarlig, and the air filled with thunder. Solid shots, hails of bullets and heavy iron harpoons flew as the arkanauts and their sky-ship let fly. Amidst the killing rain flew arrows that crackled with caged lightning, shot from the tall bows of the Judicators.

The effect of the broadside was punishing. Nurgle worshippers jolted and danced in their saddles as rounds punched into them with tremendous force. Rot flies shuddered as their chitinous plates were cracked and their fatted guts shot out in sprays of filth. Kalyani saw a bomb-like projectile punch deep into one of the flies then explode, blowing it bodily apart in a shower of rotten gore and catapulting the rider high into the air. He fell away towards the city below, his cries lost amidst the thunderstorm of explosions. She saw his body clip a jutting spire of stonework, smashing it to rubble like a falling boulder before pinwheeling away into a yawning crack in the ground.

For several heartbeats the Lord-Celestant suspected the fight was already over. Corrupted blood and torn flesh fell like rain upon Mordavia as their enemies were butchered. Yet as the smoke tattered away in their wake Kalyani saw the blightlords remained in better condition than she would have believed possible. Many boasted horrific wounds, gaping rents, disembowelments and several dismemberments that should surely have killed their victims. Yet well over half of the fly-riding Chaos worshippers remained, and now they drove their steeds on towards the sky-ship with angry bellows. The wings of the flies thrummed madly and in a moment of clarity Kalyani saw that Captain Skarlig had miscalculated. In maximising the effect of his broadside he had closed the gap too closely with the foe, and had woefully underestimated their resilience. Now his craft was sailing past and below the enemy. Aether-endrins thundered as Skarlig fought to bring his prow up and gain some altitude. His arkanaut crew swarmed over their craft like apes, assuming new firing positions as swiftly as they could. Kalyani could see it wouldn't be quick enough. A few more moments and they might have outpaced retribution.

The enemy weren't about to afford them such luxuries.

Flying hard, the blightlords came in above and behind the sky-ship. As they soared in on the attack the riders hefted suppurating orbs that Kalyani knew from bitter combat experience were severed heads. Mouths stitched shut, eyes and ears and noses all stoppered with wax, the foul projectiles were filled to bursting with diseased slime so potent that it could corrode metal and dissolve flesh in moments. Now the blightlords flung their death's heads and, as their steeds stooped into aggressive dives, so the bombardment of projectiles rained down to herald their coming.

Death's heads struck the sky-ship and its crew alike, bursting like fat pimples and spattering their lethal contents in all directions. Metal spars hissed and deck plates bubbled as unnatural plagues chewed furiously through them. Arkanauts fell back with gurgling cries, their armour frothing and their flesh sloughing away. Kalyani saw more than one courageous duardin go tumbling into open air as they lost their grip on clamber-lines and metal rungs. They followed the slain blightlords down, down, down to smash into rocky ruins or burst bloodily upon abandoned streets.

Stormcasts too were slain, several of Kalyani's hand-picked warriors struck by the deadly plague bombs. Their souls flashed away into the skies, bolts of jade lightning streaking back to the Heavens even as their mortal remains discorporated.

'Prepare to repel!' shouted Captain Skarlig. 'Fire at will!'

Bedlam engulfed the sky-ship as the blightlords fell upon it. Arkanauts fired their guns point-blank, sending rot flies spiralling past with faces blasted to craters or wings torn from their bloated bodies. Talon-like limbs lashed out to impale duardin and hold them trapped as venomous stingers lashed and slobbering mouthparts closed about their heads.

The deck shuddered again and again as Nurgle worshippers slid from their saddles and thumped down on the deck with their scythes swinging. Kalyani saw one of the grotesque flies arc high overhead trailing an enormous armoured bell that slammed into the aether-endrin with brutal force. Already, corroded rents in the endrin were belching smoke and fumes, and this impact only added another deep dent in the complex machinery. The endrins had taken on a droning note that sounded sickly to Kalyani's ear.

They seemed to be losing speed and altitude both.

She launched herself into action. They needed to drive off the boarders quickly if the arkanauts were to have any chance of getting them to the square in one piece. At these close quarters she and her Stormcasts were the best defence the duardin had.

'For Sigmar!' she roared, lightning trailing in an arc behind Song as she lashed out to lop a blightlord's head from his shoulders. The dome-like helm spun over the deck railing, leaving the Chaos worshipper's body to crash backwards onto the decking. Squealing maggots poured from it by the dozen and Kalyani directed a swift kick at the corrupt sac of muscle and meat, shoving it over the side before it could spread its filth any further.

A rot fly came at her from the right, its rider swooping down upon the deck with a glottal cry. Kalyani swung her sword in a flashing arc that hacked through the daemon's thicket of dangling limbs, then dropped and rolled aside to avoid the swing of the blightlord's scythe. She came up on the edge of a press of wrestling figures; several unseated blightlords were advancing on the helm, pressing back the handful of desperate arkanauts that opposed them. A pistol cracked, its bullet ringing a blightlord's helm like a bell. The hulking warrior took a step back, laughed and flattened the shooter into the deck with her hammer. Kalyani lunged, driving the point of Song through her victim's armpit. Stinking blood gouted around the weapon, slathering Kalyani's hands and forearms in greasy gore and wriggling white worms.

She ripped the weapon out and stepped back with a grunt of

disgust as her maimed enemy turned, still chortling. The sound stopped abruptly as a lightning-wreathed hammer head crashed down upon the blightlord's helm and drove it deep into her bloated body. Cracking booms announced more thunderous impacts as Koris the Breaker and his Retributors waded into the fight. Koris and his warriors chanted their war dirge as they swung and smote, fighting with commendable skill despite the cramped conditions.

Kalyani began to chant her own war mantra as she fought to keep her footing upon the gore-slicked deck and the sky-ship shuddered beneath her.

'We fight for Sigmar!' she snarled, channelling the red rage that burned within her breast, honing and controlling it as a master blacksmith uses the heat of their forge to temper a blade. 'We fight for the Heavens! We fight for retribution! We fight! We kill! We win!' She lashed out at the enemies around her, at the daemonic fiends that dashed themselves against the sky-ship and knocked screaming warriors from the decks with their flailing limbs.

Gunshots cracked. Bullets whined from metal and punched into flesh. One ricocheted from her shoulder guard, hard enough to stagger her.

The city's ruined buildings whooshed past below, close enough now to strike sparks from the sky-ship's hull as it scraped over them.

Voices cried out in a jumbled cacophony, war cries and battle chants and gurgling guffaws and yells of anger or fear.

The crackle of flames was audible through the pandemonium. The endrins droned and laboured.

Flies' wings thrummed. Stinking slime sprayed.

The sky-ship dropped lower, fell faster.

'This is no fight, it is bloody mayhem!' came Brightbolt's voice from somewhere to Kalyani's left, beyond the smoke and blood and heaving bodies.

'Repel the bastards!' came the captain's voice from somewhere else, maybe above Kalyani amidst the clamber-lines and throbbing pipes. 'Repel them and get to damage stations or she'll not fly another run, lads!'

'Surely there can't be many of them left alive,' snarled Kalyani as she rammed her blade through the helm of another one and out the back of his head. Yet as she tore the blade free there came a tremendous bang from behind her and a judder ran through the decking.

The Lord-Celestant spun, sure she would see the *Exactitude*'s prow ploughing into some jutting spar of masonry or ancient tower's flank. Instead she saw the helmed and grinning lord that led this murderous swarm. A monstrous-looking sapling jutted incongruously from his shoulder, its bells a-jangle. He had landed with a crash upon the sky-ship's for'ard turret, his massive bulk staving the armoured dome in and doubtless crushing the arkanaut gunner inside. Beyond the hulking lord, Kalyani could see the ship's prow wavering lower, the ruins rushing up to meet it with a speed that seemed to increase the closer and larger they grew. The Old Temple loomed, but they were going to crash before they reached it.

The Nurgle lord stepped down from the ruined turret and planted his feet. As she watched, he thrust the tines of his trident into the festering corpse that he carried in his off hand, allowing the diseased filth from the body to anoint the weapon and render it more lethal still. Then he grinned hugely at her and pointed the weapon in challenge.

From somewhere above, Kalyani heard Captain Skarlig yelling orders, but their meaning was muffled to nonsense by the blood pounding in her ears. She raised Song two-handed so that the blade was level with her face, point towards her foe.

'We fight for Sigmar! We fight for the Heavens! We fight for retribution! We fight!' she intoned and launched herself into a headlong charge even as the sky-ship lurched below her and the ruins lunged hungrily up to meet its prow.

CHAPTER FOUR

IN THE TEMPLE'S SHADOW

Mordavia, the first evening of the campaign

The Stormcast flew at him and Glumm leapt to meet her. His boots hit the airship's deck even as his trident caught her sweeping blade. Lightning exploded from the impact, staggering him back a step. Glumm grinned madly at his enemy and brandished his weapon. She was tall, powerfully built and wore a great deal of warrior jewellery that he supposed marked her out as the champion of her warband. She also moved with speed, grace and ferocity, he realised as her blade whipped in again. He swung his trident around like a quarterstaff and turned the blade, seeking to direct it down into the decking. With the Grandfather's luck, it might even stick there and afford him a killing thrust.

Glumm had no such fortune. His opponent rode the sudden redirection of her blade's motion and dropped to one knee, transforming a missed strike into a quick draw-back-and-thrust that almost took him in the gut. He stepped back again and felt his shoulder blades hit the mangled metal of the for'ard turret.

'We fight for Sigmar!' she spat. 'We fight for the Heavens! We fight for retribution! We fight! We kill! We win!'

Sudden anger filled him. Her relentless chant, her precise speed, the anger and hate he read in her dark eyes and plastered across those oh-so-clean-and-healthy features; everything about this champion of the Storm God rankled with Cankus Glumm and made him want to lash out. She was an embodiment of the order and cleanliness so anathema to Nurgle's way. She was everything wrong with the realms these days.

'Get back, y'cursed maggot!' he roared, rancid spittle spraying. Glumm levelled his trident and lunged once, twice, thrice. He knew from experience that the weapon looked clumsy, even more so for he was forced to wield it one-handed or else drop Yakob, which was something he wouldn't dream of doing. The Lord of Afflictions had wielded Benignance for centuries now, though. He knew every gram of its weight and balance, every strength and weakness of the weapon. He knew precisely how to wield it with terrifying skill. As he saw surprise flash in his enemy's eyes Glumm knew that she, like so many before her, had underestimated the threat that his unconventional weapon represented.

That said, the Stormcast managed to parry all three thrusts, blocking the tines twice by angling her blade between them then swinging hard to knock the trident's head up and away from her on his third thrust. Foul slime spattered from its tips each time it impacted her guard, yet somehow the Stormcast managed to evade that as well. A duardin behind her wasn't so fortunate, and he fell to his knees with a wail as his flesh bubbled and popped.

Ignoring the arkanaut's fate, the Stormcast danced back several steps, outpacing Glumm's lumbering advance. She weaved between bloodied corpses and struggling warriors, untouched by their brawling, focused only on him.

'We fight for Sigmar! We fight for the Heavens! We fight for retribution! We fight! We kill! We win!' she chanted, her voice made rich by some accent or dialect he'd never heard before. Glumm saw her make ready to attack again. Her footwork was sublime, he noted grudgingly. If you liked that sort of thing.

Before either of them could launch another assault, the sky-ship gave a tremendous lurch. A shudder ran through the deck. Metal groaned, complaining vociferously as it was subjected to stresses beyond its tolerance. Glumm's capacious guts roiled as he felt the prow rear behind him. He saw the Stormcast's eyes widen, saw the heaving battle at her back lose pace as combatants faltered and stared.

A shadow fell across him.

'*Um...*' said Yakob uncertainly.

Glumm spun in time to see a cliff-face of crumbling stonework loom large.

'Rottin' bones,' he cursed in exasperation before the sky-ship's prow smashed into the building's flank and a storm of shattered rubble exploded around him. Glumm staggered backwards, away from the sudden avalanche as the ship smashed through the wall. The craft bucked as it ploughed through the ancient ruin, throwing Glumm into the air. He slammed down on the buckling deck, managing to keep a grip on trident and incubatch both as rivets popped skyward around him and warriors were thrown from their feet. Rock and rubble crashed down. Blightlords and Stormcasts and duardin cried out as they were struck by flying stone and torn metal or launched over the railings into the ruinous collapse below.

Hefting his trident and driving its tines deep into the decking, Glumm hung on and hunched protectively over Yakob's helpless form as the endrins above screamed and smoke billowed.

''Ang on, brother!' he shouted, sharp teeth gritted as unidentifiable debris clanged from his armour and bludgeoned his bloated flesh. There came a moment of weightlessness, a dreadful quiet, and then a tremendous impact that slammed Glumm's helmed head against the decking hard enough to knock all thought from it.

As the towering ruin exploded over the prow of the sky-ship, a rain of rubble engulfed the deck. Kalyani lost sight of her foe. She felt a moment of frustration; they had barely locked blades and she wanted, *needed*, to cut that filthy monster apart in the God-King's name. Her sense of self-preservation prevailed as the ancient building crumpled forward to engulf the stricken sky-ship.

'Eviscerators, over the side!' Kalyani roared, running for the railing and vaulting it one-handed without even pausing to sheathe her weapon. This wasn't the way the duardin would survive this crash, but for the Stormcasts with their reforged resilience and reflexes it was preferable to going down with the *Exactitude*.

Kalyani fell like a thunderbolt into the turmoil of collapsing stonework below. Her boots hit a sagging floor, but it gave way as though made of little more than dust and memories. Balu tree branches lashed at her as she crashed through them. Falling rubble smashed against her like fists. She hit another solid surface, this one canted at a wild angle and, spotting a ragged gap ahead and daylight beyond it, she propelled herself into a furious leap that sent her smashing out through the ruin's exterior wall.

Kalyani fell another twenty feet, her hair and cloak streaming in her wake as she plummeted towards a steeply canted cobbled street. She hit hard enough to make her teeth clack together, and rolled to take the killing force out of the impact. No use escaping the crash only to wind up back in Sigmaron or, worse, stricken and maimed in the ruins of Mordavia with no one to come to her aid.

Kalyani rolled down the street, crashed through a break of nodding ferns and hit a wall at the bottom with enough force to punch the breath from her body.

She blinked, dragged in a lungful of dusty air then forced herself to her feet. Her body offered belated reports of pain from almost every angle. She tasted blood, heard ringing in her ears and had to blink more dust from her eyes. She looked down, almost surprised to see Song still clutched firmly in one hand. Her helm was lost, having come away from her belt during the fall, and her cloak was torn into tatters.

'My limbs all work, nothing is broken and I can still fight,' she said to herself then, almost as an afterthought. 'Thank you, Sigmar.'

Looking up she saw the towering ruin, now some way uphill, still collapsing by stages. Dust billowed around it and rolled down the hill towards her. She heard rumbling and crashing, the sounds echoing weirdly along the abandoned streets. There were several heartbeats of quiet as she took in the hollow windows of time-lost dwellings, fluted carvings of writhing beasts coiling up crumbling columns, many clutching hourglasses of prodigious size. Eroded gargoyles with blank masks and more hourglasses in their chests crouched above street corners and stone gutters.

Then came another boom, much louder. There was a long, groaning screech of sundering metal, several lesser explosions, and a black column of smoke drifted skywards beyond the far side of the smashed ruin.

The sky-ship must have come down in the square, she thought.

'If any of those Nurgle worshippers still live...' She was off up the hill at a run the moment the realisation struck her, banishing the last of her disorientation from the fall. The servants of Chaos couldn't be allowed to recover that weapon first!

Kalyani met Koris halfway up the hill. He was just struggling to his feet, leaning on the haft of his upturned hammer, limping badly.

He too had lost his helm; she saw it lying buckled and discarded at his feet. Blood sheeted down one side of the Retributor's face, but he looked at his Lord-Celestant with nothing but determination as she reached him.

'They crashed beyond the ruins,' he said. 'Yet listen to those gunshots. It sounds as though they're fighting just the next street over.'

'I know. For a moment I thought I had dropped straight into battle,' Kalyani replied, starting and half-turning as a war cry echoed along the street. She shook her head, seeing no sign of the combatant who had uttered it, nor the scythe blade she now heard hissing and ringing as though in response. 'Can you fight?'

Koris adjusted his hold on the haft of his hammer, slid his hand up so that he gripped it near its crackling metal head.

'We fight,' he said, and fell in beside Kalyani as she continued up the hill.

'We kill. We win,' she finished, and hoped it would be enough.

By the time the Celestial Vindicators reached the square before the Old Temple, Kalyani Thunderblade had managed to reassemble nearly half of the Stormcast Eternals who had taken ship from atop the Echolith that morning. Of Brightbolt there had been no sign. Four Retributors and six Judicators were no army, especially not with nearly half of them wounded and several missing weapons lost in the crash. Still it was a gathering of mighty heroes whose determination and martial fury were undimmed by the losses that had befallen them. It was a force more than sufficient for the task at hand, Kalyani told herself.

It had to be.

They were drawn to the square through the last tangle of streets by shouts and gunfire. Sound travelled strangely in Mordavia,

Kalyani now realised. It bounced and rolled from walls and doorways in such a way that it carried further and clearer than it had any right to.

Now, she, Koris and their surviving comrades burst into the square and saw revealed the gruesome scene that had already unfolded in their minds' eyes.

'Sigmar's hammer,' breathed Koris.

'He had no part in this horror,' replied Kalyani as she took in the wreck of the *Exactitude* lying broken and overturned in the middle of the square. The temple loomed over it as though inspecting it like some faintly curious godbeast. Strangely hued alchemical flames still leapt and danced across the sky-ship's wreck, issuing in the main from the ruin of its aether-endrin and sending choking black-and-gold smoke into the sky.

Bodies, rubble and chunks of debris were strewn where they had fallen in the wreck's wake, cast aside as it ploughed a deep furrow through the ancient cobbles of the square. Duardin and blightlords alike lay sprawled like sad and broken dolls.

It was clear that Skarlig and the last of his crew had made a stand amidst the wreckage of the ship. It was also clear, from the handful of hulking Nurgle worshippers now picking over the bodies and the depleted swarm of rot flies thrumming overhead, that the stand had ended shortly before the Stormcasts arrived.

'We abandoned them,' breathed one of the Judicators. Kalyani looked round at him with a scowl of contempt.

'They failed us. It was their duty to bring us safe to the Old Temple and to defend us from the air while we did Sigmar's work. Had they been successful their ship would currently be holding station above us and we would already be moving to seize the weapon. Instead we are here, with weapons in our hands and foes before us. Cast aside your misplaced pity and honour Sigmar, or are you not a Celestial Vindicator at all?'

The Judicator raised his battered bow and fitted an arrow to its string by way of a reply. Kalyani nodded her approval.

'All of us came into Sigmar's service by blood, and by blood shall we serve him!' she roared, not caring if her enemies heard. She *wanted* them to hear, for when the Celestial Vindicators went to battle, they cared nothing for subtlety or stealth. They cared only for the battle, and the victory at its end.

'For Sigmar we fight!' roared her warriors and, shrugging off the pain of their injuries and the sorrow of comrades lost, they followed Kalyani into the square at a run.

Cankus Glumm turned to see the Stormcasts charging from the shadowy streets and out across the echoing emptiness of the square. It was a huge space, striped amber and black by the early evening light falling through the eerie ruins all around. As Sigmar's warriors charged they passed through bars of shadow and light. Somewhere distant, Glumm heard a huge drum pounding out a relentless beat and wondered idly if it was the Stormcasts' doing.

Glumm hefted his trident and looked down at Yakob. Glumm himself had suffered a number of flesh wounds, not to mention the indignity of his gnarl-sapling being snapped clean off his shoulder guard. However, he'd ensured his pox-ridden, one-limbed brother survived the impact without losing any more of himself, and that wasn't nothing.

''Ere they comes again,' rumbled Glumm, grinning his shark's grin. 'Reckon we can take 'em?'

'*How many... are they?*' asked Yakob. '*I'd count but... my eyes are full of maggots... again...*'

Glumm chortled to himself, hefting his trident as the enemy pounded closer. A few more moments and they'd be coming into bow range. Their chieftain led them in, a look of cold fury on her face.

'There's eleven in all, including that feisty lass leadin' 'em,' he said.

'*And how… many be we?*' asked Yakob.

'Seven, not countin' our flies,' replied Glumm with satisfaction.

'*Good… number,*' rasped Yakob. '*Blessed… number…*'

'Ar, so it is,' said Glumm, his foetid heart pumping faster as the enemy drew closer. Around him his blightlords left off seeding the duardin corpses with plague spores and hefted their own weapons. One by one their rot fly steeds dropped down from on high, their riders clambering up their gangling legs to haul themselves into their saddles. Ghrottle was the last to land, surly as always but eventually willing to squat down and allow its master to mount up.

The daemon beast thrummed into the air even as lightning-wreathed arrows began to flash, the Stormcasts shooting as they ran closer. One whickered past Glumm's head, close enough that he tasted the actinic bite of the storm. Another slammed into Thrupture Bilethroat, wounding him deeply and almost knocking him from his saddle.

'Let's make 'em pay for that one!' roared Glumm to his surviving warriors. 'Let's make 'em pay for all our lost! Time fer the reapin'!'

He leaned forward, kicking his heels into Ghrottle's flanks. Yet even as the rot fly heaved its bulk through the air towards the charging foe, another cry went up, this time from the northern edge of the square.

'WAAAGH!'

There came a thunderous series of booms and a swarm of crude cannonballs whistled and bounced across the square. One knocked Shugh the Hideous from his rot fly a half-second before another burst the creature itself like an overripe fruit and swatted it from the air. Several more crashed through the ranks of the Stormcasts, smashing them from their feet. Four bright souls cracked upwards into the Heavens.

'What in the name o' the Great Gardener's this now?' cried Glumm as more cannonballs skipped from the cobbles and crashed into the buildings on the far side of the square. His blightlords had scattered, the Stormcasts too, the conflict of a moment ago forgotten under the sudden hail of fire.

Pouring into the square from the north was a mass of greenskins. There had to be several hundred, Glumm thought, all of them brandishing crude metal weapons and clad in hulking suits of jagged iron armour. With them came a rumbling spearhead of ironblasters, ogor cannon-chariots with an emphasis firmly on the cannon element, which were pulled by snorting rhinoxen. It was from these weapons that the punishing salvo had come. Even as they rattled and bounced across the cobbles he could see frantic grots scrambling over the weapons, hanging on grimly as they attempted to reload their masters' enormous firearms.

'We can't fight all that!' shouted Thrupture Bilethroat.

'You're not wrong,' snarled Glumm, frustration rising in him like bile as he watched the brutish orruks barrelling closer. He picked out mobs of Bonesplitterz in glowing warpaint, capering along in the wake of the main charge. The next moment, arrows tipped with shards of flint and knapped beast fangs were whipping around him. One punched through Ghrottle's left wing and the daemon insect gave a buzz of annoyance. Another thunked into the leprous flesh of Glumm's thigh, while a third stuck quivering into Yakob's shoulder.

'*Ow...*' the incubatch complained sourly.

Another of Glumm's favoured warriors tumbled from the air as his mount was shot out from beneath him. For a second the Lord of Afflictions considered ordering the charge anyway, whether against the orruk lines or the shattered remains of the Stormcasts. Grandfather knew it was all their hollering that had brought this lot down on them in the first place, most likely.

Glumm hadn't got to command an entire warband of Nurgle's favoured maggotkin by making rash decisions, though. Leave the suicidal charges to the Blood God's deluded wretches, that was his motto.

'The Stormcast'll keep,' he shouted. 'If'n the orruks don't get 'em first! We got a job to do for the Gardener hisself, and we shan't be doin' it dead. Come on, back to the warband!'

With a last sour look at the handful of Stormcasts now facing down the charging orruk horde, Cankus Glumm turned Ghrottle and flew away over the rooftops with Yakob clutched tight to his side and the last of his pusgoyle blightlords at his back.

'Here they come!' shouted Koris, and to Kalyani he sounded too eager by half. The orruks were bearing down on them with alarming speed, bellowing their war cries and gnashing their tusks.

'We cannot fight all these foes!' she replied.

'Then we take every last one that we can, and I'll see you beyond the Anvil!' Koris shot back, brandishing his hammer. There was a manic battle-light in his eyes, one Kalyani had seen in those of her comrades time and again.

Our boon and our curse, she thought.

'We fight! We kill! We win!' roared her warriors, and she felt the urge to join them in that cry, to cast aside all else and plunge blade first into the tsunami of foes bearing down upon her.

'No,' she shouted instead, putting every last vestige of power and authority into her voice so that it cracked like a gunshot. 'We have a duty here! It is greater than a pyrrhic death against impossible odds! Fall back, flee for the city's southern edge! Move!'

For an instant they wavered, but their respect for their Lord-Celestant was greater than their battle-lust. The orruks were almost on them when Kalyani and her warriors turned and ran.

Crude arrows fell amongst them, knocking Braegar Swift-hammer from his feet and sending his soul arcing skywards.

The cannons boomed again, and Kalyani spat a curse as Koris' head was smashed clean off by a bouncing cannonball. His body crashed down, tumbling to a stop before blasting apart with an emerald flash as his essence returned to the Anvil.

The orruks' footfalls thundered in time with her heart and the blood pounding in her temples. She wanted with every fibre of her being to turn and bring retribution to the savage beasts that had slain her comrades and driven her from her prize. Instead she ran on, into the shadowed evening streets and the tangled, shattered maze of Mordavia.

She ran until her clanging steps echoed from the looming walls, until darkness fell and the bellowing orruks were left far behind, until even the distant thump of the huge drum that she had heard since entering Mordavia was distant and muted. She ran until she and her last pitiful handful of followers were beyond the green-skins' reach, deep amidst the ruins and chasms and swaying undergrowth of the city's southern districts.

Only then did Kalyani Thunderblade stop running. Only then did she take the time to mourn her fallen, and to vow bloody revenge upon the enemies that had brought such ruin to her comrades this day.

'The swift strike has failed,' she said as they picked their way towards the distant bulk of the wooded hills to the south of the city. 'Instead they shall have all-out war.'

CHAPTER FIVE

BATTLELINES

Mordavia, the third day of the campaign

Bronvynne limped through the encampment with the clamour of military preparation all around her. Stormcast Eternals duelled amidst flashes of lightning and booms of thunder. Cavalry beasts and larger, more monstrous things growled and roared. Armourers' hammers rang upon sigmarite anvils. Aether-endrins rumbled as Kharadron sky-ships prowled balefully overhead. Most pleasing to Bronvynne's ear were the shouts and orders, the snores and singing and general conversation of the many thousands of Freeguild soldiers who had pitched their tents within the growing encampment over the past few days. Admiral Norgssen and Lord-Celestant Galabrith had been first and fastest to answer Kalyani Thunderblade's calls for reinforcement, but they had been far from the last.

As the arcanotranslocutor hurried through the tumult of humans, duardin and aelves she clutched her precious tome beneath her robes to shield it from the light drizzle filling the air. In the past days she had come to think of the book as *hers*, she realised, and felt a little foolish.

'Still, why ever not? Wasn't I the one to bring the damned thing to safety? Wasn't it my friends and comrades who suffered to help me do so?' she asked herself out loud, then had to hop aside in an undignified fashion as two hulking yaathi almost ran her down. They were hauling a heavy iron field gun behind them, and as the contraption passed her the Freeguild artilleryman clinging to the carriage gave her an apologetic wave.

'Heavens ascendant, watch where you're going, will you?' Bronvynne shouted after him.

'Sorry, ma'am,' he called back as the yaathi lumbered onward, lowing.

Shaking her head, Bronvynne forged on between drilling soldiery, hurrying messengers, stacked mountains of crates, tall wood-and-metal observation towers and row upon row of brightly coloured tents. She could see the commanders' pavilion atop a nearby ridge close to the eaves of the forest; its elevation, its mass of proudly flapping banners and the substantial observation platform that towered over it marked the huge tent out even had it not also been emblazoned with the hammer and lightning bolt sigils of Sigmar.

'Seeing it is one thing. Getting there's a-bloody-nother,' she said to herself as she was forced to step aside again to make way for a column of purple-armoured Stormcasts sat astride massive, scaled dracoths. The beasts hissed and growled as they stalked past, but Bronvynne refused to let herself shy away in fear. These creatures and their riders were allies, after all.

She was irritably shaking mud from the hem of her robes with her free hand when Tove caught up to her. Grizzled and leathery, with an assortment of scars and several days' worth of stubble, he looked like a footpad who had donned a Freeguild uniform by mistake. The scowl plastered across his roguish features did nothing to dispel this impression.

'There you are. D'you know how long it's taken me to find you?' he said in a tone of exasperated annoyance.

'Too long,' Bronvynne shot back, setting off again along the muddy path that wound through camp towards the command pavilion. Tove hastened to catch up, adjusting his tangled scabbard and pushing his drooping plume from his face as he went.

'I told you that I was goin' to finish my breakfast before we answered that summons and you was to wait!' he said.

'And I told *you*, Mister Tove, that the delay was unacceptable,' replied Bronvynne, limping determinedly through the drizzle and not deigning to look at him.

Tove grabbed her arm with a growl, and she felt the wiry strength in the soldier as he pulled her easily to a halt. She snapped her head around to stare angrily at him.

'Unhand me,' Bronvynne snapped. Tove did so, raising his hands, palms open. The scowl hadn't left his face, though.

'Listen, you can't just go tearin' off through an encampment full of soldiers when the mood takes you. This is a military operation and you're a civilian. There's orders and protocols to these things. Captain Thacker assigned me to be your bodyguard and I mean to do my job but by Sigmar you're not making it easy!'

Bronvynne narrowed her eyes.

'I made it all the way from Mordavia to Kalyani Thunderblade's bloody threshold and back without your *protection,* Mister Tove, and I dare say I shall continue to cope perfectly well without it should I choose to "go tearing off" wherever I like in future. If I must have a bodyguard then so be it, but you are that and not my gaoler, sir. Now either make yourself useful and help me get through this maelstrom of bodies to the command pavilion or go back and stuff your face at the breakfast trough. It makes no odds to me.'

Tove stared at her. The moment stretched. Drizzle fell while around them men and women marched and shouted and sharpened blades. Bronvynne had the uncomfortable sense that the man was re-evaluating her as one might size up a horse that had showed unexpected spirit.

'Fair enough,' he said at last. Giving his sword belt one last yank to get the scabbard straight, he set off at a quick stride. As he went, he shouted, 'Move aside! Clear a path! Command business! You, haul your arse out the road before I knock you in a ditch!'

Bronvynne hurried after him, ignoring the puddles she splashed through as they pressed on through the encampment at a noticeably quickened pace. The man was a swine, of that she had no doubt. Lief would have had a few choice words to say about his appearance and manner, she was certain of that much. Her brother had been… was… a brave and noble man. Still, Bronvynne would make do with the allies she had if it meant that she could do Sigmar's work, and this one might yet have his uses.

Kalyani looked up as Jeddichor Wallbreaker, her Knight-Heraldor, announced two new arrivals.

'War-scribe Bronvynne Karrobeth and Laszlo Tove.'

His stentorian voice was loud enough to cut through the hubbub of voices in the pavilion, though not enough to quiet the Freeguild officers, the senior Celestial Vindicators and Celestial Warbringers, the Kharadron captains and endrinmasters, the wizards and warrior priests and engineers, the aelven champions and minor duardin clan lords, and all the other assorted command staff filling the wide canvas space.

The pair hastened through the entrance, between the hulking Stormcast sentries and into the warm fug of the pavilion's interior. Kalyani beckoned to them and, with Tove bulling a path, they moved through the throng to her side. The Lord-Celestant gave Bronvynne a moment to fuss with her robes and check that her ancient book was dry. Tove took the opportunity to snag a goblet of pearlwine from a passing servant's tray and take a long pull on it.

'Karrobeth, how is your health?' asked Kalyani, looking Bronvynne up and down. The old cryptoscholar was wet and muddy, her wiry hair spilling out in wild curls as she pulled down her hood, but her eyes were bright and intense.

'Much recovered from our first meeting, thank you, Lord-Celestant,' Bronvynne replied. 'And you? Are you recovered after your ordeal in Mordavia?'

Kalyani heard a challenge in the cryptoscholar's tone. It brought to the fore her memories of the *Exactitude* plunging from the skies, the battle with the Nurgle Champion, the long hours of dark as she and her forlorn handful of comrades stalked down empty streets and silent ruins, leapt ragged-jawed chasms and pushed their way through hissing thickets of undergrowth, all the time nursing their injuries and watching for orruks, Chaos worshippers or whatever other mysterious perils the dead city might contain. Kalyani had felt a baleful pulse all through that dark night's hike, a sensation that had nothing to do with the distant drumbeat, the foes that she had fought or the comrades she had lost. It wasn't the pulse of anger in her temples, urging her to return to the fight, though that was ever-present of course.

No, she had thought, *this is something else and I am not the only one who feels it.*

Tempers frayed quickly in the sprawling encampment. Stormcasts and their steeds prowled as though caged, the need to do violence simmering close beneath the surface. It was the whirlpool, Kalyani knew, the dark void that she had envisioned as the *Exactitude* soared in towards the Old Temple at Mordavia's heart. One moment she thought she almost understood what it was that she felt calling to her. The next it was as though she were feeling its pull for the first time and was caught between fight or, much less likely, flight.

All this flashed through the Lord-Celestant's mind at Bronvynne's question. She was careful not to let any of it show on her face.

'I am a Stormcast Eternal, Karrobeth. We do not carry our hurts for long, and we always answer them in blood.'

'Always,' echoed Sundershield, his voice more menacing in its matter-of-fact neutrality than any amount of vehemence might have carried.

'I have a feeling you'll have ample opportunity for the latter,' said the war-scribe, brandishing her ancient tome meaningfully. 'Is it true, what we're hearing about enemies massing?' she pressed on, before Kalyani could ask any questions of her own.

'See for yourselves,' the Lord-Celestant replied, gesturing to the war orrery that took up much of the pavilion's central space. The mechanism was huge and undeniably impressive. A wide, flat map tray lay at its heart with a carefully measured inch of purified water standing within it; enchanted inks and alchemical solutions had been poured into it, swirling together to form a picture of Mordavia as though drawn out by the hands of Azyrheim's finest calligraphers. Annotated titles drifted in place to mark out certain known landmarks and designated regions of the city and its surrounds: the western lake; the Old Temple; the three forts; the southern sprawls, and others.

Great sections of the map were still blank, or close to it. Yet hour by hour those sections were shrinking as sky-ships and aetherwings flew scouting missions and Vanguard forces pushed deeper into the ruined city or fought skirmishes with the scouting parties of the orruks and Chaos worshippers. All sent back word of what they had seen, be it hand-drawn maps upon oiled parchment, the ensorcelled images captured by glimpsing stones, or visions plucked by muttering cartomancers straight from the minds' eyes of observers on the ground. As the flow of information continued, streets and ruins and chasms, tunnels and subsided districts and sinkholes and fern-forests colonised the empty patches of map like forests of wriggling black worms working their way through the water.

The rest of the war orrery consisted of dozens of brass armatures, semicircular hoops that fanned out at different heights and angles over the table. Each was inscribed along one flank in runic script, denoting everything from 'The Alignemente of Azyre' and 'The firme regarde of Aqshye and Hyshe' to 'Regimentes of Freeguilde soldierye from Celestriume' and 'The Courageous Axes of oure allies Dispossessed'. Each armature was studded along its inner face with coloured gems that shone with magical light, and as new reports came in so combat-astronomers worked the controls of the map table and delicately realigned the armatures so as to shine the gems' beams down upon the map. Those coloured beams, ascribed to the aspects and alignment of the Mortal Realms, cast broad pools of light upon the map table that turned the waters blood red, jade green or shadowy grey. Those ascribed to particular regiments or fighting forces were bright pinpricks by comparison, and mostly concentrated within the area marked out as 'Armies Encampened of Sigmar's banner' that ranged along the band between the city's southern fringes and the eaves of the forest.

A number, mostly sky-ships and Vanguard Chamber brother-hoods, could be seen ranging across the map itself like motes of dust caught by shafts of bright daylight.

There was another set of armatures, inscribed down their flanks with the names of reviled foes. 'The savage hordes of Gorkamorka'. 'The pestilential worshippers of Nurgle'. It was to these lights, clustered in disturbing profusion to the north and west of the city or scattered like festering motes through its districts, that Kalyani gestured.

'Hammer of Heavens,' breathed Tove, setting down his now-empty wine glass on the map table's edge, where it was swiftly snatched away by a beleaguered-looking servant. 'There's enough of 'em out there, eh?'

'Enough, by the accounts of our scouts, to present us battle on a scale rarely seen,' Kalyani replied. 'And that is why it is more important than ever that we understand precisely what kind of threat this weapon represents. What is it that we're fighting over? How can it be that so many armies have gathered all at once to contest the prize?'

'Is there a corner we might retire to so that we can be more easily heard?' asked Bronvynne. 'I have deciphered some details of real note and I am loath to describe them to you amidst all this background chatter lest anything of importance be missed.'

'This is not a discussion for a shadowy corner, Karrobeth, it is vital information for all those here planning our Mordavian campaign,' said Sundershield, clearly surprising the cryptoscholar. 'You shall inform us all at once. Why else did you think the Lord-Celestant summoned you?'

'Er...' managed Bronvynne before Kalyani caught Jeddichor Wallbreaker's eye and shot him a nod. Wallbreaker motioned to the Celestial Vindicator guards; Kalyani knew he would be ordering them to take up positions outside the pavilion, to patrol and to watch for eavesdroppers or spies.

That done, Wallbreaker called out to the assembled commanders.

'Pray your silent attention in Sigmar's name, my lords and ladies! Attend Arcanotranslocutor Karrobeth! She comes to us bearing fresh intelligence that you would do well to hear and comprehend.'

Kalyani watched Bronvynne intently as silence fell and all eyes turned to her. Elsewhere in the pavilion, and upon Kalyani's orders, several Judicators from the late Melandra Brightbolt's retinue would be doing the same. Judicators possessed the Sigmar-given ability to perceive falsehood and duplicity in those who spoke, and to see the taint of Chaos in another's soul; while the Lord-Celestant was more or less convinced by this point of the cryptoscholar's loyalty to Sigmar's cause, that didn't mean she would relax her vigil. She had done that before, in her previous life, and the cost had been too great to bear.

Now she watched as Karrobeth weathered the curious stares of all those in the pavilion. Some, mostly relative latecomers, looked nonplussed or even amused at the short, elderly scholar in her damp robes with an old book clutched to her chest. Those who had been in camp long enough to learn a little of her history and deeds looked on with greater respect.

Bronvynne took a moment to compose herself, refusing to be rushed by the sudden pressure of their massed regard. She unlocked the tome, laid it flat upon the edge of the map table and turned its crumbling pages gently to the first of several passages that she had marked with scraps of parchment. She looked around the pavilion, her bright stare taking in her audience at a glance and telling them in no uncertain terms that she was *not* intimidated. Kalyani's respect for Bronvynne increased despite herself as the elderly cryptoscholar cleared her throat and began to speak in the strong, clear and severe tones of a tutor lecturing a wilful student.

'Some of you are already aware of who I am, my area of expertise and how it is that I come to possess this ancient tome. To those not in possession of this knowledge I would ask you to find out later from those who do. Our time is precious, more so than any may yet have realised, as you will know once I am done speaking to you.'

Kalyani noticed the few smirks amongst the crowd had now died, replaced by looks of concerned interest. Bronvynne had an undeniable presence to her, a crackling intensity that didn't manifest itself until she spoke up. The woman was fierce, Kalyani thought, focused, driven by something. She could relate to that sensation.

'It is enough for now to say that the tome I have before me came from deep below the surface of this city, amongst the remains of a buried library that I believe dates back to the Age of Myth. Thus far I have found several passages within its contents that pertain to a weapon. I believed when I first came before Lord-Celestant Thunderblade that this weapon was of sufficiently perilous power to merit a full military response in order to ensure it was seized and sequestered as soon as possible. This I believed to be doubly important because I had already enjoyed first-hand the attentions of the orruks that even now mass upon the northern fringes of Mordavia and feared what might occur should the weapon fall into their hands.'

A few of those present shot glances at the war orrery and the vast swarm of acid-green glimmers that turned the northern edge of the city and the lower slopes of the glimmering mountains into a roiling emerald mass. Most kept their attention fixed on Bronvynne.

'Now, I fear that even my most dire warnings of peril were insufficient,' said the cryptoscholar, and Kalyani felt the atmosphere within the pavilion grow taut. They could all of them feel that dim and distant pulse of malevolence, she suspected. They would all have registered, however unconsciously, that it had become more insistent, more malevolent these past days. Now some of them would be putting that feeling together with Karrobeth's words and experiencing a growing sense of dread.

'It is my belief, based upon the words inscribed within this tome, that during the Age of Myth the people of Mordavia were strongly allied with Nagash and his undead legions,' Bronvynne pressed on. Kalyani tensed at these words. This information was new to her, too. She exchanged a loaded glance with Sundershield. 'A historical account speaks of "close ties with the Bone Lord, in whose hands is held the hourglass of sands and through whose gates flow all souls at their time of ending". Another relates how during a time of great strife when "beings of baleful countenance" bedevilled the city from "a place beyond thought", the mortal defenders of Mordavia were aided by "echo-men with no souls to steal and with witch-lights in their hollowed eyes".'

'Seems a fair enough supposition, but what has it to do with the weapon we seek?' asked Lord-Celestant Galabrith. There was no challenge in his voice, Kalyani noted, only stern curiosity. Bronvynne replaced her parchment sliver upon the tome's crumbled page and turned carefully to a later section. She scanned the new page's contents rapidly and nodded to herself before replying.

'As far as I can reckon, it was during the last days of the Age of Myth, when the creatures of Chaos were forcing passage into the Mortal Realms and Sigmar's Grand Alliance teetered on the brink, that the people of Mordavia decided to fashion a weapon,' she said. 'There was a prophecy, I believe, though the fragments I have found are in a dialect so archaic that even I cannot make it out. It is unclear whether they believed that Nagash was on his way to deliver them personally from the end of days, and so they sought to arm him accordingly, or whether they believed that by fashioning him a great enough weapon in tribute they might appease their death god and win his protection.'

'One assumes that their efforts were in vain, considering what remains of their city,' commented an aelven noble dryly. A couple of people chuckled darkly. Most ignored the comment, Bronvynne amongst them.

'I believe from what I have read here that they finished their weapon and that it was terrible indeed. However, it seems that it was Sigmar's armies, not those of Nagash that came to the gates of Mordavia. There is….' Another reverential flick through age-worn pages. 'Ah, yes, here we are. There is an account near the book's end of Sigmar "descending from the heavens in greatest wrath, and marching at the head of a mighty and vengeful host". From what I can make out, the God-King had suffered some betrayal at the hands of Nagash and was out for revenge. He came upon a city of humans who gave worship not to him but to the master of death. Worse, fearing Sigmar's fury, I *believe* that the people of Mordavia attempted to use their weapon against him rather than simply submit to their fate. It must have done significant harm to the God-King's forces for there is some crowing to that effect within this document. Yet in the end it did not avail them. Sigmar and his armies destroyed Mordavia and swept onward, and here all mention of the weapon ends. How that can be I do not know, but it simply vanishes and I have never seen mention of it elsewhere.'

'Perhaps Sigmar destroyed their weapon and moved on,' suggested Galabrith.

'Surely, he must have done so, or else taken it away and made it safe within some vault in Sigmaron,' agreed one of the Freeguild officers. 'Like as not we are here for no purpose other than to drive off some marauding greenskins.' The man's tone was a touch too obsequious for Kalyani's liking, sounding more as though he wished to win Galabrith's approbation than think rationally about the situation. From the murmuring spreading through the pavilion he wasn't the only one with this opinion, either.

Before Kalyani could speak up to silence them, Bronvynne got there first.

'I sincerely hope that you are correct, but I don't believe it and deep down I don't believe that you do either,' she snapped.

'You, some wizened old scholar, are telling me, a captain of the

Freeguild, what I do or do not think, are you?' the officer shot back, puffing himself up with indignation.

'I wouldn't need to if you would only pull your head from your backside and think for a moment,' Bronvynne retorted. There were a few gasps, a scattering of chuckles, especially from the assembled duardin. Kalyani saw Admiral Norgssen smirk through his tight-cropped beard.

'I–' began the officer but Bronvynne wasn't done.

'You feel it, don't you? We all do. That menacing undertow? That *pulse* running through the air, through the ground. Through each one of us. It tugs at our souls. It sets our teeth and our tempers on edge. Tell me, honestly, upon your oath to Sigmar himself, that you feel no such thing and I will close this book and be silent.'

For a moment Kalyani again thought she might be forced to restore order as the Freeguilder considered bulling on regardless. But he wouldn't lie, not to a tent full of his peers and betters, not on the name of Sigmar himself. They all felt it, and so did he. It was plain on his features. Kalyani watched him decide against speaking further.

The disquieted murmuring hadn't stopped, however, and Kalyani could understand why. The tale was dark and disturbing, and raised more than one unsettling question about the deity they served and the mysterious deeds committed all those hundreds of years before.

'Speculation will not aid us, only facts and decisive action,' she said, her voice pitched hard and loud to quell the mutterers. 'The weapon is still here, it is a thing made for the hand of the God of Death himself, and it is doubtless terrible indeed. Karrobeth, do you know anything more of its location or its nature?'

'Of its location? No, only the suggestion that it was located somewhere within or below the Old Temple,' Bronvynne replied. 'Of its nature I can speak a little more. I believe the weapon is fashioned so that it feeds upon death and becomes more powerful as it does so. The more death, the more powerful the weapon becomes.'

'You mean it… eh… it consumes souls?' asked one elderly battle wizard, blinking over his half-moon spectacles. Kalyani's blood ran cold at the thought; she had heard tell of weapons that could cage the essence of a fallen Stormcast, entrap it and prevent its return to Sigmaron. Such things were few, but if ever there was to be such a device it was surely here.

'I do not believe so, no,' replied Bronvynne, and Kalyani relaxed slightly as the cryptoscholar flicked to the last of her marked sections. 'There is one passage, brief and quite possibly allegorical, that speaks to the nature of the weapon itself. Make of it what you will.' She cleared her throat again then read aloud.

'The Mordavian Blade is a spectral chimaera, a weapon of the sands that flow. To steal the souls from the Bone God's table would be a sin. There is power in the transaction. There is energy in transience and the moment of the reap. As death surrounds the Mordavian Blade so its might increases. At the Bone God's word so shall the blade become its focused self and so shall that power be released, and then shall the harvest be mighty indeed.'

Silence fell as Bronvynne closed the tome with a dusty thump and carefully locked it again.

'A spectral chimaera…' mused Galabrith, sounding disturbed.

'So, it, what, becomes more powerful the more deaths take place around it?' asked Norgssen, sounding sceptical.

'That would be my reading, certainly, admiral,' replied Bronvynne. 'Though of course, more experienced military and mystical minds than I will no doubt debate the matter further. It is my task to decipher and present, rather than to analyse and put into practice.'

'To me, that sounds correct,' said Kalyani, certain that Norgssen had the right of it. 'The act of death itself lends this weapon its power, though why that power has remained hidden for so long or why it might suddenly be revealed and sought after now I do not know.'

'Perhaps it was something to do with the Necroquake?' suggested Lord-Castellant Sundershield. 'Enough death magic was released to awaken all manner of terrible things. Sigmar knows we've seen enough of them these past months.'

'If that is true then all the more reason for us to strike swiftly and seize the weapon before the worshippers of Nurgle or Gorka-morka,' said another Freeguild officer, a tall and youthful-looking man with chiselled features and a flowing cloak.

'We should at least wait until the *Freedom of Lutharia* arrives this afternoon,' countered one of the delegation of Ironweld engineers, tugging nervously on his singed beard as he spoke. 'With a cogfort at our backs who could stop us?'

'We don't need some walking watchtower, we have the might of the Stormcast Eternals and the blessings of Sigmar himself!' cried the pompous officer who had questioned Bronvynne. It was an obvious attempt to curry favour and restore face, but Kalyani agreed with the man. She was impatient to fight, to seek revenge for her lost warriors and cut a red path through to the prize in Sigmar's name.

'And what if we enter the city before it is properly mapped and find ourselves outmanoeuvred, or caught between the advance of both orruks and maggotkin?' asked a serious-faced young artillery officer. 'Spy twice the land before siting your guns, as we always say.'

'Do you question the might of the Celestial Warbringers?' asked one of Galabrith's comrades, turning to glower down at the suddenly pale young officer.

'Peace, Elenara, I'm sure that was not the officer's intent,' said Lord-Celestant Galabrith, sounding as though he were smiling behind the faceplate of his helm. 'Still, Lord-Celestant Thunderblade had the right idea when she attempted her pre-emptive strike. It was only poor fortune that prevented her from seizing victory then and there. If we believe that this weapon will become more perilous the more death that surrounds it then it is my thought that we should make our move before the orruks or the scions of Chaos make theirs. Open battle between three such massive forces would render this thing perilous indeed, no?'

'We should surely attempt to understand more,' said the elderly battle wizard, now cleaning his spectacles. 'What, for instance, does the tome mean by its talk of the weapon attaining focus?'

'It looks to me as though the matter is already out of our hands,' said Norgssen, gesturing with his smouldering pipe at the map table.

Kalyani turned to look, already dreading what she would see.

An armature had swung into motion, moved by a pair of nervous-looking endrineers who in turn were following the whispered directions of a sallow-faced cartomancer. A sea of green motes was flowing into the city from the north, a tidal wave of green light that flowed along streets, spilled through ruins, and moved south at a relentless pace. Distant but insistent, they could all hear the thumping of the greenskins' drum pounding louder than ever. It was a sound that felt as though it might carry to the ends of the realms.

'The orruks are on the move,' said Kalyani.

'We need a plan of action, now,' Galabrith replied.

'Allow me to offer a suggestion,' said Admiral Norgssen, and Kalyani saw a gleam in the old Kharadron's eye as he began to outline his plan.

CHAPTER SIX

A BEGINNING TO BLOODSHED

Mordavia, the third day of the campaign

WHUMP – WHUMP, WHU-WHUMP!

The big drum boomed louder than ever at Brognakk's back as his hordes swept into the ruined city as though feeding off the fury of their Waaagh! They flowed down the slopes like a living avalanche, orruks and ogors and gargants and grots and troggoths in numbers far beyond Brognakk's capacity to count, and never mind that that capacity topped out at 'a few'. It was time that the relic-hunting mobs stopped having all the fun, and it didn't seem like any more enemies – nor, for the moment, his big mates – were going to show up to join the fight so it was time to get on with things; that had been Brognakk's decision of less than an hour ago.

The enemy were here, everyone was waiting around and faffing about, and he wouldn't let them get the edge over his ladz with all their scouting and other sneaky, dishonest nonsense. If someone else wouldn't start the fight properly then Brognakk absolutely would!

It had been a snap decision born of impatience, boredom and a growing sense of disquiet that seemed to emanate from deep within the ruins themselves. Yet even with his bellowed insistence that the advance begin now, now, *now*, it had taken the best part of an hour for the simple order to disseminate through enough of the horde that the rest could see what was up and get the idea.

His was the biggest Waaagh! Brognakk had ever seen, huge enough to make the ground shake beneath its combined tread and churn the wet earth to mud. Meadowgrass, brakes of ferns, even stands of balu trees and outlying ruins – all were smashed flat as the army thundered into motion. Big Drekk's gore-gruntas pounded down the slope in a vast herd off to Brognakk's left, while somewhere to his right Zag Zagog and Crushes Gitz could be heard raising their ululating Waaagh! cries as they herded their vast masses of Bonesplitterz towards the city. Elsewhere Gobblagabba led his weirdnobs in a deranged Waaagh! chant that made weird tingles run through Brognakk's body. It wasn't a subtle tool, this unwieldy and ill-disciplined mass of warriors, but then subtle wasn't really Brognakk's style.

'Waaagh!' he roared, throwing back his head in exultation as he felt the brute ferocity of his hordes washing over and through him until his fingers tingled and green light sparked before his eyes. Beneath him, Smash roared too and pounded forward, massive knuckled fists leaving craters in the ground and causing luckless greenskins to scatter from his path.

WHUMP – WHUMP, WHU-WHUMP! went the big drum.

Brognakk looked down at Shrakka One-Tusk, the hulking boss lumbering forward with Brognakk's massive Waaagh! banner swaying above him like a ship's mast. Its 'sail' had a brand-new hide stitched into it, the hastily flayed and cured face of Gormm the Tyrant staring hopelessly from beneath freshly daubed glyphs.

'Gobblagabba weren't wrong, was he?' Brognakk bellowed to Shrakka as fist after fist of Ironjawz pounded past them bellowing their war cries.

'Nah, the old loon knowz his dream-fingz, don't he?' replied Shrakka in his usual dour tones. 'Humies, pointies and stunties to da south, plague wotsits to da west, and loads of 'em. Should be a good fight, boss.'

'A good fight?' Brognakk bellowed, affronted by the obvious understatement. 'It's gunna be da best scrap any of us ever 'ad, ya greasy old squig! Gorkamorka led us to dis one in person, we got da biggest army wot I ever laid my eye on, and we got da Morkagork!'

'If it can get through all dem ruinz,' added Shrakka, breathing hard as he hurried alongside the surging maw-krusha while lugging Brognakk's massive banner. Brognakk's irritation with Shrakka increased, as it always did when he was right about something inconvenient. He looked ahead to where the first waves of his horde were breaking against the city's northern edges, funnelling rapidly into the tangled streets and sprawling ruins. Already he could see punch-ups developing where too many orruks attempted to fit down too narrow a street at once, and as he swept his gaze across the vista he noted a handful of ogors borne clean over the side of a craggy ravine by the crowd-press. They vanished with gruff cries of alarm which, if Brognakk was honest with himself, restored his good spirits no end.

The towering edifice of the Morkagork was still some way from the city's edge, rumbling along as the gargants within its lowest level bent their backs to the shoving handles and dug their massive heels into the wet ground. Yet sure enough, Brognakk saw that this wasn't like pushing the rolling idol up to a castle wall and getting stuck in; there was every chance the Morkagork would get hung up on a big ruin or end up with half its wheels following those ogors down a hole before its deck crews could put their spear chukkas to use.

The megaboss' brow furrowed in concentration, then relaxed again as a suitably cunning solution came to him.

'Right, send da word, get as many gargants as you can and send 'em ahead of da Morkagork wiv clubs an' all dat. Dey smashes everyfing in front of da Morkagork flat, right? Den da Morkagork rolls down da big flat road dey makes fer it!'

'Smart plan, boss,' panted Shrakka, almost stumbling as he began to fall behind.

''Course it's smart, ya zoggin' git, I'm da boss! My plans is da smartest!'

With that last pearl of wisdom, Brognakk felt his patience run out entirely. Being boss was tiresome, sometimes, he thought. You had to deal with all the faffy bits like giving orders, thinking of plans and not letting your giant war engines fall down great big holes.

Ugh.

Well, he'd had enough of all that for now. Gorkamorka was with him, and with the Great Green God's favour the Waaagh! would take care of itself.

Brognakk spat first right then left in honour of his deity then gave Smash a good hard thump to let it know it was time to take to the air. Muscles rippled beneath the hulking beast's scaled hide and Smash leapt skyward with an ear-bursting roar. Shrakka receded rapidly in Brognakk's wake as his maw-krusha soared away. The megaboss could just make out his banner bearer coming to a grateful stop, bent double with his hands on his thighs and his chest heaving as he gasped out Brognakk's orders to grot messengers mounted on slavering snarlfangs.

Below, the vast hordes of greenskins, ogors and assorted beasts ploughed onward, their leaders bawling orders, clouting those too slow to obey and keeping the ladz all moving in the same direction with a minimum of infighting. Weirdnobs and wurrgogs moved amongst them, borne along by the tide, green lightning crackling about them and weird cries rising from their tortured throats as the Waaagh! energy built and built. A crude armada took to the air behind Brognakk as he flew, mounted on maw-krushas, snagglebeaks and other assorted flying steeds.

So great was the energy of the Waaagh! that it thickened the air like a lurid green heat-haze as the horde advanced, and seemed to amplify the drumbeats again and again. Shapes moved amongst the haze, towering two-headed manifestations whose maws roared the orruks' own bellows and whose mist-formed fists smashed all-too-real chunks of masonry from the ruins as the horde ploughed onward.

WHUMP – WHUMP, WHU-WHUMP! went the big drum.

Yeah, thought Brognakk as Smash slammed down amidst the tangled stone spars of a ruin and launched himself into another soaring leap. *Da Waaagh! will take care of itself. Time fer some fun!* He told himself he didn't care about whatever magic hoozit the other armies had come for, and fingered his Waaagh! charms at the thought. If they wanted it, though, they'd have to fight his ladz to get to it, and that was a fight Brognakk was sure the orruks would win. Ahead, still distant but thrumming closer, he saw one of the weird metal sky-ships the stunties made to hide from a good fight.

That'll do fer a start, he thought, and urged Smash on with a howl of glee.

'Into the city once again,' Kalyani murmured to herself as she strode down a sloping, ruptured street between shadowy ruins.

'Lord-Celestant?' asked Jeddichor Wallbreaker, who marched a pace behind and to her left. Behind him came retinues of

Liberators and Protectors, Judicators and Decimators, a mighty assemblage of Celestial Vindicators whose need for violence Kalyani could feel like a physical pressure.

'I left good warriors slain in my wake when I fled this city, Jeddichor,' she said by way of a reply. 'This day will see a great many more good warriors fall, but I swear that this time I shall not repay them with defeat.'

'By Sigmar's will, we shall carry the God-King's fury against these beasts and filthy heathens and through his might we shall crush them without mercy,' agreed Wallbreaker. She heard the fire of absolute conviction in his deep voice and it buoyed her own determination to succeed.

It was hard not to feel confident, she thought, borne along as she was at the forefront of so vast an assemblage of warriors. Their battle plan had been assembled hastily, it was true, but Kalyani believed that a spur to action was no bad thing; it focused the mind and forced one to discard distractions and trivialities that might otherwise have been allowed to intrude.

She and her Celestial Vindicators were at the forefront of the advance, as was their right. They were the blade-point aimed directly for the Old Temple square. Her lieutenants led more warbands forward through the nameless districts to her right and left flanks; Lord-Castellant Rojavi Sundershield led one, Lord-Relictor Alessendra Stormsmite another. Further away the Celestial Warbringers pushed forward in their turn, Galabrith's Extremis Chamber performing a swift flanking ride through the chasm-riven Sundered Quarter with the aim of sweeping into Old Temple square from the east even as Kalyani and her warriors attacked from the south. Dark shadows swept the streets from time to time as Galabrith himself and his fellow Drakesworn Templars circled over the advancing Stormcast forces.

Sigmar's reforged warriors were to be the shock-assault elements of the force, the first thunderbolt strikes that shook the enemy and threw them back in disarray. Yet that alone would not be enough, all in the counsel of war had agreed. They needed to secure the region around the Old Temple square, and to hold back the foe long enough to locate and, if needs be, make safe the cursed weapon before extracting it from Mordavia or destroying it. To complete this aim, they needed the vast manpower and potent firepower of the Freeguilds.

Even as Kalyani and her warriors had marched out through the relentless drizzle, they had seen the human soldiery massing beneath their banners while drums thundered out a martial tattoo and fifes played vigorously. She admired those warriors; perhaps not individually, for enough of them were sufficiently weak or flawed or cowardly to earn her contempt, but en masse, as a force, these human soldiers drew themselves up and marched out to face monsters and daemons and Sigmar knew what else with little more than swords and shields, handguns and crossbows and a measure of faith in their purpose and their comrades that helped them to overcome whatever dread they felt. Death was permanent for the soldiers of the Freeguilds, she knew. There would be no Reforging for them, yet they marched out anyway because their officers and their warrior priests told them that they must.

Kalyani respected that courage, even as she pitied its mortal limitations.

Thousands upon thousands of those all-too-mortal soldiers would be marching up in the wake of the Stormcast advance, regiments of duardin and aelves striking out alongside them, teams of yaathi pulling gun carriages in their midst; when the time came and the Stormcasts plunged into the Old Temple to claim the weapon, the plan was for the cannons and volley guns that the Freeguild had brought with them to mow down the greenskins for long enough to facilitate victory in Sigmar's name.

A low rumble came from overhead and the Stormcasts glanced up in time to see a substantial armada of Kharadron sky-ships plough overhead. Kalyani didn't look up, though she could picture well enough the burnished hulls slick with rainwater, the vents of the aether-endrins glowing and the arkanauts clinging to their wet clamber-lines, wiping rainwater from their goggles. She had had more than enough of the duardin and their vessels for the time being.

'There go the Kharadron, may Sigmar watch over them,' Wallbreaker said, sounding inspired.

'They don't care for Sigmar's gaze, only for profits,' Kalyani replied, unable to keep the sour note from her voice.

'Lord-Celestant, did matters go ill between you and the admiral after your return?' asked the Knight-Heraldor, suddenly angry on her behalf.

'No, and that troubles me more than if they had,' Kalyani replied.

'I do not understand, Lord-Celestant,' he replied. Jeddichor was as straightforward and honest a soul as Kalyani had ever known, and a terror on the battlefield. She liked the man, even if his repeated Reforgings seemed to have left him somewhat simple in nature.

'One of his fastest warships, one of his best crews, lost to the last for the sake of my impetuous desire to claim a swift victory,' said Kalyani, unable to keep the bitterness from her voice. 'Had the duardin responded with anger, sorrow, even recrimination I would have understood. Sigmar, I know I felt those things, feel them still. Do you know what he said to me instead? Some investments do not mature as they should, but all expenditure lessens debt. That was all.'

They marched in silence as Jeddichor absorbed this. The drizzle misted their armour. Water sluiced through ancient gutters and gurgled from cracks in crumbling stonework.

'Our allies do not think as we do, but their strength serves Sigmar just the same,' he said at last. 'And if they wish to see their debts settled then the duty they have accepted ought to pay for all.'

Kalyani glanced at the Knight-Heraldor in surprise but could glean nothing from the eyes behind his emerald-green faceplate.

'I suppose that is true, if our enemies behave as we believe they will,' she said. To the Kharadron fell the duty of guarding the western flank of the advance, not only preventing the greenskin hordes from encircling Sigmar's armies but also holding back the worshippers of Nurgle if they made their own bid for the weapon. *And they will,* she thought with grim certainty. *That champion I faced was every bit as determined to claim the prize as I, I know it.*

'The Kharadron will face their share of the fighting, and they will prevail in their own way,' said Jeddichor, as though by simply saying it out loud he could will it so. Kalyani admired his certainty.

'They will look to their battle and we to ours,' she said, doing her best to emulate Wallbreaker's conviction.

'And that will be a stern enough test, and opportunity enough for glory,' he replied, battle-hunger in his voice. 'We cannot let the Vanguard stand alone.'

As though summoned by the Knight-Heraldor's words, a Prosecutor in the colours of the Celestial Warbringers swooped in over the rain-slick stone and dropped into the street before them. His armour was rent and battered, splattered with orruk gore.

Kalyani hastened to meet him, supporting the warrior as he staggered.

'What news?' she asked.

'Heavy fighting around the Old Temple,' he replied. 'We drove the orruk scouts back and prepared our positions but…'

The warrior almost fell, and Kalyani bore him back to his feet despite his armoured weight. She realised that not all the blood slicking his rain-wet armour belonged to his foes.

'But what? Last we knew Lord-Aquilor Asperis and Lord-Aquilor Llanfier had the Old Temple and its approaches cordoned off. What has happened?' she asked, the severity of her tone causing the Prosecutor to straighten and shake his helmed head as though throwing off his fatigue.

'That is correct, we threw back their scouts but... Diseased tribesmen... they came in great numbers, berserk with some sort of frothing sickness that... They were nigh immune to pain or fear, shock troops flung at our flank to wear us down... Fresh waves of orruks moving down from the three forts and... flying beasts... Lord-Aquilor Asperis fell...'

'Is the Old Temple taken?' Kalyani asked, ice water sluicing through her veins at the thought. Bad enough that more battle, more death be allowed to saturate the weapon and render it more perilous still. But if it had already fallen into the hands of the foe despite their best efforts then the consequences could be dire indeed.

'No, still fighting...' gasped the Prosecutor, sagging again. This time Kalyani lowered him to the damp cobbles, crouching next to him. 'The situation is desperate... Lord-Aquilor Llanfier sent me to secure... any reinforcement...'

'I understand,' Kalyani replied. 'Rest now, recover your strength and let Sigmar see to your wounds. Others follow us, they will ensure you are healed and returned to camp.'

'No!' the Prosecutor insisted, trying to stand. He wobbled then crumpled again with a clatter of armour.

'Yes, you have done enough,' Kalyani said firmly, rising and looking over her assembled warriors. 'You all heard what our comrade had to say. Will we let our brothers and sisters be overrun? Will we let the foe claim that which is Sigmar's due, and turn it against us?'

'No!' roared her warriors.

'Then what shall we do instead?' she cried.

'We fight! We kill! We win!' came their war cry. Jeddichor raised his battle-horn and blew a thunderous note upon it that rolled through the ruins like a thunderclap. It was as clear a signal as they could offer to all their allies.

Battle was joined, it said.

Make haste.

'We fight!' Kalyani shouted in response, and drawing Song from its scabbard she led them forward at a run. The Old Temple square might still be as much as three miles ahead, but they were reforged, Stormcast Eternals, and they would cover that ground at speed.

'The orruks will *not* drive us from that square again!' she said furiously, not caring who heard her. 'By Sigmar's hammer they will not!'

The deck of the *Shieldmaiden* shuddered beneath Admiral Vornn Norgssen's steel-toed boots. Her aether-endrins throbbed above him. Around him, Norgssen's crew worked with slick efficiency, tending to the ship's mechanisms, balancing its chemicals, running last tests upon the workings of its guns and bomb racks ready for the fight to come. The wind sang through the pipes and struts of the sky-ship's rigging and the slowly increasing rainfall slicked every surface even as it drove remorselessly against the crew.

They didn't care and neither did Norgssen; what matter a little discomfort compared to the settling of accounts long held?

'How's her mix?' Norgssen asked, addressing the ship's aether-khemist, Skaddi Threnghist. Threnghist turned, regarding his admiral through the glassy lenses of his complex gas-helm. His voice, when he spoke, was accompanied by the rhythmic hiss and whoosh of air purifiers.

'As fine a cocktail as you could hope for, admiral,' he replied, sounding rightfully proud. 'And all the other sky-ships too, or should be so long as the captains have followed my instructions without trying to fiddle the accounts.'

'They'll have followed your guidance, aether-khemist,' said Norgssen firmly. 'I issued strict guidelines to that effect bare an hour ago. Terms understood. I'll not have some racketeer trying to scrimp on aether-gold and leaving a gap in the battleline, fear you not.'

'As you say, admiral,' replied Threnghist stoutly. The aether-khemist was ever-paranoid about his mixtures being undercut by profit-savvy captains, Norgssen knew, and not without good reason.

The admiral strode past the helmsman, Vargi, to the deck rail. He looked out over his armada with a critical eye but couldn't pick fault with anything that he saw. There they were, over three dozen sky-ships of varying weights and classes, all packed to their iron-clad gunwales with arkanauts sharp and salty for battle and profit.

'More than sufficient to pay the butcher's bill required of us,' Norgssen said with satisfaction. 'Now, where's the enemy?'

An arkanaut hurried up with a wax-treated chart, squeezing past a knot of heavily armed Grundstok mercenaries to reach his commander.

'Current positions, admiral, sir,' he panted through his mask.

Norgssen perused the battle chart as though inspecting a menu in a sky-port eatery. He produced a heavy brass-bound telescope, fitting it to one of his mask's eye-lenses and consulting the ruinous terrain below. From up here the lines of his allies' advance were like rivers of colour flowing through the streets: the emerald green and white of the Celestial Vindicators; the maroon and gold of the Celestial Warbringers; the tumult of colours and banners that marked the Freeguild masses advancing in their wake. He saw the telltale furore of battle in the distance around the Old Temple. He heard the distant pounding of that dratted drum and took in the intimidating mass of the orruk Waaagh! as it flowed down from the north to engulf all in its path. With a long, careful look to the west, he confirmed to himself that the majority of the Nurgle worshippers still looked to be ensconced in their foetid excuse for an encampment beyond the banks of the lake.

'Difficult to tell, mind, with all the flies and the miasma of filth,' he muttered to himself. Still, it wasn't his job to send ships to scout out the enemy's strength; if Thunderblade and her allies had wanted that doing, they should have stipulated it in their terms. No, his task and that of his fleet was to stymie the green-skin advance west of the Old Temple and ensure that neither they nor the scions of Chaos struck at the Sigmarite advance from that quarter.

'And that, my esteemed colleagues, is what bombs were invented for,' he said aloud, ignoring the enquiring looks of his subordinates. Pulling a wax marking-stick from a pouch on his armour, Admiral Norgssen made several small and pedantic amendments to the chart, tutting at each one. Finally satisfied he took a deep breath and allowed himself a tight smile. He turned to his first mate, Grafi Hengin, who hovered attentively nearby.

'Hengin, are the boarding parties ready?' Norgssen asked.

'That they are, admiral, reports confirmed from all skyships,' replied Hengin in his usual clipped tones.

'Acceptable,' Norgssen replied then. He consulted the time-piece worked elegantly into his right vambrace, squinted up at the dim light of Hysh where it filtered through the rain clouds, then nodded to himself. He paced back to the helm, feeling the reassuring vibration through his skyship's decks and enjoying a moment more of orderly calm before the mayhem of battle began.

'Very well then,' Norgssen said, as much to himself as his subordinates. 'It is time to settle some debts and secure a solid share of profits. First Mate Hengin, signal the fleet to sight targets and begin their run if you would please. All captains to discharge their full contractual obligations to our allies while retaining sufficient collateral resources for the primary endeavour.'

At his words, chemical beacons were lit, and their messages flashed in searing crimson, yellow and icy blue from one skyship to the next. Captains conversed through their speaking crystals. Skyships pitched and yawed as they shouldered their way into formation. Mechanisms whirred and spun as bomb racks were readied and duardin traversed their turrets into firing positions. Endrins whirring, six Grundstok gunhaulers assumed a 'V' formation at the fleet's fore, bombs hanging menacingly from their racks. Skywardens and endrinriggers swarmed in their wake, held aloft by their flight packs and tethered like bizarre bunches of metal balloons to the gunships that towed them along.

'Enemy forces sighted two points star'd,' called the *Shieldmaiden*'s lookout, relaying messages flashed back via beacon from the gunhaulers. Norgssen extended his telescope again with a snap and peered down into the city below. There they were, a massive horde of greenskins surging through the region his allies had named the Dead Towers. They flooded between looming structures that had been old when Sigmar sealed the gates of Azyr, many of them clinging to the backs of massive gore-gruntas. Their war cries were audible even over the thunder of the skyships' endrins and green lightning played above them in an unnatural storm.

'Hengin, would you say that the gathering of greenskins below us presents a clear and present risk to our allies' left flank?' asked Norgssen, knowing that his first mate would know what he expected of him. They could just have blasted the greenskins, called their job done and moved on, but there were proper forms for these things, artycles to be observed and obeyed.

'Aye, admiral, I would stand signatory witness that the aforementioned orruk forces present a contractually obligatory target for our attentions, as stated in the articles of our document of alliance.'

'Splendid. Let's be about it then,' Norgssen replied, spinning the chambers of his pistol, Restitution, and priming its mechanism with a satisfying metallic crunch. 'Fleet to attack speed, engage and eliminate the orruk forces with quite tremendous prejudice. Let us fulfil our contractual obligations and then be about the real business of the day.'

Aether-endrins howled and the *Shieldmaiden*'s shuddering increased as the ironclad accelerated to attack speed. Skyships surged around her, their prows jockeying for position in the line as their captains turned their eager attentions upon the greenskins below. The gunhaulers pulled ahead, turbines thrumming and endrins roaring as their professional two-duardin crews sighted their targets and prepared for the attack.

The *Shieldmaiden* pitched beneath Norgssen's boots and he leaned against the motion, riding it out as he had done a thousand times before. The skyship was as much a part of him as he was it, his most beloved possession and the closest thing he had to an emotional attachment in all the Mortal Realms. He enjoyed, as he always did, the slick motion as the ironclad swooped lower. Up front, Gunner Kargsson thumped his pedals and swung the fore turret to bear, cycling the barrels on the aethermatic volley gun in readiness to fire.

This, thought Norgssen, would be an absolute bloodbath.

The gunhaulers led the way in, dipping lower and lower until they were skimming over the soaking ruins with the orruks dead ahead. There came a mighty shout as the greenskins saw the skyships sweeping in towards them, and a hail of projectiles rose to meet the Grundstok gunships. Arrows, slingstones and hurled boulders flew, most falling short and dropping back to earth or else whistling wide of their targets. Sheer volume of fire ensured some measure of orruk accuracy, though, and Norgssen winced as a ravening bolt of sorcerous green energy slammed into one of the Grundstok craft and tore away its starboard endrin nacelle. The ship spun out of control, venting black smoke, its crew fighting with its controls right up until the moment it impacted with the flank of a ruin and detonated in a roiling ball of flame. Most of the skywardens trailing the craft's wake managed to unhitch and soar away from their stricken transport, but two were dragged down to vanish amidst the fire and smoke.

'Unpleasant way to go,' commented Aether-Khemist Threnghist.

Another of the Grundstok craft pulled up from its attack run as a volley of fang-tipped arrows feathered its underside and slew two of the skywardens being towed in its wake.

The rest raced low over the orruk horde. As they went, they unleashed their full firepower upon the enemy. Sky cannons and drill cannons roared, ploughing bloody furrows through the orruk masses. Aethershot carbines cracked again and again. Fragment-ation charges plunged from the bomb racks to explode amidst the greenskins, hurling torn and bloodied warriors through the air. Gore-gruntas squealed with pain as fire and shrapnel engulfed them. As the gunhaulers swept up and away the surviving skywardens unhooked their tether lines and soared free, guns blazing as they skimmed back and forth over the orruks.

Already the flowing river of savage warriors had developed whirls and eddies as the orruks milled furiously, their advance stalling as they sought ways to strike at the duardin harrying them from on high. Some tried to scale the ruins and hurl themselves bodily at their tormentors; several even succeeded, tackling luck-less skywardens out of the air and crashing back down into the horde. Bow strings twanged, sending arrows whipping through the air. Another hungry green bolt of sorcery shot skywards, nar-rowly missing a retreating gunhauler and blowing out the top two storeys of a ruined tower in a spectacular shower of blazing stonework.

'Second wave. Let's get the job done,' ordered Norgssen.

Frigates and ironclads thundered in over the orruks, letting fly with everything they had. Supremacy mines plunged from their moorings, erupting amidst the massed greenskins with catastrophically bloody results. Volley guns, harpoon launchers, bomb mortars and countless smaller firearms let fly as one, creating a steel rain that raked at the orruks with merciless claws. Bodies flew, detonated, jerked and danced as shot and shrapnel whipped through them. Blood slicked ancient cobbles and ran in gory streams into the mouths of hungry chasms. Norgssen felt a moment's unease as a dark pulse flowed from the direction of the Old Temple, something dread and ancient welcoming the bloodshed and suckling upon it.

He shook off the sensation as he sighted the greenskin shaman, even now capering and gibbering amongst the bloodied bodies of his comrades. The thing was wiry and foul, a weird crown of teeth and stones lashed to its skull. Its eyes glowed furious green and it raised its staff, unleashing a squealing bolt of energy that whipped past the *Shieldmaiden* to detonate the aether-endrins of the *Hard-headed* and send the frigate tumbling from the skies.

'Kargsson, wizard,' called Norgssen, his order relayed rapidly down the deck by his crew to the arkanaut hunched over the controls of the ironclad's aethermatic volley gun.

Without so much as raising his thumbs from his triggers, Kargsson stamped on a pedal and traversed the turret. A hailstorm of white-hot bullets spat from its spinning barrels, chewing through the orruks packing the streets like a hungry beast. Bodies toppled and flew. Blood sprayed ancient walls. Sparks blossomed as rounds skipped off cobblestones and ricocheted back up into fleshy bodies. Even as the shaman bellowed some arcane curse he was cut down by the volley gun's fire, bullets ripping into him and dissolving him into a flesh-and-blood blizzard in a heartbeat.

'One additional profit share for Gunner Kargsson,' observed Norgssen calmly. Hengin pulled out an accounts slate, marked a tally on it, stowed it again.

Below, the orruks were scattering. The effect of the Kharadron assault had been absolutely devastating. Even as the *Shieldmaiden*'s prow swung up and she thundered skywards again, Norgssen could see that any pretence at direction or formation amongst the enemy had been lost. Bodies lay in bloody mounds amidst burning craters. More than one crumbling ruin had collapsed altogether, burying orruks in hillocks of rubble. Hundreds, maybe thousands had died, packed together and unable to escape the airborne fury of the Kharadron skyships.

'Come about and give them another pass,' he ordered, dispassionate, already tallying the cost of the damage he could see to airship hulls, the aether-gold value of munitions expended and the cost of replacing lost skywardens. 'We'll hammer them into the ground, then we'll be about it.' He was comfortable in the knowledge that, by securing the true prize in Mordavia, he could more than recoup the cost of any damage sustained fighting such primitive and ill-equipped foes.

'That,' he said to himself, 'will be *quite* the payday.'

CHAPTER SEVEN

CONVERGING FURY

Mordavia, the third day of the campaign

'*It don't... like being... woke up...*' Yakob warned with customary pessimism.

'I don't give a plague-mite's dribbling arsecrack if it *likes* being woke up or no,' Cankus Glumm replied. 'The Grandfather's work's t'be done and the Slupperslythe is goin' to do it!'

He stood with Yakob upon the very edge of the lake that marked the western border of Mordavia, the eyes of thousands of Nurgle-worshipping maggotkin upon them. In Glumm's free hand he held a heavy clay pot, stoppered with what looked and smelled like rancid earwax and whose flanks were inscribed with spiky-edged sigils of what could only be described as a warning variety.

'*I'm just sayin'... it'll not... help willing-like...*' said Yakob, his tone clearly meant to communicate that whatever Glumm did next was of no consequence to him, but don't let it be said he hadn't tried.

'It'll do what it's damned well told, just like the rest of us, or it'll answer t'the Great Gardener,' spat Glumm. 'Now shut your rot 'ole an' stop embarrassin' me in front of the warband, eh, brother?'

Yakob didn't reply, but Glumm felt the incubatch's resentment baking off him like fever heat. So be it, he thought with a foul-tempered grimace. There were more important matters to worry about than Yakob's feelings. For instance, there were the sounds of cataclysmic battle drifting over the lake from Mordavia, the flights of skyships, stardrakes and other winged beasts duelling in the air over the ruins, and the very real possibility that someone else would claim the weapon before he could.

Glumm didn't want to imagine having to explain *that* one to the Great Gardener.

The Lord of Afflictions surveyed the Horns of Plenty. It had started out as a small warband, little more than Cankus and the few folk from his village with the good sense to follow his lead and embrace the Grandfather's blessings to help them fight back when Old Bones' ghasts and ghouls had come calling. In the way of all things dedicated to Nurgle, the warband had waxed and waned, its ranks swelling then decreasing, swelling then decreasing all throughout the latter centuries of the Age of Chaos. Yet Glumm liked to flatter himself that he was a strong leader and a talented gardener who had husbanded his crop well. Certainly, the warband had, on aggregate, only become larger and larger as the years rolled by and the conquests to Glumm's name mounted up. When, during the sack of Thesmor Vaults, he had earned the personal patronage of Horticulus Slimux, Glumm's name had been well and truly made.

What he saw before him now was a mighty army, *his* mighty army. It was a sprawling host that had in some cases gathered to his banner from places he'd never even heard of. Where once Glumm had known every face, every warrior, now he found it hard enough to keep track of all the tribal chieftains, aspiring Champions, beast-lords and what have you that followed his commands, let alone the thronging bands they led. Oh, he saw the Poxful Throng over there by that outcropping; the blightkings of Fecule's Filthy Few amidst the flyblown lean-tos; Gugh-Ghubb'rath and his Bloatling Beasts; Doggrul Hoxx and his maggot-gargants staring stupidly over the heads of the masses; the one-eyed rogues who had long called themselves the Noxious Ones, and followed Belladonna Blight's rotting velvet banner into battle. But a lot of the newer faces…? Glumm shook his head.

Occasionally he longed for the good old days when it had been just him, Yakob and a few dozen doughty plague-sowers out to spread Nurgle's gifts across dying lands in desperate need of them. But a horde like this, well, it allowed him to do the Grandfather's work in a far greater and more meaningful sense than ever before didn't it? It allowed him to work the will of the Great Gardener and perhaps, if he proved himself, to ascend to daemonhood! How much good could he do then, he thought with a thrill of excitement at the prospect? He would be a demigod, and a benevolent one indeed.

But first, there was the matter of the weapon, and of Mordavia. That brought Glumm back down with a bump, and he realised that an awful lot of eyes were fixed upon him. Flies droned in their thousands. Rotting matter bubbled underfoot, letting off belching clouds of gas as plague mites scampered and squirmed between the legs of the assembled throng.

Glumm cleared his throat, hawked up a mouthful of clotted slop and spat it deliberately into the lake. Slime sizzled as it met the water, then sank with a string of glottal pops.

'That's what I think o' that bunch o' gelid slugs commencin' proceedings without us,' he shouted, his shark-toothed maw stretching wide to allow his voice to boom, deep and rich as pox-ridden loam, along the banks of the lake. 'Course, you all know what's happenin' here, don't you?' he shouted, pausing to sweep his blank helm around as many of his followers as he could. No eyes didn't mean he didn't see, they knew that. 'It's the same old rot-eaten story!' he exclaimed with genuine anger. 'They looks down on us! They see the diseased, the sickened and the pox-ridden and they thinks, "Oh, 'tis only the followers o' Nurgle, don't have to worry 'bout they! Not like them wizardy-wazzerdy Tzeentch worshippers, or Khorne's skull-wallopin' nutters, eh?" They don't think we're a threat! They don't think we're as *good* as them followers of the other Dark Gods! And what do Grandfather's chosen think o' that?!'

The roar of anger that came back to him was like a solid wall, its bricks a mass of angry oaths and its mortar the rotten stench of halitosis and diseased gums. The maggot-gargants let out gurgling roars of rage, less, Glumm suspected, because they understood the insult done to them and more because everyone else seemed angry, so they supposed they ought to join in.

'Rottin' right!' Glumm roared, and around him the swirling banks of flies seemed to drone in time with his words and lend them a trembling vibrato undertone. 'Do they unnerstand how hard it is to cultivate somethin' o' worth in these accursed Mortal Realms, with gods and their followers fightin' over everythin' and the dead always gettin' up and marchin' about? No, they don't! Do they unnerstand how dangerous we are, how righteous our cause, the lengths we're willin' to go to for them? No, they rottin' don't! And are they expectin' us to come pouring out o' nowhere right into their midst with a tide o' plague-ridden slime rolling ahead of us? Hah! No, they are not! But that's exactly what we're goin' to do, and then we'll teach 'em to fear the Grandfather's reap, won't we?'

His warriors howled and roared, gurgled and slobbered in assent. Glumm grinned his too-wide grin. He had them. Now he just needed this to work, and everything would be as the Great Gardener willed it.

Glumm took a breath and set Yakob gently down on the shore, beyond the reach of the waters but close enough to Glumm that he could snatch his brother up at a moment's notice. Maggots quested out from Yakob's sloughing flesh to nose at the muddy sand and a pool of rancid fluids began gathering beneath him. Glumm gestured with both hands, beckoning to the half-dozen sorcerers of Nurgle who had waited amidst the masses for their moment. They slouched forward, several leaning heavily on rotwood staves, all clad in mounds of ragged, mildewed robes. They stopped seven paces from Glumm, and seven paces from one another, forming a ritual semicircle around him that hemmed him in beside the lake's waters.

'Here we go then. Great Gardener, if'n you wouldn't mind lendin' a hand I could probably use it,' Glumm said. He hefted the clay pot, gritted his fangs, and smashed it down hard upon a rock that jutted from the water's edge. The vessel struck the stone and its warding runes flashed green. The impact elicited a tremendous boom, far louder and deeper than such a small pot had any right to make. The thing looked to be fashioned from nothing more than crude clay, but as Glumm raised it again he saw only the merest dent and a few hairline cracks radiating out from the point where it had hit the rock.

Glumm raised the pot again, holding it with both hands now, and swung it down with enormous force. Again, there came that hollow boom, as though a boulder had fallen within a deep, water-logged cavern. Again, he raised the pot and saw that now its surface was spiderwebbed with cracks from which dribbled a grey, porridgey substance. The runes were pulsing furiously, so bright that they made Glumm glad he didn't have eyes to blind.

'Start 'er up, if you would,' he called to the sorcerers. As one, they began a mumbling chant. They shuffled from left to right, three steps one way then four the other, four steps one way then three the other. As they did so they reached into pouches of foul-smelling dried herbs and scattered them across the polluted shore.

Glumm raised the vessel one last time, shot a quick glance to make sure Yakob was still safe, then brought it down with a roar of effort. At this last strike the pot shattered explosively and from within it poured an impossible volume of grey sludge. It sluiced into the lake, spreading like a slick, frothing and bubbling as it went.

'See, what they don't realise is we ain't just been sittin' around over here watching our cysts fill up!' shouted Glumm as the substance continued to gush into the lake, spreading further and congealing into a soupy mass that foamed with reeking filth. 'Seven brave warbands been scoutin' around this lake and deep into the city. They seen what our enemies were up to and done what they could to slow 'em down. Kankher Spettle's lot even made themselves hosts to the frothjaw ague just so as they could go out glorious and disrupt the enemy's plans!'

There was a general rumble of solidarity and respect for Spettle's slaughtered tribe; it had been a brave and selfless deed, albeit one committed in the hopes of winning Nurgle's favour. The frothjaw was a one-way ticket.

'But it weren't Spettle's tribe that found us the key to victory, oh no!' cried Glumm. At his back, the grey and sludgy waters heaved and writhed as though something vast was pushing at a rotten membrane from below the surface. An awful groaning filled the air and the sorcerers around Glumm chanted louder and shuffled faster. He saw some of his followers backing surreptitiously away from the lake. The plague mites squealed in glee and hustled forward to gather in a stinking mass of eager faces and pus-plumped little bodies just outside the warding circle.

'No, t'was Oxious the Seeping and his pestigors that sniffed out the gift that Nurgle left for us to find. May the Grandfather's praise be heaped upon 'em!'

Oxious was a slime-slick beastman whose goat-like head was crowned with seven crooked horns and whose pelt dripped with the volumes of fluids that drizzled from his many sores. He leapt up onto a boulder from amidst his flyblown followers, planted his cloven hooves and bellowed in triumph. If he had been hoping for adulation, however, it didn't come; everyone was fixated on the bizarre phenomenon transpiring at Glumm's back. Giving a somewhat embarrassed bleat, Oxious slithered back down from his rocky perch.

'They discovered drowned tunnels an' caves in the western districts,' shouted Glumm, doing his best to keep his followers' attention as the heaving mass of grey-green slime behind him grew and grew. There was a strange sucking sound now, like water being dragged quickly down a plughole. He didn't need to look to know that the waters of the lake themselves would be sinking lower as the Slupperslythe drank its fill. 'They found out, with a bit o' wadin' and squirmin' and the like, that them tunnels was probably subsided streets and sewers runnin' all the way from the lakebed to the heart o' the city! And it was when old Oxious popped his horned head up and realised he was in a deep chasm and lookin' right up at the back wall o' that Old Temple loomin' over him up above, well, that's when he realised that...'

His followers recoiled, many flinching or gasping as the gruesome mass behind Glumm gave a convulsive heave and rose up in a mountain of seeping protoplasm.

'He realised that...' Glumm tried again, but there were more cries of alarm and much frantic buzzing of flies as the slime-thing leaned forward with a sound like a billion slugs being forced through a meat grinder all at once. Its shadow fell over Glumm and Yakob, and the hurriedly chanting sorcerers who were now all but dancing around them. Gelid slime and a few dead fish spattered down upon the Lord of Afflictions, who snatched Yakob up by the scruff of his neck and turned.

'He *realised* that… oh, bugger it,' he shouted, acknowledging that his moment of dramatic revelation had been upstaged by the Slupperslythe awakening just a touch quicker than he'd planned. It was never like that in the old stories of heroes and monsters he'd devoured as a child, he thought. The grand speech always got finished in time. But then, as he looked up at the rancid mass of sentient slime that he sought to ally himself with, saw the strains of liquid disease flowing through it like veins, caught sight of fish and other, larger aquatic beasts twitching and convulsing their last as they were dissolved in its mass, he had to laugh at himself. If he was the hero of this tale then it seemed as though the old stories had got a lot of things wrong.

'O mighty daemon plague, foul issue of Nurgle's cauldron, master of the flowing courses and masticator of fleshed things, hear me!' roared Glumm, throwing his arms wide.

The Slupperslythe thrashed madly, causing geysers of sludge to shoot hundreds of feet into the air before spattering back down into the rapidly dwindling waters of the lake. The sound it made was breathtakingly foul, a foetid churning and moistened slapping that filled Glumm's mind with half-formed images fit to nauseate even him. A mighty pseudopod of slime bulged from within the mass and came down upon Glumm and his sorcerers with tremendous force, only to splash apart against an invisible wall of force seven feet above their heads. The sorcerers wailed with the effort of holding their wards in place. The reeking herbs crackled and smouldered, giving off thin runnels of acrid smoke.

'*Told… you…*' said Yakob, dangling from one outflung fist. '*Not…. happy…*'

'I make you an offering, great one!' yelled Glumm. 'I present you with a feast!'

More thrashing and heaving. A boulder-sized blister rose in the slime and burst, sending a sizzling rain of goo down upon the shore. Nurglings squeaked and gibbered, squirming and dissolving into stinking mulch as the slime sluiced from the wards and spattered into the crowd beyond.

'No, not them!' yelled Glumm, doing his best to keep his calm as the Slupperslythe loomed higher, a tidal wave about to crash down and obliterate the Horns of Plenty. 'Behind you! In the city yonder! Two bloomin' great armies, big as you've ever seen, squabblin' amongst themselves and showing nought but scorn for we loyal servants o' Nurgle! They're your offerin'! They're why I freed you, O mighty flow of living rot! I offer you thousands upon thousands of flesh-clad souls an' all I ask in return is you steal away the lake an' all the water below that city and leave the tunnels behind you dry as the bones o' the desert dead. What say you?'

A lake's worth of blubbery slime hovered above Glumm and his followers. In that moment he knew that if the daemon plague chose instead to fall upon them, nothing in all the realms would save them.

A convulsive shiver ran through the monster and it slumped back down into the lakebed with a motion like candle wax melting in a blast furnace. Bubbles rose and burst upon its surface, sending grey slop and digested matter spraying into the air. Amidst a cacophony of slithering, slurping and bubbling the Slupperslythe forced itself through the tunnels in the eastern bank. Its mass drained away as it did so, leaving the bare rock of the lakebed dry but for a glistening skin that resembled the realms' largest slug trail. It clung to rocky outcroppings and gleamed amidst the exposed ruins of long-drowned structures.

All right...' grunted Yakob. '*I'll give ye that one...*'

Glumm let out a long, rattling breath as the last trailing streamers of the Slupperslythe vanished into dark tunnel mouths on the lakebed's eastern edge. His clotted heart was thumping fit to burst, and he realised he was shaking as though in the grip of frothjaw ague himself. Then a wave of elation surged through him and he grinned widely.

It had worked!

He turned towards his warriors, stepping through the ring of slumped and wheezing sorcerers to beam around at Nurgle's chosen many.

'The Grandfather favours us this day!' he bellowed. 'Make ready to advance! All those who can, we march for the tunnels. We'll pop up right under that Old Temple and find our way to the weapon like maggots chewin' their way into a ripe corpse. Those who won't fit–' at this he gave the gargants a long and pointed look, until he was sure their master had got the message – 'advance overland. Cause as much ruckus as you can and keep our enemies lookin' at the fight on the surface! An' don't worry about being outnumbered. You'll have the Slupperslythe on your side!'

The Eviscerators met orruk resistance perhaps half a mile before reaching the Old Temple square. Hearing sounds of battle ahead, Kalyani Thunderblade led her warriors into a headlong charge with the bellowed war cry of 'We fight! We kill! We win!'

She burst from a drunkenly angled side street into a main thoroughfare whose cobbles were rent by a flurry of small, dark cracks. Crumbling buildings slumped over the street, their upper floors meeting to create a cracked and partial tunnel of stone through which the worsening rainfall pattered and splashed. She saw the orruks first, a mass of muscled brutes covered in vivid warpaint and jagged tattoos. They were clustered around the dark doorway of one of the half-collapsed buildings, all trying to push their way forward to swing hatchets and clubs at the dimly visible figures holding the portal from within.

'For Sigmar! We fight for Sigmar!' yelled Kalyani as she stormed into the orruks from the rear. Some were turning, alerted by the Celestial Vindicators' war cries and trying to get their weapons up. It didn't help them. Kalyani went through her enemies like a whirlwind, every chop, slice and stab a flowing extension of the strike before it. Orruks came apart bloodily beneath her blade, heads spinning away, limbs lopped off, torsos opened and their contents spilled to the rain-slick ground. Around her, Stormcast Eternals swung crackling hammers into tusked faces and loosed lightning-wreathed arrows that smashed orruks from their feet.

The greenskins howled a war cry of their own.

'Waaagh!'

It echoed down the tunnel like the roar of an avalanche, its fury so great that it brought chunks of stonework crashing down amidst the combatants. They swung flint-bladed axes and stabbed with huge spears. Kalyani saw one emerald bolt of soul-lightning flash skywards, then another and another as the combat raged. The Stormcasts had caught their enemies from behind, however, and they had struck with such overwhelming ferocity that they drove the orruks back against the walls of the crumbling street-tunnel and butchered them.

A few greenskins turned tail as they at last registered their defeat, but the Judicators' arrows whipped after them and not one made it away to bring warning to their fellows.

'Well done, brothers and sisters, well fought!' said Kalyani. As she did, a handful of Lord-Aquilor Llanfier's Vanguard Rangers emerged from the formerly besieged structure. They wore the emerald green and white of the Celestial Vindicators, and after picking their way through the mounds of orruk corpses to stand before her, they offered Kalyani their salutes.

'My thanks, Lord-Celestant,' said a warrior that she recognised as Ranger-Prime Ottor Preystalker.

'Ottor, what news from Old Temple square?' asked Kalyani.

'The orruks have yet to bring their full strength to bear, Lord-Celestant, but the roving warbands they have thrown into the fight are already great in number,' he reported. 'We might have held them back had they come at us alone, but the sudden attack from the west by Nurgle worshippers stove in our flank. The Raptors were overrun and Lord-Aquilor Asperis was dragged down by a mob of rabid tribesmen. Rather than allow our remaining forces to meet the same fate, Lord-Aquilor Llanfier had us scatter and harass the foe wherever we could on the assumption that reinforcements would be en route.'

'Can the square be retaken?' asked Kalyani.

'By this force alone? Unlikely. If more orruks come we will not hold it long,' Ottor replied.

'We are far from the only warriors advancing upon the square in Sigmar's name,' Kalyani reassured him. He straightened a little at that.

'Then yes, Lord-Celestant, I believe that the enemy's forces are still scattered and ill-directed enough that a swift blow would drive them back and carry the square. Providing we receive reinforcement in short order, the square could be held against subsequent orruk attacks and the remaining Vanguard forces rallied.'

'Let us be about it then,' said Kalyani fiercely. She could feel the oppressive pulse of the weapon's malevolence beating against her from somewhere ahead. Her comrades must have felt the same thing, and known that the waves of dark hunger and cold hate were becoming more powerful by the minute. They needed to settle this quickly, before the main bulk of the orruk forces arrived and the battle escalated into a wholesale slaughter that might render the weapon too powerful to contain.

'Follow us, Lord-Celestant,' said Ottor, and he and his surviving warriors turned and loped away along the street-tunnel. Kalyani followed, Jeddichor at her shoulder and a force still comprising more than fifty Stormcast Eternals close on their heels.

The Rangers led them past the fallen bodies of the orruks that had fled, then sharply right through a crack that split an ancient building in two. The Celestial Vindicators trampled and hacked through the mass of wet ferns that filled the ruin. Kalyani emerged into full daylight and felt the rain now falling hard enough to plink in dull staccato from her sigmarite armour. She was at the base of a steeply sloping thoroughfare, wide enough that it had been divided by a stone channel within which trees or other greenery might once have grown. Now the channel was cracked and full of nothing but dirty water. This new street led uphill past the sagging ruins of what had once been tall and magnificent buildings festooned with statuary and huge stone hourglasses; over its crest, Kalyani could see the looming mass of the Old Temple through veils of rain.

She could see now that the street was far from empty. Another band of Rangers, this time warriors of the Celestial Warbringers, were staging a fighting retreat down the hill as a mob of blood-spattered ogors charged towards them. A grotesque monster led the huge creatures, a hulk of pallid, pierced flesh and jutting tusks wearing a bloody apron and brandishing a rusted cleaver of prodigious size.

'Into them!' roared Kalyani and launched herself into a fresh charge. The ogors, their corpulent bodies feathered with storm-bow bolts, looked up in surprise at the war cry and their eyes widened as they took in the wave of Stormcast Eternals surging up the street towards them.

Amongst their number was a hulking monster covered from his bald pate to his gnarled toes in stylised fire tattoos and wielding a black stave topped with what looked like a massive beetle's head. Kalyani pounded up the hill with arrows whipping over her, putting on a turn of speed as she saw the tattooed monster take something from a pouch at his waist and stuff it into his maw.

'Jeddichor!' shouted Kalyani and the Knight-Heraldor stopped, braced his feet and raised his battle-horn to his mask's mouthpiece. He winded the enchanted instrument at the same moment the ogor shaman heaved in a deep breath through his nostrils. The behemoth's tattoos flared with crimson light, and a billowing column of fire erupted from his mouth.

Kalyani cursed as the flames engulfed the retreating Celestial Warbringers and one, two then three of their souls shot skyward as purple-tinged lightning. The foul butcher-beast leading the ogors gave a bellow of glee at the sight.

Then the booming shock wave from Jeddichor's battle-horn whipped up the street and blew the firestorm back into the faces of the advancing ogors. Gruff roars of shock and cries of pain filled the thoroughfare. Before the hulking monsters could recover, Kalyani was in amongst them. She whipped Song around with a cry, its keen blade biting into an ogor's thick neck and shearing through flab, muscle and bone. Blood erupted from the grievous wound and the monster's head flopped half off as she wrenched her blade free. Kalyani weaved around the clumsy, if meteoric, swing of an ogor's club, taunting the beasts, goading their idiot fury.

'Slow, you are! Slow, stupid, clumsy and weak! Your gods spit upon you in disdain!'

The Celestial Vindicators threw themselves into the ogors with focused ferocity. They fought with little concern for their own safety, taking blows on shoulder guards and parrying only as an afterthought. Their aggression bore the mass of ogors back and saw skulls cracked, hearts pierced and hulking beasts smashed to the floor and trampled underfoot. Yet it also allowed their brutish foes to land blows of their own, where a more cautious Stormhost's warriors might have stymied the ogors' crude attacks. Kalyani saw a Liberator's helm crushed down into his body by a thunderous overhead blow from a club. She saw an ogor punch a Protector right in the face, so hard that the Stormcast's helm turned concave around the brute's mailed fist. Jeddichor himself was hit by a hard-flung mantrap on a length of chain, whose rusty jaws sank deep into the Knight-Heraldor's arm even as he was driving his sword into another ogor's gut. He was wrenched sideways with a yell of pain, blood welling around the awful injury as a massive ogor clad in hotchpotch armour prepared to stave his skull in with a lumpen iron hammer.

Kalyani launched herself forward and severed the mantrap's chain, releasing Jeddichor and allowing him to surge inside the ogor's guard and drive his sword point up through the monster's jaw and into its brain. At the same moment, another hurricane of fire leapt amidst the fight and Kalyani had a split second to register it was aimed straight at her. She threw herself forwards, rolling under the billowing column, and came up with a roar. Song met the fire-shaman's staff with a loud clang, and as sparks rained down Kalyani realised it was fashioned from some form of volcanic rock or glass.

The fire-shaman loomed over her, sparks dancing around his head, black smoke billowing from his tusked jaws. He leered horribly, leaning all his weight on his staff and trying to force Kalyani to her knees long enough to breathe another gout of fire all over her.

'We fight for Sigmar!' she yelled, twisting away and executing a complex sidestepping weave that slid her blade from his staff and saw its beetle-headed tip crack uselessly against the cobbles. 'We fight for the Heavens!' she snarled, hacking furiously at her enemy and forcing him to swing his stave up to block her rapid flurry of blows. He staggered back, off balance. 'We fight for ret-ribution!' Kalyani shouted as she took two running steps forward, planted one armoured boot upon the corpse of a fallen ogor and propelled herself high in a powerful leap.

'We fight!' she howled, bringing Song down in an overhead blow so furious that lightning erupted along its blade. The sword sheared through the ogor's raised staff with a crack like a thun-derbolt and hacked down through the crown of his bald head, not stopping until it reached his neck.

Landing, Kalyani ripped the weapon free and let her butch-ered enemy crash to the cobbles, black smoke and burning blood spilling from the gruesome remains of his head.

The Celestial Vindicators' charge had impacted with shocking ferocity and now, with the death of their shaman, the surviving ogors lost heart. They wavered, only for their bloody-aproned leader to wrench its cleaver from a Stormcast's twitching corpse and spit slobbering curses at them. The thing snatched a handful of rocks from its belt, stuffed them into its maw and crunched down.

Kalyani stared in horror as she heard a resounding bony crackle, and her horror redoubled as she realised that sound had not been the ogor's teeth. Instead, several of her Celestial Vindicators col-lapsed with agonised screams as their bones shattered within their limbs beneath the horrible power of the butcher's curse-magic.

Kalyani roared with wordless fury and threw herself at the butcher, hacking madly at its blubbery body and severing its fingers as it threw up a meaty paw to block her assault. Jeddichor sounded his battle-horn again, the point-blank blast hammering the butcher backwards and causing his flabby flesh to quiver and his nose to bleed. Kalyani saw realisation dawn on the monster's face that it was outmatched and, like so many bullies before it, its courage left it in a rush. It swung wildly with its cleaver and turned to flee.

Song found the nape of its neck before it had taken three paces, the blade bursting from the butcher's mouth and transfixing the gore-spattered monster. It crashed to its knees, blood jetting from its yawning maw, and as it did, the ogors lost their nerve entirely.

The Eviscerators' blood was up and their battle-lust upon them. With Kalyani and the wounded Jeddichor in the lead, they slaughtered their way uphill through the last panicked dregs of the ogor force and crested the rise amidst their toppling corpses.

'Ahead, Jeddichor, our goal! You honour our chamber with your heroism!' cried Kalyani, raising her bloodied blade high as she surveyed the scene before them. Around her, her surviving warriors answered her cry, more than thirty Celestial Vindicators so drenched in blood that their armour was now more crimson than green.

The street sloped away at their feet, down a steep hill broken by craggy stone outcroppings that had thrust their way up through the cobbles like bones through old flesh. At its base it met the Old Temple square in a trampled mass of plant-matter that had once been a break of ferns. Corpses were strewn across the vast expanse of the square, disfigured tribesmen and slain orruks and ogors scattered like offerings at the Old Temple's feet.

Kalyani saw the wreck of the *Exactitude* still lying where it had fallen in the midst of the square. Now, though, it was not the forces of Chaos or Azyr staging a desperate stand around its wreckage, but instead the orruks who had driven them off some days before. Kalyani estimated that two, maybe three hundred greenskins were crushed into a semicircular battleline around the southern edge of the wreck, from atop which several greenskin shamans were slinging bolts of green fire into their foes.

Those foes poured in from south and east; Stormcasts in their hundreds, the green-clad warriors of the Celestial Vindicators and the mauve-armoured fighters of Galabrith's Extremis Chamber.

They crashed against the hard-pressed orruks, smashing and pummelling their armoured bodies, hacking off their brutish heads and blasting them with coruscating bolts of celestial lightning. Even as she watched, Kalyani saw Galabrith himself swooping groundward upon his mighty stardrake Absaloth. The noble beast's jaws yawned, and a crackling arc of lightning erupted to blast an entire rank of greenskins to ashes.

Then came the distinctive shriek and whoosh of Freeguild rockets firing. The projectiles lofted high from a street just beyond the square, no doubt launched by some quick-thinking artillerist out to impress. They rained down amidst the orruks' rear lines, a few corkscrewing off target but most bursting with fiery ferocity right where they were needed most. Orruk bodies flew, and suddenly the greenskin line was collapsing, fragmenting and streaming back towards the yawning street-mouths on the square's northern edge.

'Protectors, guard our flanks, Decimators to the fore, focus your rage and cleave close to me,' cried Kalyani, and set off down the hill at a run with her warriors following.

A Kharadron airship thrummed overhead, trailing black smoke, its arkanaut crew desperately trying to fend off the maw-krusha that was ripping their craft apart.

Somewhere to the east, explosions flurried, lighting up the ruins and sending smoke boiling skyward.

WHUMP – WHUMP, WHU-WHUMP! came the distant booming of the orruk drum. Answering bellows of 'Waaagh!' rose from the streets to the north, loud enough to shiver the air in Kalyani's lungs.

Kalyani reached the flat plane of the square in time to see Galabrith swoop again astride Absaloth and unleash another bolt of energy into the retreating orruks. The stardrake swept so low overhead that Kalyani heard the leathery creak of its wings, felt their buffeting downdraught and smelled the actinic tang of celestial energies crackling on the air. She and her followers ran full pelt, crossing the vast expanse of the square even as Freeguild soldiery flooded in from the streets at their backs with drums a-thunder.

Ahead, the Celestial Warbringers harried the orruks back and back, driving them from the square entirely and loosing hails of bolts up at the winged greenskin beasts that flapped and swooped overhead. Their salvoes were joined by those of Rangers emerging from hold-outs and vantage points around the square. Winged Prosecutors soared in from the south in the colours of the Celestial Vindicators, hammers in hand and lightning crackling around them. They flew in 'V' formations, dozens of airborne Stormcasts racing to take the high ground of the Old Temple's cracked dome and the buildings that reared around the square.

Kalyani was into the shadow of the Old Temple itself when Absaloth rushed down from on high and landed with a whoosh of air just ahead.

'The Kharadron are doing their part, but there's a horde like nothing I've ever seen coming from the north,' shouted the stardrake-riding Lord-Celestant. 'Those orruks are going to hit us like a damned avalanche, wave after wave of them!'

'Can we hold them?' asked Kalyani as her warriors gathered around her, swiftly recovering their breath from their long dash.

'If we can get the Freeguild lines drawn up? If Sigmar smiles upon us and this rain hasn't rendered their artillery ineffectual? We'll hold for a while,' replied Galabrith. 'Long enough, at any rate, though by Ghal Maraz it is going to be a bloody battle!'

'What of the Nurgle worshippers?' she asked. 'We don't want another surprise attack from them.'

'Hard to say, whatever movements they are making are as good as invisible amidst all those flies and clouds of filth they raise. They are moving though, flowing this way under cover of their miasma. They will be on us within the hour.'

'Too slow, we will have claimed the weapon by then and be on our way out,' said Kalyani, moving to stride past Galabrith and towards the steps of the Old Temple.

'There is another thing, Lord-Celestant,' he said. 'An inexplicable thing that I fear may bode ill. The lake, to the west, the one along whose banks the Chaos worshippers were camped? It is gone.'

'Gone?' asked Kalyani, frowning behind her helm's faceplate. 'It has evaporated? Been drained?'

'Nobody saw what happened, unless perhaps the Kharadron witnessed something and have yet to tell us,' Galabrith replied. 'But wherever all that water went, I fear it may portend something ill.'

'All the more reason to make haste, then,' said Kalyani. It was then that they felt a shudder run through the ground. A dull rumble sounded. Water shook free of sloping rooves in pattering cascades, and Absaloth growled and stirred.

Kalyani and Galabrith exchanged a look.

'That is no artifice of ours,' he said.

'Drive the greenskins back,' she replied as another shudder ran through the ground and stonework creaked and groaned. 'We are going to claim this thing now. Would that we had even a handful of the Sacrosanct Chamber with us in case this goes ill.'

'Word was sent to that effect, Lord-Celestant, but as yet we have had no response from Sigmaron,' Galabrith replied.

'If wishes were warriors we would have conquered the realms by now,' she said, flicking blood and rainwater from Song's blade and jogging towards the temple steps.

'Sigmar go with you, and may you claim this dire weapon swiftly then!' cried Galabrith as Absaloth sprang heavenwards again.

'And good hunting to you, Lord-Celestant!' she replied. 'Hold them for as long as you can!'

Kalyani ran up the cracked steps of the Old Temple, feeling the heavy regard of the crumbling statues that loomed massively over it. Ancient friezes were worked into the stonework above the crooked temple doors, but whatever they had once depicted they were now little more than mingled shapes.

As she reached for the leaning stone slab of one of the doors, Kalyani felt another shudder run through the ground, a pulse more violent than any that had come before. Dust trickled down from the stonework above, and a tortured groan came from somewhere beneath her feet.

'What is that, Lord-Celestant?' asked Jeddichor, he and several other warriors taking hold of the door that Kalyani had gripped and helping to heave it open.

'I don't...' Kalyani trailed off as she saw into the interior of the Old Temple's atrium. For an instant it was as though the structure were brand new, its marble columns straight and tall, its bronzed walkways and magnificent frescoes lit by clear, cold Hyshlight. She had a fleeting impression of figures in amethyst robes striding purposefully from place to place, of high stacks of tomes and scrolls, of a massive hourglass made from brass and glass through which trickled sands of purest black.

The next instant Kalyani found herself fighting to recall what she was doing here, or even where *here* was. Her eyes roved over toppled marble, stagnant pools collecting between cracked paving slabs, ancient bones eroded down to little more than dusty remnants; what looked like it might have been a huge hourglass leaned at a crooked angle amidst the shadows, brass fixtures verdigrised and rotting, and shattered glass glinting amidst the gloom. A heap of wet, black mulch rested part within and part outside of it, looking as though it hadn't been disturbed in centuries.

Kalyani shook her head in frustrated bewilderment. What *was* this? What bizarre enchantments were filling her head with visions one moment and seeking to steal all wit from her the next?

'Is it some manner of defence?' she asked aloud.

'If so, it is a strange and ineffectual one,' replied Jeddichor. 'Come, time may be short.'

'You are right,' said Kalyani as fresh orruk war cries rolled like thunder outside and the ground shuddered like a wounded animal.

'How will we know where to find this weapon?' asked one of her Judicators as the Stormcasts filtered through the Old Temple's doors.

'Can you not feel that pulsing evil?' asked Kalyani, knowing full well they all must do. 'We simply follow that to its source, and there we shall find what we seek.'

They crossed the atrium at a jog, weapons ready, nerves tingling and eyes roving for the slightest hint of a threat. A dread feeling was building inside Kalyani's chest, an intuition of some terrible doom approaching, but she couldn't tell whether it was instinct, the effects of the weapon's proximity or some manifestation of whatever sorceries protected it.

Her question was answered as she reached the far side of the atrium and stared down a darkened stairwell into the shadowy gullet of the vaults below. Huge statues of verdigrised bronze knelt to either side of the stairway, tortured-looking humanoid figures arranged in postures of writhing torment. Each held an hourglass high and it looked as though these objects were the source of their pain.

'Down there, can you feel it?' she asked. Jeddichor nodded and shuddered.

'Such malevolence,' he said, then looked up at Kalyani as a sudden, stinking wind billowed up the stairs to meet them. The Lord-Celestant's tattered cloak rippled. A rushing, groaning sound came to them, growing louder, and the floor quivered beneath their feet.

'Run,' breathed Kalyani as the stench intensified and the rushing, whooshing sound built in fury and volume. 'Run!' she yelled. 'Back! Retreat! Out of here right now!'

She turned and broke for the temple doors at a flat-out sprint, her warriors following suit around her. Kalyani had managed a bare seven paces before the stone flags behind her erupted and a tide of stinking grey slime surged up from below to hit the Stormcast Eternals like a tidal wave.

CHAPTER EIGHT

COMPLICATIONS

Mordavia, the third day of the campaign

Deep beneath the Mordavian surface streets, something wicked wormed its way through the darkness. Slime-slick grit, old bonemeal and the shells of denuded freshwater molluscs ground underfoot as Cankus Glumm led his warband along buried roads towards their prize. Thousands of Nurgle worshippers trudged along subterranean streets and through ancient catacombs that had, until that very day, been wholly underwater. The Slupperslythe had surged ahead of them with tidal-wave speed and its grasping mass had whipped away much of the tunnels' former contents with it; still the advancing maggotkin trod on the odd flopping, eyeless cave fish, squelched through matted driftweed and dislodged dripping mineral accretions with their passage.

Where an entire ecosystem of primitive cave-swimming flora and fauna had flourished for hundreds of years, now roiling clouds of flies swarmed with a sound like bottled thunder. Where the

Horns of Plenty passed, so blooming algae and crawling fungi sprouted from the rich skim of slime that had been smeared over every surface. In their wake, Glumm knew, more complex and – to his eyes – beautiful plague blossoms would flourish, and a fecund new series of pox-rich grottos and filth-pools would take hold beneath Mordavia. Whatever else his warband might achieve this day, they had at least seeded a new bed for the Garden of Nurgle!

Many of Glumm's followers clutched rotwood torches, the oily wood squealing and popping as it burned. They spewed at least as much filthy smoke as flickering light to add to the fug filling the tunnels. Vomys Fecule and his blightkings, the Filthy Few, had muscled their way to the front of the column and formed an impromptu honour guard for their lord, nearly every one of them hefting such sputtering brands the better to light Glumm's path. Yet in truth he didn't need such crude aids to vision; his pestilent perceptions showed him every twist and turn, jag and shattered cobblestone of the tunnels with unfailing clarity.

'See them paintings?' he asked Yakob as they crossed a time-lost hall. One end of the structure had caved in under the weight of the strata above and now formed a sloping wall of crushed rubble from which jutted fragments of broken statuary and forlorn architectural flourishes. The rest of the space had survived though, its ruptured roof held up by pugnacious stone columns and its walls decorated with faded murals. The elegantly depicted figures seemed to peer out through the slick of slime left by the Slupper-slythe, wide-eyed as though in bewilderment at their strange fate.

'*Looks like… folk o' this… city… gave their worship… to Old Bones… don't it…?*' gasped Yakob as fat maggots nosed their way between his purple lips and plopped happily to the slime-coated floor. Glumm took care not to tread on the squirming insects – Yakob was rightly proud of everything he nurtured, after all – but he didn't fancy their chances beneath the tramping feet of the blightkings, diseased tribesmen and festering beasts that marched at his back.

'Does that, don't it?' he said, scanning the ancient depictions of robe-clad figures bearing offerings through shadowy gates and laying them at the feet of a towering skeleton surrounded by nine floating tomes. Many of the figures carried hourglasses, while others' faces or bodies had been replaced by them. Another line stretched away behind the crude depiction of Nagash, figures who had made their offering and were now reduced to shade-like things which drifted hollow-eyed down into a stylised pit and were gone.

'Never will understand them as worships death for death's sake,' Glumm said, shaking his head. 'What's the worth o' death without rebirth?'

'Dost thou believe, perchance, that 'tis they without the courage, nay fortitude to strive for something better?' asked Fecule, the massive blightking's voice emerging reedy and breathless from the depths of his rotting hood.

'Aye, that's likely it, Vomys,' Glumm replied, stepping through an ancient doorway and into the crazily canted ruin of a street beyond. Daylight filtered down here through cracks and rents above, illuminating the shattered remains of shopfronts and domestic dwellings long reduced to homes for subterranean fish. 'It's a cryin' shame that more ain't got the fortitude or the generosity of spirit to embrace the Grandfather's gifts. How else're we going to restore the life and beauty to the Mortal Realms, eh? Not by acceptin' our lot and worshippin' some big pile o' bones, that's for sure.'

'Thus hath it always been, my liege,' wheezed Fecule, shaking his cowled head and drizzling reeking fluids down his caked breastplate. 'The weak, the cowardly, the despairing, these are the burdens that we valiant few must shoulder 'pon our road to the Garden's gates.'

'I 'ope… them up top… are enjoyin' their road… s'much as we are…' rasped Yakob.

'I… er…' Fecule floundered, as Glumm so often found his underlings doing when Yakob addressed them directly. He had never understood their reactions; something to do with the diseased holiness of his incubatch perhaps? He didn't ask. He had no desire to make his loyal followers needlessly uncomfortable, after all.

'He means them bits o' the warband that we sent overground on account o' they wouldn't fit through these 'ere maggot-'oles,' Glumm explained patiently. 'The big lads, the blightlords 'n maggot-gargants 'n that.'

Fecule made an 'mmm' sound that suggested perhaps comprehension of the subject matter hadn't been the reason for his hesitancy.

'They have the miasmal shroud to blanket their advance, have they not, my liege? And from the substantial cacophony that floated to mine ears 'pon the winds of war a'fore we took to these darkling roads, I wouldst venture to say that our foes are much distracted wrestling one another's main strength. The Grandfather shall guide them to glory.'

'That he will, Vomys, and the Slupperslythe poppin' right up under their arses won't do our cause no 'arm, neither!' Glumm's wet laugh rolled along the subsided street, many of the blight-kings joining in his mirth.

'Sire, the way doth lighten ahead,' Fecule pointed out, and Glumm saw that his lieutenant was right.

'Ar, and listen to that, sounds like we're gettin' close to the to-do, don't it?' Where the subsided street ended it sloped up and through a fissure smeared with slime. The sounds of rainfall hammering stone washed through that gap, loud enough to be heard even over the drone of the warband's flies. Harsher and clearer still was the clangour of battle; Glumm heard blades clanging together, heavy crashing sounds, the crump and boom of explosions and a tumult of overlapping war cries. Something gave a distant fizzling crack that sounded to his trained ear like sorcery being unleashed. Something else screamed shrilly, rockets taking flight if he wasn't much mistaken. Something huge and viscid gave a gargling bellow and Glumm's smile broadened at the sound of the Slupperslythe wreaking havoc upon the surface. Through it all, thumping away like some vast heartbeat, came the WHUMP – WHUMP, WHU-WHUMP! of that enormous drum still pounding.

'*Do you… feel that…?*' asked Yakob. Glumm didn't need to ask what his incubatch referred to. *That* was doubtless the gnawing, dragging sense of malevolence that threaded through the air like a cloud of poison gas. Glumm fancied he sensed a hunger there, and the hint of some awful and incalculably ancient thing taking his measure and directing its hatred towards him.

'That'll be the weapon, then,' he said stoically.

'What makest thou say so?' asked Fecule.

'Figures, don't it? Feels bad, cold, sorta hollow,' Glumm replied, then hearing how haunted his voice sounded he swelled his chest and scowled. 'And b'cause the Great Gardener trusted me with the job o' findin' that weapon and dead-headin' the awful thing afore it could come into bloom, so I reckon I'd know it when I feels it! Now come on, this needs sortin' before it gets any worse.'

Glumm led the blightkings up the cobbled slope and out through the fissure, whose freshly shattered edges showed where the Slupperslythe had smashed it wider in its impatience to reach its prey. Behind Glumm and his retinue came warband upon warband of Nurgle worshippers, diseased tribesmen and bleating pestigors and more blightkings and more and more warriors all spilling up out of the buried city like fluids spewing from a ruptured cyst.

'*Blimey…*' said Yakob, and Glumm nodded at the sight before them.

The fissure led out into a deep chasm so long and wide that it appeared to have bisected an entire district near the heart of Mordavia. The chasm's floor was a good quarter-mile or so across, dotted with tumbled ruins and heaps of rubble now all slick with grey, porridgey slime. Its walls stretched upwards to the surface streets still more than a hundred feet above, and were layered with strata of bedrock, crushed streets, teetering old ruins and slyly glinting seams of ore. Above the tideline where the Slupperslythe had surged along the ravine there clung deep breaks of ferns, the rains pattering and splattering from their nodding leaves before trickling in rills down the jumbled faces of the cliffs.

At the ravine's far end could be seen another entrance into the underground, but this one was no raggedy-edged fissure. From the sludge-drowned remains of an ancient courtyard a flight of broad black steps led up between crumbling hourglass statues to an arch fashioned of cut onyx blocks. By Glumm's reckoning the arch was big enough for a gargant to pass through without ducking, and it led away into a dark tunnel from which raw malevolence pulsed.

Rearing above it was the vast dome of the Old Temple. Around that rose thick black columns of smoke through which airships, winged beasts and the glowing contrails of conjured spells tumbled and clashed.

'Reckon that's our route then, eh?' said Glumm.

'Verily,' agreed Fecule.

'Well, c'mon then, the beds won't seed themselves,' Glumm declared and began to march up the floor of the ravine with his army at his back.

Flies droned thick through the air, rising and spreading out into a busy roof of fat, furry bodies that kept off the worst of the rain. Still it rang tinnily upon Glumm's helm, and foul mud squelched underfoot.

'Bit exposed out 'ere, lad,' he muttered to Yakob as he marched. 'Too many flyin' troublemakers up there by half, and it don't take but one of 'em happenin' to glance into this chasm and seein' us comin".'

'Could've told you... that...' Yakob gasped, and Glumm felt his irritation flare. Perhaps it was the horrible sensations washing over him from somewhere ahead, but he was suddenly angry with his incubatch and its constant stream of cynicism and second-guessing.

'Well if you're so pox-bloomin' clever then why don't you point these things out b'fore they 'appen?'

'Not... my... job... is it...?' came the truculent reply.

'No, seems you're not much good but for lyin' around stinkin' of rot and spittin' up maggots, are you?' Glumm wasn't sure why he was so angry with Yakob, although considering how obstreperous his brother had been these last few days, he supposed he could be forgiven. Wherever the row had blown up from, it was getting louder now. He needed to win it quickly lest he look foolish in front of his followers.

'Why don't... you just... get by on your... own then, eh? If I'm so... useless...' Yakob spat at him.

'And why don't you just shut up!' roared Glumm.

'Liege...' wheezed Fecule. Glumm rounded on him, conscious that the entire army had come to a halt halfway along the ravine and were watching the argument with wide eyes.

'What?' shouted Glumm.

Fecule pointed with the pocked and rusty blade of his greatsword, and Glumm spun to see a peculiar blemish discolouring the air in front of his face. It was lurid green in colour, webbed with sickly black veins and spreading rapidly.

Glumm took a step back, hefting his trident and uttering a noise of surprise. As he did so the centre of the widening anomaly tore apart like a thin film burned by a hot flame. Stringy tatters of reality curled and blackened with a stench somewhere between hot metal and burned flesh. As they did a face was revealed, not more than ten feet in front of Glumm, hanging disembodied in mid-air. It was a long and tapering face that ended in a rat-like snout, quivering whiskers and sharp, chisel fangs. Heavy brass goggles reflected Glumm's bewildered image back at him. Red eyes bulged with sudden surprise behind them and the creature gave a shriek.

'Gnaa! Rot-things! Die-die!' The yawning barrel of an alarmingly large pistol was thrust through the widening gap. There came a hiss and a deafening bang, a flash of dirty green light, and suddenly Glumm found himself flat on his back. Groggily he raised his head and saw a massive crater had been blasted in his breastplate, from which black ichor and stringy matter were now oozing. Yakob lay in the mud to Glumm's left, spilled from his nerveless grip and left sprawled face down amidst the slimy water. Benignance lay to his right, the trident just out of reach.

'What in the name o' Nurgle...?' Glumm managed, before the rent tore wide and a screeching mass of skaven spilled from its depths.

Splichritt the Ever-most Very-much Magnificent drummed his footclaws upon the floor of his war litter and hissed with impatience. The diminutive grey seer watched as the gnawhole's exit-portal spread wider beneath the crackling lash of the Skryre burrowing-beams. Begoggled crew-rats snarled at one another as they worked bellows and spun dials, hauled upon levers and competed to be the team that forced the breach wide enough for the great Splichritt to pass through.

'Scurry-quick, gnaw-breach the hole or know my wrath!' he screeched, lashing his tail.

Already they had fashioned a wide enough breach that pack after pack of warriors from Verminus Clans Skurry and Gnashripp were pouring out of the gnawhole and into the ruined city. Splichritt could hear their maniacal shrieks, their cries of 'die-die' and the clangour as they crossed weapons with whatever foe had been unlucky enough to get in their way. Yet still the gap wasn't wide enough for the grey seer's war litter. Admittedly it might have been more practical for Splichritt to travel through the gnawhole on foot, but he had been the runt once in his life already; after those first bloody and terrifying days of tricking his bigger, stronger siblings into killing and eating one another instead of him, Splichritt had sworn he would never be small and helpless again.

'Now-now! Lazy stub-talon blunt-fang fools!' he exhorted, certain that his vehemence and anger more than made up for the high-pitched timbre of his voice.

Oh, it helped that his magic had come in quite so powerfully once his curling horns sprouted, and that he possessed such an ingrained brilliance for manipulation and bullying. But Splichritt liked to have brawn on his side as well. He had considered undergoing personal augmentation, be it the mechanical extension of his limbs or the warpstone-driven bulking out of his body, but there was no way he was going to put himself at the mercy of any flesh-twisting master moulder or half-sane Skryre warlock engineer.

No, Splichritt would not leave himself open to his many enemies in such a fashion.

Instead, he had granted Moulder Clan Thrytch the incalculable honour of gifting him their four largest, vat-bred rat ogors, to whose brawny shoulders Splichritt's armoured war litter had then been permanently sutured. It was a shame, he reflected as he inspected his talons, that the clan's master moulders had not fully appreciated the prestige he had granted them. Indeed, they had attempted to have him killed by a pack of ravening wolfrats just days later. At least, he suspected it had been them. It had seemed too likely to be coincidence. Unless it had been another rival attempting to frame them, of course, in which case he supposed their ultimate sacrifices had been more noble than he had given them credit for at the time.

One way or another, those same four master moulders had contributed one last gift to Splichritt's war litter: their heads, stitched on in place of the rat ogors' original craniums after having first been improved with a few mind-enslaving flourishes by their rivals in Moulder Clan Ruptiks. As noted purveyors of especially ferocious wolfrats, Splichritt had of course had Clan Ruptiks put to death in its entirety after the deal was done. It wouldn't do for him to look as though he had been manipulated, and after all the attempt on his life had been *terribly* convenient.

All of which brought Splichritt's fevered thoughts back around to the fact that his war litter and its hulking, armoured bearers were stuck in a still-too-small gnawhole even as battle raged beyond its mouth. It wasn't that he minded avoiding the fighting; let lesser vermin blunt the enemy's blades and face the peril of the initial assault. No, it was simply that Splichritt couldn't allow some rival to break through into Mordavia first and snatch the glory from him.

In fact, now that he thought about it, could not the incompetent Skryre breaching teams be holding him up on purpose? Wasn't it rather unusual that they still hadn't managed to force the gnawhole wide enough for him to pass? Couldn't one of Splichritt's many detractors have paid them well to blunder and falter and make him look slow and foolish?

Acid-green lightning crackled into being around Splichritt's handclaws as he drew himself up to his full, if still rather runtlike height. He stared imperiously down his snout at the frantic burrowing teams, who had obviously become aware of his mounting displeasure and were redoubling their cranking and wrenching and blasting efforts.

'You fool-fool no one, filthy turn-pelts!' he squealed. 'Rip-blast the breach this instant or die-die!'

Spraying the musk of fear, the burrowing teams abandoned all pretence at safety. They sprayed their gnaw-beams madly across the stuff of reality, erasing luckless clanrats, rival burrowing teams and the shuddering walls of reality in a great wash of green energies. There came a horrified squeal as one of the crew-rats over-cranked his weapon's mechanism then lashed and flailed as he tried to fight his way out of its straps.

Too late. The device exploded with an almighty crack and a lurid green flare that caused Splichritt to throw his handclaws over his eyes. When he lowered them and blinked into the drifting green fumes ahead, he realised that the malfunctioning burrowing engine had obliterated itself, its rival teams, several dozen clan-rats and a great swathe of the stuff of reality. The gnawhole now ended in ragged tatters through which Splichritt could see furious battle raging in the half-flooded depths of a ravine.

He sniffed and allowed himself an instant to preen; all those duplicitous agents wiped out at a stroke, his way to the battle clear, and all he had needed to do was *threaten* to unleash his powers.

'Truly, O Horned One, I am your most wise-cunning and terri-fying prophet!' he chittered. Then he turned his stare at the ranks and ranks of clanrats, stormvermin, gas-masked acolytes, minor chieftains and warlock engineers all gawping at the devastation in shock.

'Idiots! Broodwaste! Attack-attack! Gnaw-kill and gnash-slaughter! Clear a path for Splichritt the Ever-most Very-much Magnificent!'

As one, the masses of skaven that packed the gnawhole all the way back into its misty green depths raised a terrible screech-ing war cry. Motivated by a mixture of fear of their master, determination to claw their way to the top of the pile, and the heart-pounding pangs of the black hunger, the tide of ratmen surged from the gnawhole into Mordavia. Splichritt and his litter bearers were borne along with them.

Glumm was drowning in blood and slime. He was being crushed by a heaving mass of skaven whose furry, scrap-armoured bodies piled atop him and whose fangs, talons and splintered blades raked at his armour and flesh. He was frantic, not for his own life but for Yakob, who had vanished in the first seething wave of ratmen. He had no idea where *Benignance* had gone either, for skittering footclaws had kicked the weapon aside as the skaven charged.

With a roar of effort, Glumm managed to heave himself up out of the slop long enough to crush one clanrat's windpipe in his fist and drive his helm into the rabid face of another. Ten more skaven piled atop him in response, chittering and jabbering so fast that he couldn't understand a word, scrabbling and stabbing madly at him and opening fresh wounds across his body. Glumm was going cold, could feel the ichor pumping from his crushed form. His needle fangs had been smashed with fists and sword butts. His breastplate had been levered half off, Nurgle only knew how, and his innards were spilling hot and filthy over himself and his opponents alike. Something he couldn't see was *gnawing* on his intestines, causing him such horrible pain that even Glumm couldn't shrug it off.

The weapon would go unclaimed.

He had failed.

And yet all he could think about was finding Yakob, saving him from this appalling avalanche of flesh and fur and fangs.

Glumm roared again, got a fist loose long enough to punch a slathering ratman in the face. The creature, some sort of champion from its preposterously crested helm and stolen aelf blade, reared back to plunge its sword into Glumm's neck and finish him. Before the blow could land, a massive sword swung through the air and swatted the ratman aside in a tangle of limbs and broken bones. Another sword blow, and another, and the pressure on Glumm eased as skaven were smashed and broken and flung aside.

'Die-die!' they shrieked and, 'Stinking plague-things!' and they hurled themselves in maddened frenzy at Fecule and his blight-kings. Yet though more than one of Nurgle's faithful fell with razored fangs buried in their throats or rusty daggers rammed through their eye sockets, still they managed to drive back the living tide that had engulfed their leader.

When it broke, the skaven morale collapsed as suddenly as a rotting building with its foundations gnawed through. Deranged war cries turned to shrieks of panic. Ratmen clawed at one another, scrambling over each other in their desperation to escape the blightkings' ponderous wrath.

'Run-flee!'

'Aieeeeeee!'

'No, no, no, no!'

Fecule reached down and grasped Glumm's forearm to haul him up out of the mud. At that moment the skaven wavered, crashing into one another, baring their fangs in terror.

'Ratling guns! Duck-hide!' shrieked a shrill voice and then the world filled with a clattering, hammering cacophony. Glumm slapped back into the muck as a hail of glowing green bullets engulfed Fecule and plucked him backwards off his feet in a spray of diseased gore. Armour rang like broken bells. Skaven ran mad, jerking and twitching and coming apart as the merciless storm of fire chewed them and the blightkings apart with indiscriminate hunger. Viscera rained down on Glumm, and he felt fresh pain as something thwacked through his helm hard enough to bounce his head off the ground.

'Grandfather! Please!' He didn't even know what he was crying out for – aid for himself, maybe, or vengeance upon these manic ratmen who had poured from their gnawholes in a sudden storm and ruined his plans; maybe just for Nurgle to save Yakob from this bloody mayhem.

There came a sudden bang, louder than the rest, and a chorus of shrieks. Hot metal spun and whickered around Glumm, but the hail of shots had stopped. Cautiously, senses reeling and brains feeling like jelly within his punctured helm, he hauled himself up onto his elbows.

Utter carnage.

Unbelievable slaughter.

Glumm took in the mounds of corpses, skaven and maggot-kin mashed and tumbled together in drifts across the bottom of the ravine. Through a gauzy haze of smoke and droning curtains of flies he took in warbands of his warriors emerging through the fissure in the tunnel, rushing to his aid. He saw wave upon wave upon wave of skaven still pouring from the three gnawholes they had torn in reality, even as the thing he presumed was their leader was borne away upon some kind of metal raft that bobbed atop the swarm. The horned ratman was making straight for the onyx archway and the prize that lay beyond, and Glumm's ruined body and mauled army were in no state to stop him.

'Grandfather...' croaked Cankus Glumm, casting about for Yakob amongst the carnage. No sign of the incubatch. No sign of his brother, to whom his last words had been in anger.

The skaven were advancing again now. He saw it dimly, in flashes of weird colour and pestilential swirls of understanding. Ratmen advanced with bulky packs on their backs, hurling globes that shattered to release foul corrosive gases. At their backs, burning contraptions spat and popped, belching smoke into the heavens and spitting out the occasional warpstone bullet.

Strong hands grasped Glumm's arms. More tried to stuff his ruined guts back in as he was hauled backwards, away from the skaven and the battle still raging in the ravine's depths.

'The… smoke….' he said, something worrying at his mind. He needed to warn them about the smoke. Why?

'Don't worry about that now, Lord Glumm,' came a solicitous voice, clotted with phlegm and full of worry and anger.

'No. It… rising…' he said. 'Giving us away… Yakob… saw…'

And then everything went a few shades darker. Cries of panic rose around Glumm and for a moment he thought perhaps he was dying, and his followers were lamenting his loss. Then he realised the skaven were screaming too, a mad maelstrom of screeches that sawed at his nerves and competed with the hammering roar now filling the canyon.

The roar of endrins.

Aether-endrins.

'Oh… bugger it…' croaked Glumm. As they swept low overhead, the Kharadron airships unleashed their bombs and the ravine filled up with fire.

CHAPTER NINE

KARROBETH'S WARNING

The encampment, southern fringe of Mordavia,
the third day of the campaign

Bronvynne shut the ancient tome with a thump that caused Tove to glance up in surprise. She took a slow breath to steady herself, smelling wet canvas, muddy earth and the ripe smells of unwashed bodies and overcooked meat.

'I have to warn them!' she said aloud.

'Warn who about what?' asked Tove, sighing as he set down his wine cup and folded the corner of the dog-eared print-book he'd been reading.

Bronvynne was already rising, stowing the tome in her robes as her mind whirled. Panic tried to scatter her thoughts. She fought it down. Lief wouldn't panic in a situation like this. *What would he do instead?*

'Karrobeth? Warn them about *what?*' Tove said more sharply. He clearly felt her alarm even if he didn't understand it, and his soldier's instincts had driven him to his feet and brought his hand to the hilt of his sword.

'I need… a messenger! I need a messenger!' she said urgently. 'I have to get a message to Lord-Celestant Thunderblade at once!'

She felt a flash of gratitude towards Laszlo Tove as, rather than question her again, the bodyguard nodded and stepped out of the flap of the tent into the pouring rain.

'Runner!' she heard him shout. 'Runner here!'

Bronvynne stood for a moment, straining her ears in the hope of hearing approaching footfalls. There was the distant pounding of the awful greenskin drum; the distant crash and roar of warriors raising war cries, clashing blades, screaming, dying; the drone of airship endrins; the frightening roars of monstrous beasts that Bronvynne didn't wish to imagine; the thump and boom of artillery firing and firing until she imagined half the city must surely lie in ruins; and the searing shriek and crackle of magical energies being unleashed.

There was no sound of running feet.

Tove ducked back in through the tent-flap, drenched and scowling.

'Camp's half empty,' he said. 'No one around here at all, save a few camp sentries and lookouts and they're not about to leave their posts to help us.'

'But they must!' exclaimed Bronvynne, feeling frustration and fear rising within her again. This time she couldn't entirely keep it from her voice.

'You've found something bad in there, haven't you?' he asked.

'No living thing can touch the weapon!' she exclaimed.

Tove frowned.

'Well… I mean… isn't that good? That what it meant by… er… spectral?'

'What do you mean *good?*' Bronvynne almost shrieked. Tove's frown deepened and he waved a hand as though trying to grasp something from the air.

'If no living thing can touch the weapon, I mean, doesn't that mean no one can claim the damned thing? Or… Oh, Sigmar, do you mean it'll kill 'em? If they touch it?'

'Not just them,' she said, snatching up her overcloak and throwing it about her shoulders. 'Everyone! If a living being touches that weapon its power will be unleashed!'

He paled at that. Bronvynne knew Tove could feel the undercurrent of malice pulsing from within the city's heart just as well as she could.

'We've got to get word to the front then,' he said. 'Straight away!'

'That's what I've been *saying*, Mister Tove,' she exclaimed. 'Now come on, if there's no one here to take our warning then we need to get moving!'

'The command pavilion,' he said, understanding at once. Bronvynne felt another stab of grudging respect for her unasked-for guard as he squared his shoulders and turned back out into the rain at once.

She followed him out into the pelting rain, and as she left the musty bubble of the tent the sounds of distant battle grew louder and sharper.

By the time Bronvynne and Tove climbed the low rise to the command pavilion, they were both soaked to the skin and splattered with mud. As they rushed along, Bronvynne had heard the cries of wounded soldiers from healers' tents elsewhere in the encampment and had seen the nervous-looking soldiers of reserve regiments waiting under sagging awnings. She also saw, to the south-west, the enormous castle-form of a cogfort stomping along the eaves of the forest towards them upon its vast mechanical legs. Yet for all this she had had an eerie sense of dislocation, of having been left behind in a virtual ghost town while others did what they must for Sigmar's realm.

That was why Bronvynne had been digging her way through the tome with such fervour in the first place, of course. She hated to feel that she wasn't doing her part.

Well, if this message gets through then you may yet make a difference, she thought to herself. She tried to ignore the nagging voice that answered that thought, the one that said she should have found this crucial warning earlier, should have armed Kalyani Thunderblade and her comrades with it *before* they stormed off into the city chasing after the weapon that Bronvynne had sent them to find.

As they approached the pavilion, Bronvynne saw an assortment of Freeguild officers, Ironweld Engineers and flag-flapping signalmen braving the weather atop its observation tower. Some stared through long telescopes, trying to pierce the veils of rain and discern what was happening in Mordavia. Several of the signalmen were snapping their coloured flags about in repeating patterns that she realised must be intended for the crew of the approaching cogfort.

Closer to hand, a pair of masked and helmed Stormcast Eternals stood guard over the pavilion's entrance. Bronvynne recognised the teal armour of the Celestial Vindicators, though she had no way of knowing if these were warriors she had met before.

'Urgent message needs sending to the city, to Lord-Celestant Thunderblade,' barked Tove, and Bronvynne's eyebrows shot up at the sudden crack of authority in the man's voice. Briefly she wondered who he had been before donning the mantle of wine-swilling malcontent.

The two Stormcast Eternals towered over them, rain pinging from their armour, expressions hidden behind their impassive masks. The eyes that stared out at Bronvynne did not look friendly, and she felt panic rising within her again.

What if they won't help us? she thought. *What if they turn us aside? Surely Thunderblade must trust me by now! What more must I do?*

Then one of the armoured giants inclined her head and gestured towards the pavilion's interior. Tove nodded his thanks and Bronvynne followed him into the dry.

She threw back her hood gratefully, only to find herself embroiled in a wholly different sort of storm. Dozens of officers, mages, war scholars, engineers, warrior priests and assorted hangers-on filled the pavilion. If possible, it seemed to her busier than it had during the counsel of war earlier that day.

Was that really just hours ago? she thought. It felt like days.

Everyone looked busy and harassed. Messenger runners came and went with breathless speed, though not in the numbers Bronvynne would have expected. There was an omnipresent buzz of voices; voices issuing or questioning orders, voices reeling off reports, voices confirming and checking information, voices dictating updates to maps or double-checking the deployments of regiments and weapons.

'Send word for Captain Venk's batteries to move up onto the Whispering Ridge and begin enfilading fire against the orruks pushing down–'

'–no, no there's no Vanguard forces left to deploy. We'll have to move the Eighty-Sixth Cerulan Bulls up and–'

'–reports of reinforcements pushing in from the west through the Sunken District with mutant gargants at their head. What about–'

'–if we can get a force around their flank, pivot our advance about the foundations of the Gorgon's Tower, then–'

'–well haven't we heard *anything* from the admiral since he commenced hostilities? Send another–'

'An entire warband of orruks have broken through the Warbringers' advance guard! Where are the–'

'–never seen orruks in such numbers! And what in Sigmar's name is that damn great siege-tower thing they've got with them? It's moving slowly but by all the heavens if it gets its spear throwers into range of–'

'–anyone seen Lord-Celestant Thunderblade since that… *thing*… erupted out of the Old Temple? We had reports–'

Bronvynne's blood ran cold as she caught that last snatch of conversation and she reached out to grab the sleeve of the young aide-de-camp who was speaking.

'What was that about Lord-Celestant Thunderblade and the Old Temple?' she demanded. The young officer looked down at her frail hand clutching a swathe of his puffy sleeve, then up at her with an expression somewhere between alarm and anger.

'Unhand me, scholar, I don't have time for your questions!' he exclaimed. Suddenly Tove was looming at her shoulder, and Bronvynne was both irritated and glad that his presence had a more immediate civilising effect upon the aide than her own sharp-eyed glare had done.

'Answer the lady, please, there's a good lad,' said Tove.

'We've had conflicting reports from the Old Temple front,' the young officer said, eyeing Tove uncertainly. 'As best we can piece together, when the Lord-Celestant led her warriors into the Old Temple, something terrible burst out from somewhere within and attacked them. Some eyewitnesses are claiming they were spat out of the temple on a wave of… slime… or something and have been fighting in it or… against it… since. Others reckon the temple came down on them, or the orruks overran their lines. It's mayhem in there and since the enemy started targeting our messengers and aetherwings…'

Bronvynne felt dismay at the officer's powerless shrug. What if that awful tide of slime had been released as a defence for the weapon, or even *by* the weapon? What if she was too late, or the

Lord-Celestant was already dead? *No*, she told herself firmly. *Lief wouldn't lose hope, and he'd not be too pleased to see you doing so either, my girl. Think! The weapon can't have found its focus, whatever that means, or we'd all have known about it. We'd probably all be dead! And if anyone I've ever met could survive amidst whatever it is that's going on in there, it's a Stormcast they call the Once-Forged!*

'I have a message, it is urgent, and it has to reach Lord-Celestant Thunderblade immediately,' she said with new steel in her voice. However, the officer just barked a mirthless laugh in her face.

'Even *if* anyone had time to waste on some old bookwife's personal errands, we're under strict orders not to despatch any more runners to the Old Temple front.'

'Now listen here,' began Tove, but Bronvynne put up a hand to stop him and to her surprise he fell quiet.

'Young man, this is not a *personal errand*,' she said, loading her words with as much scorn and impatience as she could inject into them. It must have worked, as the young officer's face took on an expression that she most closely associated with someone getting a dressing-down from their highly disappointed mother. 'I am Bronvynne Karrobeth, the Lord-Celestant's personal arcanotranslocutor and the woman who deciphered the tome that led us all here in the first place. I have discovered new information, information of vital importance. I *demand* that you find a runner at once, more than one in fact, get them a copy of my warning each to bear and send them on their way to the Old Temple. Unless you wish to be personally responsible for our armies' defeat and our own horrible deaths?'

That helpless shrug again, and Bronvynne's heart fell as an older, broad-chested Freeguild officer with a captain's uniform and an eyepatch loomed at the aide's shoulder.

'Can't be done, ma'am,' he said in a gruff voice that sounded sympathetic, but firm. This man wasn't impressing an opinion, thought Bronvynne. He was stating an immutable fact.

'Why not?' asked Tove.

'Losing 'em at too swift a clip, sorry to say,' said the captain, nudging the aide to hurry off about his business. The lad did so with a grateful glance at his superior. 'We've put a stop on sending runners or aetherwings into any of the front-line districts. Trying to re-establish contact with the Kharadron instead and relay our information through them.'

Bronvynne felt winded, as though someone had punched her in the stomach. Her vision went momentarily too-sharp around the edges and she felt a prickle of real panic across her skin like the tautness of sunburn. She put out an arm and held onto Tove to steady herself as she thought frantically.

'You've lost communication with the Kharadron?' he was asking. 'How?'

The captain harrumphed.

'Not lost, in so many words,' he said. 'They've just stopped responding. Still bringing the fury of the Heavens down upon the orruks and the rot worshippers, mind you. But they're not picking up our signals. General Gharphyn's having chemical rockets sent up next, thinks maybe they can't make out our flags through all this dratted rain.'

'The general, if I could speak to her,' said Bronvynne, snatching at the name, but the captain was shaking his head.

'She's a half-mile closer to the city, ma'am, overseeing the messenger rocket flights in person. Can't countermand her orders in the meantime, no matter how important this information you've found might be.'

'But you don't understand, they mustn't touch the weapon or we're all going to die!' shouted Bronvynne and a hush rippled out around her like the blast wave of a bomb. Faces turned to stare.

A junior engineer dropped his stylus into the waters of the map table and cursed as he fouled an ink-swirled district.

The captain frowned mightily.

'I think perhaps you'd best take yourself away and get a grasp of yourself, ma'am,' he said, voice stern. 'Go on, take a seat over in the corner there and I'll have some wine sent. As soon as we're back in touch with the admiral and his airships we shall be sure to transmit whatever message it is you wish to see sent. You have my word. The rest of you, come along, Sigmar's war won't wait! Back to work!'

Bustle recommenced around them and the captain moved away. Bronvynne felt eyes on her, stares both questioning and alarmed. Her heart was beating too fast and her mouth was dry. Why couldn't they understand how important this was? *It's like being caught in the gears of some awful, stupid machine,* she thought. *Powerless to stop it, powerless to change its course or get them to listen to me.*

Tove took her arm and guided her away, and Bronvynne went with him in a daze. It was only when they re-emerged into the cold and wet of the outdoors, rather than sitting meekly at the corner table, that she looked sharply around at her bodyguard.

'Mister Tove?' she asked questioningly as he cast about them, shielding his eyes from the rain with a hand.

'Are you absolutely convinced that your message has to get through?' he asked her. 'You certain that we're all dead if not?'

'Well, I mean, I don't know precisely *what* the weapon will do if touched,' she confessed, and he spared her a questioning glance. 'But I'm sure that the effects will be catastrophic!' she snapped, voice firming again as her dismay turned to anger. 'At the very least thousands will die in the city. I don't doubt for a second that our army will be annihilated, and I wouldn't be at all surprised if whatever power is unleashed scours the lands of life for miles around.'

'Then we've got two choices,' he said, making a little 'ah' sound as he saw whatever it was that he was looking for. Tove jogged off downhill, leaving his sentence unfinished. Bronvynne tugged her sodden hood back over her wiry grey hair and patted the book where it lay swaddled beneath her robes. She looked up in time to see him returning leading a heavyset dray horse by its bridle.

'Artillery teams won't miss one, not with sentries that sloppy,' he said. 'And even if they do, sounds to me like our business is more important.'

'What do you intend that we do?' asked Bronvynne, shooting a scandalised glance past him and the big, waterlogged dray horse towards the half-visible cluster of tents and sheltered hitching posts from which he had stolen it. She half expected to hear angry voices raised. So far there was nothing but the distant sounds of battle and the endless boom of the drum.

'It's as I said, we've two choices,' said Tove, checking the horse over with a professional eye. It wasn't saddled, Bronvynne noted, just had a simple bridle and reins she was fairly sure were meant for leading the beast rather than riding it. 'Either you and I mount old… uhm… let's say Max… here and ride into the city to take the damned message ourselves, or we turn his head south and ride as far from this debacle as we can before disaster overtakes us.'

Bronvynne blinked rain from her eyes as she stared at him. He couldn't be serious, could he? But he was. She could see it in the set of his jaw, his hard stare.

'We… I mean, we cannot just flee for the hills and leave all these good people to die!' she exclaimed, outraged at the notion.

'Then our options just got cut in half, didn't they?' he said. Bronvynne looked towards the distant city, at the columns of boiling black smoke rising through the rain, the faint shapes of beasts and skyships duelling on high, the dimly visible moving mountain of the orruks' vast tower shuddering closer to the Old Temple all the time. As she watched there came a bright flare of purple light from somewhere amidst the districts in the east of the city. It was followed a few seconds later by a terrible wall of sound, a distant thrumming roar and screeching crackle that she knew must be powerful sorcery being unleashed. Her chest tightened and her guts felt loose at the thought of going into such peril. Hiding in her tent and praying to Sigmar had never seemed so appealing.

'Why Max?' she asked.

'Eh?' Tove replied, wrong-footed.

'Why did you just name our stolen horse Max?' she repeated her question.

'Used to have a sergeant called that. Looked like a horse. Just popped into my head,' he replied.

'And was Max a good sergeant, Mister Tove?'

'Utter bastard, but reliable as they come and a damned good fighter,' he said, and Bronvynne thought she heard the ghost of pride in his voice.

'Then how could we dishonour his memory by failing our comrades now?' she asked. 'You will have to help me up, I'm afraid, Mister Tove. I have precious little experience with riding beasts.'

'Not a problem,' he replied. 'Just hang on where I tell you, keep hold of that book, for Sigmar's sakes, and leave the riding to me.'

The journey into the city was a terrifying ordeal that Bronvynne remembered afterwards in snatches and fleeting impressions.

She recalled the strong scent of the horse's wet hair and mane, the ripple of its heavy muscles flowing beneath its skin, the tooth-rattling jolt of its footfalls and the ache that rose rapidly up through her legs, her hips and her abdomen as it pounded along. She remembered Tove hunched protectively over her, holding the beast's simple reins and directing it with a surety and skill that surprised her.

Bronvynne remembered the rain, lashing spitefully against her face, the wind rushing past, the lurch of panic each time she thought she might be about to slip off Max's back or else let the tome spill from her grip.

There were the shouts of piquet guards, receding rapidly behind them, and the hungry rumble of war, getting louder and louder as they plunged towards it.

She remembered the moment when Max's hoofbeats went from dull thumps to hard clops as muddy grass became cobbles and flagstones running with rainwater. She recalled the sound of his tread echoing like thunder from the looming suggestions of ancient buildings, and the horrible sense of familiarity that she felt at their hunched and ragged outlines. Bronvynne had been hunted through Mordavia's streets and ruined buildings for days, and she was not likely to forget the menacing feel of the place this side of the Realm of Death.

There were moments of nerve-shredding terror. Orruks, daubed in wild warpaint, bursting from within a ruined mausoleum and loosing arrows at them as they thundered past. Something huge and dripping with filth, its head that of a giant maggot, looming out of a side street and taking a ponderous swipe at Max that made the horse rear and kick. She would have fallen then, but for Tove. Instead they had thundered on, avoiding the monster's clumsy grasp. At one point a Kharadron skyship rumbled so low overhead that Bronvynne was sure it must crash down upon them. At another a vast scaled beast had plunged from the sky and slammed down in the street just behind them. Having missed its killing pounce, the thing had stomped around on its massive knuckles and let loose a bone-shaking bellow of anger that was echoed by the enormous, one-eyed orruk clinging to its back.

Bolts and bullets flew as they rode through the outskirts of furious battles. Streets were blocked with masses of wrestling, hacking figures and heaps of bloodied corpses. A massive purple orb burning with dark energy smashed through a building a hundred yards ahead of them, transforming a gaggle of fleeing soldiers into twisted statues with its touch, then smashing away again into an adjoining street.

Always the drum pounded away in the distance. Always the sense of hateful malevolence grew and grew. Danger seemed to pounce from every direction as they rode until Bronvynne was sagging and numb, half-tempted to drop from Max's back and simply curl up in a limp heap amidst the ferns and mangled corpses.

And then they were cantering up a last cobbled rise, the horse frothing and blowing, and Old Temple square was laid out before them in all its gore-soaked horror.

Kalyani met the downswing of the orruk's massive axe. Song chimed with the fury of the impact and the Lord-Celestant was almost driven to her knees. She snarled with the effort of parrying the orruk's blow then pushed upwards, shoving his axe back and away and causing him to reel. The greenskin roared at her, spittle flying between his tusks. She responded by feinting right, drawing her already off-balance foe into a ponderous sidestep before going the other way and running him through. Song's blade punched neatly through the orruk's thick, crudely beaten breastplate and burst from his back before she wrenched it back out and struck again.

Never stab an orruk once and believe the fight is done, she thought as the brute swung his axe at her again. He seemed not to feel the two ragged wounds in his torso or notice the blood jetting from them to spatter Kalyani's gore-caked armour. She whipped her blade around to parry again but was saved the effort as a massive tendril of thick grey slime swept down from on high. Kalyani was forced to throw herself clear of the descending tentacle. The orruk wasn't so quick. He was mashed into the cobbles of the Old Temple square by the blow.

Rolling clear, Kalyani spat furious oaths.

'Hammer and throne and all the damned stars in the Heavens, what must we do to kill this abomination?'

The tide of rushing filth had engulfed Kalyani and her warriors, sweeping them back out of the Old Temple and causing half of the building's frontage to collapse in the process. She had been fortunate, fighting her way free of the crushing, cloying, rancid foulness and managing to squirm away before its juices could eat their way through her armour to the flesh beneath. Many of her warriors had not been so lucky.

The thing had filled half the square by the time it finished pouring from within the Old Temple, and it had quickly become apparent that this was no flood of filth from below, but a monster that could fight and think and devour.

Lord-Celestant Galabrith had bellowed orders for their combined armies to hit the abomination with everything available. A howling storm of drake-bolts, bullets, arrows, artillery fire and magical projectiles had engulfed the slime-beast. Swathes of the filth that formed it had sizzled away into steam or been splattered across the sagging frontage of the Old Temple.

Then the orruks had arrived in force and, finding their enemies already engaged in battle, had simply hurled themselves into the fray with soldiers and monster both.

Since that moment, Kalyani had had precious little chance to command as a Lord-Celestant should. Instead she had been fighting, driven by the warrior fury of her Stormhost, a whirlwind of crackling lightning with a shining-bright blade. She had heaped the orruks up six deep all around her. She had weaved through a sorcerous bombardment to gut a greenskin shaman then set about the burly monsters that had howled with fury at his death. She had fought ogors, troggoths, grots and orruks until her muscles burned, until blood ran from her wounds and her lungs were hot bellows in her chest.

'We fight!' she chanted again and again. 'We fight! We kill! We win!'

Other Celestial Vindicators fought around her, half-glimpsed amidst the monster's whipping tendrils and the onrushing masses of the orruks. Streaks of teal and gold raced past her through the rain and the blood to smite the enemies of Sigmar with all their fury. Bolts of emerald lightning leapt Heavensward as, one by one, the warriors of her chamber fell. She heard Jeddichor Wallbreaker's battle-horn booming like thunder through the maelstrom of battle, and knew each time that he, at least, still lived. She had seen Rojavi Sundershield smashing his way through the greenskins barely five minutes before, and had hope that he was still on his feet. Yet she had a sense that the Freeguild advance had stalled before they could establish their cordon; the orruks had broken through too quickly, their numbers too great, and the seemingly unkillable abomination that had burst from the temple was soaking up an army's worth of fire on its own. It gurgled and flailed, consumed ranks of screaming soldiers and smashed war engines flat with its clubbing pseudopods.

'Only we can hold back the orruks,' Kalyani told herself as she flicked blood from her blade and prepared to face the next howling mass of onrushing greenskins. 'Only we can stem the tide until the beast is slain.'

But if it wasn't slain soon there would be no Stormcast Eternals left to go after the weapon, and then it wouldn't matter whether the Freeguild managed to anchor their battleline or not. Another power would seize that terrible device and with it they would annihilate every warrior in Mordavia.

And that will only be the beginning, she thought furiously as she hacked and parried and spun. Roaring, cursing orruk faces whirled around her. Blades clashed against hers with avalanche force, denting her armour, nicking her flesh, staggering her but never fully breaking her guard. Kalyani Thunderblade had only been reforged once. She would not face it again, here, now. Not like this, with her duty unfinished!

There came a hot rush of air and a stardrake swooped low overhead. Lightning exploded from its jaws and threw blackened orruks high into the air. Even as its rider tried to direct his steed skywards again, rotting tendrils erupted from the heaped body of the slime-beast and wound about it. The noble beast roared and thrashed as it was drawn inexorably in, and its lightning spat again and again, blasting charred craters in the abomination as the two leviathans wrestled.

Kalyani turned to lend her aid, but Jeddichor was suddenly at her side, wounded arm still hanging useless, helm sundered and blood spilling from half a dozen wounds.

'Lord-Celestant, urgent messengers for you from behind the lines,' he said. 'You must come with me.'

Kalyani glanced up the nearest northward street, at the tide of orruks and ogors spilling along it, and at the hulking enormity of the rolling war idol drawing ever closer from the north. She could hear the crash and boom as it ploughed over ruined buildings that blocked its lurching path, the repeated twang-thwack as its bolt throwers launched deadly projectiles into the fight.

'Messengers?' she panted, barely understanding the word. The need to fight and kill leapt like lightning in her veins and she began to turn away from Wallbreaker.

He grasped her arm again, shouted in her ear.

'Lord-Celestant, it is the scholar. She has discovered some terrible secret about the weapon! She says you have to know. Now!'

Kalyani felt a surge of anger and wrestled down the mad desire to strike her subordinate. If it was Karrobeth, and if the old crypto-scholar had braved the journey all the way into war-torn Mordavia to bring word of her discovery herself, then it must be important. She glanced around, seeing the remains of several brotherhoods still barely holding the line against the orruks.

It had best be, she thought. *Sigmar knows I am sorely needed here!*

'Where?' she asked. Jeddichor pointed with his good arm and Kalyani saw Karrobeth and her bodyguard huddled in the midst of a protective square of Freeguild infantry a few hundred yards back across the square.

'Hold them, Jeddichor,' she said to him. The Knight-Heraldor nodded, raising his battle-horn to his mouthpiece and sounding a mighty blast that bowled orruks backward and shattered their bones.

'Hold the line!' he roared to the embattled Celestial Vindicators. 'Reinforcements are on their way! Hold the line and fight in Sigmar's name!'

As Kalyani set off across the square there came a terrible rending crack and she glanced sideways in time to see the blackened and mangled slime-beast snapping the stardrake's spine with its putrid coils.

The Drakesworn Templar who had sat in the stardrake's saddle lunged at the monster, roaring with rage. It buried him in a wave of acidic filth, and he vanished from Kalyani's sight.

'Damn it, *damn it,*' she spat. She didn't know where that horror had come from, but it had fouled her and Galabrith's plans quite spectacularly. It had the look and stench of the Nurgle worshippers about it, and she cursed herself and all her fellow officers for underestimating them.

Kalyani had nearly reached Karrobeth and her escort, fresh regiments of Freeguild streaming past her towards the fight, when a mighty drone built up from the west. She looked up to see the Kharadron air armada sweeping in towards the square. Light gunships prowled the formation's flanks while at its centre came the *Shieldmaiden*, its massive armoured bulk scarred and scorched but still every inch the indomitable dreadnought.

'Hah, now we shall see, you rancid mass of filth,' spat Kalyani, waiting for the duardin to begin a bombing run against the diminished slime-beast. She frowned as they instead fell into a circling pattern around the dome of the Old Temple. Their guns and bombs spoke their fury, but they were firing into the streets around the massive structure, ignoring the fight in the square in favour of driving back the orruks and rot worshippers closing in from the north, east and west.

'Lord-Celestant!' she heard Bronvynne shouting over the din of explosions and airship endrins. The last thing Kalyani saw before she turned away was a skyship shuddering under multiple impacts as the spear-throwers of the orruk war tower found their range.

'Lord-Celestant!' Bronvynne shouted again, her voice hoarse and wavering. Wide-eyed Freeguild soldiers parted for Kalyani as she strode up to the old scholar. She spared a brief glance for Karrobeth's sodden bodyguard, and another for the exhausted dray horse whose reins he still clutched.

'What is it?' Kalyani demanded. 'Swiftly, the battle is at a critical stage.'

'Lord-Celestant, you have to get into the temple right away! No one must touch the weapon!' gasped Karrobeth. Kalyani frowned, her blood still up and her patience scant.

'Is this all you came to tell me? We already know that we must seize this thing before our enemies. Even you must be able to see that it is not so simple.'

Though, she thought as she watched the *Shieldmaiden* settling over the Old Temple dome and its rappelling lines uncoiling, *it may be that Admiral Norgssen is about to repay his debt to us in fine form indeed!*

'No, my lady, you don't understand,' said Karrobeth, fighting for breath. 'I… the tome… if any living being touches the weapon, if they make contact with it, then its power will be unleashed. Everyone is going to die! You *must* prevent it, my lady!'

Kalyani felt as though the ground were shifting under her feet. Fury surged through her at this sudden, disastrous revelation. Stop any living being from touching the weapon? How was she supposed to do that amidst this mayhem? Didn't Karrobeth realise that it was now just a matter of luck and willpower as to who claimed the damned thing first? Trying to stop anyone, orruk, duardin, human or rot worshipper, from seizing the weapon was like asking her to stop the falling rain from getting them wet.

'Why did you not tell us this before?' she snarled, looming over the old scholar, thunder booming behind her words.

Karrobeth quailed and Tove took a half-step as though to shield her.

'I didn't know!' Karrobeth said miserably. 'It was buried amidst the tome's most esoteric passages. There was not time to translate everything before your armies marched out to fight! I am sorry if I have failed you, whatever penance you deem fit will be mine, but we *must* act now!'

Kalyani restrained herself with an effort of will. She took a slow, deep breath and stilled the furious battle-lust within her breast. She turned and looked to where artillery batteries and ranks of handgunners were pouring fire into the viscid mass of the slime-monster. She saw emerald lightning flashing skyward as her warriors fell and the orruks spilled through into the square. She saw Wallbreaker's battle-horn hit the wet cobbles as his headless body fell before disappearing in light, Sundershield roaring orders as he sought to rally a fresh battleline.

'I am sorry, Bronvynne, but we cannot reach the weapon,' she said, her voice hollow. 'At this point, we can barely hold our enemies back long enough to bring reinforcements to bear.'

'Lord-Celestant,' said Tove, his voice stiff with fearful respect. 'If we cannot prevail then we must withdraw. Please, order a full retreat. Let us try to save as many of our warriors as we can.'

Kalyani looked at him sharply.

'Retreat? Cede the field to our foes after so much bloodshed and loss? Give up any chance of seizing the weapon before our foes do?'

To his credit, Tove did not back down nor fail to meet her gaze, though she could see he was shaking with fear at her displeasure.

'If a living being takes hold of that weapon then there's going to be nothing left living at the heart of this city. As it stands, Lord-Celestant, that means us, our army, the orruks, probably the filth worshippers too, we all take the hit. No telling what horrors that thing will unleash, but supposing its range isn't too great… well, then if we get ourselves clear thanks to Mistress Karrobeth's timely warning but our enemies don't know any better…'

'Then the foe suffers the worst of it, and we are left comparatively unharmed,' Kalyani finished for him. 'And if not, if the weapon's power is such that all in this valley are slain as you say might happen?'

'Then the ending is no different than if we'd stayed and fought despite knowing we couldn't win,' Tove replied.

Kalyani scowled. She hated this. She wanted to leave this place at once and make a dash for the weapon, gather whatever heroes remained to her and lead the charge to carve a path through to the prize. But then what? If what Karrobeth said was true then even should Kalyani somehow win through to the weapon before her foes she could not, herself, take a hold of the device and remove it from the Old Temple. Instead she would, what, fight every single enemy that came against her? Slay two vast hordes of foes and hope that at no point in the entire improbable conflict would one of them manage to lay a hand upon the weapon they all desired?

She knew it was impossible. And that left only one option.

'We retreat,' she said, the words tasting like wet ash in her mouth. She turned to the captain of the Freeguild regiment who still waited nearby for orders. 'Have your drummers sound the retreat. Break up half your regiment and send them as runners to bear the word. Fighting retreat, designated rearguard units to hold the foe back while we pull everything out. Get someone up to the engineers on the ridge and have them fire their flares to signal Galabrith and the Kharadron. And move with urgency, damn it! If we must quit this field, then let us do it with enough speed and efficiency that it is worth the dishonour.'

Drums thundered. Runners dashed off through the rain. Kalyani shot a last look at Karrobeth and Tove, then set off to martial her forces and pull them back from the fight.

She just hoped that they could get clear before Bronvynne Karrobeth's predictions of doom came to pass.

CHAPTER TEN

THE PRIZE

Mordavia, the third evening of the campaign

Grey Seer Splichritt was used to tunnels. The Blight City, his warren-lair in Skitterspike, the gnawholes by which he flitted between the Mortal Realms, and indeed virtually every fortress warren he'd ever set footclaws in were all cramped, low-ceilinged tangles of tunnels, ramshackle architecture, perilous machines and teeming masses of skaven. Yet for all this, the tunnels that wound their way up through the deeps of the old-things' city made him nervous.

He felt strangely hemmed in. His overdeveloped magical senses shrieked a constant warning at him, leaving his grey fur bristling and his tail switching like a whip. The harsh green glow of his underlings' warpstone-powered weapons caused the shadows to rear and dance as they always did, yet today Splichritt saw menacing shapes in each one. The sounds of his underlings scrabbling and jostling and hissing at one another rolled together within the confines of the tunnels, and normally that was a sound that Splich-ritt associated with safety in overwhelming numbers. Today, he had to keep restraining himself from cringing like a slave-cur as the noises grated on his highly-strung nerves.

It didn't help that the shadows concealed real dangers as well as imagined; in one corridor, stone hammers as large as pillars had swung down to crush a clawpack of clanrats like scuttergrubs; in a low-ceilinged chamber whose walls bore barely discernible man-thing murals, a crumbling statue had jerked to life with emer-ald energy burning from its eye sockets. It had waded into the swarm with its stone blade swinging, only to be blasted apart by the rock-ets of the warlock bombardiers; in a high-arched vault, a half-seen shadow figure had hissed incomprehensible words at the skaven in a voice like flowing sand until Splichritt had ordered it annihilated by the Skryre weapons teams. Whether the resultant cave-in had been the doing of the haunting presence or merely thanks to overly exuberant crew-rats unleashing unstable ordnance in a confined space, the result had been hundreds more dead. To an army with less bountiful numbers, the fiasco might have been considered costly.

Splichritt hated the smell down here, too. Something ancient and paper-dry dusted his sinuses, a barely perceptible undertone to the overwhelming reek of the grey slime that dripped from walls and ceilings.

'Plague-things have been here, yes-yes,' he muttered to him-self, and absently massaged his singed tail tip as his litter bearers lumbered up another winding, slime-slick stairway. The flying beard-things had killed hundreds of his underlings with their bombing run, but their inferior armaments had been no match for Splichritt's sorceries. Frankly, he was annoyed with himself for allowing even a slight scorching of his blessed personage. If he encountered the beard-things again, they would pay for the insult!

As for underlings, he had plenty more of those. When Blackclaw and his gutter runners had brought him their information, Splichritt's natural genius had allowed him to spot the opportunity for power straight away. Admittedly he didn't know precisely what that power *was* but when he had approached the clawlords of the Clans Verminus and the arch-warlocks of the Clans Skryre he had seen no need to tell *them* that. Ignorance was weakness, and Splichritt would never show weakness to potential rivals. Instead he had embellished the nature of the prize with just enough fanciful flourishes to snag the attention and stoke the avarice of each skaven leader he had approached.

He had, of course, also sown the seeds of mistrust as he went. Arch-Warlock Zikk's Enginecoven might not have contributed quite so many acolytes and war engines to this expedition had Splichritt not convinced them that their rivals from Clan Fumygous had provided him with a veritable *wealth* of poison-wind weaponry and the stormfiends to wield them. After such generosity, why should Splichritt not share the prize with his magnanimous benefactors of Clan Fumygous? Why, because Arch-Warlock Zikk was prepared to provide him with double the amount of weapons and warriors, that was why!

To Clawlord Slitretch he had promised a sword of such tremendous killing power that the blade need not even be drawn, merely thought about in order to see Slitretch's enemies fall dead. To the infamously cowardly Clawlord Ripwhisker he had instead told tales of a magical shield that always knew where the next hostile blow was coming from and which would interpose itself between its master and danger every single time. He had also been sure to tell Ripwhisker that his hated enemy Clawlord Skrutt had pledged thirty clawpacks of clanrats and twenty of elite stormvermin to Splichritt's venture. Unsurprisingly, Ripwhisker's Clan Skatterfang had contributed no less than *forty* clawpacks of clanrats and *thirty* of the stormvermin to the swarm that same day.

It was always thus with skaven, and Splichritt understood his querulous, paranoid race well. Every clan leader was convinced that they or their underlings would be the ones to outwit or overwhelm the other factions within Splichritt's swarm. Every one of them knew with absolute conviction that they would be the ones to claim the prize when the moment for greatness came.

At the same time, every one of them feared their rivals' cunning and duplicity almost as much as they feared betrayal by their own followers, and every last one of them hated each other for it. No wonder Splichritt had ended up commanding such a magnificent swarm! He suspected his verminous foot soldiers were still pouring out of the gnawholes at his back, flooding like a scabrous river of fur and flesh into the bomb-blasted ravine as their masters cursed and beat them for lagging behind.

Let the fools bicker-snarl, he thought to himself with a flush of smug pride. *Splichritt is cleverest, quickest, most-most powerful. Splichritt will take-claim the prize.* But only if he got out of these horrible tunnels, he knew, as his litter crested the stairway atop a flowing mass of skaven then halted before yet another featureless junction. Splichritt snarled to himself in frustration as his warriors milled and scurried, snapping and hissing at each other as more and more skaven piled up the stairway behind them and began to force the front runners off down both passages.

'Blackclaw! Come-come!' screeched Splichritt. In response, the gutter runner and his band of black-clad assassins scrambled up from amidst the verminous scrum and scrabbled over the clanrats' heads, eliciting a chorus of snarls and snapping fangs as they went. Splichritt hadn't bothered to tell the gutter runners to stay close to him once they reached the old-things' city; he knew how the agents of the Clans Eshin thought. He had been certain they wouldn't stray far from his shadow until the prize had been claimed and their payment received in full.

Probably seek-think they take the prize for themselves, he thought spitefully as the pack of gutter runners leapt down to gather like a pool of twitching shadows before his litter. Clanrats pressed in from all sides but Splichritt's litter bearers snarled at them and the masses squirmed back as the musk of fear spritzed the air.

'Where is Splichritt's prize? Speak-tell!' the grey seer demanded imperiously, looking down his snout at Blackclaw and his pack. He didn't need to be told; Splichritt could feel clearly the malevolent pulse of dark magic emanating from the left-hand tunnel. Indeed, it was invigoratingly, unnervingly close now. However, this was as good a chance as any to watch for signs of duplicity in his Eshin hirelings while simultaneously demonstrating his own incredible powers of sorcery and cunning before his still-massing underlings. If Blackclaw suggested they go right, well, perhaps he was working to lead the grey seer away from his prize, and *that* would surely mean he was in the employ of one of Splichritt's many rivals…

'Great much very-wise Splichritt, we bring you word of the weapon,' said Blackclaw, throat bared and shoulders down in a gesture of deference that, Splichritt thought, was fooling no one. 'Man-things seek it. Green-things seek it. Beard-things and plague-things seek it. Many-much power it has, but hard to find, yes-yes? Most humble Blackclaw does not know where the prize is, O great one, only that it is in old-things' city.' One of Blackclaw's beady red eyes glinted with cunning as it peered out from beneath the assassin's black cowl, and Splichritt saw sudden amusement there. 'Does Splichritt the Evermost Very-much Magnificent not know?' the gutter runner asked.

It was a simple ploy, but a lesser being might have been flustered by it. If Splichritt hesitated at Blackclaw's question his underlings would begin to mutter, to question Splichritt's abilities and knowledge. It had been a calculated risk by the Eshin agent, but one that would not pay off. It also suggested to Splichritt that Blackclaw might well be working against him.

'The spy-sneak does not know. The knives of the Clans Eshin are becoming dull-blunt, no-no?' sneered Splichritt, and Blackclaw bristled. 'The Horned One tells Splichritt every-all, Blackclaw. *Every-all*. It is this way.'

With an imperious gesture, Splichritt set his swarm in motion again and the seething masses of skaven surged off down the left-hand passage. Blackclaw and his cronies vanished into the press, but Splichritt sensed them still close by, watching him with resentful eyes.

Let them glare. It only made him feel more superior to Blackclaw, for whom he had begun to feel an intense dislike. It didn't help that the rangy assassin was so very *tall* for a skaven, and Splichritt hated those with the temerity to be taller than him.

He was still lost in his brooding and plotting when, a handful of minutes later, the sounds of furious gunfire erupted from somewhere up ahead. Splichritt flinched, squirted the musk of fear and conjured crackling green warp lightning about his staff. He straightened up again and made a show of preening his whiskers when he realised that the sounds of battle were echoing down from where the front runners of his swarm had spilled up a broad flight of stone steps and through a carved and mouldering archway at their top. His large ears filtered out the clatter of cogwork weapons, the shrieks of panicking skaven, the explosive whoomph of a warpfire thrower letting fly, the scrabble of claws and the clash of blade on blade. He heard war cries, too, in the harsh tongue of the beard-things that he had never troubled himself to learn.

There came a tremendous bang and a cloud of black-green smoke billowed from the archway. Tattered, blackened skaven scrabbled out onto the landing, several jerking and dancing as bullets caught them from behind and pitched them down the steps into the swarm. Their corpses vanished under the trampling footclaws of their comrades, or else were set upon and ravenously devoured.

From beyond the arch came a ringing beard-thing cheer that boiled Splichritt's blood.

'Beard-things think killing a few cowards from Clan Spurrik means victory!' Splichritt shrieked, sweeping his glare across the massed hordes that surrounded him. 'They think skaven are weak-weak, fool-scum, not to be feared! They think they steal-take Splichritt's prize! They are wrong! Skin them alive! Eat-gnaw their eyes while they still look through them! Kill-kill them all and bring me their beard-scalps! Kill-kill! KILL-KILL!'

Frothing and chittering, the swarm erupted up the stairs in their hundreds. Splichritt hung onto the arm of his throne with one handclaw as his war litter bobbed atop the horde like a raft upon a flood tide. A horrible leer stretched itself across his muzzle as fresh sounds of gunfire and screaming echoed from beyond the archway. Let the fools kill each other for a while. If the beard-things were here then that must mean they wanted Splichritt's prize too, but he would sweep them aside like the inferior beings they were.

Casting around, Splichritt spotted Blackclaw and his gutter runners again amidst the hordes and crooked a talon at them. 'You want-wish to prove the claws of Eshin still rip and tear?' he asked as the assassins gathered below his litter. 'The Horned One has a task for you...'

Admiral Vornn Norgssen heard gunfire erupt from the lower levels of the temple catacombs. He glanced around at his first mate, Hengin, at Aether-Khemist Threnghist and at the captains of the *Final Demands*, the *Cloudhammer*, the *Plunderer* and the *Righteous Reclamation* where they marched at his side. Their arkanaut landing party ranged behind them, more than a hundred duardin armed to the teeth. More of Norgssen's followers had remained aboard their craft to maintain the bombardment against the encroaching orruk and Chaos forces. A third group largely consisting of Grundstok mercenaries had filtered outward through the winding passages and echoing vaults of the Old Temple to act as rearguard should anything break through.

'Sounds as though the gunners are earning their pay,' said Hengin in answer to his admiral's glance.

'That sounds like a lot more trouble than routine gun-work,' commented Captain Svarfi of the *Final Demands*.

'Aye, they'll be charging for unexpected ammunition expend-iture by the seem of things, eh?' joked Captain Berrik of the *Plunderer*, raising a few wry chuckles from his colleagues. Norgs-sen didn't join them. He could hear just how ferocious the fight below them was, and he was beginning to think that perhaps his fleet's bombing run hadn't done as much to eliminate the threat from below as he had hoped.

'Pick up the pace,' he snapped. 'The overheads for this endeav-our are steep enough already. We've obligations to the Code to discharge before we can proceed to securing our operational prof-its, and there's hostile parties making their own bids from all over. We get caught in this place by a superior force, it doesn't matter how well armed...'

Norgssen's words trailed off as he reached the bottom of a sloping stone ramp, passed through an archway inscribed with crumbling stone hourglasses and found himself stood upon the edge of a huge and echoing space. The sense of malice and the pulse of sorcery were both so strong that it felt as though he had walked into a physical barrier. The sensation yielded only unwillingly and resented him for forcing passage.

'That's quite the sight,' said Aether-Khemist Threnghist as he halted at Norgssen's side. Behind them, one of the arkanauts whis-tled in amazement, the sound rendered tinny by his mask.

'That it is,' Norgssen replied, heart thumping with mingled wonder and apprehension. The chamber's floor was formed from flagstones the colour of bone while its distant walls and vaulted ceiling were formed of some night-black substance shot through with blood-red veins that Norgssen's practised eye recognised as gemstone. The huge space was dominated by an altar that rose at its heart and towered at least a hundred feet into the air. The structure's layered levels were carved from age-stained ivory interwoven with black marble and more of the red gemstones, the entire structure rendered grotesque by depictions of leering skulls devouring massed supplicants, mortal figures writhing as they transformed into fleshless golems of bone and ghoulish beings holding aloft graven hourglasses.

All of this Norgssen saw, yet all of it was rendered peripheral by the artefact that hung suspended in a corona of dark energies at the altar's peak.

'So it *is* a weapon then,' said First Mate Hengin.

Norgssen couldn't tear his eyes away from the sword, large enough for an ogor to wield, carved and worked to the most magnificent degree of artisanal perfection. His eyes crawled over its bone hilt, the crimson satin wrapped around its grip and bound in place with woven strands of what looked like silk-black hair. The weapon's blade was as dark as onyx, drinking in the light around it and giving off a faint whine of power that was audible even from its lofty position. The light that held the blade aloft shifted through the air like tides of sand that trickled and flowed in loops and whorls in defiance of natural laws. Even as Norgssen stared, the Mordavian Blade shimmered slightly within its corona, and he found to his surprise that he could almost see through it, as though it were barely there at all.

The arkanauts clustered behind their admiral, staring awestruck at the malevolent blade high above them.

'You can feel its power,' breathed Norgssen, and for a moment he felt trepidation at what he planned. But the artycles left no room for interpretation; a venture without profit was wasted, and while he had eliminated a debt by aiding Kalyani Thunderblade in her attack upon Mordavia, Norgssen didn't intend his efforts here to end with a zero sum. No, he would take this artefact that everyone else seemed so intent upon wielding or destroying, and he would sell it. Not to anyone that meant to do ill with it, of course; Norgssen was a profiteer, but he wasn't a monster. No, he had a few contacts within the Azyrheim Museum of Forbidden Antiquities who he thought would be *very* interested in acquiring... whatever this was.

'And it'll still end up safe in Sigmar's vaults, or else destroyed by them that knows best what to do with evil things like this,' he muttered to himself reassuringly. It was just that Vornn Norgssen and his followers would profit mightily from the process first, instead of letting the mercantile opportunity of a lifetime go to waste.

He might have gone on staring, except that there came again the sounds of gunfire and clashing blades from somewhere behind him. The noise of battle was growing closer, he realised. Time was running short.

'Captains, form your arkanauts up around the base of this structure and guard the entrance. Svarfi, get half a dozen of yours up the top of the ramp out there as lookouts and send another two to hunt around this chamber. Let's see if there's any other ways in or out in case we need an alternate route of egress, eh?'

As the arkanauts leapt to obey, Norgssen beckoned Hengin and Threnghist then set off up the bone steps of the altar.

'Are we not going to attempt to destroy the weapon, admiral?' asked Hengin, sounding uncertain. The Code and its artycles were everything to the Kharadron, and the contract they had drawn up with Kalyani Thunderblade left no room for creative interpretation.

'Don't worry, I'm not about to lead you into breach of terms,' said Norgssen as he slogged his way up the steep steps. Every pace was harder as he leaned into the miasma of malice that roiled around the weapon. He could feel a bone-deep chill worming its way into him through his armour and flight suit, emanating from the weapon now only a short -way above. 'All reasonable efforts, that's what we agreed upon. Hand me your pistol please, Hengin.'

The first mate complied and, without breaking stride, Norgssen raised the weapon and fired it straight at the blade. He made the gesture look dutiful and unconcerned, yet his heart was in his throat as he squeezed the trigger. *What if this actually destroys it?* he thought with a thrill of horror. *Or worse, what if this somehow triggers the winds-damned thing. Hullrust, that'd be a pitiful way to be slain, though at least we'd die fulfilling our obligations.*

The shot punched through the whirling darkness about the sword and, to Norgssen's surprise, kept right on going. He thought for a moment that he really *had* smashed the damned thing, but then he realised that the Mordavian Blade remained untouched. It was simply that his bullet had passed clean through it as though it weren't there. *Perhaps I missed,* he thought, although he knew in his heart that he hadn't. All the same, motivated by contractual obligation that ran bone deep, the admiral fired another shot. Like the first it pierced the blade's aura of dark energy only to whistle through the weapon's crossguard as though he'd fired at thin air. Before Norgssen could pull the trigger a third time there came such a furious pulse of dark magic that it drove the admiral and his comrades several paces back down the altar.

'Admiral, it's not working!' said Threnghist in a tone of alarm.

'No indeed, and as such I feel that we have discharged all contractual obligations pertaining to the use of reasonable force applied in situ in the pursuance of the weapon's destruction,' replied Norgssen, the words escaping his gritted teeth as the furious cold tried to clench itself about his heart and squeeze.

'So witnessed,' said Hengin at once.

'Seconded,' Threnghist chimed in, following the expected forms.

'My assessment, therefore, is that–'

Before Norgssen could finish his sentence there came a rattle of gunfire from down below. He looked to the arched entrance and saw arkanauts blazing away with pistols, rifles, volley guns and bomb launchers at something beyond.

'Skaven!' shouted Captain Svarfi. 'Hold the line, lads! An extra profit share for every duardin that holds the line!'

'Best hurry, admiral,' said Hengin respectfully.

'Aye, we'll just have to attend to the notary signatures once we're back aboard the *Shieldmaiden*,' grunted Norgssen. Speeding through litigation made him feel like one of the exiled air-traders you saw haunting the most rundown rust docks or dirtying themselves as virtual pack animals for the ground-dwelling peoples. That said, expediency placed highly amongst the artycles and that had to count for something.

Taking a deep breath and steeling himself against the soul-sapping cold, Norgssen reached up with his gauntleted hands to snatch the weapon from amidst its sable corona. Even amidst the flickering shadows, he caught a swift movement in his peripheral vision and reacted without conscious thought. Norgssen dropped and spun towards the movement, his hefty pistol Restitution coming up even as the black-clad skaven sailed through the air towards him.

The pistol went off with a boom and the ratman was snatched backwards, tumbling away down the side of the altar in a tangle of tattered black cloth, though not before a barbed disc had left its hand and whipped through the air to find the right eyepiece of Hengin's mask. The throwing star struck with a crunch of crystal and Hengin grunted in pain.

'Where did he… come… fr… f…' Hengin pawed weakly at his face, made a gagging sound as his limbs twitched involuntarily, then toppled backwards down the steps with a clatter of armour on bone.

'*Hrthgni*, that star was poisoned,' spat Aether-Khemist Threnghist, then cursed again as another of the projectiles rang from his armour. Norgssen looked around in shock as, one after another, half a dozen black-clad skaven popped out of thin air amidst clouds of green-black smoke. They landed nimbly upon the altar's carved surfaces, joining the handful of ratmen already advancing upon him and Threnghist.

'Rust it all,' spat Norgssen, taking another shot that sparked off the bone steps where a nimble skaven had stood a moment before. Throwing stars rang from his armour as the ratmen skittered closer.

'Behind me, admiral,' said Threnghist as he raised the nozzle of his aethermatic anatomiser. Norgssen heard volatile chemicals hiss and churn then a cloud of fumes billowed from Threnghist's weapon and engulfed the closest skaven.

Half-visible amidst the grey-blue haze, the ratmen snatched at their throats and staggered backward. Their eyes bulged as they tried and failed to drag in breaths, and their exposed flesh turned rapidly purple. One by one the skaven dropped and tumbled away down the steep slope.

Even as Threnghist was spraying chemical death over their foe, Norgssen snatched the speaking crystal from a pouch at his waist and activated it.

'Captains! Top of the altar! They used sorcery to bypass you and we're hard pressed! Supporting fire if you please!'

He leaned out around Threnghist and took another shot, which punched through a skaven's eye and exploded from the back of its skull in a cloud of bone and brains. Then three of the verminous creatures were charging up the altar through the dissipating clouds of Threnghist's blast, and the aether-khemist was cursing as his weapon chugged and churned to prepare its next load. To Norgssen's horror he realised that it wouldn't happen in time.

Dropping his crystal and holstering his pistol, the admiral snatched his steam-hammer from its straps on his backplate and swung it. The massive metal head of the weapon caught one of the skaven under the chin even as it leapt. The ratman fell away, its head a pulped ruin. Threnghist managed to catch the second skaven's curved daggers on his shoulder-plate.

The desperate manoeuvre left Threnghist exposed to the knives of the third skaven, bigger than the others and with the sense to let its underlings go in first. Now it struck, slamming one dagger in under Threnghist's arm and bringing another up under his jaw. Norgssen raised his hammer for a blow, bellowing in inarticulate anger as his old comrade shuddered and crashed to the ground. Before he could swing, the skaven's third blade, this one fused to the tip of its tail and dripping caustic green venom, whipped out towards his face. The admiral managed to duck back so that the dagger did no more than scratch a line of sparks across his face mask, but the move sent him further back up the altar towards the weapon.

Numbing cold washed over him from behind. Weakness set him shuddering. His teeth chattered and his mind filled with a sense of despair wholly alien to his pragmatic soul. Bullets whipped up from below, a bare handful of arkanauts forging up the altar's slopes to their admiral's aid. He could see they were too few, too far away, torn from an already overwhelmed battleline in a doomed bid to save the fool that had brought them to this dreadful fate. Behind them he saw arkanauts vanishing under a writhing mass of verminous foes, duardin borne from their feet with their guns still firing to be engulfed by furry bodies, stabbing blades and gnashing fangs in their hundreds.

'Rust it all...' he croaked and felt his steam-hammer slipping from his grip. This wasn't him, some part of his mind screamed. Giving up, letting self-pity and self-hatred drown his rational mind, he had never done such a thing! Norgssen rallied against the sensations, gripped his hammer with all his strength and tried to step away from the damned weapon as he wondered how he could *ever* have thought to sell this damned artefact. It had to be destroyed, now!

Three daggers struck Admiral Norgssen at once as he reeled forward away from the cursed weapon and straight into the embrace of the big skaven assassin. He felt liquid fire race through his veins as blades punched into his neck, his ribs and his groin. A dreadful gnawing pain clenched every muscle in his body tight at once, and he groaned as fever heat warred with the icy cold tearing at his insides.

Admiral Vornn Norgssen of the *Shieldmaiden* heaved a last, agonised breath as he thumped to the floor, watched the skaven step over him as his vision clouded over, felt a final pang of bitterness at how crushingly unfair everything had turned out, then slipped reluctantly into death.

Splichritt screeched with exultation as his numberless swarm overran the beard-thing gunline. Hundreds of skaven lay dead along the ramp leading down to the archway. Their bodies had formed an impromptu rampart behind which the beard-things had taken cover. That had worked until Splichritt had ordered up his stormfiends and unleashed the enormous half-mechanical rat ogors upon the foe.

The butchery that followed was spectacular on both sides, and by the time Splichritt ordered his war litter forward the archway and all its surrounds were sprayed with blood and choked with corpses. Yet the skaven could afford the exchange, for inexhaustible numbers was just one amongst the many traits of ultimate superiority that the Children of the Horned Rat displayed. Another of those traits was cunning; as he was swept into the altar chamber and looked up to see the corpses of gutter runners and beard-things scattered around the structure's upper slopes, Splichritt knew he possessed that in abundance.

As he had employed his sorcerous powers to skitterleap Black-claw and his companions into the chamber, Splichritt knew that one of two things would happen. Either the gutter runners would be wiped out, hopefully weakening the beard-things in the process, or they would clear a path to the prize and expose their duplicity by attempting to seize it first.

Now it seemed as though his second prediction was about to come true, for Splichritt saw Blackclaw shielding his face with one handclaw even as he reached out for the black and pulsing blade with the other. Splichritt's fury at this betrayal was so great that it all but eclipsed the dark wonder he felt at the incredible sight of the altar, and of the accursed weapon that hovered atop it.

Yet as Blackclaw's talons wrapped around the hilt of the weapon and the malevolent magics of the chamber howled like a gale, the grey seer suddenly appreciated how cunning he was to have sent Blackclaw ahead of him, to trigger any arcane wards or sorcerous traps that might protect the prize.

To Splichritt's eye the weapon became suddenly sharper and clearer as Blackclaw touched it, as though it had come suddenly into focus in his vision. The sable energies around the blade billowed outward in a swirling mass like the tentacles of some vast and horrible godbeast. They wrapped around Blackclaw, who stiffened and let out a shriek of horror and pain so awful that

Splichritt felt it like a physical blow. The gutter runner rose off the ground, his limbs splayed out and his head wrenched backwards as though someone had grabbed him by the whiskers and pulled. Blackclaw convulsed and seemed to *stretch*, the bones in his arms and legs lengthening, his spine twisting. The luckless skaven's flesh and muscle did not extend along with his bones, however, and Splichritt heard the gruesome tearing sound of his body coming apart even over the clangour of the battle's dying gasps.

Blackclaw resembled a ghastly scarecrow, ruined skin and torn fabric flapping madly around still-lengthening bones, blood misting the black winds around him and pattering down like storm rain. Then, before Splichritt's eyes, Blackclaw's flesh and robes scattered apart like ashes in a whirlwind. The dark hurricane of magical energy whirled outward, shadowy winds filled with what looked like driving grains of black sand swirling through them.

They engulfed the bodies of the beard-things that lay atop the altar and to Splichritt's amazement they flayed away clothing, flesh and muscle in seconds to leave only rattling, empty suits of armour. It was like watching the erosion caused by the sands of time, like cliff-faces being worn away and cities laid low, only wrought with such horrifying rapidity that by the time the grey seer had blinked in amazement the beard-things were nothing but white bone and metal vanishing amidst the expanding sandstorm.

Outwards whirled the tainted energies and Blackclaw's surviving packmates turned to run. Too slow, they were plucked up into the air and blasted down to fleshless bones by the screaming winds.

Splichritt was, for all his self-aggrandisement and his paranoid psychosis, extremely clever. His magical senses were powerfully attuned, his natural skaven instinct for self-preservation doubly so. It did not take him more than a handful of skitter-quick heartbeats to come to a deeply alarming realisation.

Something exceptionally bad was about to happen, and he did not want it to happen to *him*.

Spitting jagged syllables that caused his gums to bleed, the diminutive grey seer brandished his staff and focused his Horned Rat-given magical talents. His ears filled with the scrabble of a million claws and green-black sorcerous vapours whirled about him, his war litter and its bearers. Splichritt felt the killing cold of the ensorcelled sandstorm thundering towards him across the chamber. His nostrils filled with the acrid reek of hundreds of skaven squirting the musk of fear.

Then his skitterleap carried him out of danger, the squeals of his doomed followers still ringing in his ears.

Brognakk was having the time of his life. Smash bounded over the city in soaring leaps, each new arc ending in a violent collision with another luckless victim. The maw-krusha's boulder-like fists had sent duardin skyships spiralling groundward with their endrins mangled and their crews crushed to paste. His snapping maw had closed around the skull of a lightning-boy dragon-thing and crushed it like a squig egg even as Brognakk took its rider's head off with Krump. The two of them had swatted droning masses of giant flies from the air, sending their riders tumbling to the earth with wails of terror that put a wide grin on Brognakk's leathery old face. Around them the Gorkamorka clouds pummelled at the city with their swirling fists, toppling towers and clubbing age-old statues to rubble.

Yes, Brognakk reflected as Smash collided with a ruined building and grabbed on, *dis is da scrap I wanted.*

As Smash settled himself on his enormous roost, he dislodged most of the top two storeys of the ruin and sent them crashing down upon the orruks and Chaos-boyz battling in the street below. Brognakk barely noticed. He was busy giving thanks to

Gorkamorka for this brutal and glorious day. The megaboss spat first one side of his saddle, then the other, before dragging one long talon down his forearm and scattering the resultant drizzle of blood to the winds. Wasn't right to enjoy a fight this good without offering a bit up to the Great Green God, after all.

'Dis city is gunna be ours soon enough,' he told Smash, surveying the absolute carnage erupting on every side. Kharadron skyships still hung over the big dome-building, firing everything they had into the streets below, their crews hammering volleys off at the maw-krushas and other flying beasties still whirling around them. Orruks fought Chaos-boyz and the last luckless humie rearguard units wherever Brognakk looked. To the east he saw Crushes Gitz leading a howling charge of Bonesplitter morboyz that smashed through a plague-tribe's shield wall and painted the ruins around them with diseased blood. Just south of his vantage point, Brognakk's glowing green eye settled momentarily upon a trio of shamans driving a lone humie wizard back down a street with a volley of spells before a stampede of gore-gruntas thundered from a side street and trampled the wizard, the wounded soldiers he was trying to defend, and the shamans into the bargain.

Brognakk looked up at a sudden clattering rattle and saw the Morkagork's spear-chukka decks firing again as the war idol rolled closer; three massive spears punched through the hull of a stuntie gunship and sent it corkscrewing down to slam into the side of the temple in a roiling fireball. Another two projectiles skewered a maggot-headed gargant that had been wading through Gazblagg's ladz in the big square; the weird-looking monster crashed down into the fray and vanished under a mass of hacking, stomping, roaring orruks.

Everywhere Brognakk's gaze settled he saw masses of greenskins forging ahead, pouring through the streets over the trampled bodies of their foes. Their Waaagh! cries mingled with the monstrous pound of the big drum until the ruins shook and shuddered beneath the pummelling waves of sound.

Brognakk realised with a sour grunt that this *had* been the best scrap he could remember, but now it was running out of steam. Worst of all, his big mates hadn't even shown up for the fight, despite the drum pounding day and night. Still, that was their loss wasn't it? No point arranging a signal then not being about to answer it, was there? Meanwhile, the Chaos-boyz were completely outnumbered. The humies and the lightning-boyz had legged it, much to Brognakk's disgust. Now he realised that the stunties were doing the same. A handful of figures had appeared atop the big dome-building, waving their arms madly and grabbing onto the ropes that dangled from their mates' ships. Those ships were firing their endrins, retracting their big spear-anchors and turning their prows for the open skies.

'Not 'avin' that,' rumbled Brognakk, who could feel a rising swell of furious energies building all around him. 'Gorkamorka's angry, lad. Best punch-up in da realmz and everyone but us and da Chaos-boyz is runnin' away! Come on, let's show 'em 'ow it's done.'

Brognakk gave Smash an authoritative whack on the back of the head and in response the beast set its small, mean eyes upon the nearest stunty skyship. Enormous muscles bunched beneath Smash's scaly hide and the maw-krusha launched itself skyward, sail-like skin snapping taut as he caught the suddenly icy updraught billowing from below. Brognakk felt the old surge of exhilaration as Smash sailed through the skies, parting plumes of rising smoke and cutting through the driving rain at battering-ram speed. Below he saw old Shrakka One-Tusk bearing his Waaagh! banner at the head of a tidal wave of orruks and grots, smashing the last of the Chaos-boyz in the square and scattering their terrified remnants into flight. Ahead, the stunties saw Smash coming and pointed frantically, yelling at one another and trying to bring guns to bear even as their helmsman swung his craft wildly about.

Dat's right, panic, ya little grot-fondlerz, Brognakk thought with relish. He threw back his head and bellowed, 'WAAAGH!'

The whirling black storm erupted from within the dome-building so suddenly that at first Brognakk just thought it was more smoke, caught upon the wind. Yet even as Smash impacted with the deck of the stunty skyship and sent it yawing wildly, the megaboss realised that racing clouds of darkness were pouring from the huge building and swirling out across the square.

Bullets whipped around him, several ringing from his armour, one digging into the flesh of his neck. He whirled and hacked out with his choppa, sending two stunties tumbling back with blood jetting from enormous wounds. Yet suddenly Brognakk was as cold as he had ever been, filled with a sense of dread he couldn't explain, and all the joy had gone out of the fight. What *was* that black stuff?

'Oi, shift,' he growled at Smash and kicked his steed hard. Jaws stuffed with several dead-or-dying stunties, the maw-krusha gave a last ill-tempered swing of its fists that crippled the skyship's endrins and then launched itself skyward at Brognakk's direction. They soared again, the stricken skyship dropping away behind them. As they did, Brognakk felt dawning horror. The black clouds, whatever they were, were engulfing his ladz. Wherever they swept across the orruks and grots, war cries turned to howls of pain and fear, and then choked into silence.

'What in zog's name is dis?' Brognakk cried as Smash landed on a high spiretop, causing the structure to shudder and tilt alarmingly. Nearby, another stunty skyship was climbing hard only for a tendril of the dark storm to whip out and wind around it. Even as Brognakk watched, the crew shuddered and writhed then broke apart in puffs of ash.

If dat's happenin' wherever dat stuff goes... Panic filled Brognakk as he saw the vast majority of his Waaagh! vanishing into the whirling clouds of a giant, unnatural sandstorm. Brognakk wasn't some soft git who cared about things like casualties, but he wasn't about to see his Waaagh! gutted by some lunatic's sneaky magic tricks.

'Leg it!' he bellowed, ensuring the full, booming volume that only an orruk megaboss could achieve. Below, he saw surprised orruk faces turn up towards him. No grots, he noticed; they were already running for the hills. 'RUN, YA ZOGGIN' IDIOTS!' he roared even louder, hoping as many of his ladz as possible would hear him, hoping more would follow their example and flee. 'DON'T LET IT TOUCH YA!'

Then Smash gave a shuddering growl and Brognakk realised the tower-top was tilting, breaking, and the black storm was whirling up from below. All of a sudden it dawned on him that he and his steed were right in its path, and about to be engulfed.

'Fly, lad! Fly!' he yelled, giving Smash a firm wallop and feeling the maw-krusha launch itself out into the void. Yet the toppling tower had thrown off its leap and they flew too low, too short. Another ruin was racing up to meet them but Brognakk saw the black tendrils of the storm twining around it, boiling up from below.

'Gorkamorka! Not like dis!' yelled Brognakk. Yet he was powerless to ward off the whirling sorcery, powerless to pull Smash's head up or make his steed fly higher. Even grabbing a fistful of Waaagh! charms did nothing. Brognakk and Smash plunged headlong into the screaming sandstorm and the megaboss felt a last, all-consuming coldness take him in its talons before he was flayed to windblown ash.

CHAPTER ELEVEN

EYE OF THE STORM

*The encampment, southern fringe of Mordavia,
the third night of the campaign*

Darkness was less of an impediment to the senses of Sigmar's Stormcast Eternals than it was to the unforged humans they had once been. Tonight, with the rain abated at last and the clouds reduced to scudding tatters by an icy wind, Kalyani reflected that that was no boon. She stood atop the observation tower above the command pavilion and stared across the night-shadowed ruins of Mordavia at the abomination looming at the city's heart.

Even to the engineer observers peering through their telescopes and obnoculars around her, the spectrally lit structure must have stood out as clear as Hyshlight. To Kalyani's superhuman eyesight, magnified through an engineer's looking glass, it was rendered in excruciating detail.

Where before the cracked dome of the Old Temple had risen above the city's jumbled skyline, now a structure more than five times its height thrust up like an accusing finger towards the heavenly constellations burning bright above. It looked to Kalyani as though everything below the temple had been wrenched upwards to form an unnatural mountain whose flanks were torn and tumbled rubble. She could pick out the morbid flourishes of Mordavian architecture, heaped at crazed angles and compacted atop itself to create weird strata of rubble and jutting abutments of hollow-windowed ruins. Dark pits gaped in the mountain's sides, arched doorways and buried streets that had been dragged up whole by strange tectonics and left yawning in the flanks of the mountain. Outcroppings of heavy-fronded ferns patched the mountain's flanks, their roots still clinging grimly to topsoil now driven hundreds of feet into the sky. Why living warriors had been reduced to ashes by the storm while living plants had remained untouched, Kalyani couldn't guess.

The vast mountain of rubble and ruin swam in her vision as though it were underwater. It was wreathed in spectral illumination, an eerie emerald witch-light that described the suggestion of a towering fortress built around and atop the foundation of the city's murdered heart. More unholy light spilled from wailing masses of ghasts that flowed and swirled around the mountain's flanks. Revenant things dragged ethereal chains behind them through the glowing air; cadaverous terrors clad in tattered shrouds gave voice to piercing cries while scythe-wielding horsemen wreathed in spectral flames galloped madly upon the night winds.

'The servants of Nagash come to claim that which is theirs,' she breathed, and felt a chill that had nothing to do with the cold winds.

So much death, she thought grimly, *and all for one blade.* The thought stirred memories of her life before the Anvil, and she thrust it aside, although not before she had heard again the sound of breakers sighing across shingle, wood cracking and popping as it burned, screams and the clangour of one-sided, desperate battle.

Kalyani shook herself from her reverie and forced her eyes upwards, to the ragged peak of the mountain and the terrible altar that rose from it. She saw bone and black marble, twisted sculptures holding aloft cracked hourglasses from which unnatural amethyst sands flowed. Higher, higher, up the bloodstained steps to the pinnacle where an abomination of twisted bone crouched like some obscene gargoyle. The thing was big, perhaps twice as tall as Kalyani herself. The warped and spined skeleton that made up its body was bound together by shimmering chains of purple-tinged energy, and that same animating spark burned cold and hard in its cavernous eye sockets. Golden chains dangled, shattered, from fetters at its wrists and ankles, and a rippling cloud of shifting black energies drifted around it like a diaphanous shroud.

In one twisted claw, it held the Mordavian Blade. Kalyani had no doubt at all that the monstrous blade she saw was the artefact they had come here to claim. Its aura of malevolence was palpable even from this distance.

Kalyani watched as spectral figures climbed the altar and prostrated themselves before the bone abomination. Their death shrouds stirred around them as they offered praise to the terrible creature. In return it inclined its great head in something that might have been a nod or a shallow bow, and the energies in its eye sockets flared brighter.

'What are those creatures?' asked one observer, his voice little more than a croak.

'Sigmar preserve us, what are they doing up there?' another breathed.

'Would that we were close enough to hear whatever words are being exchanged,' said a third, older and, to Kalyani's eyes, firmer of resolve. 'Are we witnessing the sealing of a pact? The reception of envoys? Is this merely a phantasm of the past, playing out upon the winds of magic? What fresh ill does it all bode? I wish we were close enough to hear.'

'I wish we were close enough to prevent it, to hack apart that abomination and seize the Mordavian Blade,' said Kalyani. Several observers jumped as though caught in some guilty conversation.

The horror of this spectacle must be great indeed, for them to have forgotten one of Sigmar's Stormcasts stands amongst them, she thought.

'Of course, Lord-Celestant,' said the elder observer, but Kalyani heard the doubt in the man's voice. Before she could reply, clumping footsteps sounded upon the platform's iron ladder and Laszlo Tove clambered into view. He had hold of his cloak with one hand, bunching it around his neck in an effort to shut out the chill.

His eyes settled on her at once.

'Lord-Celestant Thunderblade, you're wanted for the council, if it pleases you,' he said. Kalyani nodded and crossed the platform to the ladder. As she passed him, Tove added in a lower voice, 'Mistress Karrobeth would have a word beforehand.' Kalyani responded with a curt nod then slid down the ladder, leaving the bodyguard to clamber stiffly down in her wake.

Freeguild soldiers now guarded the pavilion's entrance, Kalyani saw. They were big, heavyset veterans with zweihander swords but still, their presence attested to how few Stormcasts remained. One was wounded, she noted, brown-stained bandages bound about his brawny arm.

The interior of the pavilion was quieter now. She saw just as many aides, scholars and attendants but far fewer officers and precious few messengers. Many bore wounds of their own. They huddled in small knots, engaged in hushed conversations that reminded Kalyani of the mourning ceremonies she had attended in her unforged life. Every expression was sombre. Upon every bowed shoulder she sensed the weight of defeat and loss. Even

Lord-Celestant Galabrith wore a grim, stony expression. *And well he might, with the losses his chamber took,* she thought, then felt her chest tighten as she remembered her own dreadful casualties. The Celestial Vindicators were not known for their willingness to retreat.

'Lord-Celestant, a moment?' Kalyani looked around and saw Karrobeth hunched at a table at the pavilion's edge. She was still swathed in the same damp, mud-stained robes she had worn earlier that day and her face was pale. A half-empty bottle of wine stood by her right hand. The tome was spread open on the table before her, along with sheaves of hastily scribbled notes.

The scholar gestured to the stool that sat empty across from her. Instead, Kalyani halted before her table and looked down at the huddled old woman before drawing Song from its sheath. A moment of surprised alarm flashed across Karrobeth's features, then vanished just as quickly as Kalyani dropped to one knee, the tip of her blade driven into the straw-matted ground and her head bowed in respect.

'Bronvynne Karrobeth, I and all those gathered here owe you our lives,' she said, loudly enough to cut across any other discussion in the pavilion.

Karrobeth swallowed and made a quiet 'hem' sound in her throat. Kalyani looked up and saw the scholar shift on her stool, a stunned look on her face. Before Kalyani could speak further the applause began, steady and earnest from every corner of the pavilion.

'Here, here!' said one of the Freeguild officers.

'A medal for our brave cryptoscholar!' barked another.

Bronvynne cleared her throat, apparently unsure whether she was expected to offer any kind of speech. Kalyani saved her by standing again and sweeping her gaze around the pavilion.

'We have a war to win, and honours to award when duty is

done,' she said. 'Bronvynne Karrobeth will be amongst those heroes richly rewarded for victory in Mordavia, but she will not be alone. Gather your thoughts and discard your doubts, for the mountain is steep enough without adding to our burdens. I would have words with our scholar, but then we must lay our plans afresh.'

Now she sat as activity filled the pavilion, and Karrobeth offered her a thin smile.

'That was well done,' the scholar said quietly. 'How much was honest praise and how much a show for them?'

'A blade is sharp upon both edges,' Kalyani replied. 'You saved us today. You saved thousands of lives. Heldenhammer, you may have saved the entire Mordavian campaign, though Sigmar knows the task we face is more desperate than ever. My gratitude is honest, the honour I do you heartfelt.'

Karrobeth's smile became genuine, though she quickly covered it with a scowl and a harrumph.

'Yes, well, we scholars and our tomes are good for more than just gathering dust,' she said. A moment's silence passed between them, an awkwardness imposed by the distance that would always hang between mortal and reforged. Kalyani felt a moment's regret for the friendship that might have existed between them, then dismissed it as irrelevant.

'The weapon was triggered,' said Karrobeth.

'It must have been, though Sigmar alone knows who set a hand to the damned thing,' Kalyani replied. The familiar anger kindled within her at the thought of some fool unleashing that wave of darkness and death upon Mordavia. 'Some brute orruk? A Champion of Nurgle? Perhaps even Norgssen or one of his captains?' she wondered aloud.

'Whoever it was, they paid for their avarice,' Karrobeth sighed and sipped her wine. A hand snaked down and grabbed the bottle.

They both glanced up at Tove as he took a pull from its neck then set it down again with a thump.

'Them and every other bugger that wasn't already running away,' he said. Seeming to register that he had interrupted, Tove made a 'don't mind me' gesture then stationed himself protectively at Karrobeth's back with his hand on the pommel of his blade.

'We've few scouts left and until dawn breaks it will be hard for our observers to get any clearer idea, but our enemies were surely devastated by the blast,' said Kalyani. 'Matters look desperate, but in some ways, I believe we can be thankful. Our foes were likely ravaged worse than we. We'll know more when the council pools its knowledge, no?'

Karrobeth gave a non-committal grunt and drank more wine. Kalyani's heart sank as she recognised the scholar's expression.

'What fresh horrors have you discovered within the pages of that tome?' she asked.

'It's less what I have found, and more what I cannot find,' said Karrobeth, rifling through her notes. She muttered to herself for a moment and Tove discreetly moved her wine glass before she could knock it over with a stray elbow. The gesture was only spoiled by the fact that he took a swig before replacing it at a safe distance.

'Yes, here we are,' said Karrobeth, withdrawing a page covered in her crabbed script. It was accompanied by a hasty charcoal sketch. Kalyani had little appreciation for art, but the stark menace conveyed in the picture struck her at once.

'The altar that stands atop that mountain,' said the Lord-Celestant.

'The records speak of its construction as a monument atop which the weapon might be set, the better to present it to the God of Death,' said Karrobeth as she read back over her notes. 'The issue is that nowhere does it speak of an altar or blade being hidden away beneath Mordavia's streets, buried beneath a temple, any of that. Nor, before you ask, is there the slightest mention of the monster that our observers report crouched atop it at this moment.'

Kalyani thought for a moment, marshalling her questions before setting them out.

'Do you believe that they *would* have spoken of those things? Why warn enemies of whatever guardian creature watched over the weapon? And how can we know where the altar lay before… whatever it is that happened in the wake of the weapon's awakening? Before that mountain erupted from Mordavia's heart? Whatever magic did that could have summoned altar and weapon both from elsewhere.'

'To the first question, Lord-Celestant, I do not believe that this tome was ever meant to fall into the hands of any who dwelled outside Mordavia. It's hard to divine the intentions of its authors through the dusty veil of time, but the tone, the content, not to mention the elaborate lock, these don't speak to me of openness or disclosure. I believe that if the people of Mordavia had fashioned a dread guardian to watch over their weapon they would have spoken of it within these pages with pride. That would be doubly the case were it some creature of Nagash sent to guard or accept the blade. No, whatever that abomination is, I do not believe that it is any artifice of the Mordavians and that makes me deeply anxious for we have no way of knowing its intentions or allegiance.'

Kalyani was disturbed by Karrobeth's words, but she pressed on pragmatically.

'And my second question? The altar itself?'

Karrobeth waved a hand, clearly feeling that this was an afterthought barely worthy of their time.

'Look again at the illustration, Lord-Celestant. That's copied direct from the tome.'

Kalyani did so and grunted as she realised that chaotic swirls depicted above the structure were meant to be clouds, while the stark lines behind it were undeniably Mordavian architecture. 'It is shown beneath the open sky somewhere within the city, the blade hanging suspended above the altar and worshippers gathered all about it,' replied Karrobeth. 'No depiction of a temple, no mention of a giant bone-monster. I don't know, Lord-Celestant, perhaps the damned thing was elsewhere before today. Perhaps it went down a chasm and has been lurking somewhere in the dark, just waiting for its moment. I don't think it matters. Right now, the weapon is in the talons of some ineffable horror, surrounded by legions of ghasts atop a mountain of ruin that must surely have been raised with its power. This being even *after* it was unleashed to murder millions. Heldenhammer, perhaps it *was* those deaths that fuelled the raising of the mountain… or… or…'

She thumped the table, went to take a swig of her wine, found the glass empty and scowled. Kalyani noted that Karrobeth's hands were shaking.

'You faced great peril today, Karrobeth,' she said, refilling the scholar's glass for her. 'You saw the full horror of as great a battle as I have ever faced, and you did not flinch from it. To feel shock in the wake of this is only human.'

Karrobeth looked her straight in the eyes, and Kalyani saw suddenly that she was barely holding herself together. The dogged research had been a means to act, to try to control some aspect of the horrors that surrounded her. Instead of reassurance, perhaps some means to defeat their foes, it had only brought her more questions.

'There is too much we do not know, and I feel as though we have no time to find the answers,' said Karrobeth. 'Kalyani, what if that… *thing*… leaves here with the weapon and unleashes its power elsewhere? What if this happened in Hammerhal? What if it happened in Azyrheim? What if–' She bit the last question off and gulped wine instead. 'So many have already died, but…'

Kalyani's eyes snapped up to Tove in that moment and the two of them experienced a moment of shared understanding.

'You have done more, faced greater peril than any save Sigmar himself could ask of you,' said Kalyani, carefully taking the scholar's wrinkled hand between her armoured gauntlets. 'We will not let today be repeated. We will act upon the warnings you have given us and wrest the weapon from the grips of our foes before they can do any more harm. I swear this oath to you upon my life.'

Karrobeth put her other hand over Kalyani's, where it trembled like a frightened bird.

'Thank you, Lord-Celestant,' she said earnestly.

Tove cleared his throat and inclined his head.

'Council's waiting,' he said, sounding awkward.

'Wait, there is one more thing, and this I can tell you with some sense of certainty,' said Bronvynne, rallying. Kalyani looked at her inquiringly.

'I think I understand now the words that confused us before,' said Bronvynne, busying herself by flicking through the tome's pages. 'Yes, here…. There was mention of the blade being a spectral chimaera, and of it finding its focus. Lord-Celestant, I do not believe that the weapon exists wholly upon the mortal coil. In essence, it is part ghost, and if I am right it becomes wholly corporeal only in the moments when its amassed energies are focused and about to be unleashed.'

'A ghost blade?' Kalyani asked, frowning deeply. 'Can it then be banished through faith? Unmade by our warrior priests?'

'The tome suggests not,' said Bronvynne, shaking her head. 'It boasts that neither the artifice of the lesser gods, nor mortal sorceries can besmirch the blade-that-shall-be-offered. Everything I've seen here suggests that the blade is essentially inviolate except when its power is at its peak and about to be set loose.'

'But at such a time it could be touched? Or even broken like any mortal blade?' asked Kalyani. Bronvynne shrugged.

'In theory? Just more questions, I am afraid, Lord-Celestant.'

Kalyani nodded and stood.

'Still useful, Karrobeth,' she said. 'My thanks.'

She gave the cryptoscholar a last smile that she hoped looked more reassuring than it felt, then strode across the pavilion to join the much-reduced war council about the map table.

Bronvynne took a moment to compose herself and gather up her notes before rising to follow Kalyani. Tove laid a gentle hand on her wrist as she reached out to take up her tome.

'You don't have to, you know,' he said. 'She's not wrong, you've done more'n enough, mamzel.'

Perhaps it was the wine haze, or perhaps the way that he had so readily plunged into danger at her say-so earlier that day. Probably both, Bronvynne reflected. Whatever the cause, she didn't resent Tove's touch, but rather found it reassuring.

'I never found time for a family, Mister Tove,' she said, removing his hand. 'Duty always seemed more important. But if I had borne a son, I should not have been disappointed had he been as decent as you.'

Tove blinked and coloured slightly. He cleared his throat and squared his shoulders.

'Plenty you don't know about me, mamzel, I'm not the sort any mother wants as a son,' he said stiffly, but she thought perhaps he was pleased despite himself. Her suspicions were confirmed when he continued 'Call me Laszlo, though, eh? Mister Tove's a bit formal after all that… well, *that* today.'

'So is mamzel, Laszlo,' she replied, hefting her tome. She was sure it was growing heavier. 'Bronvynne will do.'

Crossing the pavilion, she took a spot towards the back of

the gathering. The clustered bodies of dishevelled officers and exhausted aides generated a damp warmth that mingled with the smells of pipe smoke, wet earth and cloth, dried blood and stale sweat to create a miasma around the table. What Bronvynne could see of the swirled-ink display on the table itself was in scarcely better condition. Names and emblems drifted uncertainly, some crossed through, some swimming between one location and another like shoals of hesitant fish. Great swathes of the map had simply gone blank, as though someone had dropped stones into its liquid surface and the ripples had ruined all they touched.

'...and though we lost the Eighty-Sixth Starfielders, the Fourteenth Dracolions and most of the Ninth Mountain Guard, we were able to extract fifteen regiments of Freeguild from the forward engagement areas more or less intact,' an officer was saying. She recognised him as the same scarred captain who had refused her request for aid earlier that day.

'Trailing elements have been bringing word back to camp as the day has gone on,' said General Gharphyn, taking up the thread. 'Observers in the field confirm that the servants of Nurgle have retreated into the city's easternmost districts but have not retreated altogether. Their numbers were seen to be much reduced, however, and their cohesion is reported as extremely poor. I believe we can consider them a spent force.'

'What of the kine of Gorkamorka?' asked an aelven noble that Bronvynne didn't recognise. His voice was cold with anger, and she recalled overhearing a breathless conversation between several aides barely an hour before. It seemed that what aelven forces had joined the advance had been badly mauled by ogors while pushing up through the region designated the Fernsea. 'Are we to discount the dangers they represent also, general? And what of the rumours that skaven were observed during the latter stages of today's engagement? Shall we offer up prayers to Sigmar that our foes simply do not exist?'

'Now see here–' began the scarred captain, bristling. General Gharphyn raised a hand to forestall him.

'The orruks and their allies were worst hit of all, from what we can discern,' she said. 'We retain fortified positions in the southern and eastern districts, and the crew of the cogfort *Freedom of Lutharia* are doing what they can to make observations of their own from their position in the Gateway District just north of our encampment. Both report contact with scattered handfuls of greenskins and ogors, but there is no order to them at all and many have been described as fleeing in blind panic. What skirmishes have taken place were one-sided. I believe that the wave of dark magic tore the heart from the orruk Waaagh!'

'And that dratted drum has stopped its pounding at last,' added another Freeguilder. Bronvynne started at that observation. She hadn't even noticed its absence, but the young officer was right. Now that she thought about it, the pulsing undertow of malevolence from the city's heart had also lessened somewhat, though she wondered whether that was simply because the weapon had exhausted much of its power unleashing that dreadful death wave and raising the mountain fortress. Had it even summoned the army of ghasts that now whirled around it, or had they simply been sent by some dark master to discover what had unleashed such incredible power? She felt the panic of unanswered questions grip her again and tried to focus instead upon what was being said.

'…confirm that our casualties were substantial,' Lord-Celestant Thunderblade was saying. 'Lord-Castellant Rojavi Sundershield was able to bring several under-strength brotherhoods back with him, and I extracted two more. Still, I have only nineteen warriors left beneath my banner, for we bore the brunt of the fighting in the Old Temple square.'

'Not alone,' said Lord-Celestant Galabrith. 'Barely a quarter of my Extremis Chamber managed to break away from the fighting and join the retreat. Every Drakesworn Templar I led into Mordavia is slain. The riders may be reforged, Sigmar willing, but we lost noble beasts and loyal companions this day.'

'My Lord-Celestant, we, your allies, can but extend our most heartfelt sorrow at your losses,' said General Gharphyn, and Bronvynne heard the sincerity in her voice. Everyone knew that without Bronvynne's warning and the desperate sacrifices of the Stormcast Eternals both, none of them might be stood here now having this conversation. She had heard bitterness amongst Freeguild soldiery before now, resentment at the apparent immortality of the Stormcasts and Sigmar's apparent favouritism. Not today, though. Suffering shared brought solidarity. Still, Galabrith seemed unmoved.

'Keep your sorrow, I have no use for it,' he said. 'We do not hunger for sorrow, but for vengeance.'

'For those who fell today, for all those who have fallen since this weapon awoke, and for the sake of all those it might yet send down to Shyish, we have to push back into the city at first light,' said Lord-Celestant Thunderblade. 'There can be neither respite nor delay.'

Agitation ran through the gathering like an electrical current at her words.

'What about scouting?' asked one officer. 'We need information before charging in blind.'

'Rearm, resupply and ideally reinforce!' exclaimed another, whose shoulder and arm were heavily bound and bandaged. 'We're a shadow of our former strength, even with the cogfort.'

'Until we know what we're facing with these ghasts and the rumours of the skaven...' began another, before someone else interrupted with 'And what of the Kharadron? Did any of their skyships survive? Do we even know? Can any support be counted on from that quarter?'

Bronvynne saw Lord-Celestant Thunderblade's brows lower, saw her draw breath to shout down the rising tumult of anxiety. Before she could, there came a gunshot from the pavilion's entrance. The sound made Bronvynne jump so badly that she spilled the last of her wine down the front of Laszlo's tunic. She whirled in time to see a bloodied and battered Kharadron arkanaut burst through the entrance, flanked by several more of his kin. He held a smoking pistol in one hand and for a surreal moment Bronvynne thought the duardin had come to launch some insane attack upon their former allies. Then she realised that the pavilion guards were still alive, and the arkanaut had lowered his weapon.

He wrenched off his face mask and Bronvynne's heart lurched into her throat as she saw his grim expression.

'We come… with a warning!' he shouted, sounding out of breath as though he had been running in full armour. 'We… owe a debt… and by this we repay it! We think the… drum called them. Coming up from the south. They'll be on you in moments…'

'What in Sigmar's name are you raving about?' demanded General Gharphyn.

'Mega-gargants!' the duardin shouted. 'We saw them moving north through the forest as we were making for the high airs and we turned back to warn you. We've done that and now I'm getting what's left of my crew out of here before–'

The last of his words were lost amidst a sudden tumult of screams from outside the pavilion, and a chorus of bone-chilling roars so loud that they reverberated through Bronvynne's chest. Terror gripped her as the ground shook and the sounds of thunderous crashing and rippling gunshots sounded from without. More screams came, of panic, terror and pain. Then an immense foot, easily the size of a loaded hay-wain, ploughed through the side of the pavilion in a storm of smashed wood and ripping canvas, and the world descended into anarchy.

Stormcast Eternals did not just sense better than unforged humans; they could also think far faster, consider and process more information at a greater rate and formulate their reaction with a speed and decision that mere mortals could never manage. The spark of Sigmar's divine magics crackled through their minds and souls alike, lending the speed of the striking storm to their deeds.

Even as the enormous foot came down with a ground-shaking crunch and crushed splintered furniture and screaming aides to pulp, Kalyani's mind whirled through a dozen thoughts.

The encampment is under attack by mega-gargants, in the dark and seemingly by surprise. Our forces are demoralised, many still disorganised, many more wounded or sleeping. Why did we not receive advance warning from our sentries in the forest? The sentries must be dead. The gargants' doing, or something else? Irrelevant now. How many of them are there? It sounds like utter bedlam outside, there must be a great force of them. We are in no position to suffer this attack nor to repel it. Panic and carnage will spread beyond our ability to control. It is already too late. The encampment is lost. What of the cogfort? It won't be enough by itself. No, we are lost. But our duty remains! We must salvage what we can and strike at once. How?

She looked at Lord-Celestant Galabrith, saw the same realisations sparking and racing behind his eyes, knew what she must do. What they both had to do.

The massive foot began to rise again, crushed corpse-meat and white bone shards stretching between it and the ground. The cliff-face shin above it ploughed further through the canvas of the pavilion and Kalyani heard the frantic shrieks of the observers as their platform was toppled with a metallic groan and a crash.

Men and women flailed as canvas and wooden beams tore and tumbled. The elaborate mechanisms of the map table sparked as a heavy beam crashed down upon them, knocking several brass hoops out of alignment and sending liquid splashing from the table's shallow surface.

'I will gather those I can,' she said. 'We will take the duardin skyship, if it still flies. We will do our duty.'

Galabrith nodded once.

'We shall hold these beasts as long as we can. Sigmar willing we will slay a few,' he said. The two of them clasped forearms in a warrior's handshake even as General Gharphyn bellowed orders and something outside the pavilion exploded. 'I will see you beyond the Anvil, Kalyani Thunderblade,' he said, and she offered him a humourless smile.

'But only you will have been reforged, Lord-Celestant,' she said, then she was moving, dodging a toppling beam and lashing Song through a tattered mass of canvas. As she went, she shouted, 'Celestial Vindicators! To me!'

Kalyani shouldered aside a weeping officer and vaulted a smashed table to land beside Karrobeth. Tove had one arm around her narrow shoulders and was attempting to guide her towards the nearest exit, yet even as the mega-gargant's foot tore its way out through the other side of the pavilion it brought the last of the structure tumbling down. Kalyani caught a beam as it plunged towards the two, stopping it one handed and heaving it aside.

'My thanks, Lord-Celestant,' said Tove.

'Follow me, keep up,' said Kalyani, then she was off, hacking aside wet, entangling canvas and yelling again, 'Celestial Vindicators! To me!'

She saw the Kharadron running hard down the darkened hillside and felt a stab of hope at the sight of their skyship anchored to a watchtower a few hundred yards distant. Yet as she turned her head and saw the titanic monsters looming out of the forest's eaves, that hope flickered and fled. There were several dozen of them, enormous creatures beside which a lesser gargant would seem like a scrawny child. They strode into view like men wading through tall grass, trees thrust aside or toppled before them, or else uprooted with casual violence and then hurled with tremendous force towards the encamped army before them. Kalyani saw idiot hunger in the monsters' blunt features, murderous hate burning in their huge eyes, cold moonlight glinting on teeth like tower shields and bone fetishes the size of dracoths.

In the moment Kalyani gave herself to absorb the situation she saw one of the vast creatures swing up a club made from lashed-together tree trunks and bring it down upon a half-formed regiment of Freeguild soldiery. She saw another aim a savage kick that nearly staggered it off balance, but that sent an entire watchtower cartwheeling down the hill, shredding apart and scattering debris as it ploughed through screaming soldiers, bucking horses and lamplit tents with unstoppable force.

Kalyani checked that Karrobeth and Tove had fought their way free of the collapsing pavilion and then she was moving again. She pelted downhill after the duardin, ignoring her burning desire to turn and give battle to the vast monsters that were slaughtering Sigmar's armies. Cannons boomed at a distance and shots whipped overhead, fired from the long-guns of the cogfort. The mobile structure was shuddering and belching smoke from its many stacks, and the groan of metal echoed through the night as its spider-like mechanical limbs began to move. The enormous walking castle stamped in a half-circle, alchemical searchlight beams stabbing out from its ramparts to illuminate the towering gargants as they trampled their way through the encampment.

More cannons fired from the fort's ramparts and their shots hammered one of the creatures, causing it to stagger. Its heel crashed into Kalyani's path. Gouts of blood and gobbets of flesh rained down around her from the gargant's wounds. Its roar of pain began as a subsonic rumble and rose to an ear-splitting bellow so loud that it washed out everything else. Kalyani scrambled back as the gargant reached down and closed one massive fist around a row of gun carriages to her right. Tethers snapped. Metal shrieked and clanged as the fist squeezed inexorably, crushing the field guns into a single warped mass even as it rose back into the air.

'Come on, move!' Kalyani yelled at Bronvynne and Tove, who were staggering and gaping, hands clamped over their ears. She gestured again, getting them to understand, and as the three of them set off again the gargant towering above them drew back its arm and hurled its ball of cannons. The unlikely projectile sailed through the air and hit the cogfort's command tower in an explosion of shattered masonry and tiny, tumbling bodies.

Kalyani was down on the flat now, pounding through the mud and gaining on the fleeing Kharadron. As she ran, she was joined by warriors of her chamber, Celestial Vindicators rallying to her distantly heard call. There was Lord-Castellant Sundershield, grim as ever. A handful of Liberators, Judicators and Protectors emerged from the darkness in twos and threes to join them.

'We have to get onto the skyship!' shouted Kalyani.

'Warning shots!' ordered Sundershield, and two Prosecutors loosed arrows from their bows. The shafts whipped through the night like bolts of lightning and struck the watchtower above the heads of the duardin, who were even now attaching their strange mechanical rappelling machines to their ship's ropes.

Their leader, the arkanaut who had delivered the warning, looked up at the oncoming Stormcasts and scowled.

'We've paid our debts,' he yelled. 'Look to your own flight, we've no obligation to aid you!'

'We don't look to flee!' Kalyani called back, then staggered and ducked as a massive foot sailed low overhead. It came down amidst a mob of panicked handgunners, crushing them into the ground. Even as the survivors fled, an enormous hand snaked down and scooped up a handful, lifting them screaming into the air as easily as Tove had taken the wine bottle from Karrobeth's table. Kalyani ignored the pitiful shrieks and the crunch of bones from above as she ran on.

Several duardin had already attached their rappelling machines and shot up their lines with a whirr of gears. Even as Kalyani reached him, their leader was preparing to do the same.

'We don't look to flee,' she said again, closing one armoured hand around the rope to prevent his rappelling machine from travelling up it. 'There's a duty still to be done.'

He goggled at her in amazement.

'Duty? What, the *weapon?* With what bloody army?' he demanded.

'That which Sigmar has given me,' Kalyani said as her Stormcast followers came to her side. Tove and Karrobeth brought up the rear, gasping with exhaustion and terror.

The arkanaut looked around at the carnage engulfing the encampment, then up at the waiting skyship. Only now, stood below it, did Kalyani recognise the distinctive prow of the *Shieldmaiden* as it hovered overhead.

'First Mate Hengin?' she ventured.

'Dead,' spat the duardin. 'Died along with the admiral, trying to claim that bloody weapon. I'm Vargi, his helmsman. No profit in this venture, nought but disaster. We can't help you.'

He made to engage his rappelling machine but Kalyani's hand didn't move. The duardin placed a hand upon the butt of his pistol meaningfully.

'Treble whatever you were promised,' she said. Booming footfalls sounded and a thunderous roar echoed overhead. From above, they heard the skyship's guns boom. Vargi flinched then snarled.

'They've seen her. 'Course they have. We need to go *now*, or she'll be naught but wreckage anyway!'

'Treble your reward, on my oath as a Stormcast Eternal. Sigmar himself will see your debts paid, and favourable contracts offered to your kith and kin in perpetuity,' said Kalyani and the duardin's eyes widened. She saw him calculating whether she was in a position to make such an astronomical offer, then conclude that if anyone was it was a Lord-Celestant. Avarice and fear fought a swift war behind the duardin's eyes, but in such a conflict there could only ever be one victor.

'Fine!' he yelled. 'But I warn you, I'll have the contracts drawn up en route and you'll sign before you disembark. Triple-witnessed. And I shan't risk the *Shieldmaiden*. I'll drop you part way and you can walk the rest. I'm not open to negotiation.'

'Done, Captain Vargi,' said Kalyani. He shot her a sour look.

'Passengers to come aboard, lower the nets!' he shouted up to the skyship above. Then, as Kalyani removed her hand at last, he shot upward with a whirr.

'Move,' she urged her people as weighted nets tumbled down from above, dangling down over the deck rail and providing them with a ladder by which to embark. The Stormcasts swarmed upwards at speed while Kalyani sheathed Song and unceremoniously hefted Karrobeth over one shoulder. The cryptoscholar was too shocked and exhausted to complain as Kalyani clambered one-handed up the netting, Tove labouring at her side.

With every breath Kalyani expected a rush of hot, foul air as some vast hand closed around them or a swinging club swatted them out of existence. The ironclad's guns spoke again, the repeater in its fore turret chattering as it spat rounds at dark and lumbering shapes.

Then Kalyani was hoisting Karrobeth over the railing, feeling the jolt through the netting as the anchors disengaged and reeled back in. Everything swung and swayed as the *Shieldmaiden* lifted away from the watchtower and Tove hissed as his grip slipped on the wet netting. Kalyani shot out a hand, grabbing him by his collar and heaving him unceremoniously upwards to tumble onto the skyship's deck.

She looked behind her and her blood ran cold at the sight of a towering gargant bearing down upon them. It wore a crude mask, its eyes staring madly through cavernous eyeholes of badly cured human skin. The keel of a ship was clutched in the monster's fists, spars of wood and shattered planks still jutting from it and a bundle of ballista bolts protruding from its tip to form an enormous spear.

The behemoth drew back its weapon, preparing to jab it upwards and skewer the *Shieldmaiden* from below. Kalyani turned as best she could, readying herself to leap from the netting and down onto the beast's shoulders. If she could drive Song into its eye, maybe even reach its throat…

In a sudden rush of air and crackling lightning, Lord-Celestant Galabrith was there. His stardrake Absaloth's fulminating breath exploded in a cloud that engulfed the gargant's face and made it roar with pain. They shot past, their downdraught almost ripping Kalyani from the netting before the *Shieldmaiden*'s endrins thrummed and the skyship lifted up, up, away from the rampaging mega-gargants.

'Thank you, Lord-Celestant,' breathed Kalyani as she saw Absaloth's lightning dance again in the darkness below. 'All debts shall be paid when duty is done.'

With that she turned and hauled herself over the railing onto the waiting deck as the *Shieldmaiden* sped through the skies. Back into Mordavia, one last time.

CHAPTER TWELVE

BARGAINS

Mordavia, the early hours of the campaign's fourth day

The slow drip of water grated on Splichritt's nerves. Crouching within a half-buried ruin somewhere in the city's eastern reaches, he could see through the cracks in one wall that the rain itself had stopped. Yet still its residue trickled down through the strata of ruin above him, gathered on the ceiling of this tilted chamber then fell *drip drip drip* into dark pools upon its floor.

He had considered blasting water and ceiling both with warp lightning until they stopped annoying him. That would only have caused a cave-in, however, and Splichritt couldn't risk such danger to his person. The Horned Rat would never forgive the needless demise of one of its foremost agents, after all.

Splichritt ground his fangs in frustration at the thought that he had very little else left to risk. He glanced back to where his war litter waited in the dark, its lumpen bearers shifting and growling mindlessly amidst the shadows. His spell had spirited both him and his regal conveyance out of harm's way. His idiot underlings had not been so privileged, and so far he had seen no evidence that a single one of them had succeeded in scrambling clear of the death wave unleashed by that fool Blackclaw.

'Stupid-stupid grab-snatcher,' he muttered to himself as he unconsciously twisted his tail-tip between his handclaws. 'Idiot shadow-sneak. Should have known-known magic so powerful was not for his claws. No, only Splichritt has mighty-most sorcery to wield such a weapon.'

There again, he thought with growing anger, perhaps Blackclaw had known that all along. Or at least, perhaps his *masters* had. What if the shadowy masters of the Clans Eshin had known *precisely* what Splichritt and his swarm would find beneath this dead-things city? What if they had sent Blackclaw to Splichritt in order to lure him into the radius of the deadly weapon, and fooled their gutter runner dupe with orders to snatch the blade before the grey seer could take what was rightfully his?

Splichritt's eyes widened and his agitated twitching increased as he realised that this entire debacle, the armies fighting, the weapon's empowerment, all of it might well have been orchestrated by the Clans Eshin as an elaborate trap to slay him! *Splichritt is mighty-most, maybe-maybe they see what a danger to them I am,* he thought, and his fevered imagination spiralled through a dozen scenarios in which one or other of the Clans Eshin might have determined that he, Splichritt, was the greatest and most dangerous of all the grey seers. If that was so then surely such efforts to place him in harm's way were the very least they would have made to ensure his removal.

Mighty war-war, many-much foe-things, yes this is the least they would have to do if they seek-wish to slay mighty Splichritt, he mused. A leer split his muzzle then, as he realised that despite all of the Clans Eshins' machinations, despite unleashing entire armies upon one another in their attempt to entrap and kill him, the fools had failed!

'And now Splichritt sees,' he growled to himself, his high-pitched voice echoing through the ruin. 'Now he knows the power of this kill-weapon. Yes-yes, it will be mine!'

For the next few minutes, Splichritt was transported by heady visions of claiming the kill-weapon for himself and unleashing its power upon the Clans Eshin that had sought to engineer his demise. So much devastation he would cause, so mighty would be his vengeance! Splichritt had to admit to himself that he didn't know *which* of the Clans Eshin had actually wronged him, had not in all truth even taken the time to discover which clan Black-claw and his cronies hailed from.

That wrinkle was smoothed out when it occurred to him that the Clans Eshin were sneaks of the highest order and must surely all spy upon one another such that they knew one another's plots and plans. Had any of those shadow-lurking fools been on Splichritt's side then surely they would have sent him warning, hoping no doubt to curry his favour. No, they were *all* in it together, Splichritt was sure, and so they would all pay the price.

'And then, yes-yes, seats on the Council of Thirteen open up, shadow masters too dead to sit-crouch upon them! All for Splichritt, or else maybe-maybe he takes the kill-weapon and uses it upon the council? Soon Splichritt is most-mighty master of all Skavendom! Chosen of Horned One! Conqueror of the realms!'

Splichritt gave vent to a high-pitched cackle that echoed madly around him and caused his litter beasts to incline their too-small heads in confusion. Suddenly realising how much noise he was making, and how utterly alone he was, Splichritt choked off his laughter and crouched low. His eyes darted all around, seeking the peril his instincts told him must surely be lurking in every shadow. His glands tightened and his verminous heart pattered in his chest.

When no assassin's blade or towering storm-thing emerged to slay him, Splichritt calmed. The muscles under his right eye twitched.

Yes, he wanted the kill-weapon. Oh, he wanted it *very* much.

'But how-how?' he snarled to himself.

Splichritt scrambled up a low heap of rubble and peered through the cracks in the wall. Through the clear, cold night air he saw the enormous spectral mountain rising away to the west. The sight of its whirling dead-things and the unnatural glow of its vast bulk caused his hackles to rise and his glands to clench afresh.

'Many-many dead-things, too many even for Splichritt's magics,' he muttered. 'Curse underlings for their stupidity, all die-dead just when Splichritt needs his mighty swarm.'

If he was going to claim the kill-weapon then there was no doubt in Splichritt's mind that he needed a swarm even greater than the one that he had led here. Oh, he didn't doubt for a second that the green-things, the man-things, the storm-things and *particularly* the beard-things, they would all have been much too slow and stupid to escape the kill-weapon. Yes, Splichritt was sure that he alone had possessed the skill, the sorcerous genius and the honed survival instincts required to slip free of the Clans Eshin and their dastardly assassination plot.

That still left a mountain's worth of dead-things to overcome, however. Splichritt had not got where he was today by placing himself in harm's way when he could summon others to face it in his stead! But how to gather another swarm? How to amass the power he needed, quickly enough to seize his prize before some other army of dullard surface-dwellers chanced across it and seized Splichritt's kill-weapon for their own unworthy selves?

A thought gnawed its way into his mind, a wild fancy that became a perilous temptation and then, before he could quash it, a vertiginous compulsion.

He could not summon a swarm from thin air, that much was true. But he was a grey seer. He was versed in the darkest and most forbidden rites of the Horned Rat, privy to the secrets of the scuttler in the dark, empowered to commune with beings beyond the ken of the greater mass of skaven.

He could not summon an army, but he *could* summon a greater daemon of the Horned Rat. He could summon a verminlord and then *it* could provide him with the power that he needed.

'Gnnnn no-no, very-much danger, terrible-terrible, bargains with things that gnaw in the shadows, very-much danger-risk, the price always too-too high,' he muttered to himself as he paced back and forth in the dark. 'But... power. Yes-yes. Power to make Splichritt's plans reality, and when Splichritt take-snatches the kill-weapon...'

Why, then Splichritt could obliterate anything he liked, couldn't he?

Even a verminlord.

Splichritt's frenzied preparations took almost an hour. He had to scribe the warding tridecagram from a mixture of warpstone powder drawn from a pouch, crushed snatt-beetle extract and thick dark blood let from the flank of one of his quiescent litter beasts. He had to fish thirteen skinny black wyrmwick candles from within his many pouches, experiencing several minutes of blind panic after only turning up eleven. This minor shortfall was rectified by the simple – yet, Splichritt felt, brilliant – expedient of breaking two of the candles in half, and soon enough the ruin was lit by their flickering green-black illumination. He had to crunch down several nuggets of raw warpstone, plucked from within the lead-lined tin he kept strapped to his scrawny chest beneath his robes: each was an agonising, exhilarating feast of power that felt like swallowing mouthfuls of burning glass; each caused his flesh to tremble with the barely restrained power of mutation, his nerves to burn as though electricity ran through them, and insane visions of horror and power and butchery to drown his senses in madness.

By the time his agonising feast was done, clumps of his fur were scattered across the chamber floor and Splichritt's tail had split halfway down its length. His two new tail-tips writhed like blindly questing worms beyond his control. It was an unpleasant sensation, but one he barely noticed compared to the roaring furnace of magical power now burning in his breast. Lurid black sparks danced about his claw-tips, and as he weaved his arms through the first motions of the summoning spell they left blurred after-images in the air before him. Splichritt knew that even one so mighty as he could not long contain so much dark magic without bursting apart or mutating beyond control, and the mad power of walking so perilous a line filled him with terror and exhilaration both.

Splichritt's motions became quicker and he began to hiss and screech as he placed his footclaws in the scurrying steps of the summoning rite. He chewed and spat out unholy syllables, glottal grunts and sibilant curses in an incomprehensible tongue. He felt his gums split and run with blood as the words of power ravaged them. He felt one of his fangs come loose in his mouth and, unable to interrupt his ritual and desperate not to mispronounce a single word of the binding, was forced to swallow the hard, sharp shard. His heart thundered so fast he thought it might burst. His nostrils filled with the sweet scent of corruption and he prayed to the Horned One that the stink came from beyond the veil rather than from some dreadful rot taking hold within his own flesh.

As Splichritt's incantation reached its peak, his litter beasts gave deep snarls of alarm. The candle flames burned suddenly low, then winked out one after another as though snuffed. The shadows deepened and as they did Splichritt heard a growing susurrus as though countless vermin squirmed and chittered far back in the darkness. His head snapped first one way then another as something moved, swift and stealthy and oh-so-malevolent, in his peripheral vision. The chamber went as cold as the void even as the stench intensified a hundredfold and made Splichritt gag.

As his gaze settled back upon the summoning tridecagram he gave an undignified squeak of terror and leapt back several steps. The elaborately drawn wards were now glowing with eerie green light, illuminating the monstrous being that crouched in their midst.

Splichritt took in the daemon's curling horns, its pelt thick with squirming parasites, the mist-like grey robes that flowed about its long and muscular limbs, any one of which was longer than he was tall. He eyed its wicked talons and dagger-like fangs. He felt the aura of pure malice that pulsed from it. Yet what truly held him were its eyes. Splichritt felt as though he were tumbling head over tail into a yawning well of madness and hate and endless, boundless cunning. It held him pinned with its void-like gaze as surely as if it had reached out and grasped him. Suddenly all Splichritt's boundless confidence was replaced with naked terror. He was a runt again, barely able to see, surrounded by the hulking bodies and hungry fangs of his siblings, writhing and squirming as he sought to make one bite the tail of another, which clawed the belly of a third, anything to stop them pressing in around him and setting teeth and talons to his flesh…

'*You have summoned me, little seer,*' it said, and its voice was the crack of ancient bones beneath gnawing fangs, the scrabble of a million claws, the death rattle of life itself. '*You have summoned Thrykktwyst. Why?*'

For a horrible moment Splichritt simply couldn't speak. He could force nothing from his muzzle but a reedy wheeze and he felt the daemon's anger like a physical blow. How could this thing exert such power, such menace, even while trapped within his wards?

'*Answer-answer, speak now or when I rip-gnaw your pitiful bindings I will make you screech-suffer for all eternity,*' it snarled.

Yet it did not strike, did not move at all from where it hunched like some enormous gargoyle in the midst of his summoning marks. That gave Splichritt confidence. Surely, if this terrible thing had the power to reach out and snuff him then it would have done so by now. He would have, in its place, ripped away from whatever machinations it had been embroiled in, bound by sorcery and forced to treat with one it believed its inferior. *Splichritt has the power here,* he told himself, managing to slow his skittering heart a little and squaring his narrow shoulders. *Splichritt is master.*

'I am Splichritt the Ever-most Very-much Magnificent and I summon-bind you to grant me power,' he chittered, proud of how steady he managed to keep his voice. 'I need-want the kill-weapon. To take it, I need-need an army, big swarm, biggest. Dead-things have the kill-weapon on top of their dead-mountain, and it is mine!'

The verminlord's muzzle split in a leer so malevolent that Splichritt took an involuntary step backwards. A powerful sense-memory was forced upon him of his small, weak body half-pinned under one of his still-blind siblings, its blunt fangs snapping closed a millimetre from his muzzle.

'*You seek-want the dark blade of the dead-things, little seer? You need a much-much mighty swarm to take it. Know you that others come-come for the blade also? Champions of plague-god, storm-things, tall-things, all seek-want it. I see them, closer-closer even now. Tall, big, powerful, all laughing at fool-fool Splichritt hiding in his burrow while they take away his prize.*'

Splichritt's fury at this news was incandescent, his outrage so towering that he almost forgot to fear the verminlord lurking within his wards. That others would try to steal away his prize was an insult! That they might succeed? Unthinkable! The kill-weapon was Splichritt's path to glory, his boon to seize, a reward from the Horned One himself for outwitting the fools of Eshin.

Splichritt, though, he was no fool. He knew this daemon's help would not come for free, knew the price it would demand of him would be terrible beyond imagining, but he didn't care. With the kill-weapon he could subjugate the monster, banish it if he must and when he was ruler of all the skaven, well then it would bend the knee to him just like everyone else. It would bend the knee or die! They all would!

'You fetch-bring me a swarm so mighty it can overthrow them all!' he screeched, green-black spittle flying from his lips. 'You aid-aid Splichritt in taking the kill-weapon for himself! I am most-mighty, and I command you!'

The verminlord's leer did not fade as it bowed its great horned head.

'Release me from these wards, little seer, and I will bring-bring you such a swarm that it shall darken-blight the lands with its numbers.'

'Do it, obey-obey mighty Splichritt!' squealed the grey seer and, with a single stroke of one footclaw he broke the tridecagrammatic wards.

The verminlord's laughter was the rustle of rats feasting upon the battle-slain dead. It unfolded itself like a spider from its funnelled web, limbs stretching and unbending until it loomed over Splichritt like some obscene idol come to life. It opened one taloned hand and a great mass of writhing rats' tails squirmed into being within its grip, lengthening and entwining until they formed a huge, dark staff that twitched and shuddered with horrible life. In its other out-held hand a scatter of green and black motes danced and whirled, faster and faster until they formed an orb-shaped storm that solidified suddenly into a void-dark witching ball. Splichritt saw his wide-eyed face reflected weirdly in its depths.

He looked as though he were screaming.

'*Mount your war litter, little seer, and scrabble-sneak out from your lair,*' said the verminlord, its tone mocking as it stared deep into its witching ball. '*Wait-wait but moments, and your swarm shall be yours to command.*' With that the hideous daemon vanished as though it had never been.

Heart still beating at triple speed, limbs shaking, mouth filled with the taste of ashes and stale blood, Splichritt staggered across to his litter. He had to squeak a weak command at one of its bearers to hoist him up, and as soon as he reached the safety of the litter he slumped back in its throne.

'Go-go, out now,' he wheezed, and plucked another cracked fang from his mouth. He did not ever remember being so exhausted, so hollowed out and broken. What if the thing had fooled him? What if it had gained its freedom and fled? But to what end, he asked himself? If Thrykktwyst had sought to slay him for daring to summon it, the daemon would surely have done so the moment he set it free.

No, thought Splichritt as his bearers carried him up the rubble slope and out into the cold of the night. No, the daemon was doing his bidding. Of course it was! He was Splichritt the Ever-most Very-much Magnificent!

The grey seer had barely emerged into the cold glare of the stars when dark clouds began to obscure them. The numinous masses grew and billowed with unnatural swiftness, racing to clot and swell and obscure the heavens as black-green lightning leapt amongst their depths. A racing wind swept in from the east and upon it Splichritt smelt the stink of verminous bodies, gnawed carrion and crackling sorcery. He sat up straighter in his throne, twinned tail writhing as the storm grew in size and fury. This was no contrivance of the storm-things or their God-King. No, realised Splichritt as black bolts of lightning leapt down to lash the topmost towers of the dead city and the chittering of countless rats filled the air. No, this was the work of Thrykktwyst, and by extension it was the genius work of Splichritt himself.

By the time the first gnawholes tore open in the fabric of reality, Splichritt was already on his footclaws, dancing and screeching in mad elation. The verminlord was the first to step through the torn veil, but behind him boiled a tide of skaven so vast that it surely dwarfed the swarm that Splichritt had assembled before. How such a thing could be possible in mere moments he had no idea, but nor was he about to question the dark sorcery of the being that *he* had summoned, *he* had subjugated to his will.

'Now, little seer, the kill-weapon awaits. Let us kill-kill them all!' snarled the verminlord, and so great was Splichritt's elation that he deigned to let his new servant's insubordination slide.

Just this once.

'All obey mighty-mighty Splichritt!' he screeched. 'And Splichritt says kill-kill!'

Cankus Glumm sat in his old wooden rocking chair and stared out from the porch of his farmstead. He was looking out over his southern fields, a jug of the last season's teffyl cider in one hand and a sense of contentment warm in his chest. He took a sip of the pugnacious brew, savouring its bite as he felt his limbs ache with the day's long labours.

'Worth it though, I reckon,' he said to himself as he watched the gold-and-roseblush shades of early evening painting his swaying crops and the trees of the teff orchard. Somewhere inside the house he could hear Ghallie bumping about, whistling an old harvest tune to herself as she prepared supper. She'd make enough to feed the two of them, and their boy Launce and all the field hands to boot, he didn't doubt. Always did. She was a great believer in generosity, was his Ghallie. Cankus adored her for it.

Something felt off, though, for all his sense of contentment. It made him uneasy that he couldn't quite place what was wrong. He had a feeling that something remained undone, though for the life of him he couldn't think of a task remaining to him this evening. The ghumpas were all fed and back in their paddock for the night. Harvest was going well. He'd set Jebbon and Torley on first watch, told them to ride the bounds then come back and hand over with Holsley and Pugh at third bell.

What else could there be? He wasn't due into town with his next wagonload for another three days, so that wasn't it. Still, the thought gnawed at Cankus like a maggot in a teff-root, and when he took his next sip of cider it tasted somehow *too* bitter, as though it were starting to go over.

He frowned, then looked around as he heard the boards of the porch creak under a heavy tread. His scowl became a smile as he saw his brother, Yakob, approaching. Tall, broad-shouldered and hale, Yakob Glumm had always been the better-looking of the two brothers but Cankus had never resented him for it. He just thanked his lucky stars that Ghallie had met him before Yakob, and that she preferred a level head to a handsome one.

Yakob didn't return Cankus' smile. His brother settled himself heavily in the second rocker and let out a heavy sigh.

'You left me be'ind, brother, went 'n lost me,' said Yakob.

Cankus blinked at him in surprise. He was so nonplussed by this strange pronouncement that he set down his cider and turned to face Yakob full on. The warm sensation intensified in his chest as he twisted around, and he recognised now that it wasn't satisfaction but a pain of some sort. What *was* going on? A sense of dislocation was stealing over Cankus now, a growing disquiet that rendered everything somehow dreamlike and unsettling. Or had it always been that way, and he was only now noticing?

'Yakob, what're you talkin' about, brother? Left you down in the riverfield finishin' up with Pugh, I s'pose. Looked like you were bringin' in a right fine crop 'n all!'

'Not talkin' about crops,' said Yakob, still not looking at him. Instead he stared out over the fields, and Cankus felt drawn to follow his gaze. His frown deepened as he saw the light turning turgid. Gold had turned to a sepia brown, rose to a fleshy, spoiled colour that made the crops look rotten. He saw specks whirling through the air in thick clouds and realised with a stab of revulsion that they were flies. Thousands of fat-bodied, droning flies, boiling through his suddenly blighted crops, more hatching out of the bubbling mud by the moment. Beyond the fields he saw a dark forest rising, sprouting with impossible speed to blight the horizon with its writhing lianas, gallows-like trees and fat, dripping fronds.

Cankus looked back at Yakob, mouth opening in bewilderment to demand answers or perhaps cry out in alarm. Instead he uttered a bubbling croak as the pain in his chest stabbed hot and furious. He went stiff and raised a hand to its epicentre. Cankus felt sticky wetness there. Dread filled him as he raised his hand and stared dumbly at the foul, green-brown fluid that dripped, stinking from his fingertips.

Cankus… my name isn't… wasn't… was it? Cankus? Don't sound right… It wasn't… hadn't been then… now… his thoughts whirled in confusion and shock.

'*I don't… blame you,*' came Yakob's voice, but now it was a harsh rasp. Cankus looked up and recoiled with a cry at the diseased thing his brother had become. Yellow eyes bulged and drooped in rotten sockets. Puffy grey flesh swam with fat buboes, while maggots bigger than Cankus' thumbs squirmed busily in Yakob's seeping wounds or plopped fatly to the decking.

'What in the name o' the Great Gardener is goin' on?' wailed Cankus. Just like that he remembered. It all crashed back in like foetid floodwater. This wasn't his home. His home was centuries gone and poor Ghallie and Launce and all the field hands with it. Yet in that moment the wrenching pain of their loss was every bit as terrible as it had been on the day that the dead marched through his fields and took their blades to his people. Glumm's anger and hatred burned every bit as hot. He knew again the desire to spread life to every corner of the Mortal Realms, to bury the legions of the dead in such boundless fecundity that everything they sought to build would be crushed beneath it.

'Mordavia...' he breathed, and clotted gore bubbled over his flyblown lips. Distantly, over the droning of flies and the creak and groan as the house's timbers rotted and warped, he could hear the dry voices of Grandmother Gulkh and her wose-witches. They had served the Horns of Plenty for many a year, applying their maggots and tinctures to seal wounds, encourage rancid regrowth and patch up those of Glumm's warriors who couldn't be healed by Nurgle's gifts alone. Now, he realised, they must be hard at work upon him.

'Fetch me my withersilk worms.'

'Perhaps a clottening hex? We might try a clottening hex?'

'Oh, would that we had but a phial of the fruitful bloat, that would see his lordship a'right.'

'Glopsom days, I've never seen something like this. Should it be attached in there somewhere?'

'Wither and rot, *wither and rot.*'

'*Reckon' you're dyin'* at last... *brother...*' gasped Yakob, pulling Glumm's attention back to the present, or whatever this simulacrum was. The farmstead had warped and twisted beyond recognition now, its beams and boards twisted into groaning wooden faces with rows of splinter teeth. Rusted wind-chimes and corroded bells dangled like weird fruit from the porch, their every note jarring with the next as they danced in the clammy breeze.

'Don't matter 'bout that, Yakob,' he gurgled. 'I'm just so rot-damned sorry I let you down. But 'ang on, if I'm 'ere and I'm still alive–'

'*No… such luck…*' rasped Yakob in a regretful voice. '*This… is a… dunno really, brother, it's… somewhere in between. You come from one… way and… well… I come from t'other'n. If it's any consolation… I din't half poison a few of them vermin afore they finished chewin' me up.*'

'Rot and damnation,' said Cankus, responding both to his brother's words and to a sudden ghastly stab of pain that radiated out from his chest and up into his skull. It left a strange numbness behind it that he found more frightening than anything else. It was long enough since he'd felt pain, but to experience that sudden absence of even the slightest vital stirrings within a body long riddled with bountiful plagues and parasites? That filled him with mortal fear.

And he felt anger, he realised. Anger that his duty wasn't done. Anger at the sudden, impersonal way in which he and his brother had been slain by enemies who didn't even have the decency to face them in honest battle. Just caught up amidst the mayhem, victims of poor chance and the vast battle's anarchy. An ignominious end to centuries of conquest in Nurgle's name. An ignominious failure in the eyes of the Great Gardener.

'Is he angry with me?' he asked, coughing up a wad of brownish matter. 'The Great Gardener? Is that why his gifts ain't stoppin' this? That why I'm dyin'? Punishment, like?'

For a rotting, disease-raddled corpse, Yakob did an impressive job of looking surprised.

'*Punish…ment? No, brother… you're favoured… s'why you're here… 'stead o' back in your body waitin' to perish. I been sent to tell you… you got a choice… one not a lot o' folk get.*'

Cankus took a bubbling breath and felt the cold spreading

through his limbs. The muttering of the wose-witches had grown more frantic, but it was also becoming fainter.

'Best lay it out quick-like, brother, or Old Bones'll 'ave me afore I can decide either way.'

'*Simple enough… brother,*' said Yakob, speaking with his usual rasping deliberation. '*You've earned a… place in the Garden, same as me.*'

Despite himself, Cankus gave a pained smile.

'You already walkin' the Garden, brother?'

'*Legs… arms… wind on me face and dronin' in me ears… all manner o' things I ain't had in long ages… but this ain't about me,*' Yakob replied. '*You can take your place… in the Garden of Nurgle… but if you do then your duty… won't get done. Or… the Great Gardener… can give you the gift o' life again… life enough to crush all the dead want to build… life enough to turn Mordavia into a fecund bloomin' paradise. Won't be life like you've 'ad b'fore, mind…*'

Cankus' first instinct had been to shout 'yes' with all the strength left in his failing body. Yet even as his limbs turned icy and his breathing slowed, even as his heart thumped a sick and faltering rhythm and his helpless body slumped and slid down in the splintered wood of his old rocking chair, he heard the note of caution in his brother's voice.

Won't be life like you've 'ad b'fore… Something about Yakob's tone filled him with fear, as though to agree would be to step off of a high cliff into an unknown abyss. Yet what else could he do? Accept a reward he knew he didn't deserve? Set aside his toils and leave others to fight on while Nagash and all his foul dead slaves pressed their counterattack? For all he knew they could be coming to snatch up the weapon right now, could be unleashing its powers, rendering everything to dead sterility just like they had in his village.

What else could he say?

'I'll do it,' he croaked. 'Yes. I'll take the gift of life.'

He expected Yakob to smile. Instead his brother simply glowered at him, mouth a downturned line, eyes bulging… squirming… running together into a single yellowed orb that regarded Cankus as one might an interesting specimen of plant or insect. His brother's temples bulged then split in showers of pus as long, rotted antlers sprouted from them. Yakob's body deformed, gangling green limbs growing and stretching while the rocking chair upon which he had sat bulged and swelled obscenely into a flowing mass of flesh. Some of it spread and became a green-grey slug-like body, waving eyestalks and stubby limbs. The rest hardened into a bulbous shell, and as Cankus stared in amazement Horticulus Slimux, the Great Gardener that he had long worshipped, clambered up to sit astride it.

'Good lad, thought you'd do the right thing giv'n the chance,' said the daemon in a voice like wet gravel. *'You 'ad to say yes to this yerself, otherwise the seed wouldn'a took, see?'*

'I… what?' croaked Glumm. Dimly he was aware of shapes moving all around him, slouching ranks of beings emerging from the rotted crops amidst the endless drone of counting. Huge shapes bounded and flolloped amongst them, while dark smudges filled the air above with the drone of flies' wings. Daemons, he realised as his vision became hazy. Masses of daemons, come from the Garden for… what?

Horticulus Slimux reached down and Glumm felt a fresh sting of pain in his chest cavity as the daemon drove something home into the ruined flesh there. Slimux sat back with a satisfied grunt.

'Grandfather thanks 'ee fer your sacrifice, Cankus Glumm,' he said, oddly formal. *'You might'a failed 'im as a Champion, but thy flesh'll be put to good use none the less.'*

Glumm felt the crushing weight of horror and disappointment descend upon him as he realised the choice had never been his to make. Yakob had never even been here. He had failed, and he had been tricked, and now he was going to die. He tried to speak, but his throat wouldn't work. It felt full, as though he had swallowed a wet clod of soil. He tried to breathe but his lungs wouldn't drag in air. They felt as though they were being crushed, and then that pressure was everywhere in his body, worming hot, thrusting fingers of agony through limbs that a moment before had been cold and numb. He heard again the voices of the wose-witches, crying out first in joy and then in alarm.

'Praise Nurgle, his flesh be growing most bounteous!'

'No, no, it's not his flesh, it's something *within* his flesh.'

'What in the name of Nurgle is happening? It's a plant! Some kind of plant!'

'Sisters, withdraw most hastefully! Rot and damnation, it's tearing him apart!'

'Is't a gnarlmaw, sisters?'

'Eeeegh! It has my leg! It...'

Cankus Glumm had time only to feel the utter, crushing weight of failure fill him, then his body was torn asunder.

His death, at least, was mercifully swift.

CHAPTER THIRTEEN

THE MAELSTROM GATHERS

Mordavia, the early hours of the campaign's fourth day

Bronvynne peered over the deck rail of the *Shieldmaiden* and felt her stomach lurch. They were powering in over Mordavia's southern districts, high up but headed straight for the spectral mountain at the city's heart. Their lost encampment was far behind them now, marked by scattered fires and the listing shape of the cogfort, ablaze from stem to stern.

Vast dark shapes moved through the streets behind the skyship's keel, huge and ominous as children's nightmares.

The wind howled as it sank icy fangs into the exposed flesh of Bronvynne's face and hands, and she pulled her robes tight while hanging grimly onto the rail as best she could. At her back she was conscious of the craft's surviving arkanauts hastening to and fro as they effected repairs with sparking aethertorches and loaded rattling chains of ammunition into the skyship's remaining guns. Yet Bronvynne didn't look round. She had eyes only for the dark rooftops and swaying ferns sweeping by far, far below.

'Are you all right?' asked Tove, hovering at her shoulder. 'Shall I find you something else warm to put over those robes?'

'It's less the cold and more the altitude that troubles me, Laszlo,' she replied, raising her voice so that it would carry over the singing wind. He looked at her doubtfully, then shot a meaningful glance past the scorched metal of the prow turret. She followed his gaze, strands of her wiry hair flicking around her face in the wind. The ethereal mountain filled her gaze, flowing with rivers of wailing ghasts while east of it a fresh storm front gathered with what seemed unnatural speed. Bronvynne jumped as black-green lightning leapt furiously amidst the boiling clouds, reaching down to blast tower-tops and teetering minarets into tumbling rubble.

'I think you might be better worrying about all that,' said Tove, the dryness of his tone not lost despite the wailing winds.

'I was rather trying to ignore *all that*,' she replied and clutched her tome closer to her body beneath her robes.

Privately, Bronvynne wondered how much more she could process. The sudden onset of the mega-gargants had been utterly terrifying. If Tove hadn't been there to chivvy her along she thought she might still have been crouched in the ruins of the pavilion, praying to Sigmar and cowering beneath torn canvas like a frightened animal. Since they had boarded the skyship, Bronvynne had found herself strangely numb, unable to feel a great deal of anything beyond cold and mild vertigo. Fear and panic had fled but so too had any sense of urgency about the dangers they faced. She could hear a faint ringing in her ears and felt peculiarly hazy in a way she didn't think was anything to do with the wine she had drunk. It probably wasn't good, she thought, but at the same time she welcomed the insulating blanket that had wrapped itself around her feelings. She didn't even feel the need to spur her courage with thoughts of Lief.

After all, you know deep down he's long dead, don't you, girl? she thought to herself. *And frankly unless something dreadful has dragged him back up here as one of those ghasts, what your brother would or wouldn't have thought or done has precious little bearing on the here and now.*

Normally such thoughts would have moved her to tears. Now, Bronvynne found she could confront the notion of Lief's being long dead quite dispassionately. She rather wished she hadn't thought about his ghast roaming the realms, though…

'You may not get to ignore it for very long,' said Tove. 'Whatever's happening, I reckon it'll be happening soon.'

Again, she followed his pointed look, this time to the helm where Lord-Celestant Thunderblade and the Kharadron helmsman named Vargi were engaged in what her father had used to call 'robust discussion'. A handful of Thunderblade's surviving Stormcasts had gathered at her back; splattered in mud and gore, weapons in hand, and with several sparking with celestial energies about the eyepieces and blades, they made for an intimidating sight. Equally, many of the arkanauts had slowed their work and positioned themselves within earshot with heavy tools or weapons close to hand.

'Come on, let's not be the only fools who *don't* know what Thunderblade and the duardin are having a row about,' said Tove, and the two of them moved down the railing until they could hear the debate.

'…did not promise you half the damned riches in Sigmaron so that you could deposit us a mile or more from where we need to be!' said Thunderblade, her voice hard as hammer blows. 'You captain the only functional vessel in these skies and our destination is high atop that blasphemy of a mountain. You are being paid to deliver us *there.*'

'I can have the contract read aloud to you again if you wish, Lord-

Celestant,' replied the duardin, staring fixedly ahead as he worked the skyship's controls. 'I can also have the artycles enunciated for you if that would make my position clearer. Riches are no use to the dead, and nowhere in our agreement is it explicitly stated that we have to deliver you to the pinnacle of that mountain.'

'Heldenhammer!' exclaimed Thunderblade in exasperation. 'If we lose that weapon the consequences for the enclaves of Order and civilisation could be catastrophic. Whether that abomination departs before we can corner it, or the ghasts steal the weapon away or, Sigmar preserve us, if you set us down and the gargants overrun us the result is the same. Millions could be killed.'

'And if we fly the *Shieldmaiden* into that mass of ghasts, *we'll* all be killed. No 'could' about it,' replied Vargi. 'And that's without mentioning whatever unnatural storm that is brewing up from the east. I'll not risk her in the teeth of those skies, no matter what you offer me.'

Just then there came a cry from the lookout.

'Foes engaging, ahead and below! Rust the hull, there's thousands of them!'

Bronvynne frowned, bewildered. She thought perhaps the lookout had become confused, seen foes where there were only shifting shadows. How could there be thousands of enemies still in the city? Had the orruks escaped the death wave more intact than they had believed? Had the Chaos worshippers? She remembered again the aelf asking about skaven during the violently aborted war council and her flesh crawled at the thought that the scabrous ratmen might be nearby.

Stood already at the rail, she got a good look over the side before almost anyone else. Thus, Bronvynne was amongst the first aboard the *Shieldmaiden* to bear witness to the fresh conflict now engulfing Mordavia.

'Sigmar preserve us,' she breathed.

The shadows were indeed moving beneath the racing, unnatural storm clouds. They *seethed* with motion, but it was no trick of the light. It was skaven, teeming, scurrying rivers of skaven that flowed along the canted streets and spilled through the ruins in numbers uncountable. In places the onrushing swarms were lit by the harsh green glare of crackling warp lightning and black-green warpflame. It wreathed wicked-looking contraptions that Bronvynne assumed must be weapons. The skaven heaved long-barrelled brass cannons on wheeled carriages, vivid sparks of energy crackling and dancing along their lengths. Others looked to be carrying smaller weapons but from this height Bronvynne could make out little detail. She thought she saw more ratmen scampering across the higher roof-tops ahead and was suddenly glad that Captain Vargi had chosen to make his approach so high, and with few running lanterns lit. She prayed fervently to Sigmar that none of the foul creatures would glance up and see the *Shieldmaiden* ghosting dark and distant overhead. She'd heard stories, read accounts; who knew what horrible ordnance they might deploy to shoot the skyship down?

But then, considering what was moving from the west to meet them, she supposed the awful creatures would have their attention firmly fixed to the fore.

'The Nurgle worshippers are on the move again,' said Tove. 'But... I don't... what...?'

'Daemons,' said Thunderblade, who had joined them at the railing, and whose eyes were far keener than theirs. 'Hundreds upon hundreds of the Plague Lord's daemons. The fools must have become so desperate that they made some awful sacrifice, opened the way for an entire plague legion to march into Mordavia. But what in Sigmar's name is that at the heart of their advance?'

Bronvynne strained her eyes, both wishing to understand the danger that now approached but also desperate to avert her gaze from the horrors below. The dark was merciful, for it obscured many details and left her with the impression of slumped and horrible figures slouching in vast number through the streets. They shambled through the drifts of claggy black ash that was all that remained of those who had fought here the day before. They kicked aside or trampled the empty armour of the blasted dead. The last of their mortal worshippers marched at their side, no doubt awed and terrified in equal measure.

Heavy-bodied beasts leaped and gambolled amongst them while swarm upon swarm of enormous flies droned overhead. Further back amongst the masses she saw shapes that resembled hillocks of sloughing filth, their boulder-sized heads distinguishable by the lambent green glow of their eyes. *Great Unclean Ones,* she thought as she heard the tolling of their vast, warped bells and caught snatches of the bellicose chortling that rose up from below. *Would that I knew less of these terrors.*

The darkness might preserve her from seeing the worst details of the plague legion, but it could not shield her from their combined stench, which made her gag and feel as though she might never be clean again. Nor could it conceal the titanic form that lumbered impossibly along in their midst.

'Is it some sort of… tree?' asked Tove, sounding as though he was wrestling with the desire to let out a mad blurt of laughter. She laid a hand on his arm to steady him; if any of them lost their nerve now, she thought, they might not recover it.

'I believe they are called gnarlmaws,' said Bronvynne, thinking back to the grimoires of horrors that she had studied under close clerical supervision within one of Azyrheim's chained libraries. 'But it should stand no larger than an ironoak or balu. This… well it's as though *you* had grown to the size of one of those terrible gargants, Laszlo. And in all my studies I have never heard tell of such a thing pulling up its poisonous roots and beginning to walk.'

Yet there it was, sanity-jarring and all too real, a dark and spreading presence bulling its way inexorably through the tangled streets and crumbling ruins towards the heart of the city. Jangling bells hung in their hundreds from its talon-like webs of branches. Boiling clouds of insects wreathed its castle-sized form. The cold light of stars and moons limned its pestilent trunk and the rotted fangs that stuffed its yawning maw by the thousand.

Every flash of emerald lightning from the onrushing storm revealed daemon mites swarming over trunk and branches like fleas on the hide of a diseased rat. Even as Bronvynne watched, the giant gnarlmaw gave a shudder, a peristaltic heave, and a gushing torrent of bile spewed from its cavernous mouth. She felt her own gorge rise, and had to turn away as she realised that a fresh wave of daemons had been brought up amidst the lake of vomit and were even now wriggling like maggots to find their feet and join the trudging advance.

'I think that–' She had to stop, fist clenched against her lips and take three quick breaths before she could speak without being ill. 'I think that is their gateway, Lord-Celestant. That's how the daemons have entered Mordavia.'

'And that decides it,' said Captain Vargi, who had shouldered his way through to the railing to get a look for himself. 'Daemons? Skaven? The Sons of Behemat lumbering in our wake and a host of ghasts filling the heavens? Not for all the aether-gold in the skies of great Chamon, Lord-Celestant. Not a chance.'

Bronvynne expected the Lord-Celestant to redouble her argument. Instead, she was shaking her head slowly. Terrible sounds came from below as the leading elements of the two great hordes collided. Whooshing roars, stark *zzak* sounds of energy discharge, the booming toll of bells and the clash of countless blades carried up to them on the putrid winds. Dread storm clouds stole the stars one by one.

'To think that all our efforts, days of bloodshed and conflict, thousands upon thousands of lives, and ours was not even the battle that would decide all this,' said Thunderblade wonderingly.

'Hmm, the gods do have a certain sense of irony,' agreed Vargi. 'But again, Lord-Celestant, I must insist–'

'Yes, Captain Vargi, I understand,' said Thunderblade, still staring down over the railing at the dozen or more vicious conflicts erupting below. 'And having seen all of this, I think that you are correct. Had it been only the ghasts that we had to brave then perhaps we could have run the gauntlet and seen our duty done, but it becomes clear that we are but one small set of cogs turning amidst the vast gears of a far greater doom.'

Bronvynne exchanged a glance with Tove, who looked as concerned as she felt. Had the Lord-Celestant lost her nerve? Could that *happen* to Stormcast Eternals? Bronvynne felt the weight of the tome beneath her robes heavier than ever, as though the hands of all those they had fought to save were dragging at it, trying to tear it from her hands. *Did Lief ever feel anything like this?* she wondered. *Did he ever have even half so great a weight of duty heaped upon his shoulders?*

It didn't matter, she realised. Lief was dead, and she was alive, and worrying about what her brother might or might not have done, or how he might have seen her actions, was just another way of shifting responsibility onto the ghost of someone else.

There was no one else. There was only her, and Tove, and Kalyani Thunderblade and her warriors. They were it, the last chance to stop one or other of the awful beings abroad in this storm-wracked night from stealing away the weapon and using it to wreak the gods alone knew what havoc. The truth of that cracked the numbing shell that had formed around her emotions, and she feared for a moment that the fear and panic she felt might drive her mad. Instead she clutched her tome tighter and said, 'Lord Celestant

Thunderblade? What are we to do? We cannot turn away from our duty.'

Thunderblade turned towards her as though surprised, then smiled a hard and mirthless smile.

'No, we cannot. But nor can we simply soar up there and get ourselves all killed trying to discharge it. My Stormhost is known for charging heedless into peril but I will not be another Thostos Bladestorm, throwing away my strength and that of my warriors to no benefit at all. We must be wiser than that.'

'Lord-Celestant, what are your orders?' asked Lord-Castellant Sundershield. 'We stand ready to fight.'

'And fight we shall, but not without plan and purpose,' she replied. 'Captain Vargi, do you still possess any of those devices that your admiral fashioned? The communication crystals?'

'Current inventory of the *Shieldmaiden*'s assets includes four of those devices,' he said without missing a beat. 'What do you want with them?'

'I would ask that you loan us two of them, captain. Should they be damaged or destroyed, you will be reimbursed,' Thunderblade said.

'That sounds reasonable,' replied Vargi after a calculated pause. 'But to what end?'

'Just set us down as close to the feet of the mountain as you dare, captain,' said Thunderblade. 'Then withdraw to whatever you consider a safe distance but remain on station. And ensure that you have both of the remaining devices active and to hand. Will you accede to do this?'

Bronvynne thought that the captain was going to continue haggling, and she felt frustration boil within her. Couldn't he see the bigger picture? Could this self-serving profiteer not even see beyond the end of his own nose?

'The *Shieldmaiden* will set you down as close as I deem safe,

255

but you must make your own way from there,' he said at last, his words counterpointed by the crack of lightning and the rising roar of battle from below. 'We'll wait at a safe distance for as long as we're able and, should you signal us, we will make every reasonable effort to reach your position and extract you. Do we have an accord?'

'We do,' said Thunderblade and for a moment Bronvynne felt relief. Then the Lord-Celestant went on. 'In addition, you will keep Bronvynne Karrobeth and Laszlo Tove safe aboard your craft until the battle is done. In the event that we fail, you will bear them to Azyrheim that they might deliver what warning they can.'

Bronvynne had been expecting this, yet still Thunderblade's words stung her. The thought of plunging into all that horror and death filled her with dread, but how could she turn aside from her duty now?

'Lord-Celestant, you need me down there,' she said firmly.

'You have done enough, and I have few enough warriors left as it is,' Thunderblade replied, her tone brooking no argument. 'I cannot spare anyone to see to your safety, and amidst the battle now raging you will undoubtedly be killed. You will remain on the skyship.'

'I will *not*,' said Bronvynne. Not so long ago the thought of remonstrating with an armoured Stormcast Eternal might have made her afraid. She had faced worse these past days, though, and she knew to her core that she was right. 'You need me down there, Lord-Celestant. I have translated more than two-thirds of this tome, but mysteries remain unanswered! We don't know what that being is that holds the weapon, or whether it is possible to extract the weapon... or whether it can be destroyed if not, or even how... or... or Sigmar alone knows what else we *don't* know. I am the only person here with enough knowledge of the Mordavians and their ways to understand and respond to,

I don't know, whatever unexpected things may happen when you encounter the weapon.'

Bronvynne's frustration grew as she floundered. Sigmar damn it, she knew what she meant, knew how vital her knowledge might prove, but Thunderblade looked unmoved.

'Knowledge has its uses, Karrobeth, and you have aided us greatly in this quest. But I say again, you have done your part and if I take you with me into Mordavia again you will die.'

'What if you fail?' asked Bronvynne. 'What if you fail because you need to know something that I could have told you, need to understand some inscription or answer some question that my knowledge could have unlocked? How could any of us live with the knowledge that we didn't do everything we possibly could? You say I'll die down there but believe me, Lord-Celestant, that if you exile me aboard this skyship and then fall short of your goal, you will be condemning me to death just as surely.'

'She is only one unforged soul, Lord-Celestant,' said Sundershield, surprising Bronvynne with his support. 'Her loss would matter little, but her knowledge might make a great deal of difference.'

'Every death matters, Lord-Castellant,' said Thunderblade. 'Even if you care nothing for the lives of others, every death empowers Nagash and, in this place, the Mordavian Blade also. We have not the numbers left to fight our enemies and shield Karrobeth.'

'You won't have to. Where she goes, I go,' said Tove. Bronvynne felt a surge of relief and affection for her protector, warring with guilt and fear at the thought of dragging him again into harm's way.

'Wherever any of you are going, I would appreciate if you would do so before our fuel runs out,' said Vargi, his tone arch.

Thunderblade shook her head and closed her eyes, then made an irritated gesture of acquiescence. 'There is no more time to debate this. Karrobeth and Tove will join us, then, but I believe it will be your doom. Captain, please proceed.'

Stormcast Eternals and arkanauts scattered to make their preparations, leaving Bronvynne and Tove stood alone by the railing, forgotten. She looked up at him and he smirked, though his face was pale with fear.

'Don't waste your breath, Bronvynne. Not after that speech you gave the Lord-Celestant,' he said. 'I'll keep you alive as long as I can. Just make sure we're some bloody use, eh? I don't see much sense in dying down there for nothing.'

She had no words that she trusted herself to say. Instead, Bronvynne simply took his arm in hers, clutched the tome close to her chest, and let the cold wind snatch away her stinging tears as the skyship shuddered then began its descent.

Grey Seer Splichritt chittered with mad laughter as he was borne along atop a tide of verminous bodies. His litter bearers were all but hidden from sight by the ratmen that scrabbled around and over them, eyes bulging with the madness of the black hunger, jaws frothing with foam. Splichritt didn't know from where Thrykktwyst had gathered this vast swarm, and he didn't care. He knew only that they would be his weapon of absolute victory, fighting and dying until all of his enemies were annihilated and the kill-weapon was his for the taking.

His litter spilled out into a shallow ravine rimmed by ancient, teetering ruins. Ahead, Splichritt saw a plodding mass of plague-things blocking his advance. Warpfire throwers emerged from amidst the seething skaven hordes and unleashed gouts of roiling chemical flame that consumed skaven and plague-things alike. Rat ogors tore into the enemy lines like living battering rams, rending the enemy limb from limb even as their muscles wasted and their flesh sloughed beneath the kiss of the daemons' festering blades. By the time Splichritt reached the end of the ravine the enemy had been utterly overrun, they and the skaven they had slain buried beneath an avalanche of lank fur and scrabbling claws that buoyed him up and swept him on towards the looming mountain.

It was close now, Splichritt saw, perhaps a few streets away and towering higher by the moment. He saw insane jumbles of ragged architecture, streets wending upwards as steep as cliff-faces between yawning dark maws of masonry and jutting spars of stone. It was a surreal and disorienting sight, especially with the ghostly after-images of an altogether different fortress flickering and dancing around it.

On the other hand, Splichritt could see that scaling the mountain would be no problem at all for his verminous hordes. They would surge up through its shattered ruins and drive the dead-things from their roosts then claim the kill-weapon. It would be easy, Splichritt thought as he brimmed with insane overconfidence, as easy as claiming the blade for himself, subjugating Thrykktwyst as his slave and then overthrowing the Council of Thirteen. Perhaps he wouldn't have a council at all, once he ruled. Perhaps that quarrelsome gathering had had its day. He would be Splichritt, supreme over-master of all Skavendom and chosen prophet of the Horned Rat, and even the verminlords would bend the knee before his magnificence.

As though the thought had summoned it, Thrykktwyst leapt overhead, little more than an oily dark shadow with glowing eyes that sprang from shattered rooftop to shattered rooftop. As he went, the rat-daemon flung clawfuls of dark magic into the approaching plague-things. They exploded in roiling black fire-balls or fell to gory pieces as shards of shattered darkness chopped them apart.

A huge pack of bounding tentacular beasts burst from a steeply sloping street and ploughed into the skaven like rolling boulders. Furry bodies were flung high or crushed to paste as the foolishly grinning daemon beasts lashed and flailed and emitted incongruous hoots of joy. Several of the things were dragged down and hacked apart, their gleeful burbling turning mournful and hurt as blades and fangs and claws ripped at them. Yet more of the daemons ploughed on through the skaven swarm, slowing its momentum as they forged ahead with idiot determination. The air filled with a droning roar as dozens of bloated flies the size of rat ogres swept in over a mouldering row of buildings. They drifted down upon the skaven with deceptive slowness, then struck hard and vicious as the plague-things riding them threw shrunken heads full of poison and lashed about with diseased swords.

Splichritt's muzzle twitched into a sneer of disgust as several clawpacks of clanrats broke and were overrun.

'Bring-fetch more weapons! Slay-slay the fly-things! Forward! Kill-kill!'

Rippling cracks sounded from a nearby rooftop as a battery of jezzails opened fire. Their warpstone bullets left green streaks on the air as they punched into the fly-daemons and burst their bloated thoraxes like overripe fruit. Down the street a way, Splichritt saw a squadron of doomwheels career into the battle with warp lightning leaping from their projectors. The rats in their huge armoured wheels ran madly, driving the preposterous war engines on at breakneck speeds. Their warlock engineer pilots steered them straight into the thickest press of the fighting and skaven and daemon bodies alike were crushed beneath the hurtling machines.

Still the skaven surged onward. Their sheer impossible numbers lent them undeniable momentum, those further back pushing forward with manic determination and carrying those at the fore onward towards the mountain. The battle in the street was left behind, an island in a raging torrent as Splichritt was swept towards his goal.

He squeaked in shock as a vast fat plague-thing crashed through a ruin to his right and swung a sword as long as a warp light-ning cannon through the skaven masses. Hundreds of clanrats and stormvermin piled onto the monstrous daemon, sickening and dying by the dozen as they stabbed and bit at the thing and were soaked in its virulent juices. Yet still it was buried, and its muffled roars of outrage followed Splichritt as his unstoppable advance continued.

A hail of blazing skulls whipped low overhead as he rushed down another street. They screamed in unison as they arced up into the sky then plunged down to explode amidst the battling armies. A moment later they were reborn from the fires they had raised and sailed off again to strike elsewhere. Wild magic was on the air, Splichritt thought, unleashed by the enemy's sorcerers or his own foolish underlings. He neither knew nor cared. Some-where he heard the jagged toll of a screaming bell and wondered if rival grey seers had arrived amidst this endless swarm.

If so, he would subjugate or slay them soon enough. This victory would belong to Splichritt, and Splichritt alone.

One moment his litter was surging along a winding street between tall ruins, surrounded by a solid mass of rushing skaven. The next they all spilled out into an area of rubble hillocks and sheared stone, and Splichritt found himself staring straight up at the mountain's lowest slopes.

Elation filled him. Here, he thought, here was his moment of victory!

A thunderous groan carried through the air and he spun in time to see an impossibly vast tree with a slobbering maw in its trunk bearing down upon him. Its pox-riddled bark flexed and creaked as its bloated roots bore it forward as though it moved upon a nest of giant, flesh-pale worms. A man-thing ruin col-lapsed before its bulk, rock dust and flecks of rubble exploding out in a cloud as the gigantic tree-thing rumbled closer. Around and behind it came hordes of plague-creatures, while more rode in its nooks and hollows as though going to war atop some improbable siege-tower.

Mad fury and loathing filled Splichritt. Tall rivals were bad enough. Giant enemies who came between him and his rightful victory were considerably worse!

'Die-die!' the grey seer shrieked, raising his staff and sending bolt after bolt of warp lightning crackling through the night air. The bolts struck home with actinic fury to blast burned and blackened wood in all directions. Quarts of glopping yellowy-brown slime slopped from each wound he blasted. The giant tree-thing emitted a clotted rumble of pain. Yet it did not stop coming.

'Kill-kill the tree-thing! Kill-kill the plague-things! Kill-kill them all!' screeched Splichritt, dancing a jig of apoplexy as he continued to hurl lightning blasts at the approaching abomination. Thousands of skaven surged forward at his order and if those near the front had second thoughts as they neared their gruesome enemies, if some of them even tried to turn and scramble away with lips skinned back and eyes wide with fear? Well, they were carried headlong into the fray anyway, to vanish beneath the enormous, crushing roots.

The warp storm raged overhead, its winds hot and foetid, its blasts of lightning squealing and cracking as though the Horned One himself were gnawing upon the still-living bones of the realms. Its fury was joined by coruscating orbs of warp lightning, fired from a thrumming battery of cannons. The blasts tore massive wounds in the tree-thing's bark hide, but still it came on. Skaven and plague-things were now battling all around it, fighting tooth and nail up and down the rubble foothills of the mountain, scrambling and stabbing amidst the tree-thing's lower branches.

Splichritt knew that he was the only one here with the might and intellect to stop the ridiculous daemon-tree before it crashed headlong into the mountain and spilled plague-things all over its slopes. Reluctantly he snatched another chunk of warpstone from a belt pouch and stuffed it into his mouth, crunching down and feeling weakened fangs splinter. Pain wracked his body and he whined and drummed his footclaws as he felt hot knives trying to stab their way out through his flesh. Several succeeded, blackened bone spurs ripping their way out of his skin and robes to drip blood onto the floor of his litter. Yet he mastered the power, moulded it even as green flashes exploded across his vision and fire burned through his veins.

The grey seer screeched out the holy words of the Great Horned Rat and twisted his claws into a forked sigil of ruin. As his chittering reached a crescendo the ground before his litter shuddered then cracked wide open. Poisonous light spilled up from the fuming rent as it split wider and raced away from him towards the tree-thing's roots. Hundreds of skaven screeched in dismay as the ground yawned beneath them and swallowed them up. Plague-things and their goat-thing allies gave wails of alarm as they followed their verminous foes down the glowing crevasse, and then the cracks reached the enormous tree and raced up through its roots and across its straining bark. The thing's maw yawned wide and it gave a shuddering groan of agony as Splichritt's sorcerous rift spread up its flank like a fault line.

Splichritt held the spell until he could bear it no longer then collapsed with a final shriek. The horrible glare winked out. The crack became just that, a natural, if deep and jagged, rent. The tree-thing shuddered then sagged as branches creaked and fell away to crash to the ground. The plague-things gave a moan of dismay as gallons of diseased ichor pumped from the massive wound in the tree-thing's trunk.

Splichritt staggered to his feet, his fur smouldering, his vision tinged green. He looked upon the grievous wounds he had wrought with glee, dismissing the tree-thing as surely moments from death. After all, nothing could withstand the pre-eminent might of Splichritt's magics and live!

'Now-now, strike-slay them all!' he screeched, his voice hoarse and broken. The kill-weapon was as good as his.

His heart thundered in his ears, its pounding growing louder and louder until he thought with horror that perhaps he had at last pushed even his supreme physique too far. Then Splichritt realised that the pounding was not only sounding in *his* ears. All around him his swarm hesitated, skaven cocking their heads, twitching their tails, emitting squirts of fear-musk as they tried to determine where the thunderous sounds were coming from.

The ground shook, then shook again and Splichritt screeched as a ruin not twenty feet to his left came down in a sudden avalanche. Something huge loomed through its whirling dust and for a foolish instant he expected to see a second impossible tree-thing bearing down upon him.

Instead, Splichritt saw a massive man-thing, the tallest, biggest most brutish looking man-thing he'd ever seen. The grey seer experienced a moment of sublime bemusement as he realised the newcomer held a tree-trunk in its fist, and that lashed to its end was a rope flail ending in several bludgeoned carcasses of four-legged man-thing meat-beasts.

More impossibly tall, impossibly powerful foes. More challengers for Splichritt's glory. Any sane creature would have felt naked terror as the monsters bore down upon them. Instead, Splichritt bared his shattered fangs in a ferocious snarl, raised his staff and unleashed another storm of lurid green lightning.

He would be Splichritt, much-magnificent over-master of all Skavendom. No one, absolutely no one, would stop him from seizing the glory that was rightfully his!

CHAPTER FOURTEEN

THE MOUNTAIN

Mordavia, the stolen dawn of the campaign's fourth day

Kalyani sprinted along the street, riding out the ground-shaking footfalls of the mega-gargant close on her heels. She sensed rather than saw the enormous fist come whistling down from on high, and threw herself aside. She crashed shoulder first through a crumbling wall and rolled to her feet amidst a cloud of dust. The ground jumped as the monster's huge fist smashed into the cobbled street, then swept sideways into her refuge with surprising speed. She dived aside again as the gnarled boulder of meat, gristle and bone demolished the ruin. Kalyani scrambled through a doorway, spun to lash out and score a red line across the mega-gargant's knuckles with Song, then turned and ran again. She burst out of the hollow back entrance of the ruin and ran on towards the mountain that loomed high ahead of her.

At her back the mega-gargant rose up and gave a furious bellow, shaking its wounded fist and spitting an unintelligible curse as it caught sight of her and gave chase. She risked a glance back and saw more of the enormous monsters close behind it. Their long strides ate up the distance with terrifying speed; though they lumbered like overweight drunkards, they moved fast as a galloping dracolion and were gaining on her fast.

'Sigmar lend me the wind at my heels and the storm in my heart,' she panted, wishing for the speed of a Knight-Zephyros as she ran hard. 'Let the others have evaded harm, and for all the Heavens' sakes don't let those massive brutes lose interest in the chase before I want them to.'

She could have left it to chance, could have relied upon the rampaging brutes being drawn naturally into the fighting that raged through Mordavia's streets. She had even caught sight of more than one greenskin warband or knot of gore-encrusted ogors still fighting amidst the streets and ruins as the *Shieldmaiden* came in low on its approach; she could have relied upon them to direct their fury where she wanted it to go.

Kalyani Thunderblade didn't leave things to chance. She would not rely upon the anarchic orruks to direct such a pivotal part of her plan. For all she knew the mega-gargants and the greenskins might not even be on the same side, and never mind the drumbeat that had bedevilled Mordavia for days on end. Sons of Behemat, Vargi had called them, and while Kalyani was no scholar of the Realmgate Wars she knew the names of the slain godbeasts well enough. That entity had not served Gorkamorka, so why should his lost sons?

No, Kalyani had been determined to direct matters herself. Yet she also hadn't wanted to risk the entire endeavour upon one highly risky plan. Her warriors had insisted that between them, they would be able to lead the mega-gargants much more reliably down upon the battle around the mountain's feet, and with less peril. Kalyani had forbidden it; if she was crushed for her foolishness then so be it, Lord-Castellant Sundershield would have to find another way of forging a path through the warring armies to the mountain. If they all fell in the name of her plan, who would remain to see duty done?

All of which noble sentiments had found Kalyani Thunderblade questioning her own sanity as she ran pell-mell through the streets of a dead city with sixty-foot-tall flesh-eating monsters pursuing her. She wondered at the part of herself that wanted to turn and fight them, even now, just her alone testing her martial might against these insurmountable foes. She remembered her bladesister Anjalia, how she had sought to perfect her prowess by forging the ultimate killing-blade, how the entity she bound within it had claimed her and transformed her into Anjalia the Butcher. Kalyani remembered bells tolling and bodies bobbing in the bloody surf below the jetties as she had fought to defend the last of her tribe against the possessed monster that had once been their greatest hero.

Sigmar had snatched her away from that impossible duel in a blaze of coruscating lightning, the last of her people fleeing into deeper waters as Anjalia raged and spat. Kalyani was the only one of her tribe's warriors not to die that day. Not truly, at any rate, but rather reforged, then and only then.

Kalyani still saw in her mind's eye the tragic consequences of pursuing martial might and glory without purpose or sanity. It was what had kept her alive and fighting all these years while her brothers and sisters fell and were reforged and fell again, and slowly lost themselves to Sigmar's never-ending war. It was what kept her running now, even though the battle-lust that crackled in her blood screamed at her to turn and fight, fight, *fight*.

'I will not be Anjalia,' she spat through gritted teeth, then yelled and pinwheeled her arms as the ground bucked beneath her feet. One of the mega-gargants must had stomped down hard in an attempt to knock her from her feet. To their credit, as she chased her centre of balance up the street with grim desperation, it very nearly succeeded. Kalyani heard another furious roar from behind her as she managed to keep running, then hissed in alarm as a lump of masonry the size of a shack slammed into the ground behind her, bounced clean overhead and smashed ruinously into the hollow remains of an old shrine. She dodged around the devastation feeling that soon her luck must run out. Yet now, ahead, she could hear the fury of the battle between the skaven and the plague daemons.

Surely the mega-gargants would hear it too, she thought.

'Hammer and blade, they can probably *see* it from up there,' she told herself, still running flat out as she looked for an escape route. Sure enough they let out bellows of challenge that were swallowed up by the screaming winds and the raging fury of the battle ahead. Their pounding footfalls made rubble tumble down from time-gnawed ruins and almost drove Kalyani from her feet a third time before finally she was able to duck into a narrow side alley as she ran beneath a wide stone arch.

Knowing she couldn't just cower there and hope, Kalyani ran down the alleyway. Her nerves jangled at the thought that she was now running across the mega-gargants' path of advance rather than away. At any second she expected them to smash through the ruins to her left and crush her into the ground. Their booming footfalls drew closer and she began to feel frantic as the cramped alleyway seemed to wend on without break or change for an impossible distance.

Suddenly, ahead of her she saw a dark gulf where a narrow ravine had split the alleyway in two.

'Praise Sigmar,' she said as she launched herself into a sliding skid and dropped into the throat of the ravine.

Her escape came not a moment too soon; Kalyani dropped a

good ten feet and landed in a fighting crouch amidst a ragged break of ferns. An instant later the world exploded into rubble and wreckage above her as massive, bellowing figures ploughed overhead. Ignoring the stones and dust that clattered down around her, Kalyani scrambled along the base of the narrow, foliage-choked gulley over the empty armour and fallen weapons of those slain by the Mordavian Blade the day before. Soon she was able to see out from the gulley's end directly into the area of open ruin that had once been Old Temple square.

Her eyes widened at the carnage already raging around the mountain's feet. She couldn't begin to count the foes clashing there amidst spoil-heaps of ancient rubble and newly raised hillocks of the dead. Couldn't they feel the murderous energies pulsing from the mountain's peak? she wondered. Didn't they realise that they were feeding the weapon a banquet of power that would surely be their undoing?

Or its own, said a small voice in her mind, and she quickly quashed the spark of hope she felt at those words.

Kalyani saw a tiny grey seer unleash its devastating magical assault upon the impossibly overgrown gnarlmaw, saw the grotesquely bloated tree shudder and spray its diseased fluids across combatants from both sides.

Then the mega-gargants crashed into the fight.

To her amazement, Kalyani watched as the grey seer turned towards the nearest brute and, rather than fleeing in terror, began flinging bolts of green-black lightning at it while shrieking and chittering like a maniac. Its first lightning bolt blew a bloody chunk from the mega-gargant's hip. The second scorched its chest and caused it to bellow in pain. The third hit it square in the face, and for a surreal instant Kalyani thought that the runtish ratman would succeed in besting one of the Sons of Behemat.

Then, blinded and bellowing, it tripped over the smouldering wreck of a skaven war engine. It teetered precipitously upon the edge of balance for a heart-stopping moment, then fell forward and came down to crush the grey seer and its war litter like a fleshy avalanche.

Kalyani winced as the impact threw bodies and broken stone high into the air.

'Well, that should help spread a little confusion,' she muttered to herself and set off for the rendezvous point.

She found her comrades precisely where they had arranged to meet. They crouched upon the topmost floor of a tall stone tower with distinctive scythe-brandishing gargoyles that Kalyani had spotted during the skyship's approach. As Kalyani hauled herself up through a wide crack and into their refuge, she found herself facing the unwavering points of two glimmering arrows, four sigmarite swords and three long stormstrike glaives.

The Stormcasts withdrew their weapons as they recognised their leader. They stood respectfully back while Lord-Castellant Sundershield grasped her forearm and helped her to clamber up into the shadowy space.

'There were losses,' she said, looking around.

'Three more to meet beyond the Anvil,' replied Sundershield, his voice devoid of emotion. 'A band of skaven tried to overrun us in a street just south of here. They failed. None escaped to raise the alarm.'

'Evidently,' replied Kalyani, looking around. 'Where are Karrobeth and Tove?'

'Here, Lord-Celestant,' came Tove's voice from a nook beyond what might once have been a chimney breast. She walked around to find Tove peering out of an empty window at the battle raging around the mountain's feet. Karrobeth huddled against the wall and looked at nothing.

'Scholar Karrobeth, are you still with us?' Kalyani asked. The old woman looked up at the sound of her name and offered a wan smile, but it was brittle. *She's near her limit, and this was a mistake,* Kalyani thought. Still, they were here now and there was nothing any of them could do about it. They would live or die by the God-King's grace.

'We need to move, while our enemies are distracted,' she said.

'They're more than distracted,' Tove replied, sounding awed. 'Great Sigmaron above, would you look at this butchery!'

Kalyani spared a glance out of the window and was pleased to see even more ferocity than she had imagined. Several of the giant creatures were battering at the oversized gnarlmaw, ripping off branches and stamping on plague daemons as though they were disgusting insects. More had waded into the skaven swarm and driven it back, leaving a trail of verminous corpses and smashed war engines in their wake.

The massive creatures weren't having it all their own way; several lay slain, their flesh blackening and sloughing with rot or else riddled with warp blasts and glowing craters. Still, they had more than achieved her aim of forcing the combat away from the route her small force was to take.

'We will not have a better chance than this,' said Rojavi Sundershield. 'We must make for the foot of the mountain and ascend.'

Kalyani nodded, gesturing for Tove to get Karrobeth on her feet and then dropping back down through the hole to lead her followers into harm's way.

They emerged into the full howling fury of the storm winds. Livid lightning exploded overhead; in its flash-flare the corpse-heaps, the bubbling pools of diseased slime and the devastated ruins of collapsed buildings were all lit up in excruciating detail. Ash billowed about her, and Kalyani thrust aside the question of whose remains she might be breathing in.

She had already picked out her route, running along the back of a ruined structure, leapfrogging between two huge rubble heaps then making a last dash for the concealing tangle of bastardised buildings and tunnels on the mountain's lower slopes.

Here and there, bands of skaven and plague daemons still fought while more ratmen picked over the heaped dead. None was too close at this moment, however.

'Sigmar, lend us whatever aid you may,' she prayed. Glancing behind to see that Sundershield, their nine remaining warriors and the two unforged were with her, she set off.

'Don't stray too close to the pools of filth,' she heard Sundershield hiss as they hastened along the back of the ruin.

'The taint of the Plague God cannot harm us,' a Liberator replied with a hint of scorn.

'It can and will, and that is to say nothing of our human companions,' Sundershield chastised him sternly.

'Silence,' hissed Kalyani as she reached the corner of the ruined structure and looked out across the twenty yards of open ground between her and the first heap of rubble. Bodies lay everywhere, a thick carpet of diseased corpses and butchered meat that surely couldn't help but afflict them all with the vile curses of either Nurgle, the Horned Rat or both.

'Follow, swift, quiet and low,' she whispered then broke from cover and crossed the open ground at a run while staying bent double. At any moment Kalyani expected to hear the chittering of skaven or the groans of plague daemons, but they did not come. The storm screamed and raged overhead. Unnatural lightning lashed down to blast rooftops into spinning wreckage and start furious black-green fires which the wind fanned further. Pulses of malignant energy beat down from the mountain's summit, filling Kalyani with a desperate sense of urgency lest the weapon be unleashed again.

Away to her right, the enormous gnarlmaw succeeded in tripping and then crushing one of the mega-gargants. Poisonous sap gushing down its flanks, it slammed itself into the mountain's base; daemons swarmed from its remaining branches, trying to evade the clubbing blows of the remaining giants as they scrambled up the slopes. Not a hundred yards distant Kalyani's enemies were still hacking one another apart, but by pure good fortune none spotted the small band of Stormcasts and humans slipping through their midst.

Kalyani repeated her warning before they crossed the gap between the first rubble heap and the second, but again luck was with them. Then, as they crouched in the cover of the second body-strewn hillock of broken stone, that luck ran out. Amidst a chorus of triumphant squealing and chittering, several bands of skaven converged on an outnumbered cohort of plague daemons that had been fighting nearby and overwhelmed them entirely. Panting hard, the ratmen fell upon the corpses of their own dead and wounded, greedily devouring their flesh to satiate their unholy hunger.

'They are still distracted,' said Sundershield. 'We could slip past, or else simply cut our way through them.'

'They are no more than twenty yards from our route, halfway between us and the mountain,' Kalyani replied. 'If we try to slip past them, they cannot fail to see us and attack.' She knew that, despite himself, Lord-Castellant Sundershield was hoping for just that. Stealth was not the way of their Stormhost and his warrior spirit craved an honest fight. Kalyani knew because she felt the same. As she had done a hundred times before she remembered Anjalia's monstrous visage twisted by insane battle-lust and thought, *I will never become her.*

'If we fight them, they will slay us,' she said.

'Then let me distract them,' he replied. 'I will slip back to the first of these heaps of wreck and ruin, work my way east from it as far as I can before they spot me, then keep them busy while you pass behind their backs.'

'You understand that Reforging is not always successful, or even possible, yes?' she asked him wryly.

'I may best them,' he said stoutly.

'There are more than a hundred of them, Rojavi. You will not.'

'I may,' he repeated, though she knew he did not believe it any more than her.

'Take the Protectors with you, and then you may,' she said. She could tell that Sundershield was offended, even with his helm hiding his expression.

'I offer to sacrifice my own life, not those of others,' he said.

'And yet that sacrifice will be worthless if you do not present enough of a target to hold the ratmen's attention,' she said. Turning to the Protectors she asked, 'Do any of you wish to be excused this duty?' The three Paladins shook their heads.

'We do as Sigmar wills. We fight, we kill, we win,' one of them replied.

'Lord-Celestant, the tides of battle flow again. We must move soon or be engulfed,' said a Judicator who had scaled a short way up the rubble heap to keep watch. She pointed to where fresh waves of skaven were sweeping around from the eastern flank of the mountain and driving mega-gargants and daemons alike before them.

'Damn it. The four of you, go now and go with Sigmar's grace,' Kalyani ordered. Rojavi Sundershield and his three Protectors offered her a warrior's salute and set off, making a quick dash back across the open ground. Kalyani watched from concealment as the skaven feasting slowed. Some glanced up nervously at the battlefront grinding its way towards them. Others scented the air now their hunger was sated, snouts twitching and large ears turning this way and that as they sought danger or fresh victims.

'Hurry, Rojavi, hurry,' she muttered.

Closer the battle raged, screeching waves of vermin throwing themselves at daemons and mega-gargants. Even as she watched, Kalyani saw one of the titanic monsters stagger as skaven swarmed up its shins while bolts of warp lightning blasted its chest and face. It fell with a rumbling crash and was overrun by the swarm, who drove the thinning plague daemons back even more swiftly.

The nearby skaven had all stopped eating now. The largest of them was snarling orders, gesticulating with its blade as it attempted to bully its warriors back into line. Some complied but others cringed and tried to slink away. More than a dozen made straight for the rubble heap behind which the Stormcasts crouched and Kalyani felt her heart sink. In moments they would have no choice but to fight. Perhaps she and a handful of her warriors could still make the mountain, but she didn't like their odds. The fires inside her rose hungrily and she gripped Song tight, preparing to spill as much blood as she could before the end.

'We fight for Sigmar!' came Rojavi Sundershield's battle cry. The skaven looked around in alarm at the sudden yell, then bared their fangs as they saw a mere four warriors burst from cover and charge towards them. Skaven prefer overwhelming odds, and Kalyani saw their leader's muzzle split in a calculating leer as it realised that it could legitimately lead its warriors against this apparently doomed handful of warriors instead of plunging back into the main fury of the battle.

They will not prove the easy prey you think, vermin, she thought angrily and for a moment she wrestled with the impulse to rise from concealment and howl a battle cry of her own. Even as the skaven charged down upon Sundershield and his Paladins she and her remaining warriors could hit them in the flank and–

A shuddering pulse of dark power flowed down from above, so malevolent that it made Kalyani stagger. The skaven cowered.

Sundershield took the chance to lead his Protectors headlong into them. Now was the moment, Kalyani's last chance to prise that monstrous weapon from the hands of the foe.

Biting her lip until she tasted blood, she forced herself to start running for the foot of the mountain and hoped that the last of her band were following.

Bronvynne ran as hard as she could. The Stormcasts outpaced her in seconds, pounding away across the open ground amidst flashes of green lightning and the shrieks and clangour of battle. Tove stayed with her, though, good, loyal Laszlo Tove, and she hated herself for putting him in danger.

I had to come, she thought to herself angrily. *I had to come, I might know something useful, like how to lag behind and get us both killed. Stupid, stubborn old woman!*

She ran with all her strength, but by now it wasn't much. Her knees felt like they might pop like cashva nuts in a cookfire. Vicious, aching pain pulsed from her shins, her ankles, her back. Unclean filth had splattered up her robes and burned where it smeared her skin. With every ragged breath she expected to hear verminous shrieks as she and Tove were spotted, to feel tearing agony as blades or fangs sank into her flesh. Her progress seemed painfully slow, as though she ran through deep water in the grip of a roiling nightmare. So all-consuming had the roar of battle become that it overwhelmed her senses and left her stumbling along deaf and blind. She flinched as she felt a hand gripping her, but it was just Laszlo, helping her along as best he could. He had his sword drawn and his eyes were wild with panic.

There came another lurid volley of lightning, another unholy pulse of malevolent energies from above, and Bronvynne felt her footing slip in a slick of reeking slime. Tove half-caught her and they stumbled forward, sure to fall. Panic filled her in a wordless wail then something caught her, pulled her upright and forward into darkness and numbing cold.

Bronvynne blinked stupidly before realising that it was the Lord-Celestant that had grabbed her. Gasping and shaking, Bronvynne let herself be half-lifted and borne swiftly into the concealing shadows of an ancient archway that had now become a cave mouth.

'You yet live, Karrobeth,' said Thunderblade. Bronvynne looked up at her gratefully but couldn't manage words.

'Did any of them see us?' panted Laszlo, crouching behind the broken lintel.

'If they had, we would be beset by now,' Kalyani replied.

'Thank Sigmar,' Laszlo said, sinking lower and closing his eyes.

'Save your thanks for now, for we have a long hard road yet ahead of us,' said Thunderblade. 'There is no time for rest. We must make for the summit at once and be ready to fight any foe that bars our path.'

Bronvynne felt utter exhaustion drag at her as she thought of the climb they must now make, up hundreds of feet of tangled wreckage and perilous masonry cliffs. To even attempt it would be the death of her, she knew that, but as she felt the feverish chill running through her body and the bird-like fluttering of her heart she suspected she might not have all that long to live regardless. One did not endure the touch of the Plague God's foulness without consequence.

'What of the Lord-Castellant? Should we not give him a chance to rejoin us?' asked one of the Stormcasts, but the Lord-Celestant shook her head.

'You know that will not happen, Lucio. If you would honour his sacrifice, then move swiftly and do not look back. We climb, now.'

'Lord-Celestant, I may be able to make this ascent but Bronvynne…' Laszlo's voice trailed off helplessly, then he broke into a bout of wet coughing and Bronvynne felt another stab of guilt.

Tove must be sickening also, and those afflicted by the unholy malaises of Nurgle did not live to speak of it to others.

I brought him to this, she thought miserably as the crash and roar of battle washed across them. *I dragged him into this nightmare, and for what? We shall both die here, abandoned at the foot of this ruined peak and our end shall count for nothing at all.* Tears leaked from the corners of her closed eyes, but as they trickled down her cheeks Bronvynne felt a sudden flare of defiant anger.

She would not end like this, old and pathetic and useless. She might not be some warrior hero but the knowledge she possessed was as potent a weapon as any blade, perhaps more so. She didn't know how Lief had met his end, and she had spent half her life obsessing over it when she should have been focusing on her own purpose, her own deeds and wants. She was a bloody arcanotranslocutor, for Sigmar's sakes! Now *her* deeds were what mattered, and what she wanted was to see an end to the cursed weapon that had caused so much bloodshed and sorrow.

'I will climb the bloody mountain even if it kills me,' she said, her voice weak but defiant.

'And kill you it certainly will, but you will not need to make the climb yourself,' replied the Lord-Celestant. 'Lucio, Bastus, you will bind Karrobeth and Tove to your backs for this ascent. We cannot afford for them to slow us down.'

At another time, Bronvynne might have railed against being manhandled like baggage. Now, at this desperate end, she welcomed it as Sigmar's holy warriors lifted her up and bound her in place with strong starweave cord drawn from their belt-pouches. She made sure that her tome was lashed firmly to her body beneath her sodden, slime-spattered robes then allowed herself to drift.

Bronvynne's impressions of the climb were broken and fragmented, surging in with feverish intensity before receding again like a tide.

A sense of dangling over a great drop as something hard and heavy moved behind her, jabbing hard edges into her aching flesh.

A ragged rock chimney sliding past on all sides while grunts of effort and the clink of metal on metal echoed in the half-light.

Her eyes opening upon a sudden wheeling gulf; far below the sight of armies crashing together like warring oceans; pyrotechnic blasts lighting the night as spells of unimaginable power were unleashed; blazing black-green fires consuming ancient ruins and fern forests far below, sending acrid black smoke boiling into the air.

Another moment of vertigo but this time shouting voices, violent movement, the thrum of huge wings and the howl and scream of damned things; something ethereal and half-seen swooping towards her, its face a yawning skull, swept away as something rotten and huge slammed into it from the side in a jumble of gangling limbs.

War cries. Screaming. Darkness.

'…Bronvynne. Bronvynne, come on, old girl, don't die on me now, eh?'

She blinked and weakly waved away the hand that was patting at her cheek. Thunder roared and lightning flashed green so alarmingly close that her heart almost missed a beat. She sat up with a gasp, and Laszlo sat hurriedly back to avoid her.

'Where are we? What's happened?' she croaked. The words rasped hot in her dry throat.

'We're near the peak and if we're to be any use at all it's now,' said Laszlo. Bronvynne blinked again, dragging in breaths and shaking her head to chase the drowsiness from her brain. She realised she was tucked in between a couple of large chunks of stone that jutted up from a narrow platform formed surreally from cracked cobblestones. The sky raced huge and menacing, alarmingly close above her head, and as another jag of emerald lightning split the clouds it made her cry out in shock.

The wind howled and Bronvynne was confronted with a sudden vertiginous realisation that she was very, very far from the ground. Now she understood why Laszlo's face was so white, why he clung to the stone that sheltered her with such white-knuckled intensity.

'They got us to the top?' she asked, throat still red raw and voice faltering.

'Near enough, then left us here and pressed on for the summit,' he said. 'Thunderblade told me to get you back into the land of the living if I could, then we were to follow.'

'Why didn't they wait?' asked Bronvynne, annoyed despite everything.

Laszlo paused as though marshalling his thoughts, then words spilled quick from his lips.

'About halfway up the ghasts realised we were coming up. We stayed out of the way by climbing inside the tunnels and shafts and whatnot where we could but... aye, couldn't stay hidden all the time and so there they were, suddenly coming at us.'

'I... think I remember something...' said Bronvynne with a shudder.

'Then the plague daemons were there too and Thunderblade just orders everyone to keep climbing, just defend ourselves but otherwise just keep going, let them fight each other, make for the peak. It was... desperate. Terrifying. I'm swinging my sword as best I can and the Stormcasts are doing their best to fight and climb at the same time. I swear to Sigmar if the ghasts and the daemons hadn't been fighting each other...'

His voice trailed off, and Bronvynne realised Laszlo's hands were shaking violently, his skin milk pale. Sickness or shock, she wondered? Perhaps both.

'But it worked, we survived, made it up,' she said, trying to sound encouraging even as her voice came out in a thin wheeze.

'Some of us did,' he replied darkly. 'By Sigmar's grace the

Stormcasts carrying us made it, so did Thunderblade and one of them with bows. The rest are gone.'

'Heavens preserve us,' gasped Bronvynne.

'P'rhaps they did,' said Laszlo, shaking his head slowly. 'We'd all have died, I know it, but suddenly the ghasts all gave this sort of scream and went flying upwards and the flies followed them, all still fighting. By that time the rats are coming up the mountain too, thousands of them gaining on us. Sigmar knows they can't be that far behind now. I keep expecting them to pop up over the edge of the ledge and…. well… And the Lord-Celestant shouts about hearing the sounds of battle, that someone had got there before us and now we had to move fast as we could. That's a few minutes ago.'

'And now we're here, and danger is on its way from below, and they're up above us fighting who knows what,' said Bronvynne, urgency driving back the cloying sensations of sickness and exhaustion that threatened to cast her back into the void. It would have been so good to let herself fall, but she couldn't, not now. If she did her comrades would die, and the last thing she would feel would be fangs gnawing into her flesh, claws scrabbling at her robes. The thought made her shudder with revulsion.

Dizziness threatened to pitch her backwards as Bronvynne hauled herself to her feet. Standing, she could see just how narrow was the ledge upon which they perched, how near and hungry the drop into open air. Mordavia sprawled far below, a bas-relief map seething with still-warring armies whose numbers turned the streets and ruins dark. The wind screamed and tugged at her hair and robes.

Bronvynne looked up and saw one last sheer slope of compacted stonework and statuary, above which loomed the dark faces of the awful altar. Pulses of pure malice beat down from atop it, and she realised that the storm clouds overhead boiled with warring ghasts and fly-riding daemons. She could not imagine how she and Laszlo could possibly climb up to it without being snatched away by the gale. Panic gripped her, the awful sense of having been borne up to a place she could not have reached by herself and from which there was no way she could safely descend. Her throat tried to close, and her breath came in hitching gasps.

Laszlo was there again, hands gentle but firm on her shoulders, his smile false but brave in its attempt.

'I know, eh? This is a battle for mighty heroes, in the sort of place that legend will make glorious but in truth is just a bloody nightmare. There's a sheltered stairway, all cocked sideways and broken but it's the route Thunderblade took towards the top. It'll serve us just as well.'

The wind lulled for a moment as though drawing breath to scream again. The sounds of battle reached Bronvynne's ears then, floating down from above. And from below, all too close, she thought she heard the nightmarish scrabble of claws.

'Come along then, Laszlo. What other choice do we have?' she asked, joining in the feeble game of false bravado that he had begun. It was move or freeze, and the latter meant a certain and horrible death.

'Stairway is over here, for Sigmar's sakes stay pressed up against the wall or the wind'll have you,' he said. Bronvynne thought how redundant his warning was; she wouldn't have unpeeled herself from the solid reassurance of the rubble wall for all the gold in Azyrheim.

Together they worked their way along the wall, Bronvynne hissing in fear at each vicious gust of wind that tried to snatch her up and whirl her into the void. Laszlo stepped up to what looked like an edge then vanished around the corner, causing her heart to almost stop. Shaking, she made herself take another step, then another until she reached the edge herself. Laszlo's hand came back around and took hers.

'Just step round now, I've got you,' he said. Bronvynne didn't look down, didn't think where she was stepping. Feeling panic about to overwhelm her entirely and hearing the blood pounding in her ears, she stepped out and followed the sound of Laszlo's voice. For a sickening moment Bronvynne's foot seemed to fish in open air, then she felt stone beneath her and staggered another step. She was standing on a steeply canted stone stairway, the ragged remains of a heavy stone wall still clinging to its outer edge in seeming defiance of natural laws. Just beyond it, the ghostly after-images of another wall flickered, ethereal flames dancing in long-departed sconces.

'You see, easy,' said Laszlo with a nauseous smile, which vanished as the wind screamed and the stairway shook. Chunks of stonework crumbled away from its outer edge and whirled away into the void. Thin cracks ran through the steps, which seemed to settle a few inches lower.

'We can't stay here,' said Bronvynne, heart thumping so hard it must surely burst through her aged ribs.

Taking one another's hand, the aged scholar and her bodyguard-turned-friend hastened up the shuddering stairway, towards where the last battle for Mordavia raged.

CHAPTER FIFTEEN

MORDAVIA'S FATE

Above Mordavia, the stolen dawn of the campaign's fourth day

Kalyani paused near the top of the stairway to take the measure of her foes. She and her last few warriors had one chance at this. To rush in blindly was to invite disaster.

Above her rose the altar, flanked by towering black columns that stayed upright in defiance of the screaming winds that clawed at them. Ghasts and daemons tumbled through the skies above and whirled in mad battle around the altar's upper levels. Atop the awful structure she saw the abomination, perched at its very apex and seemingly untouched by storm and gale alike. The Mordavian Blade pulsed in its grip, the energies rolling from it so unclean that even from here Kalyani felt as though ice-cold fingers scrabbled at her flesh, trying to burrow their way in.

How much death had fed that blade now? she wondered. Who knew whether the banishment of daemons fuelled the weapon as the passing of mortal lives did, but even if not then the feast of slaughter it had enjoyed must surely have been immense. Could it even be stopped now? Could she and her warriors successfully seize the weapon? Perhaps now was the time that Karrobeth had spoken of, when the blade's powers were at their peak and its focus rendered it momentarily mortal. Would destroying the Mordavian Blade unleash its energies? Could it even be done?

Karrobeth might have been able to tell her, but she'd been forced to abandon the senseless scholar a level below and she doubted now that she would see her again. Chances were, they would all be dead before that.

Moving through the midst of the mayhem, his progress steady and inexorable, was a heavyset plague daemon sat upon an enormous daemonic snail. He left a bubbling trail of slime behind him as he flowed up the altar steps. Any ghast that dared bar his way was lopped apart by his snicking, screeching shears. Kalyani knew the name Horticulus Slimux, had heard of Nurgle's Gardener who planted seeds of woe across the Mortal Realms. Now here he was in the festering flesh and, as far as she could see, he was intent on seizing the blade in the Plague God's name.

'We cannot allow the daemon to claim the blade,' she told her surviving three warriors. 'We strike him down first, and then any of us who survive rush the abomination. Slay it if you can, but that is not our priority.'

'Then what?' asked Lucio.

'We seize the Mordavian Blade, but do not let your bare flesh touch it,' she said. 'We must get it away from this place and then dispose of it however we can.'

It wasn't much of a plan, she knew, but all else had fallen away or failed and now this was all that Kalyani could see to do.

'How do we get the blade away from this place? The skaven cannot be far behind,' asked Bastus.

In answer, Kalyani held up the crystal communicator she had

taken from Captain Vargi. The other had gone with Lord-Castellant Sundershield, and she prayed to Sigmar that this last device would work as she activated it.

'Captain Vargi, we have reached the crest of the mountain,' she said into the crystal. 'Our enemies battle each other. They are distracted. Please, in the name of the Heavens and whatever honour you hold true to, we can take the blade from the enemy, but you must get us away from here.'

Long silence followed her words. Kalyani ignored the stares of her warriors, the din of battle from above and the scream of the wind as she stared at the device, willing the duardin to answer. She was about to speak again when the crystal shimmered in her hand.

'*I didn't think you would make it this far, Lord-Celestant,*' came Vargi's nasal tones, made tinny as they resonated from the strange communicator. '*I can see that the foe are engaging one another, but the storm has closed in and will make flying perilous in the extreme.*'

'We are in the heart of it, we are aware,' snapped Kalyani as lightning crackled and screeched overhead. 'Just think of the payment you will be due, the contracts, the debts owed. You will be heroes, saviours of–'

'*We hold to the artycles, but we aren't monsters, Lord-Celestant,*' Vargi interrupted. '*Several of my crewmates have convinced me that in this instance, saving lives may be more important than protecting our profits. Besides, trade would suffer if all the cities of the Mortal Realms wound up looking like this, wouldn't it?*'

'You will come?' asked Kalyani, hope reigniting in her breast. She had prayed to Sigmar that the duardin had more honour than they liked to pretend, that even they wouldn't be so self-serving as to ignore a threat of this magnitude. When Vargi agreed to remain instead of simply turning tail and sailing for clear skies, she had believed she must be right. In the end, he had not disappointed her.

'*I don't promise anything, Lord-Celestant, but if we can reach you without risking the* Shieldmaiden *then we'll get you and that weapon out in one piece,*' he replied. The crystal went dark before she could say 'thank you'.

'You believe they will come?' asked Lucio.

'I must. What other hope is there?' asked Kalyani. 'But we were not forged for hoping and waiting, my Celestial Vindicators. We were forged for battle, and now, like never before, we fight!'

Banishing her doubts, Kalyani burst from cover and charged up the altar's steps.

'We fight! We kill! We win!' roared her warriors and followed her into battle.

Ghasts screamed and plunged down towards them. Kalyani sidestepped a flame-eyed skeleton horseman, whose steed's hooves echoed upon the winds and whose blazing scythe left after-images of fires long dead as it swung. The ghast gave a hollow cry as its blade missed her. Its steed reared, hooves flailing. She lunged low to drive her blade up through its ethereal form and into the rider atop it. It felt like thrusting her blade into densely packed layers of cobwebs and a numbing cold raced up her arm as she struck the blow. Still, Song pierced both steed and rider and, with a final wail, they both tattered away upon the wind.

A crackling arrow whipped over Kalyani's shoulder and struck another ghostly horseman from his saddle. A third and fourth leapt high over Kalyani and plunged down upon the Stormcasts at her back. A blazing scythe swung, and Kalyani cried out in dismay as the helmed head of Bastus bounced away down the steps. The Judicator's body was taken by the wind, bursting into lightning and flashing Heavensward as it tumbled away.

Kalyani ran on, the need for vengeance flowing through her, celestial wrath crackling in her eyes, her veins, along the blade of her sword.

'We fight!' she shouted, leaping to a higher level to avoid the swing of a plague daemon's sword. 'We kill!' she roared as she rammed her blade through its cyclopean eye, ripped it free again and kept running.

Lucio drew level with her, charging upwards with a furious roar and hacking his way through a knot of whirling ghasts. He took three more running steps through the filthy slime trail left by Horticulus' steed, and Kalyani saw that he meant to vault up onto the snail-monster's shell. Instead Lucio stumbled as though his limbs had grown suddenly weak. He staggered sideways, trying to get clear of the bubbling slime that Kalyani saw was now creeping up the legs of his armour and seeping in through the joints between the sigmarite plates. Lucio turned towards her as black veins of rot spread up from his gorget across his face and green slime dribbled from his nostrils, then he toppled sideways and disintegrated as his soul flashed away from his body.

Another comrade taken by horror and death, Kalyani thought, fighting down the sudden weariness that attempted to close its claws about her heart. *I will not give in to despair. I will see their deaths paid back a thousandfold.*

Horticulus was only two levels below the dais now, and as his snail-monster dragged itself higher on its stubby legs he pointed his heavy shears at the bone horror that clutched the weapon. When he spoke, his voice was the wet squelch of rotted matter and the harsh clatter of scything blades.

'*That ain't yours to 'av, spirit!*' shouted the daemon over the howl of the storm. '*Don't think I don't know what they be, little foettercrack. You'm one o' them guardian things bound up to guard these dankdrip places, ain't you? Grandfather whispered it into my waxy from the lips of a little worm, an' he don't never spittle-fib to me. So what you doin' wavin' it around when you shoulda been keepin' it dank'n'secret?*'

Kalyani hesitated despite herself. Guardian spirit? Keeping the weapon secret? What was this?

'*It… is… meeee… And I… am… ittttt…*' came the abomination's voice, issuing from within the yawning jaws of its rat-like skull as its eyes flashed. '*Long did I languish…. long denied my freeeee-dom… Then came the great… shattering….*'

'**And it rottenbreak'd thy wards, did it?**' sneered Horticulus, breaking off to rear high and drive his shears through a whirling ghast. '**But thou thought to take its power for y'self, didn't you? Tricked squirmly goodlike, you was!**'

The awful spirit unfolded its gangling bone limbs and pointed the blade straight at Horticulus.

'*I am not… a slaaaaave… any… more…*' it hissed furiously. '*I… wield the… blaaaaaaade…*'

'**Slave o' Old Bones instead, eh?**' sneered Horticulus, and Kalyani realised that the daemon was keeping the horror talking while his steed squirmed closer. Could those shears cut through the abomination's bony neck? Cursed weapons like those just might, she thought.

'*Slaaaave to… nonnnnne… I take its powerrrrr… as a gifffft…*'

'**Thou'st done enough to sour'n'soil the Garden, spirit,**' retorted Horticulus, spitting a sizzling wad of slime. '**I'm destroy that'n weapon, n'destroy thee with 'er.**'

Kalyani blinked, then ducked as a howling ghast swept down upon her. Furiously she swatted the dead thing away, spinning and hacking it to tatters with Song. *The daemon means to destroy the weapon too,* she thought, her mind racing. *Can it be true?*

What if Horticulus knew she was there, had seen her coming and sought to trick her into aiding him? What if his means of destroying the weapon would in itself bring misery and suffering to those she had sworn to protect? Yet as she looked around Kalyani saw that she was alone; the last of her warriors had fallen and now only she remained to see Sigmar's will done. If it aligned with that of this daemon then was the enemy of her enemy not, at least at this desperate pass, her ally?

'Lord-Celestant!' She heard the shout distantly from below, weak and snatched at by the wind. Kalyani looked down to see Karrobeth and Tove emerging from the crumbling steps onto the lowest level of the structure. The wind whipped at them, forcing them to crawl up the side of the altar lest they be snatched away. Tove could barely keep a grip on his sword, brandishing it frantically at a ghast as it whipped low over them. Kalyani felt guilt and anger, seeing them there. How futile it had been, bringing them to this last terrible battle. How worthless their deaths would be. She thrust the thoughts aside; only the blade mattered now. Perhaps, if they survived long enough, she could rescue them and get them back aboard the *Shieldmaiden* when it arrived.

If it arrived.

For now, though, she must seize this opportunity, or they would all be dragged into damnation. *If what I am about to do does not damn me anyway,* she thought, repulsed at what she must do next.

'Daemon, we strike at the same time!' she roared, her voice carrying over the wind as she stepped from the shadows and onto the altar's penultimate tier. The two unnatural creatures both stared at her in unison, both looking as surprised as it was possible for such inhuman abominations to look. Horticulus caught on more quickly than she, it seemed, as he offered her a surly nod almost at once.

'*Thou can'st settle thy master's indebtments then,*' he said, voice bubbling with rot. Then, before Kalyani could demand to know what *that* meant, the daemon turned and drove his snail-monster up the last set of steps towards the abomination.

Kalyani leapt upwards, her feet finding the last level of the dais even as the screaming winds tried to pluck her away. Again, she heard Tove's voice, distant and distorted, yelling up from below. Again, she spared him the briefest of glances and saw him gesturing madly with his blade. Was he pointing at something? Were he and Karrobeth both? Before she could answer the question a howling ghast snatched Tove by the arm and tore him free of the altar. It bore him up, up into the storm-wracked sky and he screamed in terror as it released him. Tove's blade swung wildly, cleaving through the ghast's neck and sending it tattering away into the storm. Then he was falling, tumbling head over heels, tipped cloak flying behind him as he vanished from sight into the void beyond the mountain's peak.

Kalyani felt horror and sorrow at the brave man's awful fate. Duty pulled her in two directions as Karrobeth cowered below her and the bone abomination reared up to lock its black blade against Horticulus' rusted shears. The two unholy creatures traded a furious flurry of blows, the daemon moving far faster than he looked like he should. His snail-steed reared up and spat hissing slime across the abomination's skull face. In return the thing lashed out with bony talons, raking them across the snail-monster's face and tearing away one of its bulbous eyestalks.

The abomination swung the blade again and it pulsed with icy darkness as it struck Horticulus' shears. A black cloud of energy burst from the collision, swirling like ink in water before it lashed at the daemon and drove him back. Black patches of corruption spread across his pox-riddled hide where the death-energies struck him, and Horticulus let out an inarticulate bellow of anger. At the same time, the abomination was chanting, hissing out jarring syllables beyond Kalyani's comprehension. As it did so the blade thrummed with power and its dark pulses came faster, stronger. Kalyani saw the blade come sharply into focus, as though before it had been somehow blurred and distant and she had not realised.

Focus.

Duty. It all came down to duty, and the need to fight in Sigmar's name. What sense saving Karrobeth's life for another few moments only for the abomination to unleash the weapon's power and slay them all?

Kalyani could make no other decision. She took several running steps then hurled herself into the fight, swinging Song up in a vicious arc that intercepted the abomination's next blow. Darkness billowed as the two swords clashed, and lashing black tendrils whipped at Kalyani from every side. Searing cold bit into her wherever they struck, and in their wake she felt nothing but numbness from the wounds.

Weakness dragged at Kalyani's limbs, but she shrugged it off and struck again with a roar. This time Song bit deep into the stretched bones of the abomination's right leg, causing it to stagger and let out a furious hiss. Rusted shears bit home a second later, lopping off one of the bone spikes that jutted from the monster's body and taking a chunk of its shoulder with it.

'Entropy's the thing!' cried Horticulus, diseased spittle flying as he swung his shears about for another blow. *'Wither'n'wear, rot'n'ruin!'*

Ignore the diseased monster and fight for your God-King, Kalyani told herself sternly, wrestling with the impulse to turn and level a banishing blow at this plague daemon who spoke as though they were somehow allies. *There will time enough to destroy the plague-sower when the weapon is won.*

The abomination's blade pulsed faster and faster as its hissing voice rose. It swung the weapon with furious force, every burst of dark power withering and weakening Kalyani and Horticulus both. Yet step by furious step they drove the awful creature back, and as their blades bit deep into its twist-boned body again and again its eyes began to flicker.

Kalyani spun inside its guard and struck upward with Song,

giving a cry of triumph as she severed the hand that held the terrible weapon. The abomination uttered a hissing shriek as bony hand and pulsing blade both clattered down the steps onto the second tier.

'*Thee'll catch thy chance'n be a Champion o' Grandfather yet!*' bellowed Horticulus, drawing back his shears to ram them into the abomination's skull.

It was at that moment, as Kalyani turned furiously towards the daemon with words of denial on her lips, that she saw a dark shadow with glinting eyes rear up behind him. Talons flashed in the stuttering green light of the storm.

Bronvynne hauled herself upwards, step by step. Tears flooded down her cheeks, half-blinding her. She couldn't see, could barely think. Laszlo was gone. Poor, brave Laszlo had been snatched away and cast from the mountaintop to fall, and fall, and fall and be dashed against the ground far below. She had barely seen anything of it, just felt his presence suddenly snatched away, heard his scream and seen a flash of his wild eyes. Yet again and again her tortured imagination showed her his flailing, helpless body bouncing and crunching its way down the mountainside.

Even worse, Thunderblade had not understood them! The one chance they had had to make a difference and they had failed even in that. She had spotted it first, a hunched dark shape flowing up the eastern flank of the altar, somehow escaping the notice of all who fought around and upon it. Bronvynne cursed her own utter impotence as battle raged and the wind screamed and the pulses of dark power from atop the altar came ever more swiftly. She cursed and crawled as she saw the dark shape loom up behind the plague daemon on his massive snail and resolve itself into a huge horned rat-creature clutching an orb and a strange stave that seemed to writhe and twist in its grip.

'No… no, no, Sigmar damnit, no,' groaned Bronvynne as the rat-thing thrust its stave forward with tremendous force and impaled the plague daemon. The head of the stave erupted from the daemon's chest in a shower of rancid viscera that splattered across Lord-Celestant Thunderblade and sent her reeling.

Effortlessly, the rat-thing swung its stave and flicked the daemon from its end as though swatting away some mild irritation. The daemon's body sailed from atop the altar and as it bounced away down the slopes it broke apart into millions of wriggling brown worms that burrowed down into the altar's surface and were gone. The snail-monster that he had ridden gave a low moan of distress and turned, flailing with its stubby limbs at the rat-thing. Contemptuous, the verminous terror brandished its orb and poisonous green lightning leapt down from the clouds to blast it messily apart.

The abomination came at the rat-daemon, but one-armed and without the weapon it could do little. The staff lashed out again, cracking the abomination's skull and sending it reeling. Then Thunderblade was attacking, roaring furious defiance as she swung her sword with all her might and sheared through the rat-thing's weapon.

Still Bronvynne crawled upwards, unsure what she was doing yet utterly determined that she could not, would not fail to reach the fight. She had to do *something*. Something to make all this loss and death and horror worthwhile. She felt her tome driving painfully into her ribs with each crawling lunge upwards and wished that she had abandoned the damned thing, cast it away so that she could crawl more easily. What had it brought her anyway but misery?

Knowledge, she thought. It had brought her knowledge, and though she might not know what that awful creature was that had been wielding the blade, she knew everything she could about the Mordavian Blade itself.

Yes, it was unutterably powerful. Yes, it was beautifully crafted, a perfectly balanced and tremendously dangerous blade empowered by the passing of mortal souls. Yet now, at its moment of triumph, surely it had been rendered mortal? Now, if at any time, it could be destroyed. Bronvynne knew suddenly what she must do, while they were all still fighting atop the dais, before any could snatch the blade away.

'Shattering that blade may release all that death energy and kill every last living thing in Mordavia,' she croaked to herself as she crawled upwards, avoiding the filthy slime trails that slicked the steps. 'But it'll only happen once, and at this point it'll kill little more than filthy skaven.' She felt a momentary pang for the arkanauts aboard the *Shieldmaiden*, and for any of her allies who might have survived the sack of their camp, but matters had become too desperate now for anything else. Groaning in agony as tearing pains shot through her ailing body, Bronvynne scrambled up the last few steps and was confronted with the weapon she had fought so long to destroy. It lay there, pulsating with dark magic, its hilt still locked in the grip of long bone talons. She thought, *I have never seen a more wicked thing in all my long years*.

She tried to wrap the ragged hem of her sleeve around her hand but quickly gave this up, and gathered the last strands of her sanity and courage to reach out to grip the abomination's severed wrist. Her flesh crawled at the feeling of slick, cold bone beneath her fingers but, as she had hoped, its talons remained locked in a death grip around the weapon's hilt.

All the same, as Bronvynne staggered weakly to her feet she felt the blade's inimical aura leeching the life from her in waves. Simply being this close to it made her skin shrivel tight and begin to flake away in dust scads, and her hair turn brittle and white before falling from her scalp.

It didn't matter.

She didn't have to last long.

Just long enough.

Bronvynne turned and lurched away down the altar steps, battling against the screaming winds as she made for the precipitous drop that had swallowed Laszlo. She would follow him over the edge and take this cursed thing with her and when it shattered to shards upon the unforgiving rocks below, she would have made it all worthwhile.

Ghasts screamed overhead. The wind ripped at Bronvynne, making her stumble. Plague flies buzzed low, their riders hacking at the whirling spectres that surrounded them. Above her she heard a high-pitched shriek of rage and knew that she had been spotted. Yet they wouldn't catch her now. She was too far gone. Skin flaking away, bones splintering, Bronvynne took the last few steps.

Kalyani staggered, her body betraying her as weakness spread icy fingers through her limbs. Her guard faltered and the abomination drove its bony fist into the faceplate of her helm hard enough to buckle it inwards. She fell back, tasting blood and feeling an awful, crushing pressure on her nose and jaw. Furious, frantic, she tore the helm from her head, screaming in pain as it took a chunk of her mashed nose with it. Blood drizzled down her face. She spat broken teeth onto the black stone.

She looked up in time to see the rat-daemon and the abomination clash again. Their long claws swept and raked. Their eyes glowed with sorcerous energy and hatred. It was almost like watching the skaven creature battle its own skeletal reflection. Yet it was winning this fight, Kalyani could see it. It was stronger and faster than the hacked and battered abomination. It still had all its limbs. Whip-fast, its tail snaked out and wrapped around its enemy's skull, squeezing hard enough to crack bone.

'*Kill-weapon will belong to Thrykktwyst,*' snarled the rat-daemon. '*Yes-yes, fool-seer not have it, dead-things not have it, plague-things not have it...*'

'*Nnnone... will... have... ittttttt...*' came the abomination's grating voice, and as Kalyani followed the direction of its flickering gaze, icy dread filled her veins.

'Sigmar's hammer,' she breathed as she saw the disintegrating form of Bronvynne Karrobeth launch herself off the edge of the altar.

CHAPTER SIXTEEN

THE END OF ALL THINGS

Above Mordavia, all times and none

A storm of emotions chased one another through Kalyani's mind as she saw Karrobeth vanish over the edge in a cloud of billowing ash. She cried out, an inarticulate sound that rang with both sorrow and fierce pride at what Bronvynne had achieved. Kalyani's eyes widened and her arms fell to her sides in resignation as she realised that surely hurling the sword to its destruction in such a fashion would unleash its powers. She was doubtless about to be annihilated.

Once-Forged no more, she thought, chest tightening with fear. *I beg you, Sigmar, do not take too much from me in payment for my new flesh.*

Yet would it be like it had been with Thostos Bladestorm, consigned never to be reforged, trapped forever by some malign power to torment upon the Mortal Realms? Even if not, would Reforging mean the same searing, tearing, unendurable agony that it had before?

It doesn't matter, so long as I hold onto my self.

Looming above her, the rat-daemon let out a screech of outraged fury, even as the abomination hissed its own cry of denial.

Kalyani braced herself.

Nothing happened.

The aerial battle raged on all around her. The storm continued to vent its fury upon the mountaintop. There came no billowing wave of death magic.

Had Karrobeth failed? Kalyani thought with a sick lurch. What if she had struck the mountainside and lost her grip upon the blade? What if it had lodged, partway down, undamaged and pulsing with power where any scrabbling skaven or wailing ghast might find it and snatch it up for their masters?

Then she felt the prickle of dark magic washing across her numbed skin and looked up in horror to see the skaven daemon with its scrying orb held high. Within the strange globe swirled a miniature reflection of the storm raging overhead. Twisted syllables were spilling from the daemon's maw in a chittering chorus.

Kalyani looked back to where Karrobeth had plunged from the edge, and her heart sank into her heels as she saw the Mordavian Blade wavering back into view, held within a cage of crackling warp lightning.

'No!' she yelled and tried to drive Song through the towering daemon's ankle, but it stepped aside with a hiss and smashed her away with its lashing tail. Kalyani rolled helplessly off the altar's top tier and slammed into the stonework of the next one down.

By the time she was back on her feet, the Lord-Celestant was in time to see the pulsating blade soaring up the side of the altar to thump, hilt first, into the rat-daemon's outstretched talons.

It leered. It gave a shriek of triumph as it brandished the dread weapon high above its head. Ghasts let out terrible cries and swept down towards it, but it spat unclean words and the undead creatures were lit from within by warp lightning before being blasted apart. Plague daemons on their bloated flies spiralled madly down upon it but it gestured with its orb and suddenly plague-ridden rats were squirming from within the flies' bloated bodies, gnawing and clawing as they ate them away. One by one the gutted rot flies tumbled from the air, their riders splattering upon the altar's flanks or tumbling away into the void.

'Lord-Celestant, do you have it?' came a sudden voice, muffled within a pouch at her belt. 'Lord-Celestant Thunderblade, do you hear me? We are making our approach now! If you don't confirm we'll be forced to abort! They're all over us!'

Somewhere out amidst the storm, Kalyani heard the chatter and boom of Kharadron gunfire, the cries of arkanauts and the thrumming of aether-endrins.

The rat-daemon heard it too. With a cruel sneer it turned and raised the pulsing black blade towards the clouds, its tip pointed at where the *Shieldmaiden* was half-visible, barrelling closer through the surging clouds with enemies boiling around it.

'Sigmar damn you, no!' roared Kalyani and flung herself back up the steps. She swung Song with furious strength, forcing the daemon to weave backwards and sending its conjured bolt of warp lightning flickering harmlessly away into the clouds.

The daemon looked down at her and its mad eyes flared with anger. It opened its jaws wide to unleash another killing incantation then stiffened as there came an awful gristly crunch. Long bone talons sprouted from its maw like blood-slick tongues. It shuddered, dark red gore drizzling over its fangs and pattering the floor. Its eyes rolled as though it were trying to look backwards through its own skull, and it half-turned, raising the Mordavian Blade. Then the bone talons twisted with another ripping crunch and its body exploded into poisonous green vapours that whirled away on the wind. Before the sword could tumble to the floor those same bony digits snatched its hilt from the air and drew it possessively back.

Kalyani looked up to see the abomination looming over her, the black blade of Mordavia in one hand, unholy light pulsing in its eyes.

'Whatever you are, I command you in the name of the God-King to set down that blade,' snarled Kalyani, staggering up the steps with Song held point forward. Her body was a mass of fiery heat and icy cold, raging agony conflicting with patches of absolute nothingness. She could feel her blood pooling in the boots of her armour, the divine life force leaking from her by the moment.

She would not yield. She would fight, as she always fought, and she would kill, and she would emerge triumphant in Sigmar's name.

Yet that name did not cow the abomination as some part of her had hoped it might. Instead, it made its eyes flare with furious light and its grip tighten on the hilt of the weapon.

'I... served... the God-Kinggggg... once...' it hissed. 'Heeee left... me... formless... mindlesssss... trapped forever where I could protect... the blade... keep it awayyy from hisssss enemies...'

Kalyani shook her head.

'Do not seek to trick me with lies, creature,' she said, pacing still closer. 'I know the God-King is the greatest good in all the Mortal Realms. I serve him and I command you to do the same.' Keeping this thing talking had worked for Horticulus; it might work for her too. It seemed to *want* to speak, as though it sought to justify itself somehow.

'Noooo... The God-King... keeeeps... secretssss...' it hissed in its dead-leaves rattle, and as it did so Kalyani heard the thrum of aether-endrins growing closer, caught the cries of the arkanaut lookout as he spotted her. Perhaps if she could convince them to turn their guns on her and the monster both...?

Then came wild shrieks from somewhere behind her, and a moment later the rattle of gunfire told her that fresh battle had been joined. Kalyani didn't dare look around, but she recognised the chittering of skaven. Lots of skaven, by the sounds of things.

'Whatever you are you cannot want those vermin to have the weapon,' she said. 'They have come to take it from you, and I will not be able to stop them. It *must* be destroyed.'

'*The blaaaaade… will not be destroyyyed…*' hissed the abomination. '*It is mee…. I ammmm it… We are a gifffft for Nagash's hand… It tolllllld me… helped me seeee as it whispered toooo me… through the longgggg… years…. It showed me how to take the lifffffe… of the rat thinggggg… How to fashionnnn a body for myselffff again…*'

'A gift for Nagash? You think the skaven will let you escape this place, let you travel all the way to the heart of Shyish with that weapon? Now they know of it you will never get rid of them, and Nagash will never see his prize,' said Kalyani, one foot finding the top step of the dais again. Just a little closer and she could swipe the blade from the abomination's grasp again and make a dash for the *Shieldmaiden*.

'*Hhhhhaaaahhhaaaahhaaa…*' The thing's laughter was like the wind through dead thickets. It made her flesh crawl. '*Noooo… I doooo thissss now and we alllll go down to the underworldsssss togetherrrr… And I putttttt… the blade… in hissss hand…. myself….*'

With that the abomination raised the weapon high. Kalyani gave a yell and lashed out with Song. Had she been unwounded, had she not been buffeted by the screaming winds and weakened by the insidious gifts of Nurgle, then perhaps her blow would have landed true.

It did not. Song sheared off a long splinter of bone as the abomination wrenched its hand away then regurgitated a sibilant spew of sorcerous words that caused the blade to burn suddenly with black fire.

'No!' cried Kalyani, but it was too late.

It was done.

The blade shimmered faster and faster, throwing out wave after wave of shadows and emitting a screaming, sawing note that set Kalyani's remaining teeth on edge and vibrated through her bones. She staggered back, throwing up an arm in expectation of the expanding wave of death magic that she had seen before.

It did not come. Instead, from all around her, she heard a terrible groaning and creaking as of a ship's hull being torn apart on vicious rocks. The dais shuddered beneath Kalyani's feet. Shadows raced and strobed through the air. A tremendous pulse of whirling black sand raced outward from the blade, then another, then a third but each passed through and over Kalyani without causing her the slightest harm.

She frowned in confusion, before the tectonic groan came again. This time, from far out across the city, she heard deafening cracks like gigantic cannons firing off one by one. As she stared out over the city, flashes of lightning and leaping flames showed her enormous cracks racing through the streets. Ancient buildings shuddered as they were bisected, then fell away into the yawning black void. Entire roadways subsided, swallowing cobbles and stonework and the tiny, scrambling figures of skaven and orruks and plague daemons in their hundreds.

Kalyani looked up in growing dismay as she saw those same black cracks running impossibly through the storm-lashed sky. Even as she watched a great segment of the firmament shattered like mirror glass and fell away, tumbling down upon the shuddering city to wreak utter devastation. Where it had been there was nothing but a vast expanse of seething blackness, like a whirling sandstorm.

'What have you done?' she shouted as skaven shrieked in dismay and the *Shieldmaiden*'s endrins laboured furiously. The storm winds were whirling madly now, spiralling around the mountaintop in a wild cyclone thick with grains of onyx sand.

'I... have opennned... the waaaaay...' hissed the abomination in triumph. 'Now... we allll gooooo.... downnn to Shyisssssh... togetherrrr... and I bring Nagash... an offeringgggggg...'

All around her Kalyani could hear the groan and scream of reality being torn apart. Booming crashes rolled like thunder as districts of Mordavia fell away into utter darkness and she thought with mad horror that at last the warring armies had unleashed a power that would consume them all. The battle for Mordavia was done, and the best she could hope was that this appalling devastation did not stretch too far beyond the city's borders.

Yet she could not let this monster win. Even now there was hope, she told herself. There had to be a chance to snatch the weapon from its grasp and destroy it. She didn't know what lies it had been trying to force upon her with its talk of Sigmar, but she knew that the God-King would not want to see that weapon in the hands of Nagash! She dreaded to think what horrors would be unleashed if the abomination was borne down to Shyish with blade in hand, there to present it to the God of Death.

'We fight,' spat Kalyani, ignoring the apocalyptic devastation all around her, the cracks racing through the shuddering altar. 'We kill,' she snarled, striding back up the steps and raising her blade. 'We win!' she shouted as the screaming winds bore plague daemons and wailing ghasts and the tumbling, fire-spewing shape of the *Shieldmaiden* around and around the mountaintop. 'For all you have slain!' she howled and threw herself at the abomination with all the unfettered battle-fury her Stormhost was famed for.

Song met the Mordavian Blade with a ringing clang, then again, then again. Black energies billowed from the blade as it met hers, and its very solidity gave her hope. Surely it was still in focus. Surely it could still be shattered. Kalyani redoubled her efforts, driving the looming monster back across the dais with one hacking blow after another. It lashed out, hissing, and she took the blade on her shoulder guard before directing another flurry of blows that scythed chunks of bone from its legs and smashed one of its knee joints sideways.

The abomination hissed and the Mordavian Blade sent out a pulse of death magic. Whirling motes of obsidian sand flowed from the storm around them and bonded themselves to the abomination's body. Before Kalyani's horrified gaze it sprouted new onyx talons, the chips and cracks in its bones were repaired and its body stretched, grew, became thicker and heavier as black sand layered itself onto its frame.

Another rippling flurry of cracks ran through the air and she heard the skaven behind her screech in terror. She had forgotten the ratmen were even there, yet now she looked around to see some being plucked away and hurled into the void by the wind while others scrabbled madly before falling down the yawning hole where half the altar's slope had been. Shards of sky fell all around, and she cried out in denial as one struck the *Shieldmaiden* and sheared the doughty ironclad in half. Its blazing sections spiralled away into darkness, shedding the flailing figures of the crew as they went.

'*Yoooou... cannnottttt... winnnn...*' boomed the gigantic abomination as it stooped over her. '*Youuuu... willll be bornnnnnne... downnnn to... Shyisssssh with usssss allll...*'

Down into Shyish, where her soul would be trapped by some terrible dark magic and she would remain the Once-Forged forever, thought Kalyani. What a horrible irony there would be in that title then. And none would know what had befallen Mordavia, nor the armies that marched here. Not until this doom came again to some other enclave of Order that Nagash chose to consign to damnation.

'I will not allow this,' she said. She might not be able to win this fight, but she could at least choose how she lost it.

Lightning crackling around her blade she charged again, leaping up to hack at the abomination whose legs alone were now taller than her. She struck it a furious blow that sent it staggering. It hissed in fury as it stooped and swung its weapon, death magic pulsing again from the blade to send hissing motes of dark sand driving at her.

Kalyani danced away, praying to Sigmar that her body, and the shuddering mountain, would hold together long enough. The abomination swung again, conjuring another pulse of the blade's energies to lend its strike unnatural speed. It caught Kalyani a glancing blow that sent her tumbling away down the steps. She crashed into several ratmen who were scrabbling upwards to escape the altar's collapse. They snarled and scattered, scratching and biting at her until she surged back to her feet with a roar and sent them skittering away.

She looked up, bloodied but unbowed as the abomination stomped down the steps towards her. The Mordavian Blade pulsed darkly in its fist, and to Kalyani's horror she saw that its outline was wavering as though slipping slowly out of phase with all around it. The abomination was spending its power, she realised. She had to end this now, before her victory slipped beyond her reach.

'*Whyyyyy do…. you… fiiiiight…?*' it hissed.

'I fight for Sigmar!' she spat and ran up the steps to meet it. The Mordavian Blade swung down like a shadow-wreathed guillotine and she leapt aside, allowing it to strike sparks from the shuddering steps. Kalyani lashed out at the abomination's wrist and it pulled its hand back again, wary now of having the weapon severed from its grasp. She had been counting on it doing precisely that, and as the abomination swept its arm upwards so she leapt and grabbed on with her free hand.

Kalyani was borne upwards. She leapt from the monster's arm

and wrapped her armoured fist around the bones of its branch-thick ribs. The abomination hissed furiously as she found footholds amidst its ribcage. It staggered back up the steps as stonework fell away before it and another great chunk of the sky tumbled down to rain across the shaking altar. Kalyani felt as though the entire mountain was descending now, plunging downwards into deepening darkness as chunks of statuary and sundered city districts whirled and tumbled around it.

The abomination swept one huge fist outward and swatted back in, trying to crush her against its bony chest. Kalyani swung aside, allowing the monster to pound its own bones hard enough to crack them. She uttered a furious yell of, 'We fight!' then used the momentum of her swing to carry herself up and ram the point of Song through the creature's jaw and up into its skull.

The abomination tottered and gave a hissing groan. The lights in its eyes flickered and Kalyani felt sudden acceleration as it toppled forward and crashed down upon the steps. She let go, pushing herself desperately away to avoid being crushed beneath tons of iron-hard bone. Kalyani hit the steps hard and awkwardly, and tasted blood. She felt her bones snap at the impact, felt sharp pains tear through her as she rolled away, felt a sudden horrible void beneath her that she knew meant she had rolled clean off the edge of the crumbling altar. Kalyani shot out her free hand and grabbed a jutting spar of stone.

For an instant she hung over a yawning, whirling void of racing sands of pulsing shadows. Remnants of Mordavia still spread out below her like a jigsaw puzzle smashed by a frustrated child. She thought she saw figures still huddled together within those weird islands of architecture and whipping ferns, desperate to cling to a few more moments of life, perhaps hoping for some miraculous deliverance that would not come. Unbelievably, some were still locked in battle.

Then she was hauling herself up, bones grinding together, muscles and sinews protesting furiously as she forced her body to move, to support her weight, to heave itself up and onto the edge of the crumbling altar again. She screamed with the pain of it, but she did it all the same. Kalyani drove herself to her feet and staggered drunkenly towards the fallen abomination. Already the monster was stirring and hissing. The Mordavian Blade pulsed and shimmered as it drew in waves of sand that layered themselves over the abomination's wounds.

'No, not yet,' spat Kalyani.

She had one chance, and she couldn't waste it. Pushing herself to a final effort she staggered forward and swept Song down double-handed upon the Mordavian blade. Her life was already forfeit, but she could stop this monster from delivering the weapon into the hands of the Great Necromancer.

At the last instant the abomination reacted, snatching for the blade, clumsily striking its pommel with bony talons. Song whistled down and struck true, right at the base of the Mordavian Blade where it met the crossguard. The blow should have sheared the weapon in half, and Kalyani howled in dismay as it instead passed through the insubstantial weapon and sparked against the altar's steps.

Jogged by the abomination's desperate lunge, the Mordavian Blade clattered with ghostly echoes down the last two steps and out into the void. It was snatched by the darkling winds and whirled away, a gleaming point of light soon swallowed amidst the void.

Kalyani felt all the strength leave her. She dropped to her knees, and Song clattered to the ground at her side. She had failed. She had *failed*.

Yet have I? The sudden thought shot through her in a jolt of realisation. Who knew where that blade might land now? Who knew how long it might be lost again amidst the maelstrom, where it might come down amidst all the myriad underworlds of Shyish. If she could bear warning of its existence back to Sigmaron then she might yet see a questing force find and secure the damned thing before it ever came to Nagash's hands.

At last Kalyani knew what she had to do, and she faced the knowledge with staunch determination.

'*Whaaaaat haaaavvvve… you donnnnnneeee?*' screeched the abomination as it pushed itself back to its knees and snaked out its remaining hand. Its talons wrapped around her and lifted her up, and Kalyani offered no resistance. '*The blaaaade… is lossssst… in the abyssssss…. I cannnnotttt… you havvvvve….*'

'I have put it beyond your reach, and that of Nagash as well,' spat Kalyani.

'*IIII… ammmm… ittt… and it issss… meeeee…*' hissed the creature. '*I willll… finnnd itttt…*'

'It used you, and now it is gone. Look at yourself, filth,' said Kalyani with a hard smile.

'*Nooo….*' howled the abomination as it realised what Kalyani was talking about. With the blade gone the dark sands were flowing away from its form again, its long bones eroding as though aeons of howling winds were eating them away.

'I will find the blade. I will warn all Sigmaron of its power, and together my comrades and I shall find it and destroy it once and for all, just as we destroyed you,' she spat, and with a last vicious twist she wrenched her blade arm free. Ignoring the agony that screamed through her body she hurled the sword as hard as she could. It plunged into the abomination's right eye socket and the fires there flared explosively then winked out.

The monster gave a hissing roar and squeezed hard, crushing Kalyani in its fist, before dropping her broken body to the altar steps. She tasted blood in her mouth, felt unbearable agony throughout her dying body, but there was nothing but a grim sense of victory within her mind. The blade might not be destroyed, but once she had been reforged she would quest for it with absolute determination. The armies that had fallen in Mordavia would be as nothing to the legions of foes she would gladly slay to see the Mordavian Blade put beyond Nagash's reach once and for all.

We fight, we die… we win, she thought as her vision faded, and then lightning coursed through her mind, she heard a thunderous crack, and Kalyani Thunderblade was Once-Forged no more.

ABOUT THE AUTHOR

Andy Clark has written the Warhammer 40,000 novels *Fist of the Imperium, Kingsblade, Knightsblade* and *Shroud of Night*, as well as the Dawn of Fire novel *The Gate of Bones* and the novella *Crusade*. He has also written the novels *Gloomspite* and *Blacktalon: First Mark* for Warhammer Age of Sigmar, and the Warhammer Quest Silver Tower novella *Labyrinth of the Lost*. He lives in Nottingham, UK.

An extract from
Realm-Lords
by Dale Lucas

Ferendir stumbled on loose rock resting in dry soil. He first fell forward, overcompensated by shifting his weight backwards, then felt gravity – sure and inexorable – seize him. There would be no course correction – he was falling, and the steep, thinly wooded slope was about to thrust him away from its cold, sere face as though disgusted by him. In desperation, Ferendir whirled his arms, hoping to save himself from a painful impact and a merciless slide back down the steep incline. Further on, ahead and above him, he saw his master, Serath, turn back to stare.

Surely that was the worst – not the slip, not the fall, not even the impact to come, but Serath's cold, appraising glare and silent disapproval.

Then a gentle pressure upon Ferendir's back steadied him. His fall was arrested, his humiliation postponed. His other master, Desriel, had stopped his backward fall with an outstretched hand. Regaining his balance and planting his feet widely to stabilise himself, Ferendir lowered his eyes. Deep within him, buried beneath layers of physical conditioning and mental inculcation gained throughout his years as a supplicant to the mountain temple, he felt the seething, roiling forces of his emotions, like subterranean waters warmed by geothermal vents, made turbulent by a sudden underground tremor. Embarrassment, relief, fear, self-loathing – all were so close in that horrible instant, so present just beneath the mask of calm he fought to project to his mentors, that he could almost taste them.

Breathe, he ordered himself inwardly. *Just as they taught you. Regain your composure. Centre yourself. It was just a misstep... an understandable accident.*

But was it? He raised his eyes to Serath again, further up the slope.

Serath makes no such missteps, does he? That is why he looks upon me with such disdain, such disappointment. Nothing I do will ever be good enough for him.

And Desriel. Quiet, compassionate, supportive Desriel. He makes a good show of believing in me, maintaining his patience no matter how often I make mistakes, but he is probably ashamed of me on some level, as well... certain that I'm unequal to what's ahead.

The trial. My final *trial.*

Perhaps my final anything.

Stop, that cold, quiet voice within him said again. *Fear will destroy you. First things first, now – just get up the mountain without another fall.*

Ferendir forced himself to follow the voice's command. He continued to breathe evenly, consciously, to count slowly backwards as he did so, inhaling on the even numbers, exhaling with the odd.

Inhale. Exhale.

His heart rate slowed. The subtle tremors in his hands disappeared and the sweat upon them began to evaporate.

'Shall we continue?' Desriel asked quietly.

Ferendir opened his eyes. Looked up the steep incline of the mountainside. Saw Serath up ahead, silently impatient, still watching, radiating a vaguely disdainful air.

'Onwards,' Ferendir said, and resumed his climb.

Today, he faced his final initiation rite as a supplicant and acolyte of his Alarith temple. He could not afford to let a single misstep, a single, foolish mistake, ruin the calm and confidence he had worked so hard to cultivate within himself in preparation for this final, harrowing rite. He must be present, mindful, ready for anything yet expecting nothing.

Today, he would suborn himself to the mountain's will and beg its blessed sanction.

Today, he would be buried alive.

If the mountain accepted him, he would survive the ordeal. If, on the other hand, it found him unworthy...

'We linger too long,' Serath said from above.

Ferendir forced himself not to raise his eyes or meet Serath's disapproving gaze. From behind him, Desriel answered.

'Patience, Serath,' his master said. 'Our young supplicant was simply recomposing himself.'

Serath persisted. 'Had he stepped carefully, noted all possible impediments to his passage and skilfully avoided them, he would not have slipped, or fallen, or lost his composure.'

He could hide no longer. Trudging on, never breaking stride, Ferendir raised his eyes to meet Serath's, however difficult doing so might prove.

'I beg pardons of both of you, my masters,' the supplicant said. 'Please, let us continue.'

He lowered his eyes to the path, set one foot before the other and said no more. He leaned into the steep slope and chose his footholds swiftly but carefully.

The terrain they moved through – deep in the Ymetrican mountains of the realm of Hysh – was sparsely wooded and dreary, slate-grey knobs of cold stone and dry, subalpine soil scattered with towering sentinel trees and blanketed here and there with cushions of moss and islands of sedge. Hand- and footholds were not hard to find – there always seemed to be some jutting stone, the gnarl of a tree root or a narrow shelf of tightly packed earth awaiting his employ. Ferendir concentrated on finding the best of these, determined not to slip again simply because he had failed to closely examine where he planted his feet. As he trudged onwards, he sometimes used his small, delicate hands to assist in his ascent. He could still hear the burbling rush of the last stream they had crossed before beginning their climb, far below them, because the wind-wracked forest around them was so deathly silent, so funereally still.

Ferendir stole a glance upwards at Serath, to see if his stoic mentor yet lingered above him. To his chagrin, Serath had not moved. His master stood, bedecked in his shining white plate armour chased in gold, leaning upon his long-handled stone mallet. One of Serath's booted feet was braced upon a bleached-white tangle of deadfall wedged between two thin, sickly trees, and the stoic Stoneguard stared down at his long-time apprentice with his familiar reproachful glare. Ferendir could not tell if that expression – so subtle, so inscrutable – was a sign of complete disdain or simple pity. Serath held Ferendir's upturned eyes for only an instant, then turned his back and began to climb again.

Behind him, Ferendir heard Desriel begin to hum quietly – a slow, melancholy tune. Ferendir recognised the sombre melody at once as one of the temple's hymns, a wordless song taught to all the servants of the mountain. Its dolorous melody and slow, lilting cadence were designed to sharpen one's senses, to suppress one's conscious thoughts and widen one's consciousness – a sort of musical state of meditation, useful when undertaking laborious physical tasks such as a slow climb up a steep, wind-scoured mountainside. Ferendir was tempted to join Desriel in humming the old hymn – he had always loved the sense of plaintive peace that it stirred within him – but a part of him was reticent.

It was Serath. Though Ferendir now bore down upon his master with his senses and struggled to listen closely, he could not hear Serath humming. Serath, apparently, was centred, focused and fully present without the benefit of the hymn's quiet, hypnotic power. Therefore, Ferendir, determined to earn Serath's respect if not his affection, would do as *he* did, and remain silent, no matter how much he wanted to join Desriel in his song.

They had set off in the early hours of the morning, when the dim Hyshian twilight that constituted night was yet upon them and most of the temple Stoneguard and acolytes yet slept. His masters were each fully armoured and carried their personal weapons – an elegant diamondpick hammer for Desriel, a massive, long-hafted stone mallet for Serath – while Ferendir himself, facing a trial, wore a supplicant's tunic and had only been permitted to bring along his well-worn yew staff and a small dagger. Their path led them north-west, along one of the many narrow hiking trails that criss-crossed the rolling ridgelines and deep valleys of the mountain, taking them far from the lovely, well-hidden, tree-packed dell in which their temple resided towards the thick, shadowy forests that blanketed the mountain's western slopes. After hours of following the hill-hugging trail, they finally came to a rocky stream tumbling down out of the woods. At the stream, they left the path and followed the wending waters deeper and deeper into the shady hollows and rough-hewn gullies that formed the uneven geography of the mountain. Just as the full light of day began to bleed back into the world – Ulgu's darkness waning at last before the imminent glow of the Perimeter Inimical – they finally came to the lower edge of the thinning subalpine forest that marked the beginning of the end of the mountain's life-sustaining lower slopes. Whereas before the rolling, climbing landscape had been thick with intertwined, leafy decidua and tall, needly dream-pines shading banks of shaggy verdibrush and beds of sprouting toadstools, the world above the stream suddenly exhibited signs of weariness and surrender. The spaces between the trees widened. Green turf and fronded ferns were replaced by dry soil, bald stone and isolated beds of spongy moss or obdurate sedge.

Hour by hour they climbed, the light invading the thinning woodlands growing brighter and brighter, even as the gusts blowing down from the mountain's heights grew colder and more insistent. The world stirred little, only a few lonely birds offering sad songs while from the last clinging shadows beneath the thinning trees they heard the rattle of tiny claws on stone and the soughing, subtle passage of small, fleet bodies. The moribund forest, the steepening mountainside, the air above and around them – everything, no matter how austere and faded it appeared, showed signs that it was alive, awake, hungry. This was one of the most basic lessons imparted to young supplicants of the mountain temple – or any temple, for that matter.

There is life in everything, desire in everything, will in everything. One forgets that fact at great personal peril.